Celtic Shadows

BLUE FEATHER BOOKS, LTD.

To those sleeping Amazons who have
awakened to the call and sharpened their swords:

It is to these modern day Warrior women who
are putting their lives on the line to defend
our freedom and liberty, that we raise our goblets in toast.

And to Elaine who, no less an Amazon, was so looking forward to this, our second book in the Shadow Series. Unfortunately, she was taken from us, and resides now with the Amazons, in their land.

"Accept the things to which fate binds you, and love the people with whom fate brings you together, but do so with all your heart."

-- Marcus Aurelius

ALSO BY K.C. WEST & VICTORIA WELSH:

SUPERSTITION SHADOWS

Celtic Shadows

A BLUE FEATHER BOOK

by

K.C. West and Victoria Welsh

CELTIC SHADOWS

Cover design by pinfeather
Cover art by Felicia M.
E-mail: Felicia_M_Arts@yahoo.com

A Blue Feather Book
Published by Blue Feather Books, Ltd.
P.O. Box 5867
Atlanta, GA 31107-5967

www.bluefeatherbooks.com

ISBN: 0-9770318-6-1

First edition: December, 2006

Printed in the United States of America and in the United Kingdom.

Acknowledgements

The stalwart friends who performed so admirably for us with *Superstition Shadows* continued to read, comment, and lend us expertise where necessary for this book. Thank you Arly, Lisa, Mary, and all the great folks at the online forum. To Heather Blakey, owner of the *Soul Food Café,* we extend our gratitude for her continuing support. For sharing her wisdom, humor, and artistic talents with us, and for serving as a daily example of the Amazon Spirit, we send our appreciation to Felicia.

We'd be remiss if we didn't add a husband, two daughters, and a life partner to the list of those who encouraged us. Also, our two former publishers, Anne and Sam, and our two new publishers, Caitlin and Emily, deserve our gratitude. We thank Caitlin and Em, too, for putting up with these two often impatient authors. And special thanks to Jane Vollbrecht for her invaluable editing skills.

Finally, we offer our deepest thanks to the readers of *Superstition Shadows.* We value your kind words and suggestions, and we hope you enjoy this second book.

Hugs to all,

K.C. and Victoria

Chapter 1

"You said cottage, PJ. Your words were crystal clear. You told me that plans had changed and we were meeting your dad in Newport at the cottage."

"Okay, let me—"

"This place is huge. It must have twenty or thirty rooms."

Kim's jaw hung open as she stared at the house. She raked her fingers through her short, dark hair, and I watched the sun glint off strands of silver in the gentle breeze. Tall, tanned, and muscular from years of working dig sites, my partner was not easily cowed by man or beast. Facing the evidence of my financial situation, however, often left her disturbed.

"Thirty-four, to be exact," I said, hoping to lessen her apprehension with an abundance of details. "But you see, these places have been called cottages from the day they were built, which in the case of Grandma Jo's place, was in the 1890s."

We were standing on the paved driveway inside the compound leading to the south entrance of Windswept. My grandmother's summer retreat was a mansion set high on the hillside overlooking Rhode Island Sound and, beyond that, the Atlantic Ocean. It was a late Victorian structure with a wide, wrap-around porch, cross-gabled roof, and Palladian windows.

Grandma Jo's retreat was shingled with cedar on the upper floors, but its first level was encased in native stone. The exterior shutters and trim gleamed with a fresh coat of Wedgwood blue paint. The rugged stone and weathered cedar gave the house a patina of rustic charm that spoke of permanence, despite decades of exposure to the elements.

Warm sunshine bathed the flagstone terrace to our right. Wrought iron tables and plump chaise lounges awaited casual dining, conversation, or sunbathing. I had whiled away many summers on that terrace, gazing out toward the horizon, pondering my future.

Pup, Kim's fifty-fifty blend of wolf and German Shepherd, made a thorough circuit of the terrace, sniffing and whining at every stray insect or wisp of sea grass that had the audacity to cross his line of sight.

"Pup seems to be enjoying himself," I said, as we started through the walkway. "You know he's a good judge of character."

Kim shifted her daypack to her other shoulder. "I never said it wasn't a lovely place, just big."

"Once you know the people who live here, you'll think of it as a home like any other, only with more bathrooms."

She laughed. "Yeah, right."

"Please try to like it, if only for my sake. We won't have to stay long if it bothers you too much."

We gazed at each other for several seconds.

"I'm sorry," she said, giving my shoulder a squeeze. "You know that I come from a small, narrow-minded family that was only too glad to see me leave. I forget what it's like to be loved and welcomed."

My free arm circled her waist. "I thought I was doing my best to convince you of both of those, especially the love part."

She gave me a hug. "You certainly are persuasive. Please tell me more about this clan."

"Okay. Where was I?" We entered by way of the sun porch, walked through a sitting room, and went into a long hallway. "The place has been in my father's family for generations." I opened a door and we peeked in. "When she was eighteen, Grandma Josephine Lane married Will Samuel Curtis right here in the grand ballroom."

We crossed the shiny oak floor to the large windows and admired the view of rugged coastline below. "Dad was born two years later and spent a great deal of his summers here, fishing, sailing, swimming, and racing motorcycles up and over the narrow roads along the coast—much to the dismay of his parents." I moved to another window and waved in the direction of the nearest mansion. "Fortunately, the neighbors lived on estates of their own and didn't concern themselves with noise or reckless youths. When Dad married my mother Rachael, her mother, Priscilla Ludlow, joined the Curtis family groups spending summers here."

Fearing I had put Kim to sleep with my ramblings, I turned to apologize and found her still staring at the shoreline and its breaking waves.

"This place is amazing. Every window has a million-dollar view."

Oh, shit. I retraced my steps. "Don't worry about the size or the view, okay?"

Kim's brow furrowed, and she aimed one of her withering stares at me. "Easy for you to say. You aren't entering the land of the rich and famous for the first time."

I dropped my bag and put both arms around her waist, hugging her close. "Kimmy, please. You'll get used to it, I promise. You've been to the town home in Boston several times. That can be intimidating."

"That place isn't as enormous, and doesn't have the Atlantic Ocean in its backyard. And besides, I was in Boston to see your father about work. He and the Curtis Foundation provided the funds for several of my expeditions, and that intimidated me more than your ritzy digs in Back Bay."

"Comforting thought, since Dad's here, too."

"Don't remind me." It came out as one long groan.

I rubbed my cheek against her shirt, inhaling her distinctive, spicy scent. "I'm sorry."

She ruffled my hair and kissed the top of my head. "We'll manage somehow."

I looked up at her, grinning. "You may even grow to love the place. Plenty of aunts, uncles, and cousins have relaxed inside these walls. The Lane, Ludlow, and Curtis clans all congregated here during the summer. I'm just sorry that I never got to know my grandparents very well before they died. Grandma Jo lived the longest. She inherited the place and lived here year-round, through several hurricanes and countless blizzards, until she and two of the servants were killed in a boating accident in 1971."

"That's sad. She sounds like she was a pretty feisty woman."

Still embracing, we turned and looked down at the water. "I imagine she was," I said. "I'm named after both my grandmothers, though I shortened my name to PJ as soon as I could."

"Why's that?"

"Too many relatives made comparisons and always found me lacking."

Kim's arm tightened around my shoulder. "I understand, sweetheart. But, you have no reason to feel that way. You're the bravest, boldest, most intelligent—"

"Yeah, yeah, give me a swelled head. You aren't exactly unbiased, you know."

"Most beautiful, most sexy—"

"Jesus, Kim, you're good for a woman's ego."

Pup joined us, having apparently explored some terrain below the terrace. His black muzzle was peppered with damp, sandy granules, and pieces of seaweed and beach debris clung to the fur on his narrow legs.

Kim used a tissue to wipe the sandy residue from his head and scratched his ears in the process. "Geez, Pup, you can't go around looking so grubby. This is a fancy place, and PJ's ancestors may be looking down on us right this minute, shaking their heads in dismay."

I laughed. "I'm sure there are plenty of my living relatives who'd criticize me for the life I've chosen, but I'm more resigned to it now." I looked into Kim's dark eyes, and my heart overflowed with love.

I'd found what I really wanted. I'd found my knight in shining armor; only she'd turned out to be an Amazon warrior archaeologist in khaki cargo pants.

She had been waiting for me in Arizona, searching for a lost tribe of Amazon warriors. All I'd had to do was earn her respect and convince her that our initial distrust could change to love if given half a chance. The fact that we both thought I was straight slowed the attraction that grew between us, but eventually I wore her down. Displaying a patience I'd never known I had, I convinced her that she was the person I wanted to live with and love for the rest of my life.

We did have our differences. Not the least of which was what I liked to call the "wealth issue." I'd been blessed—or cursed—with it all of my life, but Kim had to work her way through college and graduate school, earning her honors and degrees with academic scholarships and part-time jobs. In matters of finance, she was proud, frugal, and fiercely independent. In the six months we'd been together as lovers, I'd learned to compromise—a lot.

Pup seemed bored with the ballroom and sniffed the air for hints of more exciting discoveries. He had been Kim's companion and protector for many years. To my surprise and delight, once he stopped trying to scare me away from his mistress, he became my friend and extended his protective services to include me.

"Come on." I touched Kim's forearm. "Mitch can't stay, and we need to get the luggage."

We went back to the Mercedes and helped our pilot and chauffeur empty the trunk. Without another word, we shouldered the lighter bags and followed Mitch back into the house.

We finished our quick tour of the downstairs, breezing into and out of the main room, dining room, kitchen, two bathrooms, library, and Dad's spacious suite of offices. Kim peeked at the screened-in porch, with its comfortable chairs and love seats, and her tension seemed to ease.

"Now, that looks comfortable. I could live in one of the rocking chairs, or on the loveseat."

"Sweetheart, you can live any place here that you want, except for Dad's office and his suite."

"Suite?" Kim chewed her lower lip. "I'm getting nervous about staying in a place that rivals Buckingham Palace." She looked up at the high ceilings and ornate crystal chandeliers. "Must be a bitch to clean the cobwebs from those."

I put my hand on her shoulder, giving it a rub. "Relax, okay? I'll be with you every step of the way. But first, we need to dump our things in my suite and get changed."

Her body tensed. "There's that word again. You both have suites?"

"Mine's only three modest rooms, overlooking a corner of the bay." I nudged her hip. "Come on, we can leave breadcrumbs to find our way back, if you want."

"Very funny." She gave me a weak grin. "All this opulence is making me a bit queasy, that's all."

I kissed her cheek. "The salt air will fix that right up. We can change into jeans and sweatshirts and take Pup on the Cliff Walk up to The Breakers. That's three miles along the coast, with a view of several mansions. It'll get your blood flowing again."

"Breakers? Does the ocean get that rough up here?"

"The Sound is choppy, but— Oh, The Breakers." I smiled. "No, actually, that's the name of the biggest estate up here, a retreat for the Vanderbilts—Cornelius, the second, I think. It has twice as many rooms as this place."

Before Kim could react to my statement, Dad walked into the main room and paused. Workouts in his private gym and frequent games of tennis and golf kept him fit, especially for a man in his sixties. Though not tall, he stood and walked with confidence, and his thick, white hair was cut in a casual, boyish style that I had always liked. Despite our difficulties, I was proud of him. My heart ached for the close bond we once shared, and I wondered if we could ever get it back.

A tentative smile twitched the corners of his mouth as he patted Pup on the head and turned to Kim, pouring on the charm. "Welcome to Rhode Island, Dr. Blair. Did you have a good flight?"

Kim nodded. “Very pleasant, thank you.” She waved her arm to indicate the large room with all its furnishings. “This is very impressive. Thank you for inviting me.”

Dad walked over, and they shook hands. “The pleasure is all mine.” Then he turned to me, his arms outstretched. “And Priscilla, thank you for coming.” When I hesitated, he lowered his arms. “I’m so glad you agreed to meet with me. I’m just sorry so many things kept getting in our way.”

“Yes,” I said. “First one thing and then another.”

“That problem with the oil spill took forever to clear up. I just couldn’t—”

I held up my hand. “I understand, Dad. It’s okay, really.”

“And then you two got busy.”

Kim nodded. “I promised PJ a trip to see some very old trees in Colorado. Bristlecone pines.”

“And then we went to Mexico to… uh…” Oh, shit. That wasn’t business. That was pure pleasure. Me and my big mouth. “We went there to work on…” I could feel my neck and cheeks flush.

Kim rescued me. “Glenna Rhoderick asked me to write a chapter for her new book about warrior women. That took several weeks and some more traveling to sort out.”

I shot her a grateful smile. “But well worth the effort.” I turned to my father. “Kim is going to collaborate with a very distinguished archaeologist.”

“Yes, I read about that. Quite a feather in your cap, Dr. Blair.”

Kim looked embarrassed. “Thank you, Mr. Curtis. And I wish you’d call me Kim.”

He grinned at her. “Only if you stop calling me Mr. Curtis. It’s Frederick, okay?” He stuck out his hand again.

“Okay.” She grinned back and clasped his hand.

“The whole deal is great publicity for the foundation,” I said. “I don’t know if you realize it, but Glenna Rhoderick is a hot property in our field.”

“As is Kim,” Dad said, giving her shoulder a squeeze.

Oh yeah, was she ever. Hot. Hot. Hot.

Kim glanced at me, apparently reading my lecherous thoughts, because she blushed. “It isn’t a done deal yet, but we discussed the project and did some preliminary groundwork.”

“And then we couldn’t leave Arizona before Sandy and Laine got their doctorates.” I smiled, remembering our group’s festive reunion at Mrs. O’Brien’s.

My father's expression grew serious. "No matter how overdue it is, you're both here now." Moisture glittered in his eyes, and the lines on his face softened. "We began this on the phone when you were in Arizona, and now I'm ready to talk it all out and make a fresh start. I want to settle our differences, if you'll give me the chance."

"I'd like that too, Dad. When you called and told me that you loved me, it helped a great deal. I think we've been out of synch for too long."

"And it shouldn't have taken an earthquake to convince me that we can't go on like we have. I want to fix that, or at least make a start." He held his arms out again. "Please, let me try."

I moved into his embrace with such speed it surprised us both. He stumbled, but gave me a hug and a delighted laugh. "Welcome back, Princess."

"It's great to be back," I mumbled into his shirtfront.

We stood squeezing each other for several seconds, then I released Dad and stepped back.

"You get Kim settled," he said. "Change into something comfortable, and we'll talk."

I wiped my eyes. "That sounds good. We have a lot to talk about."

* * *

An hour later, I found Vivian, Dad's personal assistant, working at her desk in the alcove next to his office. She was elated to see me. "Such a lovely tan, Priscilla. And you look so happy. I guess all that danger and excitement in Arizona must have agreed with you."

"It was a bit scary at times, but I wouldn't have traded the experience for anything. Is he ready for me?"

Snow-white curls bounced as her head bobbed vehemently. "Go right in. If you ask me, this chat is long overdue."

"Wish me luck."

"You'll be fine. Just remember that he loves you, and he always has. He'll take forever to say it, but that's what he means."

"Yeah, well… I wish I had your faith." I squared my shoulders and walked through the door.

His office hadn't changed much since the last time I had been in it. Although upgraded and updated, the computer, fax machine, copier, and file cabinet rested in their usual places against one wall. His huge, solid cherry desk stood alone in the center of the room, and framed antique maps and paintings of sailing ships cluttered most of the wall space. Aged brass seafaring instruments gleamed on glass-enclosed shelves on either side of a large picture window.

Everything looked just as I remembered it, but something had been added. On one corner of his polished desktop, next to the ugly clay pipe holder that I made for him in first grade, were three framed photographs. Two of them were familiar. I had seen the one of Mom and Dad on their honeymoon in Tahiti and the one of me as a child of five or six, sitting on my father's lap in his New York office, pretending to dictate a business letter. The look of pride on my father's face was enough to bring a lump to my throat. I used to matter to him so much.

I stared at the third photo, a group of smiling people in a restaurant. When I moved closer, I recognized Kim and me, standing in the middle of the group. It was one of our earliest gatherings at Mrs. O'Brien's. How in the world did he get that? Kim must have sent it to him. What a sneak. What a sweet, adorable sneak.

"Is Kim all settled in?" Dad asked, startling me.

"Yeah. She's reading on the porch. We'll do the Cliff Walk when I'm finished here."

"Good." He put aside his paperwork, moved to the sleeper sofa along the far wall, and sat down. After my mother's death, Dad had worked many nights in here to the point of exhaustion. He would crash on that sofa when he was too tired to climb the stairs to his own room. Now, he patted the space beside him. "Won't you join me, Priscilla? I can vouch for the cushioning. It's very comfortable."

I perched on the edge, gripping my knees. "Dad, I noticed that new picture—the one of our Amazon-hunting group."

"Yes. Quite an energetic bunch, wouldn't you say?"

"Absolutely. They were the hardest workers I've ever had the pleasure of being around. We had some great times. I miss them a lot."

"I hope you don't mind. Kim sent me the photo with one of her reports. She knows I like to keep up with you, see how you're getting along."

I felt my face flush and looked away from him. I hadn't realized he was keeping tabs on me. Should I have been flattered, or worried?

Dad cleared his throat. "I can see this is going to be awkward for both of us."

"Yes, I'm sorry. I guess there's still a lot of tension."

"Should I ask Francine to bring us tea, or something stronger?"

My laugh sounded strained, even to my own ears. "Maybe some bottled water. My throat is a little dry."

"Of course." He rose and moved to the intercom on his desk.

His summons was answered immediately, though the voice wasn't Francine's. "Yes, Mr. Curtis. What can I do for you?"

"Megan, please have Francine bring two bottles of water to my office."

"Yes, sir."

"And have her visit the porch and ask Dr. Blair if she needs anything."

"Right away, sir."

That would probably freak Kim out, I thought, then I giggled. Oh, hell, she might even get to like it.

Dad returned to the sofa. "Something funny?"

"I'm just wondering how Kim is going to react to being waited on."

He grimaced. "She's not used to any of this, is she?"

"No. It isn't really her style."

"She's a fine scientist. I'm impressed with her work. Sending you down there to Arizona was the best thing I ever did."

"I couldn't agree more."

He directed his gaze at me for several seconds, head cocked to one side. "You know, she's done wonders for you. The reports you've faxed me, the grant money you gave those kids— All of that showed so much initiative, so much professional maturity."

"Thank you, Dad."

He touched my knee, giving it a squeeze. "And you've settled down, tamed your wild social behavior. Ending that pointless relationship with Stephen was for the best."

I hoped he would agree when he knew the whole story. "Yes, it was."

"In short, you've blossomed."

"Whew." My cheeks were flaming with all this sudden praise. "I appreciate the sentiment, but really, I owe it all to Kim."

He slid closer and put his arm around my shoulders. "If that's the case, you stick with her."

"Oh, I intend to." Night and day, through thick and thin. Until death did us part, I would stick with her.

He hugged me against his chest and kissed the top of my head. "Good."

"Actually, that's part of what I wanted to discuss with you."

"Right. You mentioned something in your last e-mail."

There was a brief, but firm knock on the door, and Francine entered, carrying a tray loaded with two chilled bottles of water, two crystal goblets, and several slices of lemon. It also held crackers, cheese, fruit, and a glass bowl with a generous supply of whole cashews. Both Dad and I reached for a handful and laughed as our fingers collided.

"Guess you can tell we're related," he said.

Francine smiled at me. "Welcome back, Dr. Curtis. It's wonderful to have you at Windswept again."

"Thanks, Francine. I'm happy to be back. How is Dr. Blair doing?"

"Oh, she's quite content. I'm bringing her a pot of tea and some fresh blueberry muffins."

"If you spread the muffins with honey butter, I know she'll love it."

"I'll be happy to." She turned to my father. "Will there be anything else, sir?"

"No, thank you, Francine. Just have Vivian hold my calls until further notice."

"Of course, sir." She moved to the door just as Vivian brought in a bundle of mail.

"I wouldn't have disturbed you, but the top letter came Air Express and was marked urgent." Vivian handed the mail to my father and gave me a reassuring smile. "I must say, it's wonderful to see you back in here with your father."

I seemed to have a cheering section among the staff. I grinned back at her. "Thanks, Vivian. Dad and I really needed this time to talk. I'm just sorry we were delayed for so long."

"You're here now. That's what counts." She watched as Dad returned to his desk and slit open the letter. "Will you need anything further?"

Dad looked up at her, frowning. "Not just now, Vivian. Stay close, though. I think I may need your assistance in a few minutes."

"Of course. I'll be right outside." With a brief nod of her head and a wink in my direction, she was gone.

I took another handful of nuts and chewed them while Dad drummed his fingers on the desk, lost in thought.

"Problem?" I asked, getting up from the sofa and flopping into one of the two chairs in front of his desk.

He passed me the paper. "Do you remember the Morrisons?"

I looked at the ornate embossed letterhead and gave the name some thought. "Should I?"

"I think you saw John a time or two when you were very small, but I met him long before you were born, sweetheart. We first ran into each other, literally, in a bookstore in Oxford during my junior year abroad. He backed into me, and I knocked half a dozen books onto the floor. We began laughing, and when we couldn't stop, we were escorted out of the building for creating a disturbance."

I smiled, still chewing.

"That was before he met Jenny and I met your mother. When they got married, I was his best man. It was quite a posh affair. Through the years, we kept in touch as best we could, but when your mother died… well, we lost touch. Now it seems they're someplace in Wales, living on his family's estate."

"Wow. Quite the upper crust."

"Yeah. Lord and Lady Morrison."

I finished reading the letter. "I have to admit, it sounds intriguing… some sort of mystery. But where do I fit in? How did he even know I'm an archaeologist?"

Dad shrugged, his attention focused on a small pile of papers. "I guess he must have read about it in a news article, or something."

"I see. Still, I'm sure there are better-qualified people right in his own backyard. He's talking about a Celtic warrior and some kind of connection to ancient relatives." I sighed. Now, where had I heard that before?

Dad shifted in his seat, making the chair squeak. "I'm sure he wouldn't ask for help if he didn't really need it." He rubbed his chin in thought. "You would be doing me a favor, if you'd assist him." He paused a moment, and then his expression brightened. "What if you and Kim were to go over there together? How would that be? You could work on it as a team for a couple of weeks and then take a holiday."

"You'd have to ask her, but I'm sure she'd be very helpful."

A tiny smile played at the corners of his mouth. "You seem to know a great deal about what Kim likes."

I sank back into my seat on the sofa. "We got to be very good friends while we were in Arizona."

He stared at me for several seconds. "Yes. I imagine you did."

I handed the letter back to him. "I need to talk with you about Kim and me. It's important."

"Why don't you go get her, and we'll discuss it together?"

"No!" The word came out with more vehemence than I intended. "That is, I—uh, we thought that I'd better tell you alone… first."

He frowned. "About you and Kim?"

Jesus. Did he have any idea what I was going to say? He looked so stern. I was going to blow it. I just knew it.

"Priscilla, do you have something to tell me?"

"Oh, sorry. Yes, it's about Kim and me. We became friends in Arizona. Good friends. And then things changed between us. Our friendship grew into something stronger. I know it might come as a shock to you, but… I fell in love with her."

His expression never changed, and I couldn't tell how the news had affected him.

"Dad? Did you hear what I said?"

He leaned across his desk and stabbed the intercom button. "Vivian?"

Her cheerful voice contrasted with the tension in the office. "Are you ready for me now, sir?"

"No, not yet. Please find Dr. Blair and have her report to me at once."

"Right away, sir."

Oh, shit! I had messed up. I did a mental review of our conversation. The stuff about Wales had thrown me off, made me rush. I had freaked him out. Damn it, I only told him the truth.

"Dad, please. I—"

He stood and held up one hand. "Let's just wait for Kim to get here, so I can talk to both of you at once, okay?"

I sat in silence, hands clenched in my lap, blinking back tears. If he wouldn't accept us as a couple, then that was that. He could forget about reconciliation. I loved her. If he forced me to choose between the two of them, I'd take her side in a heartbeat.

There was a knock on the door, and Kim entered the office, looking brave and incredibly beautiful.

Chapter 2

Despite the opulence that surrounded me, I was quite relaxed, drifting from the pages of my book into a dreamy, nap-like state. A light breeze ruffled my hair.

Pup, lying on the floor beside me, also seemed, in his own doggie way, a little overwhelmed by so much wealth. It was probably just my overactive imagination, but I could have sworn that his eyes widened the first time he was served water in a crystal doggie bowl and food in a fine china dish that was trimmed with colorful hand-painted doggie images.

"Don't get too used to it," I warned him. "When we get back home, all this luxury will disappear, and it'll be back to Wal-Mart's finest plastic." He arched his eyebrows in what I took to be condescension. Francine's arrival interrupted my reverie. She carried a silver tray with tea in a cozy-covered teapot and a delicate Royal Doulton tea service. My eyes focused on the plate, which held two of the most delicious looking, and what I assumed were homemade, blueberry muffins. "Ms. PJ—I mean Dr. Curtis—thought you would enjoy some refreshments."

"Thank you, Francine, and please thank Dr. Curtis for me."

Francine prepared to pour the tea. "Cream or sugar?"

"Both, please."

"Two cubes or one?"

"Two, thank you." It wasn't my usual practice to have sugar in my tea, but I could not resist those sweet little cubes, especially when I visualized dipping them into my tea and then sucking on them. Mmm. Made me think of PJ. I felt my face flush at the unbidden erotic connection.

The cream was the real thing, too, not the two-percent stuff I used most of the time. If I wasn't careful, I could get used to this lavish lifestyle.

Pup fixed his big, yellow eyes on me as I picked up a muffin.

"No, Pup. Too much sugar for you, my friend."

"I haven't forgotten you, Pup," Francine said, patting his head. "I have some freshly baked dog biscuits for you, so why don't you come with me and see whether they've cooled sufficiently?"

Pup trotted into the house alongside her. Just like a male, I thought. Couldn't resist a pretty woman.

After enjoying my tea and muffins, I lay back and allowed my mind to wander.

This situation wasn't good for me. I needed to be working, not sitting on my butt living the good life.

I wondered how PJ was doing. She was going to break the news to Frederick this morning, so the good life could be over for me before I knew it. *Oh, PJ.* I hoped she wasn't making a mistake, springing it on him too soon.

I must have fallen asleep then, because the next thing I was aware of was Vivian waking me. "Dr. Blair, Mr. Curtis wants to see you in his office right away."

"He does? Oh, dear." I stood and straightened my clothes. "Where's PJ?"

"She's with him."

"Vivian, how is his mood?"

She gave me a strange look. "Fine. Business-like, as usual. That man works way too hard."

As I made my way to Frederick's office suite, I took little notice of the exquisite artwork hanging on the walls. PJ's mother had been a connoisseur of the arts, and her collection, displayed here and at their Boston home, revealed her good taste. I doubted that I would have the opportunity to admire this part of the collection. For now, I was too absorbed in wondering what awaited me, what Frederick's reaction would be. I was in a state of limbo, not knowing what kind of future was in store for us, or if there was any future at all.

Frederick was a powerful man. With little effort I could visualize him as an enforcer who could, if need be, hire someone to make sure I was no longer a "threat" to his daughter.

Geez, I hated dark alleys, but that was where I was going to end up. Stop it! Frederick was nothing if not an ethical businessman. He wouldn't stoop to criminal activity to get rid of his daughter's lover. More than likely, he'd try to pay me off with a generous sum and a one-way ticket to Outer Mongolia.

My mind returned to the present as I entered the office suite. Vivian had taken a detour to the kitchen, so there was no one at her desk to announce my presence.

I straightened my shoulders and tried to take bold steps to the closed door of Frederick's private office, his inner sanctum. My knock sounded too firm.

"Enter." It was a command rather than an invitation.

"You wanted to see me, Frederick?"

"Yes, I do."

I glanced at PJ. She was sitting across the desk from Frederick in one of the leather chairs. Her face was red, and her green eyes glistened with unshed tears. Her golden hair was mussed, as if she had been running her hands through it, in desperation perhaps.

Frederick hadn't looked at either of us. Instead, he added his signature to a sheaf of papers.

I wanted to get on with it, get it over with. Why was he prolonging the punishment?

Finally, he replaced the cap on his pen and carefully placed it on the desk. He leaned back in his chair, looking first at PJ and then at me. There was no trace of a smile on his face.

I glanced at PJ. She made a discreet movement with her finger, drawing it across her throat. Frederick caught the gesture and froze her with his gaze. She dropped her hand into her lap and looked in my direction. Pleading, I thought, for me to make things right.

I felt sorry for her distress, but what was done was done. We'd have to live with the consequences, whatever they were.

"We need to talk." Frederick stood up and came around his desk to stand in front of me.

"Yes, sir."

PJ rose and moved to my side. Her fingers sought mine and held on to them.

Obviously, she'd made up her mind, but did this have to happen just as she and her father were rebuilding their relationship? I glanced toward her, my eyes questioning. Was I worth her risking continued estrangement from her dad?

The rift between them had started when PJ was fourteen. Her mother had been killed in a plane crash in Egypt while on assignment as a photojournalist. Apparently, PJ and Frederick had never worked through their grief successfully.

Frederick didn't say anything. He looked first at me and then at PJ.

"I can explain," I said, "and I hope you can find it in your heart to understand."

"Dr. Blair, what is the extent of your relationship with my daughter?"

"Dad, it's like I told you."

"Priscilla, I want to hear Dr. Blair's version."

"I love your daughter, Frederick," I said. "I love her more than anything or anyone in this world, but if it means that she's going to lose you again—" I hoped the catch in my throat wasn't audible "—I'll walk out of here alone and never turn back."

"Kim." PJ dropped my hand and swung around to face me, forcing her father to step aside. "You can't mean that. You wouldn't, would you?" Tears overflowed onto her cheeks.

"Yes, if it comes to that, PJ. I have to do what's right, what's most beneficial for you."

"If you think that walking out on me is the right thing to do, then your priorities are severely screwed."

A chuckle alerted us to the fact that Frederick was smiling.

"That won't be necessary," he said, drawing us both into his arms. "Welcome to the family, Kim. You're good for Priscilla. I know that, and I'm proud of the two of you."

PJ slapped him on the chest and then wiped at her tears. "How could you? That was cruel, acting like you disapproved. I almost had a heart attack."

"I'm sorry. I was only teasing you both. Forgive me for allowing it to go on so long."

"Jesus." PJ's voice shook with emotion, but she finally joined in the group hug. "Did you know about us all along?"

"I had my suspicions, but I waited. I knew that sooner or later you would say something."

"I think I've lost ten years off my life."

"You and me both," I said, grinning with relief.

Frederick smiled. "I won't say it didn't concern me at first."

PJ looked up at him. "Oh?"

"You do have a history of being headstrong. I was worried that you hadn't given sufficient thought to your actions, and about what the fall-out might cost you. If you hadn't spoken of it this soon, I would have broached the subject myself."

"I have thought about it. Kim and I talked long and hard about the situation. She even tried to dissuade me."

"You realize, don't you," he said, leaning his hips against his desk and half sitting on it, "that you'll face disapproval in some circles and downright discrimination in others?"

"I know that. Kim made sure I understood what I was getting into, and what to expect."

"And children, Priscilla?"

"We've talked about that, too. Right now, we both want to concentrate on our relationship and our work. If we decide later that we want a child, there are ways, and you know it." PJ put her arm around my waist. "It's quite common these days for couples like us to adopt, or use scientific methods, so don't rule out being a grandfather."

"Ah, 'tis a brave new world," Frederick said. "One that I don't always presume to understand. What I do understand is love, and if that's what you and Kim share, who am I to deny you the right to such a powerful emotion?"

"I love Kim." PJ squeezed my waist and gazed into my eyes. "And I know she loves me."

I kissed her on the forehead and looked at Frederick. "I tried to dissuade her. I really did, because I can't imagine what she sees in an old fossil like me."

PJ gave me a nudge. "Stop that. Don't you even think those thoughts, not even in jest." We grinned at each other, lost in the moment, until Frederick spoke.

"For what it's worth," he said, standing up straight, "you have my blessing."

"Thanks." PJ kissed him on the cheek. "And your blessing is worth everything, so much more than you can know. I can't tell you how happy we are that you understand and support us."

Caught up in the emotion of the moment, I pecked him on the cheek, too. "Thank you, Frederick. You have my word that I'll do my best to make her happy."

He laughed and kissed me back. "She'll be a handful, Kim. I hope you're ready for that."

"Hey!" PJ poked him in the ribs.

"Oh, I'm looking forward to the challenge, believe me."

Although PJ's eyes gleamed with mischief, I saw anger in them, too. It was directed at me.

"That may be so, Kimberly Blair, but wait until I get you alone. For starters, what were you thinking when you said you'd leave me?"

"It would have been for your sake. After all, you and your father were just getting reconciled."

"My sake? You would have done it for my sake? What about my happiness? Doesn't that mean anything to you?"

"Priscilla, stop. Kim was only trying to do right by you, which proves to me that she really loves you. And now, my dears, I suggest we see if we can make some noise about lunch."

* * *

The dining room overwhelmed my down-to-earth sensibilities. The long mahogany table, with its high-backed chairs, breathed formality, as did the seat cushions, woven of a braided material with subtle ship designs. Standing against one wall was a huge sideboard, where food would be placed before it was served, or so I assumed. A silver coffee service sat at one end of it, gleaming in the midday sunshine.

Outside the picture windows, gardens flourished in a glory of color. Beyond them, the blue haze of early summer lay over the Sound. It was a picture-perfect setting and a far cry from the dusty Arizona desert. PJ evidently sensed my discomfort and moved toward me, taking my hand in hers.

"Dad, if you think you're sitting here at the head of the table and sending me down there, you're mistaken." PJ pointed to the other end of the table. "Not when it's just the three of us."

Frederick pulled out the chair to his right. "No, you're going to sit here."

"Thank you, Papa."

"Don't you 'Papa' me." He gave her hair a playful tousle.

I stood, unsure of what I should do.

"Please, Kim, relax." Frederick came around to me and pulled out the chair to his left. "Have a seat. This isn't a formal affair. We're just having a spot of lunch, family style."

"Thank you, Frederick." I glanced across the table at PJ and swallowed the lump that was forming in my throat.

"I'm not through with you," she said, pointing a finger at me.

"Now, Princess," her father said, "be nice."

As if on cue, Francine arrived along with Bridie, her assistant, to oversee the serving of lunch. We started with sherry-laced lobster chowder, a platter of assorted crackers, and chunks of sourdough French bread.

Frederick and PJ helped themselves to crackers, but I couldn't resist the still-warm bread. Slathered with butter, it was a banquet to the palate.

During the pause between the soup and the main course, Frederick took a letter from his pocket and handed it to me. "Kim, this is from Lord Morrison, an old college friend of mine. Unfortunately, we've grown apart in recent years. You know how it is, both of us being involved in business pursuits. Anyway, we drifted in opposite directions, and for the most part, we've been out of touch."

I scanned the contents of the letter. "What is his business?"

"He's involved in a number of charities, and he's Chairman of the Board of the Royal Society of British Antiquities."

I read the letter again with careful deliberation. I tried to read between the lines of what I thought was a strange request.

My frown must have been evident because Frederick interrupted. "He asked for Priscilla, but I want you to go with her. You can make it a working, all-expenses-paid vacation."

"Wouldn't he be better served by going straight to the police?" I asked. "This is a matter for their expertise. We're not detectives. Besides, we'd be going in cold. I don't know how much help we'd be."

"I agree, but he made a specific request for Priscilla, so he must feel he has need of an archaeologist's expertise."

Our conversation was interrupted by the arrival of the main course.

Francine and Bridie served us sandwiches that consisted of the most delicious-looking grilled Virginia ham I'd ever seen, together with honey mustard, Swiss cheese, and romaine lettuce, all on marbled rye bread. The sandwich tasted even more delicious than it looked.

"This is fantastic," I said, wiping a bit of mustard off of my chin.

"Isn't it?" Frederick said. "There's a restaurant on Front Street that serves these. I had Megan gather the ingredients and hound the chef for his secret recipe." He took a huge bite and chewed it vigorously.

I thought of the meager meals I had eaten after Terry, my ex, had left and before PJ had come into my life. I was a good cook, but looking back, I knew I could have done better for myself. Living alone, with no one else to think about, I had become careless about my nutrition.

Francine filled our glasses with wine, snapping me back to the present.

As soon as she had left us alone, Frederick raised his glass. "To you, Kim, and Priscilla. May your life together be a long and happy one."

"Thank you." PJ took his hand. "I love you, you know."

"And I you, Princess." He reached for my hand. "I'm happy for both of you."

The conversation drifted to other things, as PJ and her father caught up on each other's lives.

"I'm afraid that this is of little interest to you, Kim," Frederick said.

"Not at all. I just regret for your sakes that you saw so little of each other during those years."

"I regret it, too. I missed so much of Priscilla's growing up because I grieved for her mother in all the wrong ways. I lost sight of my daughter's pain and what her mother would have wanted for her."

"That's all in the past now," PJ said.

"Yes it is, isn't it? And in a roundabout way, Kim, I have you to thank for bringing us together."

I blushed at the unexpected and important compliment. This reconciliation was a gift in itself, even if I had done nothing else for PJ.

We topped off lunch with Chocolate Banana Purses, which were crispy won tons filled with dark chocolate and banana slices, served with vanilla ice cream. If I wasn't careful, my waistline would transform into a huge doughnut around my middle.

"Is this another recipe from that restaurant?" I asked Frederick, as he scooped up several of the tasty treats.

"Yes. Megan managed to capture their unique taste rather nicely."

As we finished our meal, we made plans for our coming trip to Wales. Frederick said he would call Lord Morrison and let him know when we'd arrive.

* * *

After a long walk along the cliffs, PJ and I settled down to make lists of the supplies, clothing, and research material we would need for our hasty flight to Wales. The list of research material was skimpy, because we weren't exactly sure of what we'd be facing or what we'd be expected to do.

I was concerned about looking for a missing Celtic chieftain. My expertise was with Amazons, and although I hadn't discussed it again with PJ, I felt we weren't through with them yet, nor they with us.

Chapter 3

Following the directions of a village policeman, I turned right onto a narrow street, and then left into a small courtyard. PJ's excitement seemed to rise at her first glimpse of The Royal Lion Inn, which appeared out of the fog like some ghostly apparition from times past. A short, irregular stone walk led to the front door, and the stone walls were blanketed by a thick growth of ivy. Colorful flowers invaded the path's right-of-way, brushing the legs of those entering or leaving.

"It's delightfully quaint," I said, stepping from our rented Range Rover.

PJ's face was flushed. "It is indeed. Do you think they'll have a room for us?"

"I hope so." Perhaps it was foolish not to have made reservations. We elected to have Frederick's corporate jet drop us off in London, rather than a closer airport, and PJ thought committing to a definite arrival time would have limited our freedom of travel to Wales. We rented a car and made good use of our time, taking in the sights of the English and Welsh countryside. Frederick had suggested, after all, that we combine our business with pleasure. We were doing that in spades.

The lobby smelled of fresh baked bread.

"Ooh! Isn't this wonderful?" PJ took my arm, and we peeked into the main sitting room.

A robust fire blazed in the massive, gray stone fireplace. It was a welcome sight after our drive through a heavy overcast that all but obliterated any sight of the surrounding hills. The gleaming brass handles of the fireplace tools reflected the flickering flames. An ancient bellows lay on top of a brass coal scuttle, now filled with logs. The large, blackened iron pot, hanging on a hook above the grate, reminded me of Shakespeare's *Macbeth*: "Double, double toil and trouble; Fire burn and cauldron bubble."

The cozy lobby showed no hint of the bard's Three Witches, with their secret ingredients of "eye of newt and toe of frog." Neither was there any indication of "wool of bat and tongue of dog," except for Pup, who I hoped would be a guest in this old-world hostelry. Antique bed warmers, huge stirring spoons, and other utensils adorned the walls that flanked the fireplace.

A number of easy chairs were arranged in a semicircle in front of the hearth. According to a placard supported on a sturdy easel and placed in the center of the lobby, tea would be served at four o'clock.

"Oh, how very British," PJ said, all but cooing over the Welsh atmosphere. "They have to have room for us. They just have to, that's all."

A rosy-cheeked young woman, whose brogue was as Welsh as the country was ancient, greeted us at the reception desk. "Prynhawn da," she said, then repeated in English, "Good afternoon."

"Prynhawn da."

I smiled at PJ's Welsh response. No one could say she didn't get into the spirit of the place.

She caught my amused expression. "It's such an ancient language, and so beautiful."

"I'm sure it is, if you can pronounce the words."

I turned my attention to the clerk. "This is our first visit to Wales, so we'd like your nicest room," I said as I glanced at her nametag, "Arwel."

"I'm so sorry. We have nothing suitable."

I cursed myself for not insisting we make reservations.

PJ's shoulders slumped. "It was a good idea while it lasted. Maybe we can come back here later."

"It's the sheep dog trials, you see," Arwel said. "The Welsh National Championships." She consulted her register once more. "We do have one room. One of the early entries was disqualified and left this morning. The room is smaller than the others, mind you, and has only one bed, a double."

Trying hard to be serious, I glanced at PJ. "Why not? I don't mind if you don't."

"Are you sure?" PJ's green eyes sparkled with amusement.

"We allowed the occupant's dog to stay in the room with him. I don't know if it will smell as fresh as it could." Arwel frowned as she looked from PJ back to me.

"That wouldn't be a problem. Kim's dog is traveling with us and would prefer to stay with her." PJ gave me a wink.

"How nice." Arwel continued in her singsong dialect. "It has a lovely view of the gardens and the mountains. You can see the river, too. And it is one of the few rooms we have with a private bath."

"I think we can manage." I turned to PJ. "A private bath's a rarity in this part of the world."

"Mmm, if that's the case, I suppose we should take it," PJ said.

* * *

We entered the room from a small lounge that was accessed from the ground floor by a narrow wooden staircase. The center of each riser was worn down by centuries of footsteps. Several of the stairs were slanted, but despite the lack of modern uniformity, the structure had withstood the test of centuries.

PJ dropped her bags and flung herself across the bed, laughing. "You think we can manage, do you? Just you wait and see how we manage."

I lay down beside PJ, then on top of her. We traded kisses while my hand sought her breast.

She writhed beneath me, panting and gasping. Suddenly, she stopped. "Geez, do you hear that?"

"Hear what?" I was too busy teasing PJ's breasts to hear or to sense anything other than the quivering of her breath.

"Stop, Kim. This bed creaks so much they'll hear us all the way down to the cellar."

I slid my hand under her shirt and unclasped her bra. "Not to worry, these old buildings have stout walls."

"Wait!" She rolled out from under me, fastened her bra, and tugged her shirt back into place. "I just think we, um… should have afternoon tea first."

"Tea? Instead of me?" I pouted. "Okay, so break my heart." I took a deep breath, trying to settle the pounding organ in question. "I guess the honeymoon had to end sooner or later."

She took my hands and replaced them on her breasts. "Sweetie, just wait until later, okay?" She gave me a tender kiss. "I promise you're going to have a lot more than tea to deal with. Maybe I'll smother myself in some of that delicious Devonshire cream, and you can dip your strawberries and—"

"God." My imagination filled in the remainder of her sentence as she moved from the bed to the window.

"Oh, come look. It's gorgeous."

I stood behind her, my arms locked around her waist, my head resting on her shoulder, as we looked out at the carefully manicured gardens with their beds of colorful blooms. "It's like an old painting come to life." I nuzzled the hollow of her neck. "Are you happy?"

"Incredibly."

"So can we continue where we left off on the bed?"

She turned and pulled me into another breath-stealing kiss before pushing me toward our luggage. "I promise. After we get settled in and have some tea. You're going to need all your strength for what I have planned for you, my dear."

"Let's get busy then."

We unpacked and hung our clothes in an antique, freestanding wardrobe that smelled faintly of mothballs. PJ ran her fingers along the smooth wood of the old-fashioned dressing table. The mirror was ancient, the image distorted. "I'll bet this old furniture could tell many a tale."

"So could the bathroom." I peeked around the door. "You'll have to see it to believe it."

The claw-footed tub stood on a six-inch-high platform. PJ giggled. "I'll need a ladder to get in and a grappling hook to get out."

"I'll be happy to assist you."

"My hero, always willing to help a naked damsel in distress."

"It's a tough job, but somebody has to do it." I wandered to another section of the large bathroom. "Wait till you see the toilet."

PJ looked behind the partition. "Good grief." It, too, was raised onto a platform. She practiced getting on and off while I stood by, driven to hysterics by her antics. The only way she could sit on the toilet was to back up to the stool and hop onto it. Once seated, her feet dangled free of the floor. "I can see that my morning ablutions are going to be an adventure in themselves, and heaven help me if I have to get up in the middle of the night."

"And you'd better have your toilet paper in your hot little hand." I pointed to the roll holder that was mounted on the wall just out of reach. At this point, she could barely talk for laughing.

"Oh, geez. All this talk—now I've got to pee." PJ's expression was pained, but her words were lost in her laughter as she jumped off the commode to pull down her pants before struggling back on again.

"You forgot already," I said, handing her some toilet paper. "Next time, you're on your own, kiddo."

"Hey, where's my Soft and Lite? This stuff is like a page out of Playboy."

"You could use a hair dryer."

"Very funny." None too gracefully, PJ hopped down and pulled up her pants. "Why do you suppose they raised everything like that when the Welsh are said to be small in stature?"

"It was probably designed by an Englishman. There's still some rivalry between them, you know, the English and the Welsh."

"How do you know that when you've never been here before?"

"I saw them play a soccer match against each other on TV. It was pretty tense."

"Humph."

I glanced at the pull chain, with its china handle painted with tiny pink rosebuds, and was astonished at the workmanship someone had devoted to something so utilitarian, an object destined to spend its life in the loo. I wondered how many visitors, if any, ever took time to marvel at such fine art in this gallery of lesser human arts.

* * *

We sat on a love seat directly across from the fireplace. Two middle-aged couples, prim and proper in demeanor and dress, sat on either side of a low antique table. They glanced toward us from time to time, turning away when we returned their stare.

Responding to PJ's stage whisper, I looked at the two elderly women seated in wing-backed chairs next to the fireplace. Each of them balanced a fine china cup and saucer in one hand, and nibbled ginger cookies from small, matching plates on their laps. I had noticed their disapproving glances when we were making our selections from the table spread with so many delicious looking goodies, and again when we sat down with our tea and Princess Anne Sandwich Cake.

"Our attire must be inappropriate," I whispered. PJ's jeans, loose-fitting shirt, and multi-pocketed vest weren't exactly parlor wear. Neither were my cords and wool sweater.

"They probably blame it on the fact that we're Americans and don't know any better."

"How do they know that when they don't know us?"

PJ giggled. "Easy, we don't poise our pinkies."

I snorted.

"That, too. It's only uncouth Americans who snort like that."

I suspected that my laughter was a little too loud, as all heads turned in our direction.

"Sorry." I shrugged and raised my hands palms upward. My smile was met with stony glances.

It was PJ's turn to snort.
She did.

* * *

The hostelry was early thirteenth century and delightful in spite of the rain that fell in sheets during our first night. From my reclining position, I watched the water cascade down the windowpanes. The glass was old, greenish in color, and uneven, distorting the deluge's downward path.

PJ lay in my arms, asleep after a wild and wonderful session of lovemaking. God, she was a passionate woman. I melted from the fire that burned inside her. My body was still throbbing in remembrance. I kissed her thick, blonde hair, and she stirred but didn't awaken.

A flash of lightning lit the room. Pup, who was on the floor beside the bed, raised his head and growled.

Seven months ago, we left the Superstition Mountains of Arizona and the Amazon remains we had discovered there. I had spent the better part of my professional life searching for the Lost Tribe of the Amazons, and when I finally caught up with them, I learned much more than I could have dreamed I would. Finding Marna, a key member of the tribe, and recognizing that she and I were one and the same, except that we were travelers in a different time, had brought me peace, but I felt that something was missing from the equation. I couldn't put my finger on what it was, and I was reluctant to discuss it with PJ.

I planned to write about the project, and I had material to contribute to Glenna Rhoderick's book. Since events beyond our scope of explanation controlled so much of our experiences, the writing wasn't an easy task. Even PJ had come to believe, in a limited way, that the spirits of the old Amazon Goddesses were alive and well. And while I was no longer as driven as I had been about the Amazon tribe, I was no less dedicated to the job at hand—helping Lord Morrison with his Celtic warrior project.

Beside me, PJ stretched and yawned. "What are you thinking about?"

I looked into her sleepy, half-opened eyes. "You and me and that special something we have together."

"It is special, isn't it?" PJ draped a leg across my hips, an arm across my midriff.

I wanted and needed her as much now as I had that night when we first made love.

"So special, it takes my breath away." I brushed her bangs off her forehead.

"Oh, that's unfortunate. About your breath, I mean. I was just thinking that since we were already in this warm, cozy bed, and since we were already naked, maybe we should make love again. But if you don't have any breath left—"

I slid my left hand across her abdomen, pausing to tickle her navel, making her squeal. "Don't you worry about me, my love. I think I can keep breathing long enough to satisfy you. Just say the word."

"Okay, if you're sure."

I rolled on top of her, delivered moist, tender kisses along her neck and downward, and paused at the center of her collarbone.

"Oh, Kimmy, you're not going to—?"

I licked the hollow and started to hum against her sweet-smelling skin.

"Ohhh!" PJ gripped my head and moaned. "That drives me crazy. And you know it, don't you?"

"Guilty as charged." I hummed a bit more before kissing my way down her body. "Are there any more strawberries left, or did we consume them all?"

PJ gasped something that I couldn't understand. "What's that, my sweet? Don't tell me I've taken *your* breath away?"

"You're a tease, Kim Blair," she managed to say between pants. "But I love you anyway."

"And I love you, too." I stroked the inside of her thighs and then slipped my hand between her legs. "Always and forever."

* * *

When I awoke later, I thought about the mission that had brought us to Wales. We had left Newport and Windswept, the cottage overlooking Rhode Island Sound, three days after reading the letter Lord Morrison had sent to PJ's father. His request was vague, at best. A retired Royal Fusilier Colonel and a descendant of Owain Glyndwr, he was a reportedly eccentric amateur archaeologist who had spent many years tracing his lineage back into the dark and shadowy past of Wales's tumultuous history. Glyndwr himself had disappeared in 1412 and hadn't been heard from again. While his disappearance wasn't a purely archaeological matter, we wondered if Morrison's mysterious request had something to do with it. If that were so, then instead of digging through the sands of time, we would be excavating musty records in a dark cellar somewhere.

Wales, I had heard, was a land of mystery, and she guarded her secrets. The country was as old as she was beautiful; wild in places, and lonely, but I had read that she imprinted her spirit on those who dared get to know her.

Right now, it was enough that PJ filled my mind and my arms. There would be time tomorrow to set our sights on the new project. At the moment, I was content to study my love's relaxed features, as flashes of lightning danced upon the walls and the magic of the old inn wrapped itself around our two loving hearts.

I fell asleep, but awakened again in the middle of the night and glanced at my watch. 2:10. PJ slept with her head on my shoulder, her breathing deep and regular. I managed to ease my arm out from under her so that she slept on, and I got up and went to the window. The combination of antique windowpanes, lights at the end of the walk, and pouring rain presented an eerie effect.

As I stood there in the dark, my stomach churned. Why was I so nervous? My thoughts turned to the Amazons, as they often did. Though they had affected my life in so many ways, I understood them and the hold they had on me. Now I was about to play detective in an ancient and mysterious country that I knew little about. But surely there was no reason to feel this apprehensive. Maybe it was just one of those feelings we get sometimes, that usually amount to nothing at all.

"Can't you sleep?" PJ sat up with the down comforter around her shoulders.

"I wondered if it was still raining."

"I can see it is from here. You didn't have to get up and stand there. You'll catch your death of cold."

I realized then that I was chilled and scurried back into the warm bed. PJ yelped when I snuggled up to her back and put my freezing hands around her waist.

"Sorry, go back to sleep."

"Yeah, with Ice Woman."

Chapter 4

I backed into our room carrying a breakfast tray. Kim was in the bathroom, so I placed the tray on the table by our bed and poured us each a cup of Earl Grey from a china teapot.

"Breakfast is ready. Do you want me to bring you some tea?"

"That's okay. I'll be out in a second."

I heard the gurgle of water rushing down the bathtub drain and Kim's contented whistling. She sounded chipper this morning. It was good to hear that she wasn't too exhausted from last night.

"And just what are you smirking about?" Kim came out of the bathroom tying the sash of her terrycloth robe, her hair still wet and curling at the tips. My heart gave a lusty little flutter. My woman, standing there all dewy and delicious. I wanted to lick every bit of mango and pear lotion from her moist body.

She accepted her tea with a smile and a peck on my cheek. "Ta, love."

"You have the lingo down, don't you?" I took a long swallow of my tea, climbed onto my side of our bed, and eased back against the headboard. Kim claimed the other side, fluffing the pillow at her back.

"I figure 'when in Rome,' you know. And you haven't answered my question."

"What? Oh, the smirk?" I felt my cheeks flush. "It's nothing, really. I heard you whistling and thought that maybe you were thinking about last night, how much fun we had."

She smiled. "I did have fun last night." She put her cup down and touched my cheek. "Any time we can be together is a special time for me. You make me happier than I have any right to be."

"Aww—"

"I mean that." She placed her hand over mine. "We've been together, what? Seven months?"

"Almost."

"Every time is magical, like we couldn't be closer."

My throat tightened and my eyes filled with tears. "For me, too, Kim. I love you."

She grinned at me. "I love you, too. How about a pre-breakfast kiss?"

"Just one," I said and giggled. "Our food is getting cold."

Her lips tasted warm and spicy from the tea. I nibbled on her lower lip and slid my tongue inside her mouth. "Mmm. Who needs breakfast?"

Kim pulled back and shook her head. "It's the most important meal of the day. I don't know about you, but after keeping up with your escapades last night, I'm famished."

"Say no more, my dear one." I slid the tray in between us, so she could select her plate and utensils.

"Thanks. This looks delicious."

I watched her pick up a thick slice of toast and slather some marmalade on it. "You really did work up an appetite."

"Okay, maybe we both got a bit carried away." She forked a large piece of bacon onto her plate, then added eggs and grilled tomatoes. "I'm going to blame it on the big, soft bed, the pounding rain, and your intoxicating scent."

I laughed. "Goodness. I think Wales has cast a spell of enchantment over you. I've never heard you sound so romantic." I offered her a piece of my scone, which she took into her mouth along with my finger.

"Mmm, perhaps. Yum. Is that strawberry jam?"

"Yes, and I'd like my finger back."

Kim gave it a final lick and relinquished it.

"Geez, this is unnerving."

"Whatever do you mean?"

"Don't get me wrong. I love it when you get all romantic and sexy, but you're acting like the female version of Casanova."

Kim gave me an indignant look. "This is supposed to be a working holiday. I'm merely getting into the holiday mood."

"I see. It was all an act."

"Not so."

I swallowed the last of my tea and noticed that her cup was empty. "Do you want a refill?"

"Sure." She held out her cup. "This is a lovely way to start the day—good food, good conversation." She waggled her eyebrows at me. "Good company."

"I'm about to change the subject on you. When I called the Morrison estate earlier, I was told that his lordship was away on unexpected business."

"Oh?"

"We can't see him until Friday morning. What kind of business would be keeping him?"

She shrugged. "Any number of things, I guess."

"But his letter to Dad sounded so urgent. And he did ask us to come all this way."

"Yes, he did, didn't he?" A shadow passed across Kim's face.

"What?"

"I didn't say anything."

"You didn't have to. I can see from your expression that something's bothering you."

"It's nothing you need worry about, my darling."

"Hmm." I broke apart another hot scone and buttered it. "Anyway, we have some free time now. What would you like to do?"

"Well…"

"Apart from that."

We laughed and Kim considered my question. "We could go to the library and do some research on whatever it is that we're supposed to identify, except we really don't know what that is, which leaves us at a dead end. For now, anyway."

"Perhaps. He is being very secretive." Kim's eyes narrowed. "You have problems with that, don't you?"

"With what?"

"The fact that he might be doing something illegal and he'd be dragging us into it."

"I'm not sure I'm concerned about whatever it is being illegal. I really don't know what is bothering me. There's too much that we don't know yet."

I pushed the tray farther down the bed. I slid closer to her, picked up her napkin, and wiped a crumb from the corner of her mouth. "There. That's better."

She snatched my fingers and grinned. "Thanks, Mom."

"Don't mention it."

"You could have kissed my lips clean."

"Oh, no. That might delay our plans for the day."

"What plans? We don't have any, do we?"

Our fingers interlaced, and we found ourselves giggling over a playful tug-of-war.

"You are so frisky, and you have been since we arrived here," I said. "Not that I'm objecting, mind you."

She pulled our hands across her body, dragging me closer.

"Careful, Kim. I'm going to fall on top of you."

She smiled. "And that would be a bad thing?"

I gave her what she calls my lopsided grin. "No, but the tray might get knocked over and spilled."

"Oh, no, we can't have that. That would be tragic."

We continued to grin at each other. "Come on, little one," she said. "I could use another kiss."

"Oh, so now you need kisses when we wake up, when we part, before, during, and after breakfast?"

"Uh huh. Pucker up, gorgeous."

I gave her a chaste kiss. "So demanding."

"Whoa, you can do better than that. Here, let me show you." Kim wrapped her arm around me, crushing my lips with hers, then finishing with a bit of gentle tongue tangling.

My heart fluttered in my chest. "Whew! So that's how it's done."

She laughed.

"Being your partner sure is challenging."

"I'll give you plenty of time to get used to it. Fifty or sixty years ought to do it."

* * *

After breakfast, we spread some travel brochures out on the bed and made plans to drive out into the countryside to explore and soak up the Welsh atmosphere.

"Kim, why don't you gather up these guidebooks and maps, pack up our overnight bags, and grab a couple of water bottles? I'll exercise Pup and meet you at the Range Rover."

"Sounds like a good idea. We'll need to stop first in the village and buy some gas."

"You mean petrol. We're in Wales, now. We'll need several liters of petrol."

"Right. Now who's tossing the lingo around?"

We planned to head north, to explore quaint spots and sample local cuisine at our leisure.

Ten minutes later, I opened the back door to the Rover and Pup bounded in, checking out both side windows before settling down behind the driver's seat. I helped Kim load the gear, and I remarked that she had thought to grab our hooded raincoats.

"The sky looks too threatening to leave without them," she said.

"Good thinking." I opened the door to the driver's side. "Do you have the keys?"

"You're not going to drive. Remember how you nearly got us killed driving through England?"

"How can you say that?" I took a step toward her.

"Because it's true."

"Jesus." I ran my fingers through my hair. "One time, that's all. One time, I forgot and drove on the right."

"And that one time a truck was headed right for us." Kim feigned panic.

"Oh, come on. We missed it by several feet."

"We missed it by inches." She leaned in close to me, our noses almost touching, and pointed to a narrow streak of silver in her hair. "You see this? It's white. And it wasn't there before we got to Wales. It turned that color because, like a fool, I allowed you to drive partway across England."

I pretended to inspect the hair in question, planting a kiss on the top of her head. There were other gray hairs among the dark ones, but they only made her more attractive to me. Sexy to the max, in fact. I didn't dare tell her that, though, or her ego would be out of control. "It makes you look distinguished."

"Humph. It makes me look old. And no, you're not going to flatter your way into driving, and that's final."

"You are so bossy."

She smiled and climbed into the vehicle. I sighed and walked around to the co-pilot's seat with maps, tour guides, and notes in hand. Pup was already asleep.

As we pulled away from the inn, Kim kept glancing in the rearview mirror. A wave of uneasiness crept over me. "Are we being followed or something?"

"What makes you think that?"

"You. You're looking in the mirror like they do in the movies, when the good guys are being followed by the bad guys."

Kim glanced at me. "Your imagination is working overtime. I'm just being extra careful because I'm driving in a foreign country."

"Yeah, sure. I almost believe that."

We planned to tour parts of Snowdonia National Park, hike, find a nice place for lunch, buy souvenirs, and check some historic sites.

As the kilometers passed, however, the clouds thickened. We decided to wait for a clearer day to see Mount Snowdon.

"Damn," I muttered, "Snowdon is supposed to be the 'spiritual heart' of the Welsh people."

"Is that so?"

"Yeah, and it's guarded by a dragon. Now that would be cool to see."

"I'm afraid the only thing we're going to see today is fog and rain."

I sighed and turned to other pages in my guidebook. "Says here, the Druids were able to conjure up 'mists and storms, bring slumber upon people, and perform other feats of magic.'"

"I don't think we'll find any Druids around here, but we could look for some sacred wells and make an offering, if it makes you feel better. Maybe that would bring us better weather for traveling."

I smiled at her. "I'd love to find a well or two. In the meantime, we'd better try Plan B."

"And that would be?"

"See some sights in the area of Portmeirion, and when it rains, go inside."

"Sounds like a plan. Which way?"

"Head north."

We drove in and out of villages, noting clean, tidy stone houses, gardens with brightly colored blossoms, hillsides carpeted in wild flowers, and lush green grass. Cattle nestled in the valleys, and sheep with cute little tails were so plentiful on the hills, an insomniac would be hard-pressed to count them all.

"Why do most of the sheep here have tails and at home they don't?"

Kim shook her head. "You ask the darnedest questions."

"Inquiring minds want to know."

"Yeah, *your* inquiring mind."

"Poor sheep. That's an indignity, having your tail chopped off. I like them better with tails."

"The term is 'docking,' and it's done to prevent sheep poop from clinging to the tails and attracting flies."

"Ewww."

"I know I shouldn't ask, because I'm likely as not to get a smart answer, but what do you suppose they do with the tails?" She glanced sideways at me. "Do you think they use them for anything?"

"Hmm." I thought for a moment. "Okay, you've heard of ox tail soup, right?"

Kim rolled her eyes. "I knew it! Only you would suggest sheep tail soup."

* * *

We found wells tucked into moss and fern-festooned havens, in forests, and sometimes just squatting in peaceful splendor along the roadsides as we drove. I made Kim stop several times to examine them, so we could toss coins into each one and wish for sunny skies.

"Did you know that in the old days, sick people would come and sleep beside the wells? Then, come morning, they'd be cured of their afflictions."

"Truth or fiction?"

"Supposed to be the truth, for some wells anyway. Then there are stories about the skulls of saints being submerged in the water."

"Humph."

Unfortunately, the clouds remained, so we searched for some original Celtic standing stones and discovered that Christian inhabitants had carved most of them into crosses long ago.

"You'd better be careful," Kim said, "or you'll fall under the spell of the mystical Celtic spirit. I can almost feel it clinging to the landscape."

"It wouldn't take much. You know, the folks around here believe in fairies."

"Fairies, huh? Do you mean the limp wrist kind or the little people with wings?"

I giggled. "Maybe both."

We promised ourselves one more sacred well because the guidebook said it was in a secluded wood not too far from the main road.

"Look, PJ. It has to be there, at the bottom of that hill to our left."

"Where?" I peered in the direction of her outstretched finger.

There wasn't much room to park, but she managed to get the car off the road near an old and well-worn stile. The fence that held it in place was still there, though hidden beneath the lush greenery that had grown up around it. The wooden structure blended so well with the foliage that it had become one with it. I hopped over, managing to avoid the brambles on either side.

"I think stiles are so much nicer than gates," Kim said, straddling the top rail and assuming a not-so-graceful pose.

"Wait, this calls for a picture." I reached for the camera I always kept in my daypack.

The path that led toward the woods was barely visible. "I don't understand," Kim said. "If there's a well here, it must not be visited very much."

The mist closed in on us, adding to the sense of mystery. We looked around while Pup, nose to the ground, did some searching of his own.

We could see no grotto-like circle, no small stone arch. "I think we're out of luck," I said, more to myself than to Kim.

"Don't give up yet," she said. "Some wells are so old that even though they're listed on an ordinance map, you can only see the faintest impressions of where they were."

"That's tantalizing. So where, Dr. Blair, eminent archaeologist that you are, do you suppose this well was?"

"Hey, you're as eminent as I am, so let's just conduct a field survey and look for traces." Kim walked off, head down, searching for clues. She was in her element. I followed, scanning right and left, looking not for a grotto like the last one we'd visited, but for a depression maybe, or a seepage that might indicate a well.

"We'll be hard put to find a spring, after all the rain," Kim said.

We gave up.

"Sorry, PJ. I know you were hoping to see another grotto. That last one was perfect. Being on church property, it was well maintained and in pristine condition. If there ever was one in this vicinity, it's long since gone."

She put her arm around my shoulder. "Come on. Let's go back to the Rover."

"I suppose."

We started walking back, when something caught my eye. I stopped and peered to the left, into the mist.

"What?" Kim said.

"A hawthorn tree. 'A solitary thorn.' They're often found near wells."

I hurried toward that lone tree with Kim at my heels.

It was a scraggly specimen, though it appeared healthy enough. The depression we'd been looking for in the woods was here, out in the open, guarded by a solitary thorn.

With our bare hands, we dug into the ferns and grass and found pieces of stone that could have been part of the well.

I dropped onto one knee, which sank into standing water. "Rain or not, there's seepage here." I stood and shook my sodden pant leg.

"You know," Kim said, "this one's an ancient, wild well. In a way, it's more exciting than the others. At least it is to me."

"You're right. I wish we had our tools with us. I have an itch to dig."

"We have some in the Rover, but I don't know what local ordinances we'd be breaking."

"Yeah, I suppose." I gazed at the depression, wishing. "Nah. Better we leave it alone… a sanctuary for the spirits who haunt this place." I took a couple of digital pictures, but saw no apparitions in the little display window. "Besides, I've seen enough wells now to last me awhile."

Kim pulled me to her and guided my head to her shoulder. "This is a sacred place. I feel it, more so than at any of the others."

"Me, too." I rubbed my cheek against her damp jacket, my nostrils filling with her distinctive scent. I was aroused again.

I forced myself to concentrate on my surroundings. "Remember that lady who told us dragons are sometimes associated with wells?"

"Yes, and there's one watching us from the woods. His eyes are big and red, and he's stoking his fiery breath so he can come get us."

"If that's the case, let's go." I didn't look back.

When Pup and I reached the stile, my partner was only halfway up the hill. "Come on, Kimmy, what are you waiting for?"

"I had to go back for something."

"What?"

"This." She pressed a small piece of stone into my hand. "I wanted you to have something from your mysterious, dragon-guarded well."

"Thank you." I tucked the stone into an inside pocket. "Maybe it will bring us good luck. We could use some."

I pulled a pair of pants from the bag of spare clothes we had tucked into the vehicle for just such occasions.

"Need some help with those?"

I nodded and she helped me into the dry cargoes.

"This is a switch for me," Kim said with a laugh. "I'm usually helping you out of your pants."

"Shh. You're getting me a little too stimulated with that kind of talk."

I tossed my muddy pants into the Rover and waited for Pup to climb in. Kim nuzzled the back of my neck. "That can be taken care of, my sweet."

I pushed her away, grinning. "Not here. It's too dangerous."

"You're afraid of a few ghostly apparitions?"

"No, I'm afraid of that fire-breathing dragon you saw in the woods. Besides, we've got to get to Portmeirion. There's a fabulous hotel with a world-class dining room."

Kim gave my butt a caress before shoving it up and into the passenger seat. "You and your stomach."

I reached for her hand, thoroughly kissing each knuckle. "Just you wait until later, gorgeous. You can breathe a little fire of your own."

She hopped into the driver's seat and revved the engine. "Oh, yeah. Let's get the show on the road."

* * *

Portmeirion surprised us. It looked more like a village in Italy than a quaint Welsh hamlet. We visited a subtropical garden and purchased jams and chocolates in the gift shops. At teatime, we peeked into the hotel, which was modeled after a Victorian villa. According to our guidebook, it had opened in 1926 and played host to George Bernard Shaw, H.G. Wells, and Noel Coward. It was not going to host us, however. We weren't dressed in proper attire, we lacked reservations, and we were accompanied by a dog. Pup would have stayed in the Rover, but after receiving several dubious looks from the management, we decided to leave.

"Too bad," Kim said, as we tried to locate another eatery. "I really had my mouth set for that 'seared salmon on Niçoise salad with balsamic dressing.'"

"I think you'll miss the 'orange cheesecake or banana and mango mousse with chocolate sauce' even more."

Her stomach rumbled. "We'd better find a place to eat and spend the night, before it pours."

Of course, as soon as she said it, the rain started in earnest. After several unsuccessful attempts to locate a nice hotel room or bed and breakfast, we managed to secure one room in a midsize farmhouse. Again, we were asked to share a double bed.

"No trouble," I said. "We can manage for one night."

Kim frowned. "I'm not sure," she muttered after a sideways glance at me. "She snores, you know."

That remark would earn her a poke in the ribs when I got her alone. I swallowed my indignation and presented an innocent face to our hosts, Mr. and Mrs. Fielding. She was a small, round woman with rosy cheeks and thinning light-brown hair, pulled back into a bun. Her apron was sparkling white over a flower-print dress. "The Mister," as she called her husband, was tall and lean, with huge, sinewy, tool-gripping hands. His voice, soft as a dove's coo, had a delightful, melodious ring. Mostly he said, "Yes, luv," and "Ta, luv," to his wife.

They showed us to a small room at the top of their house. Mrs. Fielding explained that four other couples were guests for the night: one couple upstairs in the room next to us, and the remainder in rooms on the second level. Each floor had its own bathroom.

"Now, mind you, this is a working farm. The Mister will be calling on the lot of you to pitch in with the chores come morning." Mrs. Fielding smiled, and two dimples appeared in her cheeks.

We replied with grave nods, having no idea what we were in for, and shuffled off to unpack our bags. Pup had the choice of sleeping in the barn with the family dogs or joining us. After a slight hesitation, he went with his new canine pals.

Our room had a small chair and dresser besides the double bed. I bounced on the mattress to test it for squeaks and was pleasantly surprised to find none. A grin appeared on Kim's face when she realized what I was doing. She sat beside me and nuzzled my neck.

"Ah, not so fast, bucko," I said. "Let's get one thing straightened out, shall we?"

"What? What's the matter?"

"You know perfectly well what's the matter. I do not snore."

"Yes, you do."

"I do not." I folded my arms. "Be very careful how you respond to that, Dr. Blair, if you know what's good for you."

Kim paused. "Hmm. Perhaps I spoke in haste, Dr. Curtis."

"That's better."

"You do not snore."

"Exactly the answer I was looking for." I wrapped my arms around her and rewarded her with a kiss. One led to another and before we knew it, our hands were tugging at buttons and belts, exposing skin. I pushed Kim down onto the comfy bed and was slipping my hands under her bra, when a bell rang from somewhere downstairs.

"Jesus Christ!" We broke apart, startled.

"Dinner will be at half past the hour!" Mrs. Fielding shouted. Flashes of lightning and a loud clap of thunder accompanied her announcement. Rain pelted the slate roof above us.

"Damn," Kim said. "Not enough time for any further bedroom games. Wonder if I can grab a quick shower?" She winked at me. "It might have to be a cold one."

"Aw, did I get you all hot and bothered?"

"You most certainly did."

"Good," I said, giggling. We buttoned each other's shirts. "I imagine we'll have to work out a timetable for the bathroom."

"Yeah." A gleam came into her eyes. "You know, it would probably save everybody on this floor a lot of time and water if we doubled up on the shower."

"You're a genius. I wonder who I can get to shower with me?"

She swatted me with the towel she had pulled from our dresser. "Don't you even *think* about showering with anyone else but me."

I was about to answer when we heard moans coming from the room next to us. I started to giggle again. "These walls are so thin, Kimmy. What are we going to do?"

She made a face. "Can we be very quiet? I mean, it's one thing for them to make that sort of noise, but it would kind of freak out a few people if we made noises like that, too."

Since we assumed that our floor mates would be occupied for a little while, we grabbed towels and decided to try out the shower. Nice hot water flowed over us.

"Now, this is more like it," I told Kim, pointing to the fixtures. "You notice everything is at normal height."

"It's quite modern compared with what we have at the inn."

"Maybe we can survive the night after all. It won't be the first time we've made love in a shower. We can just cuddle quietly in bed, after dark. No problem."

"Sounds good to me."

Then, the lights went out… and the water turned icy.

"Ah!" I cried, shivering. "Scratch that plan. Looks like you got your wish for a cold shower."

* * *

Supper was a large bowl of lamb stew with plenty of brown bread drenched in herb butter. The storm had caused a power outage and everyone dined by candlelight around a huge oak table. Mrs. Fielding prepared tea with water boiled in a kettle over the stone fireplace. Our dessert was rhubarb pie smothered with what we learned was Bird's custard sauce. I thought Kim was going to swoon right on the spot. The meal was lovely, in spite of the circumstances.

Once the dishes had been cleared, we all chatted awhile. We were the only Americans, and the other guests seemed eager to talk to us. Some Brits were as fascinated with the American lifestyle as we were with theirs. We weren't so different, though, except for language. We'd discovered that there was a big difference between the Queen's English and American English.

"Americans are a brash and loud bunch," Kim said, speaking to some of the guests, "but our hearts are in the right place. You Brits are generally more refined. The gap is narrowing though, as we all become part of a world community." She sighed. "No matter where you go anymore, there is commonality. Local culture is being swallowed up by strip malls and fast food outlets."

The others agreed, lamenting the disappearance of individuality. Several of them thought it a crime that the Welsh language had fallen into disuse in so many parts of Wales.

A mousy, middle-aged woman had been silent throughout the conversation. She seemed to be intimidated by her overbearing husband. "I think travelers have to be like archaeologists," she said quickly, when her husband got up to get a bottle of pale ale from a sideboard that doubled as a bar. "They have to dig to find the local culture."

"You are so right," I said, smiling at the woman's obvious pleasure in contributing to the conversation.

"Are you interested in archaeology?" Kim asked.

"Yes. I've read a little about it, and I've always thought—"

"Now, Sadie, you don't know a thing about it, so don't pretend you do." Her husband returned to the table, and she retreated into her shell.

I wasn't ready to let it go. "I have some books that I don't use anymore. If you'll give me your address, I'd be happy to send them to you."

"She doesn't need them," he said, squelching any further discussion on the subject.

Afterwards, as we climbed the stairs to bed, I let loose. "Why, that no good son of a bitch!"

Kim shone her flashlight back toward me. "Hey, don't get yourself in an uproar. There's nothing you can do. She's allowed herself to get into this situation, and you're not her therapist. Let it go."

"I know, but it makes me angry. Makes me think of Stephen. That's the way I would have ended up if I'd gone with him that day on Superstition Mountain."

"But you didn't." Kim gave my shoulder a squeeze. "You chose me instead, and look what that got you."

We both laughed.

"I think I'd better thank Stephen for being such a crass and disgusting creep."

Kim grinned. "I'd rather not hear any mention of Mr. Cresswell while we're having such a pleasant time."

We were anxious to get a good night's rest for the next day, so we grabbed our flashlights, shuffled off to the bathroom, then crawled into bed.

Under layers of warm blankets, Kim and I snuggled together in our T-shirts and panties.

I felt very over-dressed.

"Nos da, sweetheart," I whispered against her cheek.

She turned her head and kissed me. "And a good night to you, too, love."

Chapter 5

The clanging of a bell woke us out of a sound sleep.

"What the hell is that?" Kim grumbled.

I sat up, rubbing my eyes. "Must be a fire somewhere—and in the middle of the night."

The bell rang again, louder this time.

"Bore da! Good morning, lads and lassies!" Mrs. Fielding's way-too-cheerful voice reverberated off the walls as if she were using a bullhorn. "Time for milking!"

I rolled over and snuggled under the quilt. "Can't be. It's still dark outside. I bet the cows aren't even awake yet."

Kim threw the covers back and climbed out. "Come on, sleepyhead, it's time to play farmer."

"Whose bright idea was it to spend the night on a working dairy farm?"

"As, I recall, it was yours."

"Oh, yeah." I swung my legs over the side of the bed.

I heard Kim try the light switch, but the power was still off. "Damn," she said.

I stumbled to the dresser and felt around for my jeans. "It just keeps getting better and better. Remind me never to do this again, okay?"

Kim laughed softly. "Indeed I will."

"What time is it, anyway?"

"Early." She flicked on her flashlight and laid it on the dresser.

"Brilliant. I figured that out all by myself."

She put her arm around my shoulder and pulled me into an embrace. "You really don't do mornings well, do you?"

"I'm sorry, sweetheart, but the thought of cold water for washing and a cold breakfast doesn't help my mood."

"Geez, I forgot about that." Kim finished dressing. "My feet are freezing. Have you seen my boots?"

"They're under the bed, I think." I searched for the rest of my clothing. "No full Welsh breakfast, no hot shower, and I can't find my sweatshirt."

"No whining, PJ. There's no whining in dairy farming."

I gave her a dirty look, which was wasted, considering the faint light. "You're just a barrel of laughs sometimes."

"I'm only trying to make the best of a bad situation." She used her light to help me locate my missing shirt. "Here you go. Can't have you going out to work half naked."

"Thank you. You're so thoughtful." I tugged the shirt over my head and squinted into the mirror. "Hold that light over here, would you? I don't suppose there's time for me to put on makeup."

"Don't worry, the cows won't care what you look like."

"Wrong answer."

"Oh. Uh—you look beautiful without any makeup at all." She kissed me on both cheeks and my forehead.

"Nice recovery, Doc." I returned her kisses. "Sorry I'm such a grouch."

She tousled my hair. "You're forgiven. Besides you're adorable when you're sleepy."

We heard other guests moving down the hallway. "Come on." I pulled her with me to the door. "We can't keep those cows waiting."

"Those poor animals. What have they done to deserve us?"

* * *

Having made good use of the fireplace again, Mrs. Fielding had hot tea and some sort of glutinous porridge ready for her guests in the kitchen. In various stages of wakefulness, we assembled around a massive oak table that emitted the faint scent of beeswax. There was just time for a few gulps and swallows before our hostess gave us further orders.

"Stop at the shed first, mind you. It's wet underfoot, and you'll need some Wellingtons. There's cow dung, too, in the milking shed. You'll not want to ruin your good shoes."

Once at the shed, we climbed into the rubber boots. She divided us into teams and sent us to the barn.

One team was assigned to tend the chickens. Another team cleaned and replenished hay in the stalls, but the really lucky ones—Kim and I among them—got to hand milk the cows.

When I entered the milking shed, I wrinkled my nose. It was a knee-jerk reaction, one that I hoped the others hadn't noticed.

"What's the matter?" Kim asked, taking a deep breath and patting her chest. "Is your pretty little nose sensitive to this healthy aroma?"

"Oh sure, there's nothing like a little Eau de Barnyard to start off the day." I appreciated the Wellies. The concrete gutters in the milking shed brimmed with water, urine, and cow dung.

Mr. Fielding was most apologetic. "There's naught but to do it the old-fashioned way, I'm afraid." His soft, melodious voice barely carried over the din of mooing and shuffling cows. "The modern milkers use electric power, you see. We've none of that now, and the cows'll not wait."

Fortunately, there were four other helpers besides us, and after many false starts and much noisy commentary from the restive cows, we got a handle on the situation, so to speak, and filled our pails with milk. Balancing on a three-legged milking stool was a feat I was not very good at, but I managed when I saw the farm boys balancing on one-legged ones. Everyone—except the cows, of course—had a good laugh over our efforts.

After all the chores were finished, we enjoyed a parting cup of tea and thick slices of bread and marmalade. We packed up the Rover, settled Pup into the back, and left the farm with fond memories and Mr. Fielding's surprising compliment ringing in our ears.

"You'll both make fine farmers' wives some day," he had assured us as we bid the couple farewell.

"Yeah, when pigs fly," I said, once we had rolled up our windows and driven the length of the lane to the paved road.

"Could be something to fall back on," Kim said, "if the current arrangement doesn't work out."

I gave her ribs a poke. "Nice try, partner. But I'm in this for the long haul."

"Speaking of long haul, where to now?"

I consulted the map. "Just head south for a bit until I sort out these brochures."

"Don't take too long. Wales isn't that big a place."

* * *

"Wasn't that dairy farm a real trip?" I asked after several kilometers of uneventful driving.

She shook her head, grinning. "I'm never going to forget that place."

"Oh, sweetie. Were the cows too much for you?"

"No, the cows were a snap. It was that couple next to us. They must have been at it all night long."

"Maybe they were on their honeymoon."

We laughed and headed toward the coast and Caernarfon to the creameries and cheddar cheese making.

"You know what milking those cows reminded me of?" I asked Kim, as we drove through patches of sunlight and shade. The Rover's leather seats gave off a fragrant oily scent from the interior's increasing warmth.

She grinned. "I'm afraid to ask."

"Nothing bad. I was nervous at first because I didn't know how the cow's teat would feel, and if I could get the milk to come out."

"And we had to make sure our hands were warm so the cows would be comfortable."

I laughed. "Yeah, that, too. Anyway, it felt like the last time we gave Pup a bath, and my rubber glove got a leak in it. Do you remember that?"

"Sure, you squirted me with soapy water."

"Yes, but before that the glove filled up with water, and it was smooth and firm. Just like those cow teats."

"At least you didn't squirt me with milk. It took us long enough to fill our pails, without clowning around."

"I wasn't about to do anything like that." I picked up a travel brochure and flipped through the pages. "Here we go. This lovely tearoom will cheer you up." I shoved the page under her nose. "And for dessert, there's Cadwalader's ice cream, the best in Wales."

"How do you know it's the best in Wales?"

"Says so right here in the pamphlet."

She laughed. "Ask a stupid question..."

"We'll just check it out for ourselves. I've got a whole stack of interesting brochures. We're going to have to make several trips out into the countryside while we're working on this Morrison project." I pointed to a stone fortress looming out of the cloudy mist. "That, for instance, is a castle that Edward the First established in 1283, after his armies had defeated the princes of North Wales. The guidebook says there were numerous revolts against English rule here, and that the place became one of Cromwell's strongholds."

Kim pondered that information. "I have to admit, it's impressive."

I flipped a page in the book. "They have tours daily, but it could take hours to wander through it and see all the arrow slits and such."

"Let's wait for a sunnier day." She guided the Rover around the traffic circle, or roundabout, as it was called in Wales. "I'm getting hungry right now."

I smiled at her. "No problem. There are all sorts of dairy products to sample."

"Okay," she said, grinning. "Give me directions, but leave out milk. I've seen enough of that for the time being."

* * *

We were so full of sharp cheddar cheese and chocolate ice cream sundaes that we decided to skip lunch and drive through to Llandudno. The Rover now smelled of delicious food items as well as warm leather and slightly damp dog. We opened more windows.

Kim tugged on her seatbelt and twisted her head to look between the headrests and out the back window. "I can't explain it, but I feel like we're being watched. When we came out of the ice cream shop, I could swear someone took our picture. And now I wonder whether someone's following us."

"Hey, it was probably a tourist. Look around you. There are lots of people visiting these quaint little villages, doing just what we're doing. Maybe someone noticed Pup and took a picture of him."

"Pup?"

"Yeah. You know, maybe they thought he was a full-blooded wolf, or something."

Pup shoved his head between our bucket seats and huffed.

"I guess he doesn't think much of that possibility," Kim said, shrugging. "Anyway, I don't see anybody with a camera pointed at us now."

She gave Pup a pat on the head and started the Rover. As we navigated the narrow, winding lanes, I kept looking to the sky for signs of the sun. "There isn't going to be any sunshine today. We're just lucky the rain let up."

My remark was followed by a moody silence that mimicked the weather. "I was hoping we could get a good glimpse of Mount Snowdon, maybe get to climb it." I sighed and folded my arms. "We'll just have to come back on a brighter day."

"You don't want to try it today?"

"The books all say not to attempt it in bad weather. If those clouds hang around all day, it will only get worse. There will be too much fog and probably more rain."

"Cheer up." Kim gave my arm a squeeze. "We'll do it another time. We're almost to Llandudno, anyway."

It was late afternoon when we pulled into the parking lot for the Martins Hotel and Restaurant. Once again, we were too shabby, although they didn't come right out and refuse to seat us. We took one look at the patrons in the dining area and rejected ourselves. I managed to snag a menu as a souvenir of our brief visit, however.

We decided to find another place and got back on the road. After a while, Kim's attention focused on the rearview mirror.

"What is it? More bad guys?" I asked, teasing her.

"I know you'll think I'm paranoid, but there's been a blue car behind us for several miles."

I turned to peer over my seat, but Kim grabbed my wrist. "Don't look."

"Is the car that close?"

She hesitated. "I guess not, but I don't want to take any chances."

"Geez, you sure are jumpy. This is so unlike you."

"It's probably nothing. Ever since we left the Superstitions, my imagination has been working overtime. And don't ask me to explain why that is, I just don't know."

A few raindrops pelted the windshield. "Great," I muttered. "Just what we need. More rain."

Kim rubbed my thigh. "Look, sweetie, let's head back toward The Royal Lion. Our last stop is the brewery, anyway, right?"

"That's right." I consulted the map. "Take the A470. It's the Dolgellau Bypass. I'll help you find the turn off to the Bragdy Cambrian Brewery."

After we made the turn, she breathed a sigh of relief. "The blue car went on by."

"There, you see. No spies out to get us this time."

The rain intensified, drumming steadily on the roof and chilling the car's interior. "I've got to close these windows a bit," I said. "Can you get the ones in back from your control panel?"

Kim looked at her left-side armrest and pushed a few buttons. "All done. You'd better turn on the fan, though. It's starting to get steamy in here."

I adjusted the controls, but our visibility was reduced to two front patches and a rear window section. I slid an anxious glance in Kim's direction. "Can you see well enough?"

"I'm fine, thanks. Try the A/C for a few minutes. The defroster's making it too warm."

I pushed more buttons. "Any better?"

"Yeah. I think the rain's letting up now, anyway."

I relaxed into my seat and read the menu from Martins.

"What?" Kim asked, after a few minutes.

"What, what?"

"You keep giggling and murmuring under your breath."

I pointed to the menu. "I can't help it. You won't believe the meal we could have had."

"Please, don't tell me."

"Oh, I must. 'Fillets of wild Conwy salmon on a couch of sorrel and laver bread, pursued by shameless concoctions of cream and chocolate, exotic fruits, and enchantments of pastry.'"

We were giggling so hard that Kim had to pull off the road and take some deep breaths. "Do they give prizes for that kind of writing?"

"I'll bet it has something to do with those Taste of Wales banners we've seen—the red dragon on the black circle with a white background. Each village is trying to outdo the others for tourists' money."

The Rover's wipers made monotonous sweeps across the windshield as the rain continued. We parked close to the entrance to the new brewery, avoided several puddles, and took a quick tour, sampling a pint of their ale and buying a few bottles for later on. Feeling somewhat mellow from the beer and too little food, we stopped at a fish and chip shop for a "takeaway" order.

"Home, sweet home!" Kim called, as we rolled into the car park at the inn. We unpacked the Rover and grabbed everything. "Race you upstairs."

Once out of the rain, in the privacy of our room, we peeled off our wet clothing and slipped into our robes.

"I'll get a fire started in the hearth, if you'll feed Pup." Kim bent to stuff kindling into a pile and pulled a long match from the stone mantel.

I took a towel and tried to rub our pet. He shook himself first, sprinkling me with moist droplets.

"Pup! Geez, I'm trying to help you here. Now stand still while I wipe you down."

He finally rolled onto his back, exposing his belly.

"Ah, now you catch on. Now that I smell like wet pooch." I tickled his tummy, and he whimpered. "There you go. All dry. Want some dinner, sweetie?"

He rolled over and sat up.

"I'll take that as a yes." He gave me a tiny yelp. I filled his bowl with dry food and broke off a piece of fish fillet, making sure there were no bones. Then I filled his water dish from the bathroom sink. Remembering the day I had first met him, I wondered how I could have been so afraid of this pussycat in wolf's clothing.

Kim finished with the fire and pulled pillows and a blanket from the bed, so we could lie near the warmth of the fireplace while we ate.

"Oh, it looks so cozy." I washed my hands and joined her on the blanket, pausing to wipe damp bangs out of my eyes. "Let's see what we have here." I unwrapped our sumptuous, though now tepid, meal and licked the grease from my fingers. Kim was stretched out beside me, her eyes closed.

"This is more like it," she said.

I slid my fingers between the folds of her robe and rubbed her stomach, leaving the robe open when I withdrew my hand.

She smiled. "Mmm. Are you going to feed me, or just tease me?"

I broke off a piece of our main course and placed it on her bare skin. She opened one eye, but didn't say anything.

"Fillet of nondescript white fish on a couch of Arizona sun-baked abdomen," I said.

Kim snickered.

I added a handful of greasy chips to the indentation of her navel.

She opened both eyes and giggled.

"Golden, lard-fried slabs of potato, delicately nestled in an enclave of belly button." I was laughing hard now.

"Stop!" Kim's stomach shook. She picked up the fish and chips and ate her meal with slow, deliberate movements, smacking her lips. "Yum."

I tried to snatch a piece of her fish, but she slapped it out of my hand, and it fell down the front of my robe. "Darn it. Where did that pesky thing go?" I untied my belt to look for it.

Kim rolled to one side. I heard paper crackling.

"What are you doing?" I asked, climbing over her to get a better look.

She broke pieces of something and wrestled me onto my back. I could smell chocolate. "Are those Halo bars? They're delicious, and I love them, but I'm not sure—"

Tiny chunks fell onto my breasts and belly. It tickled. Kim started licking up the pieces. Now, I was almost hysterical. Grinning, she said, "Pursued by shameless fragments of chocolate."

"Stop! Enough 'pursuing.' It tickles too much."

"What about the exotic fruits?" Kim asked, after licking most of the chocolate from my body.

"Hold on… just one minute." I crawled, still laughing, to our souvenir purchases, opened a jar of strawberry preserves, and smeared a handful over her breasts. She giggled.

Now, it was my turn to sample the fruits of my labor, so to speak. "Yum. They make a mighty fine fruit spread at Portmeirion."

"Hey, I like strawberry, too." Kim pouted.

I held out the jar and was soon plastered in jam. We took childish delight in cleaning each other up. Then, yawning, we banked the fire, took a bath, and climbed into bed.

Kim sighed as we lay holding each other in the dark. "A most delightful day."

"We missed the cream and enchantments of pastry," I said, trying to sound forlorn.

"Another time, sweetheart. Another time."

I nuzzled the hollow of her neck, kissing and licking until she moaned. "Can I be your little tart?" I whispered.

She hooted. "Oh, good one!" She rolled me onto my back, her hand making a slow, erotic journey down the length of my stomach, belly, and farther south.

It was my turn to moan.

Chapter 6

"I didn't know that squash was a beverage, Kim. That's why I gave Arwel that funny look."

"Yeah, I must admit that one puzzled me, also." I grinned at PJ as we pulled up to the entrance to the Morrison estate. As we made our way through the winding lanes and narrow side roads, our conversation had centered on the differences in British and American words. I stopped the Rover just outside the gate, and before we could push any buttons or ring any bells, the barrier swung open.

"Now, that's service," I said.

"Impressive." PJ looked around, but stone walls and tall hedges obscured our view beyond the gatekeeper's cottage.

I pulled to a stop as a short, rather stout man ambled out to greet us. He had a handlebar mustache and florid complexion. "Good day to you both," he said, looking us over. "You'd be Dr. Curtis and her colleague, from America?"

"That we would," PJ assured him.

His tweed shooting jacket and knickers were a bit overdone, in my estimation, but who was I to judge?

"Would you like us to show some identification?" I asked him.

"That won't be necessary," he said, wheezing. "His lordship is expecting you." With considerable effort, he walked to the side of the Rover and pointed out the direction to the main house.

"'Tis a mite winding, but keep to your right once you round that bend and you can't go wrong."

We pulled away slowly, in second gear because of the loose gravel.

"So, where was I?" PJ ruffled her bangs. She seemed obsessed with the language differences, but I always enjoyed her enthusiastic and thorough observations. "Oh, yeah. Napkins are serviettes and panties are knickers. The trunk of a car is the boot, and the hood is the bonnet. A drug store is a chemist's shop. And that fellow back there—the knickers he's wearing are called plus fours. I'll never get it straight. If I ask for a napkin, I'm liable to be handed a diaper." She gave me a weary sigh. "Life can be difficult."

"Poor you," I said, smiling at her flair for the dramatic. "But just think, here you can ask the desk clerk to knock you up at seven in the morning and not encounter any embarrassing repercussions. Try that in the States."

"Ha!" She gave my arm a poke. "Trust you to find a sexual reference in all of this."

"Me? I was only contributing to the conversation."

Our attention focused on the well-graded driveway, flanked on the left by lawns and flowerbeds. To the right of the driveway, a manicured privet hedge fronted well-tended fruit trees. In the distance, the spray from a fountain caught the late morning sunlight.

"Wow! Look at that," I said.

"All those chimneys." PJ craned her neck. "They must have at least fifty fireplaces."

"One for every room. Old houses like that are often cold and drafty." I had stopped the car, giving us time to take our first view of the three-story, gray stone structure that must have covered at least two acres and appeared to grow out of the surrounding landscape.

"And I thought Windswept was something. It would fit into one wing of this place."

"Add a couple of turrets and a moat, and it would qualify for a fortress." I eased my foot off the brake and allowed the car to roll forward.

* * *

A pull chain off to the side of the massive front door operated the bell. We could hear it jangling from deep within the bowels of the structure. I was about to pull on the chain again when the door was opened and a dour, middle-aged woman, whom I suspected was the housekeeper, indicated that we should follow her. PJ and I glanced at each other as she led us down a long, mahogany-paneled hallway. Between doorways, trophy heads gave us baleful stares as we passed under them.

Everything smelled musty, as though it had been closed up for too long a time, like a tomb just opened. The hair on my neck prickled, and I looked over my shoulder, half expecting to see someone, but no one was there. PJ and the housekeeper were several yards ahead of me, however, so I hurried to catch up.

We were shown into a large drawing room, where more dead animals glared at us from walls covered with embossed maroon paper. Several overstuffed chairs, two sofas, a heavy, ornate coffee table, and a sofa table were arranged in haphazard fashion on a colorful East Indian rug. It alone saved the room from the monotony of maroon, gray, and navy blue. One of the overstuffed chairs, the only one upholstered in leather, appeared to be well-worn.

"Does this guy still have a wife?" PJ asked after the housekeeper had left.

"I think so, but you know more about the Morrisons than I do. They're *your* father's friends."

"I don't think I ever met them, although Dad said I did when I was very young. I don't remember even hearing much about them."

"You're a lot of help."

"What can I say? I doubt that Dad had seen or heard from them in thirty years or more. Until he got the letter asking for my help, that is."

"Life sometimes forces people apart, and it's easy to lose touch."

She grasped my hand. "That's not going to happen to us."

"No way, my darling." I gave her hand a squeeze. "You can count on that."

PJ dropped into an overstuffed chair, almost disappearing into the folds of the cushions. She sneezed as gray dust rose around her, metamorphosing into bright, jeweled flecks. We watched them float about in the thin beams of sunshine that fought their way through gaps in the velvet drapes.

"This is a museum," she said.

"That it is." The man's voice startled both of us and embarrassed my partner. Lord Morrison was a tall, well-muscled man with graying hair and a full mustache.

"I'm sorry," PJ said. "I didn't mean—"

Morrison waved off her apology. "It *is* a museum, Dr. Curtis. Jenny and I live in the East wing when we're here, but we prefer to be at our cottage in Conwy."

"You know me? I mean, you know which of us is which?"

"Why, yes. Frederick talked about you all the time. He even sent the occasional picture."

I frowned.

He turned to me. "And you must be Dr. Kimberly Blair. I wasn't expecting to have the services of an archaeologist of your reputation. It is an honor."

Now, I was uncomfortable. "Thank you."

"You must forgive me if I stare," Morrison said, turning again to PJ, "but you are so much like your mother—a beautiful woman, if I may say so. You have her eyes, you know, so alive."

"Thank you," PJ said.

"Your parents were a most handsome couple. It was a terrible thing for all of us when we heard about your mother."

PJ's eyes glistened. "Thank you, again."

"Sit down, please." Morrison pulled the bell cord on the wall before settling his bulk into the leather chair. "I'm delighted you agreed to come." He crossed his legs, revealing red, white, and blue Argyle socks. "I must explain my reason for asking you to come here, to Wales."

"Yes." PJ gave me a quick glance. "Your letter to my father didn't give us much information."

"I need your assistance in solving a mystery."

"We'll do what we can, of course," I said, "but I'm not altogether sure that it's archaeologists you need." I perched on one end of the dusty sofa.

Morrison held up his hand. "Please hear me out before you decide."

The door opened and a petite young woman in a dark dress and white, lace-edged apron appeared, bearing a tray with tea and a plate of plain and chocolate cookies, which the British called biscuits. We sat in silence while she poured the tea, handed us each a plate, and served us. She met my smile with a stony expression.

Morrison stood up, his back to the empty fireplace. He pulled at his thick mustache. "I don't quite know where to start."

"The beginning is good," I said, seeing that PJ's attention was focused elsewhere.

"Quite so." Morrison cleared his throat. "As you know, this is my ancestral home. The house is twelfth century. Nothing much has changed through the years, except, of course, some of the furniture. I couldn't stand to live here all the time."

"Neither could I," PJ said with a shudder. "All these animal heads. It's criminal. What did they ever do to spend eternity in this mausoleum?"

"PJ, please, not now."

"I suppose the brave hunter who shot him," she continued, pointing to a Bengal tiger skin hanging on the wall, "was on the back of an elephant." Her finger stabbed at a black bearskin rug. "And he was probably bagged from an airplane."

"That's not for us to judge."

"The hell it isn't. This man is so proud of his ancestors, and they were nothing but a bunch of—"

"PJ, that is enough." My tone must have registered. She turned to face Morrison. "I'm sorry. I shouldn't have said that."

Instead of appearing stricken, Morrison grinned. "By God, woman, you not only look like your mother, you have her fire as well. Frederick must be damned proud of you."

"Lord Morrison," I said, trying to steer the conversation back on track, "what exactly is it you want us to do?"

"First, you must call me John. This Lord business is a crock."

"All right, I'm Kim. And, of course, you know that this young lady is the incomparable Priscilla, or PJ."

She threw me her best "wait-until-I-get-you-alone" look.

"How about another cup of tea?" Morrison asked.

"Not for me, thank you." The British regimen of serving tea at the slightest excuse was giving my bladder fits.

"You'll have your work cut out for you." Morrison poured another cup for himself and one for PJ.

"What do you want us to do?" she asked, reaching for another chocolate cookie. "We're still a little fuzzy on the details."

"You know, of course, that I'm a descendant of Owain Glyndwr, though as Americans, you may not have heard of him."

"I believe my father mentioned your relationship," PJ said, "but don't underestimate us. Our schools may suffer from violence and lack of funds, but some of us still manage to learn something. If I remember correctly, Glyndwr led a rebellion around the year 1400. Unfortunately, Henry the Fourth of England forced his retreat. I guess that's all I know about him, but it's something."

"You're right." Morrison paced slowly back and forth across the room. "What you don't know is that he disappeared around 1412, leaving Wales in turmoil."

I glanced at PJ. She met my gaze, but shared no hint of her thoughts, so I turned back to Morrison. "You want us to find out what happened to him?"

"Oh, no. I have another, very different project for you."

"And what would that be?" I wondered what the discussion of Owain Glyndwr had to do with anything.

"Follow me." Morrison turned and strode rapidly out of the room. I extended my hand to PJ and pulled her out of the deep chair in which she was foundering. She grabbed another cookie before following me, her hand cupped beneath it to catch the crumbs.

At the end of the hall, a low door opened to a flight of stairs that led down to the cellar. It was cold, a natural refrigerator. Racks of cobweb-covered wine bottles lined one wall. "You must take a couple of bottles with you," Morrison said. "There are vintages in there that are over three hundred years old."

"Wow! A glass of that would short circuit your bionics." PJ winked at me. "Maybe we could crack one open for our anniversary," she added, loud enough for me alone to hear.

"I'm a scotch man myself," Morrison said. "Scotch on the rocks."

He opened a door into a dark, windowless room. "There's no electricity in here, but if you'll wait just a moment, I'll have some light for you."

Four gas-fed torches flamed, a pair on both of the longest walls. Their flickering shadows enhanced the already spooky atmosphere. Dark soot marks on the ceiling indicated that the torches had burned often throughout the centuries, but that they had not always been gas-fed. In the center of the otherwise stark room, a marble pedestal held a glass case, the top slightly askew.

"Take a look and tell me what you think."

PJ and I glanced at each other before circling what, on closer inspection, was a glass coffin. The padded, satin-covered bottom was imprinted with the shape of a body. I turned to Morrison. "Who was in here, and where is he or she now?"

"I believe the body was that of a Celtic chieftain."

I heard PJ draw in a breath.

"As for his whereabouts at the moment, I don't know. He was stolen."

PJ's eyes widened. "Stolen! By whom?"

"That's why you're here."

I frowned. "We're not detectives. This is a police matter."

"I don't want them involved."

"May I ask why not?"

"The Welsh authorities wouldn't approve of the interment of an important Celtic chieftain in a private home."

"I'm inclined to agree with them," PJ said. "Private ownership of historical treasures, human or otherwise, robs people of their history, the ability to reveal the past."

"I disagree. Families like ours..." He stared at her. "We shouldn't have to share everything with the unappreciative masses."

I could see PJ's jaw tighten, and I had to bite my own tongue.

"Please don't include my family in your assessment, Lord Morrison." Her voice was firm. "Neither I, nor my father, share your feelings on that subject."

"Are you certain of that, my dear? Perhaps you've been estranged from Frederick too long to judge."

"You know about that?"

Morrison gave her a confident smile. "Of course. Frederick and I are close friends."

I watched and listened to the exchange while doing my best not to get caught up in a discussion that really was none of my business. My mind, though, was bursting with questions. I was building up a dislike for this man. Friends? What could he and Frederick still have in common? And what about his Welsh heritage? If his feelings for Wales were so strong, surely he would want to share such a treasure. Why was the Celt here in the first place? How had he gotten here? Then, I had a more scientific thought. "How well-preserved was the body?"

Morrison appeared surprised, as if for a moment he had forgotten I was in the room. "Uh… very well. The features were distinct. Hair, skin, even some bits of clothing were still intact."

"That might not be true anymore," PJ said.

He looked from one of us to the other, brows knit. His expression showed that he was in unfamiliar territory.

I pointed to the glass coffin. "This would have been airtight. If the remains were not immediately replaced in another airtight container, they probably would have disintegrated by now. They would have suffered damage just being removed from one container to another." I shook my head. "Chances are the thieves weren't experts in the preservation of human remains. That being the case, your Celt has been lost to everyone concerned, including the masses."

"That's my reason for wanting you two to take charge of this investigation."

PJ and I looked at each other. She said nothing; her expression revealed even less.

"All right," I agreed with reluctance, but questioned my decision when a vision of Marna appeared in front of me. She was standing, legs apart, with a drawn sword held crosswise and flat bladed across her chest. I shook my head to clear the vision, which faded quickly. "Uh—let's just say that we'll see what we can do. We won't promise anything, though, until we have more information."

Morrison appeared relieved. "That's all I ask."

Despite my reservations, I was curious. "Where did the body come from originally?"

"My great, great grandfather's man discovered it in Cors Caron, the Tregaron Bog. He, my ancestor, murdered his man to prevent the discovery from being revealed."

"Nice ancestors," PJ murmured.

I walked around the coffin, looking for smudges that might indicate fingerprints. The glass appeared to have been cleaned and the crime scene obliterated. "And you know for a fact that the remains were those of a Celtic warrior?"

"Yes, and according to my ancestor, an important one."

"One more thing. Was the body filled out?"

"What do you mean?"

"If the bog was acidic, the bones would be poorly preserved, but the organic remains would survive very well." I glanced at PJ. She seemed lost in thought and content to let me take the lead. "To be preserved as well as you say he was, he would have been treated with chemicals after he was removed from the bog."

He stroked his mustache. "I'm afraid I still don't follow you."

For someone who supposedly dabbled in antiquities, he didn't seem very well-informed.

PJ turned toward him. "Bodies have been discovered in bogs before, here and in Ireland. The last one, I believe, was discovered in Ireland in the seventies. These bodies are well-preserved and appear tanned like leather. The chemical makeup of the bog dictates the degree of preservation. One of the most famous was the Tollund Man, discovered in 1950 in a peat bog in Denmark. It was determined that he died two thousand years ago. He was so well-preserved that he appeared to be asleep. Because of limitations at the time, they were only able to preserve the head, that being soaked first in formalin and acetic acid, then alcohol, toluol, and wax." She looked from him to me. "I doubt these thieves had knowledge of such techniques."

"I can only tell you what I know," Morrison said. "As for the condition of the bones, I never actually touched the body. It was always just there, in the case."

PJ and I shared a look. She seemed to want me to make the final decision. "We'll do what we can," I said.

"Fair enough."

"We'll probably need to come back and look around, to check windows and doors for possible entry," I added, as Lord Morrison escorted us out of the room. "I assume you'll give us freedom of access for that."

"Of course. Call me when you're ready, and I'll be here."

"By the way, John, how is your wife?" PJ asked, as we climbed the stairs.

"Jenny's fine, except that she's under the weather today."

"Nothing serious, I hope."

"Just a bad cold. It's being here, you know." He waved his arm, encompassing the dark and dreary décor. "She gets chilled."

PJ and I shared another look. This time I had no difficulty reading her mind. The place gave us chills, too.

Lord Morrison escorted us to the door. "Until we meet again, and that will be soon, I hope."

We shook hands all around.

* * *

"Phew, I'm glad to be out of there," PJ said, as we climbed into the Rover. "It's freaky. Even you looked like you had seen a ghost."

"I know."

"What do you know?"

"What if I told you that Marna appeared to me in there? I wonder if it was a warning of some kind."

She pinched the bridge of her nose and gave a weary sigh. "Oh, not again. I thought we were done with the Amazons. I know that at some level you're not ready to let them go, but you must—and you will."

I wasn't about to argue the point. For her, the Amazon chapter was closed. I wished I could be as certain.

"How long is it since your father has seen Morrison?"

"Geez, years. Many, many years. Are you thinking what I'm thinking?"

"That all is not what it appears to be."

"Yes. Something's screwy, but I can't put a finger on it."

"For one thing, Morrison's younger than I expected."

"I thought that, too," PJ said.

"Mmm. And your father hadn't heard from him in years."

"Right."

"Morrison said they talked all the time. But if they weren't corresponding with each other on a regular basis, why would he say that, and why would Frederick be sending him pictures of you?"

"He wouldn't be. Maybe Morrison saw my picture in People Magazine, or worse, in some supermarket rag."

"But he knew about your problems with your father."

She nodded. "Same source, I expect. What are you getting at?"

"Nothing tangible."

I pulled the seatbelt across my shoulder and started the engine.

"There's something else," PJ said, after several moments of silence.

I guided the vehicle back along the drive and through the iron gates, waving to the gatekeeper. "What's that?"

"He told us to call him when we were ready to return."

"What about it?"

"The difference, my dear Kimmy, is between the Queen's English and American English, like boot and bonnet. Americans call, Brits *ring.*"

"Maybe it's a Welshism."

"I don't think so."

"Now who's suspicious?"

We reached a fork in the road, and I pulled off to one side and stopped the car. "Are you saying the man we spoke with is really an American?"

She shrugged. "I don't know. It may be my imagination, but his accent didn't ring true."

"If he isn't Morrison, who the hell is he?"

She chewed her lower lip in thought. "I'm going to call Dad to see if he has any recent pictures—newspaper clips, perhaps—of his lordship."

"Good idea." I steered back onto the road. "And what was all the talk about Owain Glyndwr? It has no bearing on the Celtic riddle."

"Name dropping, Kim. For the Welsh, having Owain Glyndwr in your family tree would be something special."

"Or he may have cooked up the story just to throw us off."

PJ tilted her head and frowned. "Off what?"

"I have no idea." I paused for a moment as we reached another bend in the road. "But, speaking of ideas, it's such a lovely day. Let's take a drive and stop at a pub somewhere for a sandwich and a glass of ale."

"Ah, you've a hankering for some Bass Ale?" She gave me a knowing look.

"You know me too well, my love."

"All right. Under one condition." Her green eyes sparkled. "We go back to the inn afterwards for a bit of hanky panky."

"I suppose that could be arranged."

Chapter 7

Kim was supposed to be working on her laptop, but I caught her glancing in my direction as I dressed. It felt good to know that I could distract her with little more than a wiggle of my hips as I pulled on my jeans. Oh, yeah.

Trying to be as casual as I could be under the circumstances, I let my fingers brush across my breasts when I buttoned my shirt, and her gaze lingered on my chest. I smiled, still pretending not to notice, but left the top two buttons undone. Uh-huh. I could see her swallowing.

I struck a sexy pose.

She frowned.

"What?" I asked.

"Where's your medallion?"

"Oh, that. For a minute there, I was afraid I'd lost my irresistible charm."

Kim grinned. "You? Never. So, what happened to your medallion?"

I tucked my shirt into my jeans and buckled the belt. "The clasp is loose. I was afraid it might fall off, so I put it on the dresser for safekeeping."

The laptop gave a tiny ping, and her look was diverted to the screen. Damn. My charm was resistible after all.

I closed the distance between our bed and her chair and leaned in to kiss the back of her neck and run my fingers through her hair. "Must you work right now? I thought maybe we could have some fun."

"Perhaps," she said, turning and giving my mouth a nibble. Then her eyes refocused on the monitor. "Hang on, Hot Lips. We have an e-mail from your dad."

"Finally." I slid onto her lap so I could read the message as she brought it up. "Maybe he's sending that photo of Morrison I asked him about."

There was a soft knock on our door, and I scrambled to a less compromising position.

Kim chuckled. "If that's Arwel, you don't have to put on an act. I'm pretty sure she knows about us."

I fastened one more button on my shirt and finger-combed my hair. "Us?"

"Our relationship."

"Oh." My hand was on the doorknob. "How perceptive of her."

"The woman has eyes. It probably didn't take much effort."

"Hi, Arwel." I smiled as she handed me a tray laden with breakfast goodies.

"Bore da, ladies. Here's something to start your day."

I accepted the tray. "Thank you, and bore da to you, too. This smells divine."

She bobbed us a curtsey, as if we were royalty. "Cook says the marmalade is fresh made and the scones hot out of the oven. Oh, and the tea is Earl Grey, just the way you like it."

"How wonderful," Kim said, smiling at her. "You're spoiling us with such good service."

"Not a bit, Dr. Blair." Twin rosy spots bloomed on Arwel's cheeks. "You two are no trouble at all."

"You Welsh folks don't seem to worry much about carbs or calories, do you?" I inhaled the fragrant aroma coming from the tray.

Her puzzled expression answered my question. "You wouldn't need to," I hastened to say, "with all the nice footpaths you have in this country."

I thanked Arwel again and set the tray on our bedside table. She and Kim exchanged pleasantries before our hostess left to assist her other guests.

Unable to control myself any longer, I spread generous amounts of butter and marmalade on a hot scone and took a bite. "Mmm." I tore off a chunk for Pup and then licked the sticky residue from my fingers.

Kim turned to watch us. "You know, too much sweet stuff isn't good for him."

"I know, but how do you resist that look?"

"It isn't easy, but I try. Besides, I see it often enough on your face that I should be immune."

"Moi? You've got to be kidding."

She laughed. "You're doing it right now."

Damn. Another secret weapon gone. Was there anything left in my arsenal? I sighed and poured our tea, carrying the cups and a plate of scones to Kim.

She ate and drank while I moved to the back of her chair and peered over her shoulder.

"What does Dad have to say?"

She swallowed the last of her scone and put her cup down. "See for yourself."

I maneuvered into a comfortable position on her lap, leaning into the warmth of her embrace. "Ah, this is nice."

"Make yourself comfortable, why don't you."

"Thanks, I have. Can you still reach your tea?"

She shifted under my weight and groaned. "I think I can manage. Let's get to your dad's message."

We read the e-mail together.

> *Ladies, we may have a problem. My security people have warned me about some threatening messages that have been coming in. These threats, though not specific, extend beyond me to my staff and family. I'm taking the usual precautions to safeguard all of us. Since you are out of the country, I'm sending a couple of fellows to keep an eye on both of you. Geoff Hunter and Trevor Poole are trusted employees and part of my personal security team when I'm in the UK. They are aware of and comfortable with your private relationship. I'll keep you posted and will try to get some photos of Morrison age-enhanced for you shortly. Just be careful, okay? Priscilla, you know the drill. Love to you both, Dad.*

I eased back against Kim's chest. "That's interesting."

Her body stiffened. "Interesting? Is that all you can say?"

"Easy. It's no big deal."

Her arms tightened around me. "He sounded serious. Maybe we should head home."

I broke her fierce grip and stood up so we could face each other.

"Will you please relax?" I picked up her teacup. "Here, finish your tea."

She took it, but only long enough to stand and replace it on the desk. "I can't think about tea now." Her body still radiated protective vibes. "And what does 'you know the drill' mean? Has this sort of thing happened to you before?"

I shrugged. "Once or twice."

"Jesus." She grabbed me again, tighter this time. "That does it. We're leaving."

I pushed her back, breaking contact. "No, now wait. Listen to me. Dad has been through this before and he knows what to do. Let him handle it, okay?"

She gripped my hands and pulled me into another suffocating hug. I wanted to make a joke about being some sort of human yo-yo, but her body was trembling too much. "How can you be so casual about a threat like this?" she murmured against my cheek.

I gave her what I thought was a lighthearted laugh. "It's the downside to being rich. I'm afraid having money makes craziness happen. It's a curse, sometimes."

"I wouldn't know about that." She pulled back and stared into my eyes. "I'm not used to this kind of thing, so please humor me. I'm concerned about your safety and your father's."

"I know you are." My eyes stung with unshed tears. "Please don't be upset."

She fretted over me, stroking my hair, patting my bangs, and kissing my forehead. When she spoke again, her voice was husky. "We've only just found each other, and if anything happened to you, I don't know what I'd do. I can't imagine life without you. I think I'd go insane. Do you realize that?"

"Yes," I said, my throat tightening. "I feel the same way about you."

She was my fierce, independent, Amazon warrior, so alone against the world before we met, and now so vulnerable because of loving me.

Her fingers dug into my shoulders. "I love you so much." Tears welled in her eyes and spilled down her cheeks.

"I know you do," I whispered.

Funny, wasn't it, how love could hurt? One minute you were alone and aloof, playing the field, tossing lovers aside with abandon, feeling no pain, no worries. And then you found the special one, and everything changed. What you had together was so precious that you feared losing it, even when you were safe and secure. Even when you knew that both of you were together forever and always, there were moments when you feared it could all disappear.

I looked into the depths of those glistening brown eyes. "And I love you more than anything. Don't ever doubt it."

We were silent for several seconds, holding each other, reining in our emotions. "Good," she said, giving my back a final rub. "Then, it's settled. We'll call Frederick and tell him that, under the circumstances, we can't stay any longer."

I pushed against her chest, clearing space between us. "Whoa. Hold on a second. I don't recall us making that decision."

"There's no other sane way to deal with this, PJ." She turned away from me and paced in front of the door. Pup whimpered and tracked her progress with growing agitation.

"Look, you're getting Pup all worried." I stood in her path, raising my hands to her shoulders and forcing her to halt. "Kimmy, sweetheart, read my lips. Do not worry. Okay?"

Brown eyes, which had been so full of love just seconds ago, now darkened, and her jaw tensed.

Jesus. The Great Stone Face. I took a long, cleansing breath. "Look, I know you're concerned. And I'm flattered beyond measure, really I am. But we're not in some third world country. We're in a small, peaceful place, in a town most people can't even pronounce, let alone find. Dad is sending us bodyguards. They'll make our lives miserable with all their attention, but with them dogging us, we'll be safe."

Pup made a noise. "Sorry, Pup. I meant no disrespect."

That made Kim chuckle. "Like he knows what you're talking about."

With her tension diffused, the rigidness left her face and her brown eyes lightened and filled with love again. "I suppose you're right." She sighed and moved into my outstretched arms. "I just don't want anything to happen to the people I love."

"Oh, honey." I rubbed the small of her back. "I know, and I appreciate that. And I love you for it, believe me." My arms circled her waist. "But right now, I say let's get on with our lives."

"Well…"

"We won't have much time to ourselves once our security gets here."

"True."

"How about we take a drive to check out that National Library? We wanted to see what kind of research facilities they had and make ourselves known to the higher-ups and such, so we can learn more about Owain-what's-his-face, right?"

"Right."

"I bet that big, stone building has just what we need to get to the bottom of this Morrison mess."

Kim picked up her teacup and drained it. It had to be cold by now, but it seemed to settle her. "I'd like that, as long as we're cautious." She grabbed her purse and jacket. "A trip to Aberystwyth to scope out the library, followed by a nice Welsh tea someplace will work for me."

I gave her big smile. "Me, too."

"And when we get back, we'll take Pup for a stroll around these lovely hills."

"Throw in some shopping, and it sounds like you have a plan, Doc."

She cringed. "Shopping? I don't recall promising—"

"Shh." I put my fingers across her lips. "You love me, remember?"

"Oh, yeah." She sighed, giving my fingers tiny kisses. "But shopping?"

"It goes with the territory." I pulled my fingers back and gave her a long, lingering kiss.

"Wow," Kim said when she could breathe again.

I smiled. "And that goes with the territory, too."

* * *

The large neo-classical building that housed the National Library of Wales was an impressive structure that dominated its hillside location. It overlooked the seaside resort of Aberystwyth and resembled a palace. Its interior was warm, spacious, user-friendly, and inviting. The Main Hall was big, almost overpowering, and there was even a restaurant on the premises.

Hampered by the probable illegality of Morrison's possession of the corpse of an ancient Celtic warrior, we avoided confiding in anyone during our search for information. We were able to locate numerous promising history books in the reference section and made appointments to speak with several heads of departments in the near future. Kim made notes on the entire visit, so that we could plunge right into work once we had formulated a plan of action.

Then, of course, we had the Owain Glyndwr connection to examine. We didn't know what to think about that, or why it had been brought up at all. Glyndwr had been a hero, complete with accompanying myths and legends. We looked forward to separating fact from fiction wherever possible.

I made a few discreet inquiries about Lord and Lady Morrison, but nobody could recollect the last time they had seen the couple. We were led to believe that the Morrisons spent most of their time away, at their other homes, and weren't recognized locally.

“Why don’t they know these people better?” I asked Kim, once we were in the Rover on our way back down Penglais Road, looking for the turn onto A44.

“You heard what they said about them not spending much time here. But frankly, I think those folks know more about the Morrisons than they care to share. They were keeping their opinions to themselves. For some reason, they didn’t want to discuss anything. Maybe it’s just that we’re too inquisitive for their taste.”

“You think?” I gave her a grin. “I thought we were nice and subtle about it.”

Kim wanted to explore some of the hills and valleys around Dolgellau, so we spent a relaxing hour driving to scenic overlooks, walking Pup along bike paths, and admiring several duck ponds.

Afterwards, we found a spot to park the Rover, near one of Wales’s famous footpaths. We walked along the path for a couple of miles before heading back to the Rover.

“You can walk from village to village,” Kim said, “or, if you want, from county to county. Ideal for those on extended holidays from South Wales to North Wales.”

“England, too. Am I right in thinking that you’d enjoy that kind of a holiday?”

“You know me.” She laughed. It was a tight little giggle, the laugh itself lost in whatever or wherever her thoughts were. “I’m a sucker for seeing what’s around the next bend in the road or footpath. Preferably footpaths. They were the highways of our ancestors.”

I raised my eyebrows. “Uh oh, you’re thinking Amazons again.”

“No, I wasn’t. Not this time.”

It suddenly began to rain, heavily, and we dashed to our vehicle. We had parked in a secluded grove, surrounded by trees, rocks, and thick, moist ferns. The heated air inside the Rover reeked of rich, dark soil and fragrant wild herbs. Kim and I listened to the drumming rain overhead and slid closer together.

“This is cozy.” I stroked her thigh.

“That it is.”

“The rear seats fold down, you know, if you want to get more comfortable.” I tried to give her a loving smile that wasn’t too obvious.

She sighed. “I’m afraid this body isn’t as limber as it once was. Besides, we really should get back to the inn and load this material into the laptop.”

I imitated her sigh, exaggerating it. "Poor old thing. I guess you're right." I glanced out the rain-drenched window. "You'll just have to give me a rain check."

With a snort, she started the Rover. "Funny, PJ. Very funny."

* * *

We had an early supper and retired to our room. Kim worked on the computer and I stretched out on the bed, reading some Welsh history that we had downloaded and printed out earlier.

The afternoon activities must have tired me more than I realized. After several minutes of reading and rereading the blurring lines of type, I gave up and dozed. The sound of muffled voices woke me. I sat up and discovered Kim and Arwel in the doorway, whispering. Kim took a bundle of clothing and some boots from the young woman and thanked her. When she turned in my direction, she seemed startled, but made a quick recovery.

"Ah, you're awake."

"What's happening? What have you got there?"

She picked up several papers from the desk where her laptop usually sat. "Your father sent these." She handed me what appeared to be photos of an older, very thin man who had gray hair and a mustache.

"Morrison?"

She nodded.

"Then who the hell is the guy we talked to?"

"That's what I'm going to find out." She pulled out her daypack and stuffed the dark clothing into it. "There wasn't any answer when I called the estate."

"Wait just a minute, here." I blinked and shook my head to clear the cobwebs from my sleep-filled mind. "If you think you're going to sneak off into the night like some kind of commando, without me, think again."

"After what your dad said about—"

"No, no, no. Uh uh. We are in this together, Kimberly Elizabeth Blair." She tried a series of stern expressions on me, but I cut her off. "Don't even try that with me. I'm going with you, and that's final."

"Damn it." She handed me a set of oversized camouflage pants and a matching shirt. "Arwel rounded these up for us. I guess she figured you'd never listen to me. Please, I want to search that estate, but not if it puts you in harm's way. Your father is wondering about this fake Morrison, too. He's thinking maybe there's a connection to the missing chieftain."

"And I'm sure he doesn't intend you to go sneaking around the estate by yourself."

"Maybe not."

"So, that's all the more reason I should go along to help you solve this mystery and keep you out of trouble."

"Keep *me* out of trouble? That's a good one." She put her arms around my waist and kissed the top of my head. I let my cheek rest against her chest. Her heart was racing. "All right, but a quick in and out. Just fact-finding, that's all."

I giggled, inhaling the faint scent of mango body wash from her skin. "Captain Kim and her sidekick, Corporal Curtis. What a team we'll make."

Chapter 8

"I was gung-ho at first, but now I'm not so comfortable with this," PJ said, as we each pulled on the British Army camouflage suits and smeared black goo on our faces. We looked like commandos about to storm the bastion. In a way, we were. Maybe not commandos, but we were preparing to raid an enemy stronghold, and that was reason enough for me to have a case of the jitters. Apparently my partner, despite her earlier bravado, was also nervous.

"I know," I said, pulling on my gloves. "But something fishy is going on in that place. And now that we know the man we spoke with isn't Lord Morrison, I want some answers."

"On the one hand," PJ said, "it's breaking and entering. On the other, it's trying to find out what happened to the real Morrisons."

Hearing the indecision in her voice, I tried to offer some comfort. "Your father mentioned they have several homes, so they could be anywhere."

"I suppose." She gave me a lopsided grin. "I love you, but don't ask me to kiss you with all that crap on your face."

I wrinkled my nose at her. "You're not a picture of loveliness right now, either."

We had driven the Rover into a narrow lane and parked it behind some heavy shrubbery about half a mile from the Morrison estate. After two days of steady rain, we needed our Wellies. The only time PJ had worn them before was the morning we milked the cows, so she had no experience walking in them for any distance. The pair that Arwel had found for her was too big. The wide tops thumped against her calves, and the bottoms slurped as the muddy track tugged at her feet.

Thump, slurp. Thump, slurp.

"So this is what they mean by the music of the night," she said. "Thanks, but no thanks."

I suggested she fold down the tops of her Wellingtons. "That way they'll fit your trim legs better."

“Thank you, Dr. Blair, but my trim legs do much better in other situations, if you get my drift.” We weren’t using our flashlights, so all I could see of her face was the mischievous gleam in her eyes.

“Later, dear. You can show me.”

“Yeah, that’s if we get out of here alive.” She ran up alongside me. Thump, slurp, slurp, thump, slurp, slurp. “We do make beautiful music together.”

I stopped and took her gloved hand in mine. “Sweetie, you don’t have to go along with this, you know. In fact, I’d prefer you didn’t. You can go back to the Rover and wait for me there.”

“No way. Where you go, that’s me, babe, right there with you.”

“What about the threats against you and your dad?”

“He can handle it. Besides, that has nothing to do with this situation.”

“How can you be so sure?”

“Because Morrison asked Dad if I would help him with something. The request was legit. It was on his personal crested notepaper.”

“Humph.” This wasn’t the time to voice my concerns, however.

We started again.

Thump, slurp.

The old stone wall that surrounded much of the estate halted our progress. It was too high to scale, so we followed it up the road, ducking into the ditch a couple of times when we heard cars coming. Luckily for us, the water didn’t top our Wellies.

“James Bond, where are you when I need you?” PJ whispered. The question sounded like a shout in the dark.

We paused at the tall, green, solid-wood gate that served as the back entrance to the estate. I remembered seeing it when we were on our way to Clarach Bay for tea and Queen Anne cakes. I sure hadn’t figured we’d be trying to break into the estate from this side.

Giving myself a mental shake, I tried the gate latch. As I’d expected, it was secured from the inside. Just beyond the gate, the wall angled right and away from the road. We were at the southwest boundary of the estate’s gardens. A barbed wire fence continued on, separating the public roadway from the private fields.

“Come on, but be careful,” I whispered. “You can get a nasty cut from this stuff.”

With my long legs, I made it easily over the fence. I was too late, though, when I turned to help PJ. She had snagged the crotch of her camouflage pants. “Good thing I’m not a guy,” she muttered. “If I were, there would be extensive damage to my hanging garden.”

“Shh!” I put a gloved finger in front of my mouth for emphasis.

She mimicked me. “I’m shh-ing, damn it.”

A dog barked from a distance, but seconds later, he was on the other side of the wall, barking and growling. Convinced we were about to be discovered, we froze in our tracks, barely allowing ourselves to breathe. After what seemed like an eternity, the dog lost interest and left.

“If Pup were here, he’d make hamburger out of that mangy mongrel,” PJ whispered. “And speaking of Pup, why didn’t you want to bring him along?”

“We don’t know what we’re going to run into on the other side of that wall. He might be more liability than help.”

“Like me.”

“I didn’t say that.” I gave her shoulder a squeeze.

“You didn’t have to. Still, I’d feel a whole lot better if Pup were with us.”

“I’m afraid it’s just us two commandos.” I moved forward. “Come on, let’s get this over with.”

We followed the wall north, walking between it and a line of giant oaks. The wet ground muffled the sound of our footsteps and we were able to move right along.

A hoot sounded from a branch right above us. PJ jumped. “What the hell?”

“Relax, it’s just an owl.”

“What, you think I don’t know an owl when I hear one?”

“Shush.”

“Shush yourself.”

We continued until the wall right-angled again and headed east. We had found no way to gain entry to the gardens, let alone the house. And to make matters worse, it began to rain steadily.

“This is not fun,” PJ said.

“I didn’t say it would be.”

I was about to call it quits and take my chances face-to-face with Morrison’s impostor, when we came to a low door in the wall. I tried the latch, and it gave under my hand.

We were in the upper garden. It was very dark, but here inside the wall, I dared not flash my light. As my eyes adjusted to the darkness, I could make out, to our right, the outline of a small outbuilding.

We made our way toward it and slipped inside. It was filled with garden paraphernalia. Small tools hung from hooks on the walls, and larger ones, including rakes, hoes, shovels, and garden forks, leaned against the sides. A workbench was strewn with empty flowerpots and a trowel. Partially used bags of fertilizer were stacked under the bench. A wheelbarrow leaned, upended, in the corner across from the door.

We sagged against each other for a moment, taking the opportunity to catch our breath and slow our heart rates. "You okay, sweetie?"

"Never better." PJ's voice was heavy on the sarcasm. "Here I am—heiress to one of the most prestigious companies in the United States—in the midst of trespassing, nearly soaked to the skin after that shower, about to break and enter. All things considered, I guess I'm in great shape."

"You were the one who insisted on coming." I wiped the dirty windowpane with my gloved hand and peered into the blackness. "No one twisted your arm."

The clouds parted just long enough for the waning moonlight to illuminate the outline of a stone cottage, probably the home of a chauffeur or grounds keeper, and beyond it, the main house. It appeared massive and forbidding until it disappeared again into the darkness when clouds covered the moon.

"If you think I'd let you wander alone into enemy territory without my help, you'd better think again."

"Help? What help?"

"Thanks a lot. I don't know how to handle all that appreciation."

"PJ, it's not that I don't appreciate your help. It's just that with you along I have to worry about both of us."

"Okay, if I'm such a liability, you just worry about yourself, and let me take care of myself."

I turned and took her into my arms. "It's only because I love you so much, and I can't bear the thought of you being hurt."

"I know. I'm sorry I was grouchy. This just looks so easy on television when the good guys do it." She squared her shoulders and took a deep breath. "Let's just agree to take care of each other and ourselves, okay?"

"Deal."

I released PJ and put my hand on the latch. "Time to go. Me first." Before she had a chance to object, I eased through the opening, stopped immediately, and backed into the shed, shoving her behind me.

She tripped over a spade, and it clattered to the floor.

"Jesus," we both said in a frightened whisper.

I pulled the door nearly closed and peered through the crack. "If they weren't aware of our presence before, I'm sure they are now."

"You scared the shit out of me," PJ said against my back. "What happened?"

"Someone opened the cottage door. Now please, hush up."

A bright shaft of light fell across the garden and lit up the shed. The beam illuminated the interior, too, passing like a spotlight through the circle I had wiped clean.

The dog, barking and growling, was making a beeline for our hiding place.

"Rex, put a sock in it." The voice was masculine and irritated. "Get back in here, damn it." I was sure Rex was not convinced, but at the sound of his master's gruff tone, he headed back anyway. The fresh cooking smells wafting through the open door probably had something to do with his lack of attention to duty.

"You keep away from that shed," the voice said. "There's poison in there for the rats." We could hear the man scolding the dog all the way back to the cottage.

The door slammed shut and all was quiet, except for our breathing.

PJ gripped my waist. "Did he say rats?"

"I believe so, yes."

She pulled me around to face her. "In here? With us?"

"Now, calm down."

"No." Her head swiveled from side to side, seeking evidence of furry rodents in each of the four corners. "I don't want to be in here another second."

I put my arm around her. "The fact that there might be rats in here saved us, don't you see?" She was shaking in spite of my efforts. "And we're ahead of the game because we know where Rex is, at least for now."

"Ye-yeah," she stuttered. "He's in a nice warm house, chewing on a fresh bone, and we're out here in the rain and mud, freezing our asses off with the rats. Pup is looking pretty smart to have stayed at the inn. He's going to love this story."

When I looked at her, I realized that the sudden shower had made her camouflage outfit cling to her body in all the right places. "I don't suppose it would help if I said you look incredibly sexy in those wet clothes."

She made a face. "Nice try, pervert."

* * *

By taking a wide detour around the cottage, we crept to the south side of the main house. I tried a couple of doors. They were bolted. "If I have it figured correctly, this is about where the basement room should be. We need to get in there to collect samples from that glass coffin."

"Yeah, and while we're at it, I could use a bottle or two of that three-hundred-year-old wine to warm me up."

I was relieved to hear PJ regain some of her feistiness.

She knelt on the soggy ground beside a small basement window. "Over here. I think we can get in, but I need help with this window."

She had forced it open partway, but it was stuck. Warped, I thought, from lack of use. We knelt together in the mud and tugged on the window frame until it finally opened, giving a loud creak. We froze as somewhere in the distance, a dog barked.

"Shit," PJ hissed, "not again. Rex will want to chew on us for dessert."

"Relax, little one. We're much too tough for Rex."

We remained motionless for several seconds. I was cold and miserable, and I knew PJ felt the same. "Come on," I said, squeezing her hand.

"Yeah, yeah, where you go, I go. Remind me again why I'm doing this?"

"Because you watch too many James Bond movies."

I heard a smothered giggle. "You've got that right."

Chapter 9

"Are we having fun yet?" Kim and I were crouched in the mud outside the small basement window, making final preparations to climb through. Her quiet acceptance of the damp, cold weather only made me more irritable. As if things weren't difficult enough, my bladder began to protest.

"I don't suppose we could take a bathroom break before we do this?"

Kim put a gloved finger to her lips and shook her head. "Follow me."

I gripped her shoulders. "Don't you think a smaller person should go first?"

Ignoring my question, she switched on her flashlight and scanned the basement room. "Damn, I need new batteries." She withdrew her arm from the window and played with the switch. The light faltered and dimmed but didn't go out. She shook it and the beam brightened.

"Looks like a loose connection."

"Yeah, but it'll have to do. You have yours with you, don't you?"

"Yep." I pulled it out of my pocket. The light snapped on bright and steady. "Compared to yours, this is a searchlight."

She scowled at me.

"And since I have the better light, I should go first." I gave her hip a nudge. "So move over, Rover."

"Not so fast. It's easily ten feet to that stone floor, and with your short legs, you'd never have a chance. I'm going first and that's final."

I bit my lower lip. Damn. I hated it when she was right. I'd huddle here and worry the whole time.

"Your concern is appreciated." Kim gave my shoulders a quick squeeze, seeming to read my mind as she often did. She backed in and lowered herself through the narrow opening.

I leaned in as far as possible, gripping her arms as she hung on to the window ledge.

"Let go."

"No, I can't."

"Damn it, PJ, let go!"

"Okay, okay."

Everything happened in slow motion. Her hands slid off the ledge, and after what seemed to be an eternity, there was a soft thud on the stone floor. I could see the yellowish beam of her flashlight flick over a pile of boxes and crates along one wall. I aimed my much brighter beam into the room while she stacked some of the boxes under the window so my entry would be easier.

"Pssst!"

I stuck my flashlight back in my pocket. Time to join Kim. The windowsill was filthy. Powdery mortar dust made my nose itch, and bits of granulated stone flaked off under my gloves as I slipped butt-first through the open window. For a few seconds my legs flailed about, searching for something solid to stand on. Kim guided one foot to the edge of a box, and I put all my weight on it. It gave a little, but held until strong hands gripped my hips and the rest of me slid into Kim's waiting arms.

"There." She kissed my forehead. "That wasn't so bad, was it?"

"Piece of cake," I answered, gulping for air.

We waited, hugging each other, listening. I couldn't tell whether it was Kim's heartbeat I felt thudding against my chest, or my own.

Kim let go and picked her flashlight up from the box it rested on. "How about getting that spotlight of yours out?" she said.

I held it up high like the cops on TV do, as if it were a knife in striking position. We found a few more boxes filled to capacity with Styrofoam-like packing beads. Ghost turds, I called them. We added some of the boxes to those Kim had stacked under our window, forming a crude, but unobtrusive, staircase.

"Our stairway to freedom," I whispered.

We had determined before entry that there were no other lights on in the basement area, and that the section above our window was dark. Once inside, though, I could hear faint voices and soft music.

"Do you hear that?" I asked.

"Yeah. I was hoping we'd have the place to ourselves."

"So, what's our plan?"

"Same as before. Find the coffin, check it further for clues, and get the hell out of here with our skins intact."

"Okay. That works for me, but what are you expecting to find?"

"I haven't the foggiest," she said. "Clues. Anything that looks out of place."

"Ha!"

"What?"

"You haven't a clue, but you're looking for clues. That's sort of amusing, don't you think?"

"Let's just get on with it."

"Yes ma'am, boss."

I started down the hallway to my right, but Kim grabbed the back of my commando shirt. "Whoa. The coffin room is this way."

"Are you sure?"

"It's to your left. I'm positive." She gave my shirt another tug. "You and your sense of direction."

"Hey, I found *you*, didn't I?"

I was rewarded with a tiny chuckle. "Can we please get moving?"

"Of course." I turned left. "Right this way."

We followed the corridor past several closed doors and a stairway. The cold air made us shiver, and hanging cobwebs added an eerie touch of mystery to our mission.

Just a fact-finding expedition, Kim had said. I'd bet the only fact we would find was that we didn't belong in this basement.

The second door beyond the stairway creaked open to reveal the coffin's marble pedestal, shrouded in shadows. We angled our small beacons downward to view what was immediately in front of us. What we needed, but didn't dare use, was a lantern to illuminate the room. We inched our way toward the empty coffin, listening for any sounds from above.

Our beams lit the coffin simultaneously. "Jesus!" I gasped.

Kim made an unidentifiable sound and recoiled.

Occupying the casket was a tall, thin man, dressed in a modern suit and tie.

"Oh my God," I whispered. "What the hell?"

"Who the hell, I think you mean."

"One thing's certain, it's not Owain Glyndwr."

Kim pocketed her flashlight, which was all but useless. "Shine yours over here."

I did as she asked, but all I wanted to do was get the hell out of there. She examined the body, taking care not to touch anything.

I didn't want to admit it to Kim, but I was creeped out. What if the mud on my Wellies glued me to the floor, and I couldn't move? I'd be trapped in here forever with Kim and the corpse. Being with her was one thing, but the dead man wouldn't do much for our love life.

Trying to get a grip on myself, I studied him, too, forming a physical description. Height? About six-one or -two. Weight? Maybe one-sixty or -seventy. Short, gray hair and a thin mustache.

Kim looked over at me. "You okay, sweetheart?"

"Yeah. Keep on with what you're doing. I'm just verifying in my mind what I'm seeing."

"You're seeing it all right. We're both seeing it."

"No distinguishing facial features, unless— Oh, geez, Kimmy, there's a bullet hole in his left temple."

"I know. That was hard to miss."

In the pale light, I detected scrapes and bruises on his hands.

"I can't see," Kim said.

I had allowed the light to wander over the body instead of illuminating her work area. "Sorry."

Kim moved to my side and refocused the light. "I know it's hard, but try to concentrate, okay?"

"Are those defensive wounds?" I pointed to the scratches and bruises on his hands.

"Probably." She stared at me. "I'm almost finished. Can you make it?"

I took a deep breath and tightened my grip on the flashlight. "This man was murdered, Kimmy. Somebody's got to pay for that."

"Somebody will, if we have anything to say about it. Now, I think it's time we left."

"You don't have to tell me twice." I leaned my head against her shoulder for a few seconds. "It's Lord Morrison, isn't it? The real one, I mean."

"He matches the pictures your dad sent." She gave me a comforting hug and a kiss on the cheek.

"Dad's going to be—"

I was interrupted by the sounds of a door opening on the floor above us and heavy footfalls on the stairs. I covered most of the flashlight's beam, and we moved quickly into the hallway.

The voices were closer and louder. Two men, making a lot of noise, were now between us and freedom.

"How many bottles does he want this time?"

"Two at least."

Oh, shit. We weren't going to make it. I turned toward Kim, my heart thudding in my ears. She pushed me ahead of her into a small, closet-like room, and I buried my face in her shirtfront. The men's voices faded, and they moved on into the wine cellar next to the coffin room.

"Whew!" My breath came out in a rush. "That was too close."

Kim opened the door just enough to peek down the hall. We were poised to make our escape, when we heard one of the guys shout, "Hey, what the hell?"

The second man responded. "Now what?"

"The door to the room where we stashed old Morrison was shut, and now it's open."

"You're imagining things. I told you not to read them horror stories."

"No, I'm sure. I closed it myself, I did."

"No way anyone can get in. Just forget it, okay?"

"Bloody hell. I was so sure. Let's get upstairs. I feel I'm being watched."

"That's the stiff giving you the evil eye."

"Don't kid around. You know I'm not comfortable with this whole business."

"Being paid enough, aren't you?"

"Yeah, the money's good."

"So clam up, and let's get what we come down here for."

We heard some bottles clink together, and Kim pulled the door closed just as the guys entered the hallway.

I kept my cheek against her chest. "I'm scared."

"Yeah, me too." She put her arm around my shoulders and squeezed. "As soon as they go back upstairs, we'll get the hell out of here and call the cops." She kissed the top of my head.

"Sounds like a plan." I smiled, feeling safer. "You know, sleuthing with you can be quite a turn-on."

"You're crazy, you know that? Sexy as all get out, but crazy all the same."

The tiny closet grew stuffy. I stepped back, giving us breathing room, and stumbled over some clothing that was piled on the floor. When I shined my light over the pile, I had to stifle a scream. A woman stared up at us from one dusty corner.

Kim crouched down and felt her neck for a pulse, but shook her head.

"Jesus, there's a corpse in every room."

"Easy, PJ. Don't freak out on me now."

"But this is bad."

"I know." She gave me a reassuring smile. "You've seen remains before."

"Yeah, but they were long dead."

"Just a couple of minutes and we'll be out of here. Okay?"

I took a deep breath. "Okay."

By flashlight, she continued to examine the body. "Gray hair, blue eyes, and a small caliber bullet wound to the head."

"It has to be Jenny Morrison."

Kim stood up and opened the door far enough to stick out her head. We held our breaths, but we heard nothing.

"Come on. It's time to let the police take over. We're in way over our heads with this escapade."

I patted her hip. "Right behind you, love. Let's get out of here, before we become part of the body count."

She eased herself out of the closet and into the hall.

"All clear," she whispered, taking my hand. We threw caution to the wind and ran for our crude staircase of boxes. It seemed like hours since we had forced open that little window.

"Stop right there!"

We froze at the bottom of the stairs and turned in slow motion toward the voice. A man stepped out of the shadows above us. Something glinted in his right hand, probably a gun.

"Hey, Davy, I was right, someone's down here."

I heard a muffled "God damn it to hell!"

"Run," Kim whispered. "Run like you've never run before." With that, she bolted, dragging me by the hand.

Just as we reached the escape room, there was an explosion. I was blinded by the flash and deafened by the noise. Kim hauled me to the boxes. We could hear the men running down the hall after us. They were shouting, two voices close by, and a third barking orders in the distance.

Kim pushed against my butt. "Climb up and out. Hurry!"

"What about you?"

"I'm coming. Just *go*."

I don't remember the mad scramble upward or the tight squeeze through the window, but I was outside and Kim was climbing close behind. She paused, and I heard her kick the top box back into the room. From the noise and the cursing, I figured some of the other boxes had fallen, too, spilling their contents. The guys must have been falling all over the ghost turds.

Racing in Wellies wasn't easy, but I managed. Kim, running just ahead of me, seemed to have no trouble. Hers must have fit better than mine.

"Shit!" I yelled. "I'm getting a blister. A couple, I think."

"Better blisters than bullet holes," she called back.

Her comment fueled my tiring legs. With a burst of speed I wouldn't have believed possible, I pulled ahead of her and we cut across the vegetable garden and through a flowerbed or two.

As we ran, panting, through the green gate and along the row of oak trees, we could hear shouting and barking coming from the gardens. Barbed wire ripped at our clothing when we scaled the fence, but all we could think about was getting to the Rover. We scrambled in, and Kim, key at the ready, shoved it into the ignition. She jammed the Rover into gear, spun the tires in the mud, slowed to get traction, and then hightailed it for the road. Our tires squealed onto the pavement. The vehicle rocked, and for a second or two I thought we'd tip over. When I was able to look back, I saw flashlights bobbing up and down in the road.

"God, that was close."

"Tell me about it." Kim reached for my hand. "Are you okay?"

"I am now." I started to peel off my Wellies. "Damn. My right heel isn't so good, though. The blister broke and bled into my sock."

"I'll help you clean it and cover it with gauze when we get back to the inn. Right now, we've got to go to the police station and report a couple of murders."

"We don't have our first aid kit with us this trip, so where are you going to find gauze at this time of night, huh? Tell me that."

She reached over and chucked me under the chin. "I'll tear a strip off my petticoat."

"F-u-n-n-y."

"I'll bet Arwel has something we can use."

"Arwel, if she's like any normal, sane person, will be in bed asleep."

"I'll find something."

I snuggled up to her as best I could over the gearshift. "You can jolly well kiss it better."

"You sound just like a Welshwoman." Kim planted a kiss on my forehead. "But sure, I'll do that, too."

Chapter 10

"Time to face the music," I said, giving PJ's cold hand a reassuring squeeze.

She grimaced. "Yeah. How bad can it be?"

"I don't think I'll answer that."

"Probably best that you don't. My imagination is working overtime as it is." She shuddered and took a deep breath. "That looks like the place, up ahead on the right."

I slowed and put on the turn signal. In the pre-dawn, there was little traffic to battle, but it still felt weird turning right from the left lane. I guided the Rover into a visitor's parking slot and engaged the brake. My body ached from tension and lack of sleep. Our sleuthing and near capture had taken its toll on me.

By the looks of it, PJ was no better. A dirty smudge graced her chin; the sleek-fitting commando outfit, so sexy and butch on her just hours ago, now showed evidence of our panicked escape from the Morrison estate.

We entered the police station with trepidation, pausing just inside the door. I turned to PJ. "You know, we committed a crime by breaking and entering, so I don't know what kind of a reception we'll get. They could just lock us up."

"Don't say that."

"We have to be prepared."

She sighed. A sign of resignation on her part, I thought.

The lobby was stark but clean. There were no pictures or anything colorful to brighten the white walls. Wanted posters and other notices were pinned to a few oversized corkboards. A wooden bench and a couple of straight chairs told me that this was the waiting area.

"Do you want me to do most of the talking?" I asked her.

"Whatever you think best. This is a new experience for me. I haven't been in trouble with the law since my college days, when I racked up a few thousand dollars' worth of unpaid parking tickets."

"Ooh! What a big, bad criminal. You'd better keep quiet about that, or they'll lock you up and throw away the key."

She tugged me into a corner near a set of stairs. "Look, I know you're trying to make light of this for my benefit, but it's just not working."

I pressed my palm against her lower back, needing to keep us physically connected for as long as possible. "I'm sorry. I blame myself for all of this."

"No. We decided to go there together. It was the right thing to do under the circumstances. We thought we were checking into the missing Celt story and why someone was posing as Morrison. That impostor guy told us to come back. It wasn't our fault that they didn't answer the phone. Besides, we didn't know there were murderers in that house!"

PJ's frayed nerves had given added volume to the last sentence. Several heads turned in our direction. Before we could create further mayhem, I walked up to the front desk, which was at chest level, and cleared my throat. PJ followed me.

The desk sergeant, a thin, balding man with a beak-like nose, eyed us with mild interest. "Yes, miss?"

"I'm Dr. Kimberly Blair. I—that is, we—want to report a murder."

"Two, actually," PJ added.

"Yes, two." I swallowed hard. "At the Morrison estate on the White Way over by—"

The sergeant held up his hand. "I'm familiar with the place. You say two people were murdered at the estate?"

"Sergeant…" I looked at the nameplate pinned to his uniform pocket. "Sergeant Jenkins, I can't say for sure they were murdered there, but the bodies are there."

He took out a form, scribbled a few words, and then glared at each of us. "And just how would you ladies be knowing about that?"

PJ leaned against the scarred wooden desk. Its height kept all but her shoulders and head hidden from the sergeant's view. "We know because we saw the bodies with our own eyes."

He tapped his pen against the form and gave her a bemused look. "Did you now? And who might you be?"

"I'm PJ Curtis. My father is Frederick Curtis of the Curtis Foundation." There was a hint of confrontation in her tone.

Sergeant Jenkins was not impressed. "Isn't that interesting?"

He pushed a buzzer just below his left hand, and part of the wooden barricade swung open. "Why don't you two step through and have a seat over there on the bench? I believe some members of the investigative squad would like to chat with you about all of this."

"Certainly, sir." PJ turned to me with a tired grin. "Now we're getting somewhere."

"Somewhere," I said, as we stepped behind the wall, moving deeper into police custody. "But just where is that?"

The bench was as uncomfortable as the one outside the counter had looked to be.

After a wait of ten minutes, two men in dark suits introduced themselves as Constables Renfrew and Gardiner. They took our names, examined our passports, made copies of our photo IDs, and searched our daypacks, after politely patting us down in case we had weapons.

"Cop a feel," PJ muttered, "and I'll smack you."

"Excuse me?" Constable Gardiner was young and pink-cheeked. He hadn't taken his eyes off PJ since he was called in to "process" us, and I could see he was smitten. I couldn't blame him because, despite her smudged face and dirty and torn commando suit, she was a lovely, sexy woman.

"Nothing," she said.

After determining that we weren't wanted for anything, they were eager to hear our story and prompt to order several constables to the Morrison estate. Once the flurry of activity over the murder report ended, we cooled our heels on the bench again, while the two constables conferred with a third member of their group, a young woman with reddish blonde hair.

Since we were cautioned not to talk to each other, we settled for some encouraging smiles and unobtrusive handholding.

The woman had a delightful Welsh lilt to her voice. Under different circumstances, I could imagine her swapping stories with us and hoisting a few pints at the local pub. Alas, we were far from such a casual scenario now. Even though her eyes hinted at friendliness, there was a firm set to her jaw and wariness in her posture. "Dr. Blair, Dr. Curtis," she said, making eye contact as she addressed us, "I am Sergeant Blodwyn Jones. Constables Renfrew and Gardiner and I will take your official statements now."

We both stood up. "We just did that," PJ said.

Sergeant Jones smiled at her. "That was just preliminary, so if you, Dr. Curtis, will accompany me, please."

PJ turned to me. She hadn't expected us to be separated. Fear shone in her eyes, but only for an instant.

I touched her hand.

"It'll be okay," we said at the same time, then smiled. I watched them walk down a long hallway and disappear into a room at the end. PJ paused long enough to give me a parting glance before she stepped out of sight.

Now that we were apart, I felt a rush of panic. The two constables ushered me into what could best be described as a cell, but was in fact an interrogation room, then excused themselves to join their partner in questioning PJ. I gave them a confident nod, but as soon as they left, I sank onto one of the hard wooden chairs at the table and cradled my head in my hands.

Oh, little one. What had I gotten us into?

How would PJ manage? It was three against one.

I rubbed my tired eyes and looked around the room. The furnishings were sparse; there was a scratched-up table and three other chairs, besides the one I occupied. The linoleum on the floor was cracked and faded. I assumed that PJ had been taken to a similar room, though maybe the Curtis name had merited better accommodations.

An hour passed before a middle-aged, dark-haired officer, wearing a somber gray suit, entered the room.

He pulled back a chair at the opposite end of the table and sat down. "Good morning, Dr. Blair. I'm Detective Chief Inspector Derek Mann." He was soft-spoken and, so far, nonthreatening.

"I guess it is morning," I said, in response to his greeting. The tiny barred window near the ceiling showed it was still dark.

DCI Mann set up a portable tape recorder. "Can I offer you a cup of tea before we get started?"

"Thank you, I'd like that."

He left and returned moments later carrying a battered tray with a cup of tea, a tiny sugar bowl, cream pitcher, and—in the saucer—a slice of lemon.

I gave him a brief smile. "You British and your tea. Do you treat all your criminals so well?"

He smiled back. "You're not accused of anything yet, though breaking and entering is a crime, one that we cannot overlook." He paused and waited for me to add cream to my tea and take a sip.

"I know who you are, Dr. Blair, and I know who Dr. Curtis is. I can't imagine either of you doing what you did with malicious intent."

"Is Dr. Curtis okay?"

"She is very well. In fact, she demanded a doughnut with her tea."

I laughed. That was my PJ. "And no doubt you obliged?"

"I'm afraid the best we could offer her at this early hour were some stale ginger biscuits. She'll be finished with her statement soon. Right now, I'd like to hear what you have to say."

He instructed me to relate the evening's activities in my own words, including the events leading up to them. My statement would be recorded for posterity on tape.

I did as he asked, trying to provide every detail, including the letter Morrison had written to Frederick, the age-enhanced pictures, and our early suspicions of the fake Morrison's identity.

"You realize," he said afterwards, "that in playing detectives you both committed a crime?"

"Yes, I do. But, it was all my idea. PJ—Dr. Curtis—had nothing to do with it, except that she was concerned for my welfare and didn't want me going out alone."

His brow furrowed. "This isn't one of your archaeological mysteries. She would have been better served if she had restrained you altogether."

"She tried, but I was being stubborn."

His lips twitched, revealing a hint of amusement. "Your stories ring true. They're similar, but obviously not rehearsed. So, I'm letting you both go. The fact is that your crime uncovered a greater one." DCI Mann stood and escorted me to the outer office. "Our people are investigating that as we speak."

He walked me back to the long bench where I could wait for PJ. I felt the need to explain our actions a bit further before he left.

"You know, Inspector, this all started as an archaeological investigation. We came to Wales looking for a lost Celtic warrior."

"A Celt, eh?" He rubbed some stubble on the tip of his chin. "It appears that you got more than you bargained for, Dr. Blair."

Sergeant Jones came out of the room at the end of the hall, grinning. When she noticed her boss with me, the grin vanished.

"All finished, Jones?" he asked as she drew closer.

"They'll be ready in a tick, sir."

"Fine." He exchanged information with her in quiet undertones and then turned to me. "I'll leave you in Sergeant Jones's capable hands and go see what's keeping the rest of them."

"Thank you, sir, for going easy on us." I shook his hand.

He wandered back down the hallway, and I waited to see if Sergeant Jones had any questions for me.

"Your friend won't be much longer," she said, joining me on the bench.

"That's good to hear."

She laughed. "We'd have been finished a lot sooner, but she wittered on so."

"I beg your pardon. 'Wittered on?'"

"Sorry. It means chatted a bit too much about things."

"When she gets nervous, she tends to do that."

"I thought so. In our experience, when a person talks too much about anything, they either have something to hide, or they're just really nervous."

"And with PJ you thought—"

"That she was probably nervous. I don't believe the inside of a police station is familiar territory for either of you."

"You've got that right. We've had enough excitement this past night to last us a long, long time."

Her expression softened, and she lowered her voice. "I can see that you care for each other quite a bit."

My breath caught. "And?"

"I thought it was sweet the way you both tried to take the blame for your unlawful entry last night. You told the inspector it was your idea, and Dr. Curtis assured us it was hers. You're protective of each other, and you care about each other."

"Yes, we're friends as well as colleagues."

The door at the end of the hallway opened, and Inspector Mann led the group toward us. PJ's smile widened when she spotted me.

"Are you okay?" she asked when the group reached me.

"Yes, I'm just fine."

"I trust that you'll check with us," DCI Mann said, "if you're going to leave the area."

"You can count on it," I assured him.

"And please, in future, leave the detective work to those of us trained in such matters."

"I don't need lightning to strike me twice," PJ said. "Oh, and thanks for the ginger cookies. They were delicious."

* * *

When we returned to the inn, PJ handled the sad task of informing her father that John and Jenny Morrison had been murdered. I left her talking on the cell phone, consoling her father, and went down to the kitchen to wangle a tray of cold meats, cheese, bread, and fruit to bring up to our room.

"You look like you've been through the wars." The speaker was a buxom woman who was up to her elbows in flour.

"Mavis," she said, flourishing a rolling pin like a weapon, "give the lady what she wants and give her some of that bread pudding with rum sauce. Heat it, mind you, so they can have it warm."

"Yes, Cook, right away."

Mavis appeared timid and terrified of Cook, as she called her. It must have been the rolling pin that was so menacing. She looked motherly, otherwise, though a bit overbearing.

"Thank you," I said. "You're very kind."

"Kind nothing. I don't know where you've been or what you've been up to, but you look like you're in need of some comfort food and rest."

"You're right. Food and bed is all I can think about right now."

Cook turned again to Mavis, who was setting up a tray of food. "Get a move on, girl. Can't keep the lady standing here all day."

Mavis scurried over with the loaded tray. "Can I help you with this, ma'am? Carry it upstairs for you?"

"No, thank you, Mavis. I can manage."

The tough part would be staying awake long enough to eat.

* * *

PJ and I sat by the fire and nibbled our food in silence. She was subdued from her phone call, and I was too tired to keep a conversation going. We perked up a bit when we tried Cook's bread pudding and rum sauce. It tasted as delicious as it smelled, but we were too tired to do more than sample it.

We were still in our commando clothes. Neither one of us had the energy to change and get cleaned up. The whole eventful day and evening required discussion, but it would have to come later.

PJ stood and stretched. "I know I should eat. We both should, but I'm too tired and too dirty."

I put my glass of water down. "Me, too. It's hard to decide which to do first. Eat, sleep, or wash? We're in need of all three."

She knelt behind me and slipped the soiled shirt away from my shoulders. I felt her fingers working the stiffness from my knotted tendons.

"Bless you. That feels wonderful."

"You don't seem to be any hungrier than I am right now," she murmured against the back of my neck.

I twisted around, smiling. "Maybe later."

"I think we both could use a long soak in that huge tub." She gave me one of her lopsided grins and caressed my cheek. "How about it? Want to scrub my back?"

"I can't think of anything I'd rather do." I captured her hand and kissed her palm.

Her eyes moistened. "I want you to know how much I appreciated having you with me today."

"There's no need to say anything."

"I would never have been able to go through all that alone."

"Anything for you, baby. I love you."

She kissed me, and I replied in kind.

The kiss was a tender expression of love and commitment. There was nothing lusty or tongue tangling this time, just two souls re-affirming their closeness, forever and always.

"I love you, too," she whispered, her voice husky. "So much it frightens me sometimes."

She padded to the bathroom and filled the old tub with fragrant raspberry bubbles. I took Pup outside for a quick visit to the shrubbery and settled him in front of the fire with the tasty soup bone that Arwel had brought for him earlier.

PJ and I stripped off our grubby clothing, piled it in a corner of the bathroom, and placed thick terrycloth towels beside the tub. I helped her step up and into the steaming water. I arranged myself at her back, with my legs stretched out on either side of her hips.

"Ah, my own personal cushion." With a contented sigh, she leaned against my chest.

Languidly, we soaped and rinsed each other until the water grew cool and our bodies demanded sleep. Then, exhausted, we rubbed each other dry, dropped our towels on the floor, and tumbled into bed.

I kissed PJ's forehead, eyelids, and nose while she giggled and responded with sleepy endearments.

"Snuggle up now," I said after our motions grew sluggish. "We've had a hell of a day, and we need sleep. Don't fight it anymore."

PJ rolled toward me, draping her upper body across mine. Stroking her firm, smooth back, I guided her head to my collarbone and sighed, feeling her heart beating in time with my own.

She yawned. "Okay, my love. I surrender."

* * *

A tap on our door woke me up. My watch indicated that we had been asleep for four hours, though it seemed just minutes since we had curled up together. Another, more insistent knock came, and I slid out from under my partner.

PJ moaned and smacked her lips. Her hand brushed my breast. "So good."

I grinned. "Hold that thought, okay? There's someone at the door. Probably Arwel."

She opened her eyes. "Arwel? At the door? Okay, let her in."

I was up and pulling on pants and a sweatshirt. "Not quite that easy, sweetie. We're not exactly dressed for company."

"Jesus, we're naked."

"There you go."

She shot up to a sitting position, giving me a splendid view of her chest. "Wait. What should I do?"

I found her robe and tossed it at her. "Get in the bathroom and run some water. Pretend you've been in there awhile. I'll get the door."

She finger-combed her unruly hair and flashed me a saucy grin. "Very clever. You act like you've done this sort of thing before."

"Not now, PJ."

The knock sounded again, louder this time. "Coming," I called, making shooing motions at my partner.

She entered the bathroom, and I opened the bedroom door.

"Arwel, hi. Sorry to be so long. We had a rest after our long night and were just getting up."

She dipped her head. "Dr. Blair, 'tis I who am sorry to trouble you, but there's a telephone call from the police station. An Inspector Mann, I believe he said. He left this number for you to ring him back." She handed me a piece of paper.

"Oh, yes. We've been expecting that. Thank you, Arwel."

"Certainly."

"Just let me find my shoes."

There were sounds of running water coming from the bathroom now, followed by splashing, and PJ's off-key rendition of… something. I think it might have been an Indigo Girls song, but it was hard to tell.

I rapped on the door and shouted, "I have to take a phone call."

The singing stopped just long enough for PJ to say, "Okay," then started up again. Way more role-playing than we needed, but I appreciated the effort.

I followed Arwel down the narrow wooden stairs to the reception area hallway and dialed the number. "Hello, Inspector," I said when he came on the line. "Sorry to be so long getting back to you."

"That's quite all right. I wanted to let you and your colleague know what we found at the Morrison estate. I know you gave me your mobile phone number, but I don't trust them for relaying sensitive information."

I looked around the deserted hallway. Arwel and her assistants were busy at the reception desk.

"I can talk, Inspector. Were you able to locate those men?"

"No, I'm afraid the grounds were empty when we got there. The bodies, though, were exactly where you said they would be. We've transported them to the Medical Examiner's office for autopsies, and we're in the process of notifying the family members, so someone can make a positive identification."

"Such a terrible thing to have happened. I'm so sorry the perpetrators got away."

"Rest assured that we will track them down and arrest them."

"I'm sure you will, Inspector. Thank you for letting me know. I'll relay this information to Dr. Curtis."

"Oh, and one more thing, Dr. Blair. The estate has been sealed off for crime scene investigation. It's off limits, and that means to you, too."

"Don't worry. We're not about to go back there."

I hung up, and drummed my fingers on the reception desk for a few seconds. If only I could get PJ to stop singing, we could get a few more hours of sleep.

Chapter 11

"They got away?" I stretched back on the bed, laced my fingers behind my head, and stared at the ceiling, processing what Kim had just told me. "Then we messed up by going there."

"Not necessarily. If we hadn't gone there, we wouldn't have found—"

"Yeah, that's another thing. Two people dead." I exhaled and sat up. "Maybe they would still be alive, if we hadn't come to Wales."

Kim sat down beside me. "Hey, where is all this coming from? You were calm and collected when I went to talk on the phone with the inspector, and now you seem to be riding a huge wave of guilt. You have nothing to feel guilty about."

I leaned forward, braced my head in my hands, and my stomach tightened. "That's the trouble. I don't think I was feeling anything before. I think I was numb. It hadn't sunk in, what happened. But now—Jesus, this is such a mess."

Kim put her arm across my back and drew me in. The warmth of her embrace further undermined my emotional resolve, and I embarrassed myself by bursting into tears.

"Honey?" She patted my back.

I snuffled and hiccuped in an attempt to stop the flood. "I'm—I'm sorry."

"Shh. It's okay. This has been building up inside you, and it's time to let it all out." She guided my head to her chest and rocked me gently, offering a tissue when I finally stopped.

I blew my nose, sat up, and managed a weak grin.

"Feel better now?" She smoothed my hair and dabbed my cheeks.

"I do. Thanks. I know things are still a mess, but I feel a bit better."

"Sounds to me like the guilt you were carrying just burst loose. You and I, and your father, too, are victims of circumstance. We have nothing at all to feel guilty about."

I leaned my cheek against Kim's neck and inhaled the familiar, spicy scent of her skin. "I know that something went horribly wrong. It wasn't supposed to turn out this way."

"Yeah, and we can't leave town yet. But we can go home as soon as the police finish with us."

I stood up and took a few steps to the window. "I've been thinking about that. I don't know what would be best right now. Dad thinks there'll be a big funeral back in Gloucestershire when they've finished doing the autopsies. He plans to fly over for it."

Kim joined me beside the window. Sunshine slanted into our room, and a light breeze ruffled the curtains. "Is that wise? I mean, with the threat still hanging over him, over all of us?"

"I don't know. He seems to think it's okay." I searched her eyes for some hint of her true feelings. "What do you want to do?"

She stared past me, down at the garden with its colorful flowers. "I think we need to talk about this, but I'd like to do it outside." She took my hand, curling my fingers in hers. "Want to go for a walk in the garden with Pup and me?"

"You know I'd go to the ends of the Earth with both of you. Just let me fix my face and grab a jacket."

* * *

The air was filled with the scent of tea roses and the drone of honeybees making erratic sorties in search of pollen. Pup walked beside us, his ears twitching and muscles rippling, prepared to pounce on anything out of the ordinary. The biggest threat we encountered was a small gray mouse, scurrying through the rosemary in the herb garden.

"Let's look at this whole situation in a calm, logical fashion," Kim said, as we settled onto a wide stone bench, our hips touching. She held up one finger. "Your father got a letter from his old friend asking for your help." She held up a second finger.

"And," I said, "he alluded to some sort of mystery about a Celtic chieftain. Without saying as much, he led us to believe that the mummified remains in his possession had been stolen."

"Right," she continued without raising any more fingers. "So we came over here, and for a little while I thought there was somebody following us."

"But we couldn't prove that."

"No. It was just a feeling that went away once we visited the Morrison estate."

"Where we met someone posing as John Morrison. What's more, he knew who we were and quite a bit about us, enough to convince us he was genuine."

"True." Kim scratched her head. "He showed us an empty glass coffin and continued the charade about the lost or stolen chieftain."

"Correct."

"Why?"

"That's the sixty-four-thousand-dollar question. And when we called him, there was no answer. We went back to see what was going on and found several strange men—one of them with a very nasty gun—and two dead bodies."

"Indeed. So, what does it all mean?"

We pondered that question.

"What worries me," I said, "is that maybe we somehow caused this to happen."

Kim covered my hand with hers. "How could we have?"

"I mean, what if Morrison really had a valuable dead Celt, and when he contacted us, somebody found out about it? What if they came and tried to steal it from him? Maybe he put up a fight, and they killed him and his wife."

"Where do we fit in?"

I thought some more. "We came along right after the bad guys had killed the Morrisons, but before they could get away with the Celt."

"Interesting theory, but where was the Celt? Once out of that air-sealed case, he would have disintegrated." Kim stood up, still gripping my hand. "Come on, let's walk some more while I digest that possibility."

The breeze stiffened. We were forced to walk with our heads down and our hands thrust into our pockets. Kim remained silent until we returned to the welcoming warmth of our room and hung up our jackets.

"Do you think," she asked, "that we could have forced the issue? That somehow they knew we were coming, so they had to kill the Morrisons when they might just have stolen the remains instead?"

"I hope that isn't the case, but I'm afraid it could be. It makes me sick just thinking about it."

"I think there's more to it than that, but we may never know what happened until the killers are caught."

"If they're caught."

There was a knock on our door, and Pup stood, tail wagging.

"Someone he knows," I said.

It was Arwel, and she had two men with her. Pup's wag turned into a growl.

"Pup, back here, boy." Kim gave him a firm command. "Sit." He obeyed, but he didn't take his eyes off the two men.

"These gentlemen wish to see you," Arwel said. "They've booked a room on this floor. I trust that is all right."

Oh, shit. Our bodyguards. I'd forgotten all about them. "Yes, thank you, Arwel. That will be fine." I smiled at the young men. "Please come in."

Arwel left after announcing that tea would be served in the drawing room in fifteen minutes.

Kim closed the door. "There's not much room, but you're welcome to have a chair here or over at the desk." She came and sat beside me on the bed, all the time keeping a firm grip on Pup's collar. Feeling more than a little paranoid, we assured ourselves that their credentials were in order by reading the letter Dad sent with them and examining their identification.

Both of them were tall, blond-haired, and muscular, suitable for a game of rugby or the rescue of damsels in distress. Since neither event seemed imminent, they sat down, keeping a wary eye on Pup.

"Everything seems to be genuine." I returned their documents with a smile. "I'm PJ, and this is my partner, Kim, but I guess you figured that out." My laugh sounded a bit forced, but they joined in.

"Geoff Hunter," said the blue-eyed guy nearest me.

"And I'm Trevor Poole." The taller and more deeply tanned of the two men near Kim nodded. "Your father told us about the animal," he cast a quick glance at Geoff, "but we weren't expecting such a formidable presence."

I ruffled Pup's fur and he gave my hand a lick. "There's no need to worry, gentlemen. He only bites bad guys. Right, sweetie?"

Pup made a snuffling sound, and the men shared a nervous laugh.

"I have a question," Geoff said. "What if one of us had to make a sudden move to grab you or push you out of the way? How would he react?"

"Allow me to formally introduce you." Just as she had cautioned me the first day I met Pup, Kim instructed the two men to remain motionless. Still holding Pup, she allowed him to sniff them and recognize their scent. It was as if he was checking for evil in the air or on their person. Like he could smell it if it was there. After a few seconds, he sat at Trevor's feet, his tail wagging.

"And I thought airport screeners were bad," Trevor said.

"That was intense," Geoff agreed. "Is he a full-blooded wolf?"

"No, but he has most of their characteristics," Kim said.

Trevor leaned forward and put a tentative hand on Pup's ruff. "Wow! He's really something."

I grinned. "So, you think he'll make a good member of the security team?"

"Let me put it this way," Geoff said. "I'm glad he's on our side."

Everyone relaxed after that, and Pup curled up in his favorite corner by the fireplace.

I leaned closer to Kim, and she put her hand against my lower back. "I guess now would be a good time to fill you both in on the latest happenings around here."

Trevor held up his hand. "Not necessary, Dr. Curtis. Your father briefed us just this morning."

"Yes," Geoff added. "Are the police finished with their questions, or do they want you to return?"

I looked at Kim, but she deferred to me. "We've given them our statements, but they told us not to leave town. I guess they may have more questions for us."

Trevor noticed me eyeing his blazer. He unbuttoned it and spread both sides open. "We're not carrying guns, Dr. Curtis. Your father said you were adamant about that."

"Yes. I'm sorry, but that is a stipulation I insist on."

Kim's arm tightened around my waist.

"What?" I asked, turning to her.

"You never mentioned that little detail."

"Is it a problem?"

She thought for a moment. "I sure hope not. The guy we saw on the stairs had a gun, but other than that… It's your call." She glanced toward Geoff and Trevor. "I assume these gentlemen are prepared to defend us in other ways."

Trevor nodded. "We're both proficient in several forms of martial arts, attaining black belt levels in—"

I held up my hand. "We believe you. We also hope you never need to prove it."

Geoff's expression turned serious. "We just want to assure you that we can protect you, no matter what the situation."

"How are you at shopping?" Kim said, smirking. "PJ probably has more black belts than you do in that activity."

"Oh, aren't you funny." I poked her in the ribs and smiled at Geoff and Trevor. "She's exaggerating."

"Only a little," Kim muttered.

Geoff looked at his watch. "I believe the manager said something about tea?"

We all stood up.

"Are you going with us?" I asked.

Geoff got a nod from Trevor. "Yes. Our orders are to go everywhere you two go, within reason. Do you have any problems with that, Dr. Curtis?"

I shrugged. "I guess not, but there is one thing."

"Yes?"

"I'm PJ, okay?"

"And I'm Kim."

"Whatever you say." Geoff offered me his arm. "Do you take cream and sugar in your tea?"

I laughed and glanced over at Kim.

Her face held a bemused expression. "A person could get used to this."

Just wait, Kimmy, It's going to get old really fast.

* * *

Geoff and Trevor kept as low a profile as possible, considering they were charged with seeing that no harm came to us during the rest of our stay in Wales. They were serious, soft-spoken, and very attentive to our routine. As Dad had promised, they accepted our relationship, giving us as much private time together as they could. Having Pup as a live-in guard meant they didn't need to be in our room at all, just close by.

Arwel and the staff at the inn gave them curious looks at first.

"She thinks she's figured out that we're a couple," Kim told the guys one evening, as we sipped pints of Guinness at the local pub. "When you two came along, she couldn't figure out how you fit in."

We all laughed.

"I just told her that you guys were Dad's business associates and that you had come ahead of him to provide security."

Geoff nodded. "Not far from the truth."

"Right you are," said Trevor, draining his glass.

I smiled. "I find a half-truth is often better than an outright lie."

Kim's eyebrows arched. "And just how often do you indulge in this subterfuge?"

I patted her hand. "Oh, with you never, of course."

"Yeah, right."

I stood up. “Come on, you three. The dartboard is free. Let’s see if Trevor’s luck holds out for a second night.”

“Luck?” Trevor said. “I’ll have you know that it’s pure skill. There’s not a bit of luck involved.”

“Is that so?” I cast a quick glance at my partner. “Would you care to place a little wager—say, guys against the gals—and the losers buy another round?”

Geoff grinned at Trevor and flexed his biceps. “It’s a pity to take her money, but I guess she’s well enough off. She can afford to throw it away.”

Kim sighed. “Now you’ve done it. PJ can’t resist a jibe at her financial status.”

I picked up two darts and handed one to Trevor. “You and I will throw. Highest score starts.”

“Suits me fine.” He took his dart and twirled it in his fingers. “I think I’ll have something especially expensive to drink after we win. How about it, Geoff?”

“Whatever you say, mate. Just remember that her father is paying our salary.”

It was a close game, but Kim landed a shot in the ring around center on her last try to win it for the gals. We told the fellows that we’d wait for another night to collect our drinks.

* * *

Several days passed, and we settled into a working relationship that allowed us to move about, act like tourists, and retain some of our freedom. Geoff and Trevor accompanied us to town, the police station, on walks with Pup, and to the National Library of Wales where we met with several research librarians.

When Kim and I traveled together, sometimes one of them would protect both of us, and the other would take some time off. Their most serious vices seemed to be reading the Sporting News, playing darts at the pub, and watching the cricket matches on the television or listening to them on the radio.

By the end of the week, though, Kim and I grew weary of the extra attention. I felt hemmed in, and Kim had not been feeling well, so that might have added to her crankiness. At first she suffered from just a sore throat and headache, but then she developed a cough. I dosed her with medicine we had brought with us, but the cough persisted. It was keeping both of us awake at night.

I made her spend a day in bed while I nursed her with Cook's special herbal soup.

"You know, you're a lousy patient," I told her, spooning up some broth and attempting to force it into her mouth. "Come on, love. Please try to get this down."

Kim made a face and stuck out her tongue.

"Oh, that's mature." I put down the spoon and pushed the tray to the side of our bed.

"Sorry. It hurts to swallow." Her voice was raspy. I tested her forehead with the back of my hand.

"I know, and I'm sorry, too." I patted her cheek. "Just rest, don't talk anymore." I searched through our first aid kit for more potent medicine. "Damn it. Nothing's working. You were awake half of last night with that cough."

I gave her a few sips of water and fluffed her pillow. "I'll be right back. I'm going to ask Arwel to direct me to the local drugstore." I kissed her feverish brow and headed down to the lobby.

* * *

"You can't go out without an escort," Kim said, when I returned with the directions. "Remember the rules?"

"Shh, no talking. Save your throat."

"The hell with my throat. This is your safety we're talking about."

I grabbed my wallet and buttoned a heavy wool shirt over my T-shirt as I spoke. "Arwel said the drugstore—I mean chemist—is just down two streets, left at the church, through an alley, and next to the greengrocer's. I ought to be able to find that, once I figure out what a greengrocer is. We can buy cough syrup with codeine here without a prescription."

"PJ, stop."

"I'll be back before you have time to miss me."

"Please call Geoff or Trevor."

"It's just a quick trip to town. I don't want to bother them. They shadow us every day as it is. The poor things must be worn out from all this babysitting. Nothing's happened, and it's been a week since Dad's e-mail."

"Maybe nothing has happened because we've taken precautions."

I sighed. "I could have been there and back by now. Don't worry so much."

"Then take Pup with you," she rasped.

"Pup is with Trevor. They went on a long walk in the meadow behind the inn. You just lie back and close your eyes. You need stronger stuff to help you sleep, which will help me sleep. You see how it helps both of us?"

"But—"

"Love you." I blew her a kiss and slipped out the door. "I'll be back soon."

* * *

The air was cool and damp, a stark contrast to our warm, cozy room. Lights from the village gave a faint glow to the surroundings. It looked like a Thomas Kinkade painting, with the fog meandering its way up from the river and making everything look fuzzy. I turned up the collar of the wool shirt and picked my way over the uneven stone path that led down a very winding, narrow street toward town.

The chemist's shop wasn't too hard to find. In addition to the cough syrup, the pharmacist suggested a bag or two of lemon and honey drops for Kim's throat. I stopped in the Sweet Shop for them and threw in a couple of Halo bars, just to keep up my strength. Pure milk chocolate and only ninety-five calories. I'd become addicted to them.

The fog crept through the narrow streets as it made its way along the side of our peaceful valley. I mentally reviewed the route I had taken, hoping I could retrace it to the inn without losing sight of landmarks. Why was it that everything always looked different on the way back? It didn't help that so many of the quaint row houses resembled each other.

A few villagers passed me, walking briskly through the mist, no doubt headed for home and hearth. I thought of Kim waiting for me in our comfortable room and smiled. Seven months now, and my heart still somersaulted when I looked at her. How did I get so lucky? Kim was the best thing that ever happened to me. I only hoped I deserved her.

The streets were almost deserted now. A few cars crawled along, adjusting to the fog. I nodded to a couple of young men on bicycles and stopped to let them turn the corner in front of me. They crossed the street and glided down a hill where they paused to consult a map.

I heard a vehicle slowing down behind me, so I waited at the curb, expecting it to turn the corner, too. A car door opened and there was a shuffling sound. Before I could turn around, somebody grabbed my arm, dislodging the bag of cough medicine. Little yellow lozenges scattered in all directions, and the bottle of cough syrup crashed to the pavement.

"Hey!" I cried. "What are you doing?"

"Shut up and get in the car."

I twisted free and caught a glimpse of a man with a ski mask pulled over his face. I started to run in the direction of the bike riders. The car and the man followed me. I looked around, but except for the bicyclists, I saw no one.

"Stop it! Leave me alone!" One of the young men was looking toward me over his shoulder. He shouted something to his companion, and they turned their bikes around. The man who was chasing me grabbed my shoulders and hauled me toward the car.

"Damn it! No!"

His gloved hand clamped over my mouth.

"In the car," he repeated, breathing hard.

I fought to catch my own breath and used my elbows and feet to poke and kick him, trying everything I could remember from the self-defense classes I had taken as a student in Boston.

The bicyclists were pedaling uphill toward us. One of them called out a question that I couldn't quite hear.

"Mind your own business!" my assailant shouted in their direction. "She's run away from her husband, and we're taking her home!"

The car's front door opened. "Shit, what's taking you so long?"

"She's a— Ow! A goddamned hellcat. Give me a hand."

As I grappled with the first assailant, the driver joined us. I felt a stabbing pain in my hip, and a cloth covered my nose and mouth, forcing me to inhale a strong chemical. I kept biting and struggling, but my vision blurred, and everything started moving in slow motion.

One of them pinned my hands behind my back, and I couldn't feel my legs touching the ground. The bicyclists wouldn't reach me in time.

Kim was going to kill me.

My head made contact with something hard in the backseat, and everything went dark.

Chapter 12

The fever held me tightly in its grip. My head throbbed, my eyes burned, and my throat felt like it had been scraped with a rusty razor. I lay on my side, then on my back, but no matter which way I turned, I couldn't get comfortable. Hell, I didn't need this now.

It didn't help that I was worried about PJ. I told myself that I was worrying over nothing. The threat was real, though, and we had been warned. Now I was imagining the worst.

PJ had made light of it, saying there were always threats of one kind or another. Even though her dad was an ethical businessman, he made enemies. It was the nature of success.

A spasm of coughing left me exhausted and breathless. I closed my eyes and slept fitfully for what I thought was a few minutes, but when I awoke and looked at my watch, it was eleven o'clock. I'd been asleep for three hours.

"PJ?"

Hearing no response, I called out, "Did you get the medicine?"

There was only silence.

"Are you in the bathroom?"

Pup came whining to my bedside. I remembered PJ telling me that Trevor had taken him for a walk. Either she or he must have returned him to the room while I slept.

"What's the matter, boy?" I put out my hand, and he nudged it with his head. "Do you need to go out again? Where's PJ?"

My voice was raspy, and every word hurt my throat. Damn. Why did I have to come down with the flu, now of all times?

I raised my head with effort and glanced at our travel alarm. It agreed with my watch. Shit! PJ should have been back ages ago.

Her shoulder bag was on the chair. She was probably chatting with Arwel, giving me some peace and quiet.

I lay back down. After a moment or two with the soft pillow cradling my aching head, a frightening thought crept into my mind.

She hadn't taken her bag, just grabbed her wallet. Oh, my God!

Pup made a beeline for the door. He scratched at the panel, turned toward me, and whined again.

Forgetting that I was weakened by the fever, I got up too fast. The room started spinning. I groped for the edge of the bed and sat down, waiting until I regained my equilibrium.

I called Geoff and Trevor's room. A sleepy voice answered the phone.

"Sorry if I woke you, Geoff. What time did PJ return from the drugstore? And where is she now?"

The silence on the other end of the telephone chilled my insides. Despite the fever, I shivered.

"Geoff, are you there? I want to know what time PJ got back. I need to know where she is."

Geoff was still a little slow on the uptake. "Yes, Dr. Blair, I'm here. You said that Dr. Curtis went to the chemist?"

"You mean you didn't know?"

"No. She didn't ask either of us to accompany her."

"Oh, my God, Geoff, she's been gone over three hours." I looked around. "I know something's wrong. Pup senses it, too. He's very unsettled."

I heard Geoff say something to Trevor before getting back to me. "We'll go and look for her."

I hung up the telephone with a muttered, "Thank you."

Twelve precious minutes elapsed before Geoff knocked on the door, opened it, and stuck his head in. His face was drawn. "We've checked the inn and the courtyard. She's not here."

"Damn it, Geoff, where could she be?" I was still sitting on the edge of the bed, sweating and shaking from fever and fear. My head continued to throb, and I desperately wanted to lie down and sleep. "Damn her anyway, I told her to have one of you go with her."

Geoff entered the room and closed the door behind him. "Look, there's probably nothing to worry about. We'll find that she went for a walk or something."

My fingers curled into fists. "I'm going to kill her with my bare hands."

"Yeah, after I do. Trevor's out looking for her, tracing her steps into the village." He started to pace the small area in front of the door, raking thick fingers through his hair. "Maybe someone saw her, though it's a real pea souper out there. There won't be many people on the street, and it's late. The chemist is always on call for emergencies, though I doubt he gets many around here, not like in the bigger towns. Still, we'll wake him if necessary."

"She took this threat too lightly."

"Exactly when did she leave?"

"I've been pretty muzzy since this bug hit, but I think it was a little before seven o'clock."

"Bloody hell! Why didn't she come for one of us? That's the reason we're here—to look out for you two. If you don't cooperate with us, we can't do our job."

"Don't tell me. You know PJ. She has a mind of her own." I wiped a hand across my sweaty forehead, stood, and staggered toward the chair.

"Go back to bed," he said, turning me around and urging me back toward the big, old-fashioned bed with its heavy head- and footboards.

I shook my head and winced at the resulting dizziness. "I have to get dressed."

"Not yet, you don't. We don't know for sure that Dr. Curtis is in trouble. Even if she is, you're not going to be able to help her if you're sick with pneumonia."

I groaned. He was right. There was little I could do. I'd try to look on the bright side. She'd show up any minute and wonder what all the fuss was about.

Geoff pushed me gently onto the overstuffed mattress and covered me with the fluffy quilt. I was in no shape to argue. I sank into the bed's soft comfort, telling myself the fever was making me overly anxious.

Fifteen minutes dragged into thirty and then a whole hour. Geoff sat, staring into space. I wondered if he worried that the night had swallowed up his partner, too.

Finally, I could stand it no longer. I sat up and flung the quilt to one side. "Where the hell is Trevor?"

"I don't know, but—"

His cell phone rang.

I fell silent while he answered it. "Yeah. Oh, bugger! What? Where? You're where?"

I was on my feet, my fever forgotten. "Please tell me what the hell is going on."

"I'll be right there." He hung up the phone. "Trevor's at the police station. I'm going there now."

"Not until you tell me what's happened. Where is she? Is she okay?"

His hesitation terrified me. "Now, Geoff. I want to know *now*."

"It appears she was abducted."

"Oh, shit!" A terrible, gnawing emptiness gripped my belly. "I knew it. I just knew something was wrong."

"You should have called us earlier."

"I was asleep, damn it!"

He lifted his hand, palm toward me. "Sorry. I'm just—" He stopped and started again, his voice more controlled. "Look, there were witnesses, a couple of bicyclists. Maybe we'll find out exactly what happened and get a description. All we know so far is that she was on her way back from the chemist when she was pulled into a car." He tried without success to push me back into bed. "You stay put. I have to join Trevor at the police station and see what else we can find out."

"I'm coming with you," I said, and promptly broke into a fit of coughing.

"You stay here, damn it. If PJ had followed instructions, we wouldn't be in this mess."

"I can't just do nothing."

"You can ring Frederick Curtis. Tell him what we know so far. Tell him that Trevor or I will contact him as soon as we have some more information."

"Take Pup with you. He'll know her scent. Maybe there's still a trail."

Geoff grabbed Pup's leash, and I had my cell phone out before the door closed behind them.

Frederick was still at his office. "Jesus!" he said, his voice bellowing through the earpiece. "That daughter of mine will be the death of me yet. What else do we know?"

"Not much, I'm afraid. Geoff and Trevor are at the police station now. There were witnesses, so we should be able to get a description of the abductors. It was dark, though, and very foggy."

"Kim." Frederick's tone was commanding. "Priscilla e-mailed me that you haven't been well. I want you to stay put. You aren't going to be any help to her if you have to be hospitalized."

"But I—"

"But nothing. I've been monitoring the weather over there, and it's as cold as Boston in late September. Not at all what you're used to."

Despite our predicament, I was forced to smile. We had all changed so much in the past seven months; Frederick Curtis was no exception. "You stay there," he said. "You hear me? I'll be there as soon as I can."

"I'd appreciate that," I said, rubbing my eyes, which had filled with tears.

"I know you're worried about her and want to get out and look for her yourself, but it's important that you stay put to answer any calls. It's possible the kidnappers could call the inn with ransom instructions."

I thought it highly unlikely, but I supposed it was a possibility. "Yes, sir."

"Don't you 'sir' me. We're family. I have to hang up now and get things in motion from this end. And, Kim…"

"Yes."

"Don't worry. Allow Geoff and Trevor free rein. They're good men. We'll get her back."

With that, he hung up, and I was left alone with my own frightening thoughts.

I crawled back into bed and pulled the covers up around my neck. They provided little comfort. I felt so useless, but I guessed it was for the best. I'd be more hindrance than help, out there. I pulled PJ's pillow close and fell into a fitful sleep.

I dreamed I was back in the Superstitions and saw Marna rise from the rubble of the earthquake-triggered landslide. She wore a flowing white robe and carried an ornate dagger at her waist.

As she glided toward me, I extended my hand. She took it and began to chant. I couldn't understand the words, but they were comforting. I thought it might be a prayer of some kind, one that caused me to slip into another dimension. Her long dark hair spilled around her face, leaving it in shadow, keeping me from looking into her eyes, which I longed to do.

Then she was gone, and I was back in my bed, awake. My fever had broken, and though I was still terribly weak, I felt better. When Arwel checked on me, I asked her to bring me a bowl of hot soup and some thick slices of wheat bread to go with it. If I was to help find PJ, I had to regain my strength… and soon.

Chapter 13

I was aware of pain, overwhelming pain, and though it was a total body experience, it was most intense in my throbbing head and aching right side. My ribs felt like I'd been kicked by a mule. Make that several mules. My cheek rested against a padded seat. Through it, I detected the rhythmic thrumming of a car engine, punctuated with bumps and sudden, shifting turns. The vehicle was moving fast, with no regard for my comfort.

Some kind of rough material covered my eyes, making my face itch. My hands were bound behind my back with something tough and smooth—maybe plastic or nylon straps. It felt like the same stuff bound my feet. I was trussed up like a hog for the market. *Oh, Kimmy. I really screwed up this time.*

There had to be a way out of this predicament. With effort, I ignored the discomfort and temporary blindness and tried to focus my remaining senses. A faint odor of stale cigarettes and fried food lingered in the fibers of the fabric-covered seat where I lay.

I could hear tires swishing on pavement, light rain on the back window and roof, the hypnotic hissing of windshield wipers, and the tense voices of my captors, as we drove through the darkness.

Darkness? Was it still night outside, or did it just seem dark because of my blindfold? How long had I been unconscious? Such a stupid thing—going out without the guys or Pup. What must Kim be thinking? I knew she'd be mad, and I didn't blame her. I was just so incredibly sorry for the grief this must be causing her and Dad.

Hot tears leaked from under my blindfold. The itching turned to burning. I moved my head and inhaled a strong chemical. That must have been what they put over my face—chloroform, or some modern-day equivalent. We made a quick turn, and my stomach roiled, bringing a wave of nausea so great that I gulped repeatedly, trying to keep my last meal down. I don't remember moaning, but the front-seat occupants reacted as if I had.

“You got a complaint back there, Blondie?” His voice sounded surly, with a hint of wicked amusement.

“Stop the car. I feel like I’m going to throw up.”

“Oh, shit.” The other man’s voice was thick and muffled, as if he had a cold. “We can’t stop now.”

There was a cranking noise and some cool air rushed over me.

“Breathe that in and shut up,” the first guy said.

In the midst of my discomfort, my brain registered some interesting information. They were American.

Another wave of nausea hit, and I started retching.

“Damn it, she’s going to puke up the car!” The thick voice was alarmed.

“So what? We’ll ditch it anyway.”

“What if she chokes? She could die before we get to the cottage. The boss’ll have our heads.”

With a screeching of brakes, the car slid to one side of the road, and it sounded like both front doors flew open. I felt a cold chill on my skin and heard the wind rustling in the trees above us. Woods? A forest? I didn’t hear any rain now, but the air was heavy with moisture.

I was hoisted out and shoved to the ground, landing on my injured side. Wet grass and pungent earth smacked my face, and the dampness seeped into my shirtsleeve and pant leg.

“Here.” One of the guys crouched behind me and tugged at my wrists.

My arms sprang apart, and a tingling sensation raced to my fingertips. There was no time for gratitude. Bracing myself on elbows and knees, I waited for the inevitable: my body’s surrender of lunch, breakfast, and what seemed like all ten toenails.

I actually felt better afterwards, and pressed my forehead against the wet ground, reinforcing my tenuous bond to Mother Earth and all her living creatures. The thudding of helicopter blades sounded overhead. Was someone searching for me? No, it was too soon to expect help.

The kinder guy pushed a cloth into my hand.

“Thanks,” I mumbled, wiping my mouth and chin.

His arms wrapped around my waist. “All right. Up you go.”

As I tried to balance on my hobbled feet, I recognized that another bodily crisis was imminent.

“Please, wait,” I gasped. “I have to go to the bathroom.”

He released me with a grunt of disgust. “Jesus H. Christ. What next?”

I dragged myself a few feet away from him. "Please. I have to pee. Really. I won't take long, I promise."

There was a thrashing in the bushes on the left and heavy footfalls. "What's going on?"

His buddy sighed. "Would you believe she has to take a leak? How do we work that?"

I started to speak, but the mean guy's swearing drowned out my words. "For two cents, I'd wring her skinny neck and leave her here to rot. She's more trouble than she's worth."

"Come on, give her a break."

"You're sticking up for her? She broke your nose back there. You should be pissed."

I heard a bit of jostling. "Just shut up. It was a lucky kick. Besides, it's not broken, just real sore."

I managed a snicker before my bladder protested again. "Hey! If one of you could just untie my legs, I could crawl into the bushes or something, and I'd be finished in no time."

There was a moment of silence.

"All right, bitch. But I've got a needle full of that stuff that put you out before. You do anything funny and I'll use it, you hear me?"

"Loud and clear. I'll behave, but right now, I *have* to go."

I felt a tug at my ankles, and my feet came free. He pressed his hand against my lower back and expelled hot, garlicky breath next to my ear. "Keep the blindfold on or you're dead. Understand?"

"Perfectly." I swallowed bitter-tasting saliva.

"Okay. Take about five steps and turn to your right. There's a tree big enough to give you some privacy. We'll be watching both sides and listening for any funny stuff. If you try anything, you'll wish you hadn't."

I attempted to stand, but the ground wouldn't stay level. My legs felt as though I'd been pedaling one of the mountain stages of the Tour de France. I crawled the rest of the way, using an outstretched hand to locate the tree and maneuver around it.

While relieving my bladder, I listened, trying to locate the two men. I could hear one of them off to my right, but the other was quiet. Too quiet. I pulled up my pants and took an experimental peek from under the blindfold. It was still night. The only real light came from the car's headlights, off to my left. We had stopped in a wooded area. As my eyes adjusted to the low level of light, I saw plenty of shadowy rocks and thick brush to shield my escape, if I chose to try it.

Should I go for it? I wished my legs felt stronger. I wished I knew where "Garlic Breath" was right now. Most of all, I wished Kimmy were here to help me. She'd know what to do.

I took a deep breath. Tugging the blindfold downward so it rested around my neck like a bandana, I stepped off to my right, keeping the tree's trunk between the glow of the car's headlights and myself.

After a few steps, I paused to listen before moving on. Even my heartbeat seemed magnified in the damp night air.

A noise from my left meant that the one guy was moving, too. "Come on, Blondie. Finish it up."

I could sense rocks and tall brush ahead of me, and I took longer strides to reach them. Breathing hard, I slipped into the wet foliage and listened.

A whistle pierced the stillness, making me jump. The guy I had eluded was shouting something to his buddy.

Time to pick a direction and make a run for it. I did a mental flip of a coin, turned left, and slipped between two large rocks, ducking under a low-hanging tree branch.

"Jesus, I hope my luck holds," I muttered under my breath.

The tree branch moved and an arm snaked around my neck, immobilizing me.

"Sorry, your luck's all bad tonight." His arm tightened, cutting off my breathing. "Ain't life a bitch?"

Bright, flashing lights danced in front of my eyes. I felt a needle jab into my hip, and the lights disappeared.

* * *

"Easy does it, I'm just trying to help you." A woman's gentle Welsh lilt floated above me, and a cold cloth pressed against my forehead. Her hand touched my cheek. "Awfully warm," she said. "Are you in a lot of pain, miss?"

I was tied up again, and the blindfold was back in place. My left side was still numb, and my right side still ached. Instead of the backseat of a car, I was lying on some sort of moldy mattress. I hadn't felt this spaced out since I'd had my wisdom teeth pulled.

"Miss? Can you hear me?"

I tried to swallow. My tongue was thick; my saliva tasted like vomit and blood. I licked my dry lips and discovered that they were split and swollen. My cheek was sore and my jaw throbbed. One of those guys must have punched me. I was going to have one hell of a bruise.

A hand shook my shoulder. “Miss?”

“I can hear you,” I croaked. “Can you untie me and tell me where I am?”

The hand rested on my right shoulder, warming it. “Sorry, no. I have to do what they tell me. I’m a captive, just like you.”

I tried to move a bit on the mattress and felt the familiar prickling of pins and needles along my left side as I regained feeling. Good news for once. My feet weren’t tied. When I wiggled my toes, I discovered my shoes were missing.

“Could I maybe sit up? How long have I been here?”

The woman exhaled. I could detect the faint fragrance of lavender.

“Sorry, luv. I really have no idea. A few hours I suppose. I could try to help you move, if you’re certain you aren’t too injured.”

I took a deep breath, testing my body. “Headache and a pain in my ribcage, on the right side. Otherwise, I’m okay. I think.”

“All right, then.”

Her strong arms gripped and twisted my upper body when I slid my legs and feet off the bed. I let out a long moan as my ribs protested the new positioning, and the prickling along my left side seemed to go on forever.

“Thank you,” I said when I could take a breath. A wave of nausea alarmed me.

“What’s wrong? You’ve gone all white.”

“Sorry, but I’m going to be sick again.” I tried taking slow breaths, but the feeling only increased.

There was a hurried shuffling and scraping, and a metal container was thrust into my lap. “There you go. It’ll be all right.”

She held my head and braced my hips as I vomited again. This time there was little left to contribute, but I continued dry heaving for several seconds until my stomach settled. Damn, what was in that stuff they had shot into me? Sweat coated my face and chest. I was hot and cold at the same time.

“I’ve been drugged,” I told the woman.

“Aye, miss. That you have.” I heard her rinse the cold cloth again, and she dabbed at my mouth, avoiding my puffy lip and bruised cheek. “And, by the looks of it, you’ve not taken too kindly to whatever it was.”

She offered me a drink of lukewarm water and held the cup to my lips while I sipped. My stomach felt better now that it was empty, but my brain was another matter. The throbbing continued. Even when I sat back on the mattress, keeping my head level, my internal gyroscope tilted out of control.

"I can't stay here," I told the woman. "I've got to get out of this—this—whatever it is."

"It's a cellar we're in, in some sort of country cottage, I believe. They brought me here in the dark, blindfolded like you. Put me in a room upstairs and told me I was to see to a woman, fix their meals and such, and that I was not to try to escape. They said if I did exactly as they told me, they'd let me go free."

"And you believe them?"

"I have to."

"I see." The poor woman was scared to death. Not that I could blame her. I was pretty terrified myself, but fear didn't have to immobilize us. Maybe we could help each other. "I'm PJ. What's your name?"

"Sarah." She finished wiping my face and neck. "Do you want more water, PJ?"

"Not right now, thanks."

She busied herself making me as comfortable as possible, straightening and smoothing the rough blanket that I was lying on.

I wondered if she was what she seemed, or if she was one of the gang. "What can you tell me about the men who brought us here? I know about two of them. I think they're just thugs. They mentioned a boss. Have you heard about him? Do they have guns or weapons? Have they talked about their plans?"

She inhaled sharply. "So many questions."

"I'm sorry, it's just that they may not leave us alone too much longer."

I heard her move the metal container to one side. "Your wounds need attention, and you should rest."

"I know, I know. But, it's more important that I find out what you know."

"Very well." She cleared her throat and put her arm around my shoulders. "I've seen three men. Two roughnecks to do the dirty work like capturing us and tossing us about, and one a bit more refined—a gentlemanly sort, by his speech."

"Is he American also?"

"He didn't say much, but now that you mention it, I believe he is."

"Okay. Go on. Did they discuss any plans in front of you?"

"I can't—"

There was a sound of a door opening to my left, and Sarah fell silent. She withdrew her comforting arm and stood up.

"She awake, finally?" It was the man with the sore nose.

"Yes," Sarah said, "but she's hurt. And whatever you gave her upset her stomach. She needs medical attention."

"Hey, this isn't a hospital. She's going to have to make the best of it, just like you."

Sarah sat back down beside me and put her hand on my knee. "You're wearing a ski mask. Can't I at least remove her blindfold and bandage her injuries?"

"Yeah, how about it?" I put in my two cents. "Even the Geneva Convention calls for better treatment of prisoners."

"All right, all right. Wait a minute. I'll go see what can be arranged." He turned and left, muttering curses under his breath.

I managed a small grin of triumph, and Sarah gave my knee a reassuring squeeze.

"There's a big bathroom upstairs. You could take a hot bath, or maybe a shower if you can stand. I'll take a look at your ribs and see about something for your headache. You'd need a CT scan to rule out a concussion, but I could do a few checks."

"You sound like a doctor. Have you had medical training?"

"I studied to be a nurse, but my parents divorced and there wasn't any money left for my schooling. That's when I found work as a servant on a rich man's estate. Don't worry, I've got enough first aid skills to make you more comfortable."

"I'm not worried. Just tell me how you became involved with these guys. Why did they kidnap you?"

"Because I was there, handy."

The door opened again, and we both fell silent.

"The blindfold can come off, and I can untie her hands while she's locked in the cellar."

"Good," Sarah said. She removed the cloth covering my eyes.

The light came from a single, bare bulb, but it was bright enough to make me blink and squint until my eyes adjusted. I tried to see everything at once without appearing too inquisitive. The room was small and had several tall, fully-loaded bookshelves, as well as the moldy cot and chair. Sarah was a little taller and thinner than I was, and a little younger, too. Her short blonde hair was just a bit darker than mine.

The guy with the sore nose was very tall, and had a muscular build. A green ski mask covered most of his face, but his eyes looked dark, and his lips were thin. Only the tip of his red, swollen nose was visible.

"I'm sorry about that," I said, pointing to my own nose.

"What?" He waved his hand. "Oh, forget it."

"Do you want Sarah to look at it?"

"No, it's fine. I've got some instructions, so listen up. If you want to stay alive and healthy, you do exactly what I say. When you have to use the john, yell for one of us, and we'll walk you up there. The girl can help you, but you have to be tied up for the trip up and down. Since you tried to escape, you can't be trusted, and we gotta be careful."

"I understand."

"Good," he said.

"Your boss's orders?"

"Yes."

"Can she go upstairs now to the loo?" Sarah seemed bound and determined to treat my wounds. Not that I was complaining. "I'd like to fix her some tea. I can fix all of us some tea. How would that be?"

"Yeah, whatever." The guy helped me stand. I caught a whiff of a woodsy scent on his clothing, pine maybe. He took hold of my shirt collar and elbow and escorted me out of the room.

"Take it easy. I'm not a sack of flour, you know." My legs were still shaky, and I had trouble walking, but I tried to act fearless.

Sarah took my other arm and we climbed fifteen steps to the first floor.

Garlic Breath met us in the hallway. He sported a bright red ski mask and a black T-shirt tucked into tight jeans. When they stood next to each other, he was about three inches taller than "Woodsy." Both of them had thick biceps and well-developed pecs. No wonder I hadn't been able to get away from them back in the village. They were huge.

"What are you staring at, Blondie?" Garlic Breath asked.

I could hear the sneer behind the knitted mask, and his eyes took their own sweet time moving up my body. It took all my concentration to keep from shuddering.

"I'm taking her to the loo," Sarah said in a firm voice.

Garlic Breath stepped into our path, taking up a position on my right side. Sarah gave me a weak smile and went ahead of us down a narrow hallway.

"Eyes straight ahead." He tugged my elbow, so that I stumbled and fell against him. "Oops. Here, let me help you."

"I could manage just fine if you'd keep your filthy paws off of me." I tried to right myself and prevent him from groping me at the same time. He slipped one hand under my wool shirt and squeezed my left breast.

"Hey!" I dipped my shoulders and twisted away from him.

"What's the matter?" Woodsy asked. He'd seen me stumble, but he hadn't noticed his partner's roaming hand.

We all stared at each other for a few seconds. Sarah had reached the door to the bathroom and turned. "Here we go."

"If you'll excuse me, I can take it from here." I walked as quickly as I could to the doorway.

Woodsy caught up to me, but Garlic Breath had the knife. He made a big show of sliding it down my back to my bound hands.

"Hold still. I wouldn't want to cut any of your finer body parts by accident."

"Heaven forbid," I muttered. The plastic tie came away and my wrists were free again. They were scraped and bleeding from the tight restraints.

"Come on, relax." He stroked my jaw. "You're not going anywhere for a while. We got a little business to conduct with your old man, but in the meantime—"

"In the meantime, stay as far away from me as possible."

He patted my shoulder and let his hand trail down the front of my shirt. "Maybe I should help you get cleaned up. I'm not sure we can trust the girl to do a thorough job."

Woodsy stepped between us. "You go ahead, miss. We'll be right out here. The windows are nailed shut, so don't even think about leaving."

I glared at Garlic Breath while rubbing my sore wrists. Then, I nodded in Woodsy's direction. "I'll take your warning under advisement."

Sarah filled the sink with warm water and helped me clean up. She found gauze to wrap my wrists and antibiotic ointment to ward off infection. My T-shirt and pants were soiled with mud. We left them soaking, while Sarah pulled a pair of jeans and a clean shirt from a shelf in the bathroom closet.

"I don't have much," she said. "They gave me some toilet articles, and I found some clothes in my room here. I guess they belong to the owner. They're men's, but they aren't too bad a fit. I'll wash your things as soon as we get you bandaged up."

My eyes filled with tears. "Thank you for your kindness. We'll get through this okay, you'll see. And after we do, I'm going to see to it that you get back into that nursing program."

"Sit right there, PJ. Don't go on so about rewarding me. I intend to get out of here alive, so I'm just doing what I'm supposed to do, nothing more, nothing less."

While I sat still on the toilet, trying not to whimper, Sarah examined my ribs, pronounced them bruised but not broken, and made neat bandages for my wrists. With gentle movements, she pulled the shirt over my head and helped guide my arms through the sleeves. Then, she steadied me while I climbed into the jeans. They were about six inches too long, so she rolled the cuffs for me.

"There you go. Almost good as new." The emphasis was on the almost.

She gave me a quick hug. "Let's get the tea kettle on and fix you a proper meal."

"Okay."

She bent to tidy up our medical station. I took a moment or two to search the room for possible escape aids. It looked like the guys had cleared everything nonessential out of the place. There was a cabinet behind the mirror, and I eased it open. It made a slight squeak of protest, but wasn't loud enough to raise an alarm. Two or three bottles of medicine were stuck in some yellow goo to the bottom shelf. I couldn't tell what had been in them, only that the expiration date had long since passed.

Sarah looked at me. "What—"

I put my fingers to my lips and whispered, "Just checking on a couple of things."

She nodded.

The top shelf held a more current bottle of something called Ambien. I read the label: *Ten milligrams. One tablet by mouth at bedtime, as needed.* The bottle contained warnings about drowsiness and avoiding machinery. Must be a sleeping pill. It was prescribed for Mr. Peter Gibbs of—

The door rattled and I quickly closed the cabinet, but not before memorizing the name of what I hoped was the town of my captivity—Llanrwst.

Chapter 14

It had been two days since PJ's kidnapping, and the police remained in close contact with me. Geoff and Trevor spent a lot of time working with them, in addition to snooping around on their own.

Reporters got wind of the event, but after breaking the initial story, they backed off and cooperated with the police. I suspected Frederick had something to do with that.

Ransom notes surfaced, but so far, all of them had proven to be hoaxes. I felt as though my wheels were spinning in useless effort.

My health improved; the flu bug that weakened me was almost out of my system. My brain was functional and my stamina increased daily. The one person, besides PJ, that I really needed to talk with was her father. I had been waiting all day to hear from him. We hadn't spoken in nearly twenty-four hours, and to tell the truth, I was annoyed that he hadn't kept in more frequent contact. Didn't he understand that just talking to him helped me cope with PJ's disappearance?

Arwel stopped by the room to say that Frederick had left a message telling me there were developments, but ones he didn't feel free to discuss on the phone. I found myself pacing between the desk and the door, much to Pup's annoyance.

What had he meant by "didn't feel free to discuss?" Why hadn't he talked to me directly? Because he knew I would demand to know what had developed? Didn't he realize that we were in this together, that PJ's safety was of paramount importance to both of us?

Obviously, he had his reasons. And since I trusted his motives, I had no choice but to wait to hear from him later.

It just wasn't like him to avoid following through in a timely fashion. That was probably why I felt so uneasy.

When a knock came at the door, it startled me so much my heart was thumping in my ears as I opened it. The two police officers looked smart in their dark knit sweaters and sharply creased slacks. The man was tall. He removed his cap with its black and white checkered band, revealing a head of closely cropped black hair. The young woman was our freckle-faced friend from Aberystwyth, Sergeant Blodwyn Jones.

"Dr. Blair, may we come in?" she asked.

Icy fingers of fear raced through me, settling in my gut. "Yes, of course." I stepped aside.

"This is Constable William Thomas," Blodwyn said. We nodded at each other. Apprehension had formed a giant lump in my throat. I searched Blodwyn's face for some explanation for their visit. She met my gaze and held it. "Detective Chief Inspector Doreen Edwards has been in touch with Mr. Curtis. He asked us to speak to you. He didn't want you to be alone when you got the news."

Oh, Jesus. A wave of nausea washed over me. "What news?"

"I think you had better sit down." The sergeant motioned me to a chair.

I sat, glancing from one to the other, willing my nerves to settle down. This couldn't be good news. They were too formal, too polite, too damned considerate. "Please, get on with it. Tell me what's happened."

The sergeant and the constable exchanged glances before she continued. "We have an unidentified body in the morgue. A woman."

"No! No, please. It's not PJ. There's some kind of mistake."

Sergeant Jones crossed the distance between us and put a hand on my shoulder. "We don't know for sure, but the general description fits your colleague."

"No." The room darkened and began spinning. I bent my head and covered my eyes, trying to combat the dizziness. The sergeant put her arm around me and steadied me until I regained some control.

I wanted to cry. I needed to cry, but I couldn't. Damn Frederick. Why hadn't he told me right away? I had slept in our bed last night thinking that PJ was a captive somewhere, but alive. And now to have found out that she—

"We need you to come with us," Constable Thomas said, in a clipped, business-like manner.

I stared at him, not comprehending.

"To identify the remains."

Drowning in a black pool of confusion and despair, I gathered up my jacket and shoulder bag, only vaguely aware of Sergeant Jones helping me into the police car.

"We have to go to Aberystwyth," she said as she slid into the backseat beside me.

"Aberystwyth?"

"That's where she was found, on South Beach."

"How did she—?"

"Gunshot." The sergeant hesitated a moment before continuing. "She was shot and then dumped in the ocean." Her warm hand rested on my arm. "We have reason to believe she was still alive when she went into the water."

"Stop!" I motioned with my hand, and the car came to an abrupt halt. I stumbled out and vomited into the weeds at the base of an ancient rock fence.

* * *

It was all a mistake. She couldn't be dead.

I thought it when they first told me about the body, and I continued to think it as we walked into a forbidding, gray stone building that reeked of disinfectant.

Not my PJ.

I was shown into the anteroom, and I steeled myself for what I knew I had to do. I wondered if I was capable of viewing her with all the light and vitality gone from her eyes.

She was too young, too loving, too full of life.

My knees started to buckle. Sergeant Jones held on to me, guiding me to a hard metal chair.

It was only then that I became aware of another woman in the room. "What the hell are you doing here?" I asked.

"Frederick Curtis hired me to help with the investigation."

Sergeant Jones shot me a puzzled look. "Dr. Simms is one of the best known forensic anthropologists in your country."

"Oh, I know all about Dr. Simms." My tone was not kind. I couldn't stomach the idea of Terry Simms being around right now, no matter how impressive her credentials. Even after all these years, my feelings toward her were still raw. Why did Frederick think this woman could help with anything? There were plenty of dedicated medical examiners in Wales. And frankly, I'd trust any one of them over her.

PJ's father, though, had no way of knowing that Dr. Terry Simms and I had been lovers for many years, until Terry left with a younger and, in her words, "livelier woman." I did not want to share my grief with her.

"We'll be with you in a minute," Sergeant Jones said, leaving the two of us alone in the charged atmosphere of the bare room.

"So, how have you been?" A faint smile played around Terry's attractive mouth.

"You dare to ask me that now?"

She shrugged. "Sorry, I'm just making conversation."

"Then save it."

"Is that the best you can do, when we haven't seen each other for, what, almost a year? As I recall, you weren't very friendly then, either."

I folded my arms and turned away from her, remembering the night she had showed up unexpectedly at my motor home in Apache Junction, basically announcing my sexual preference to PJ and Sandy. "It's the best you're going to get."

"By the way, is there any truth to the rumor that you've been sharing a mattress with Curtis's daughter? Quite a catch. How'd you manage that?"

I turned around and glared at her. "What I do is none of your business."

"Was she as good as I was?"

I turned away again, livid.

Terry gave a dramatic sigh and began to pace. "But then, you had to *teach* her, didn't you? She was new to the life as well as new to you. Such a drag, having to tell someone where and how to touch you."

I balled my fists and turned on her. "Terry, shut up before I shut you up."

"Struck a nerve, did I?"

"And stop referring to her in the past tense."

She held up her hands in mock surrender. "Sorry. Really, I am. I'll change the subject. Perhaps, when we're done here, I can interest you in some lunch."

"Damn lunch and damn you!" I wanted to slap the smirk off her face. "As far as I'm concerned, the less we see of each other the better."

"Hey! I'm not the enemy here." Terry flopped onto one of the scratched and dented chairs and propped her briefcase against a table leg. "Curtis hired me as part of his team to help find his daughter."

"I'm sure Mr. Curtis is making it worth your while."

"He's paying me well." She leaned back against the chair, arms folded. "For as long as I'm here, I'll do my job to the best of my ability, with or without your help." For a moment, she was serious and almost sounded believable.

"See that you do."

* * *

Sergeant Jones led us into a cold-storage locker room and introduced the assistant medical examiner. His name passed by me in a blur. The body, covered with a white sheet, lay on a bare metal table. The smell of disinfectant overpowered everything else.

This couldn't be real. It was a nightmare. Any moment now, I would wake up. PJ would be with me and everything would be all right.

Terry, thank the gods, had the presence of mind to stand behind me, out of my line of sight. Sergeant Jones stood next to me, her hand on my elbow. "It won't be easy," she said quietly. "Being in the water hasn't helped. I suggest that rather than seeing her face, you look for distinguishing birthmarks or scars. It might be easier."

"Yes, of course, but I'd like to see her face."

"It's not a pretty sight."

"I understand."

"I'm not sure you do."

"Please. I must see her face."

"Very well, you tell me when you're ready." The assistant medical examiner stood beside the table, his hands on the sheet, ready to fold it back for my inspection.

My mouth went dry, and a buzzing sound filled my ears. I felt like an actor, going through the motions, as if on stage in a Shakespearean tragedy. Soon, I would walk off into the wings and the show would be over, and so would this nightmare.

Or was my nightmare just beginning?

I nodded and braced myself for what I was about to see.

The assistant folded the sheet down to her shoulders. Her face was blue, bloated, and damaged beyond recognition. I swayed. The sergeant's grip on my arm tightened, her other arm circled my waist. Bile rose into my throat, cutting off my breath, choking me.

The hair was the right color and length. I shook my head, trying to dispel the vision. "I'm just not sure. She has a tattoo of a shamrock," I whispered to Sergeant Jones, "on her buttock."

"Which side?"

I couldn't answer. My mind had ceased to function.

"Check her bum for a tattoo," the sergeant instructed the assistant.

He covered the face before rolling the body forward, away from him. After a thorough examination, he shook his head. Then, he walked around the table to check the other side. He shook his head again. "No tattoos."

"No tattoos," the sergeant echoed.

All the apprehension I'd been struggling to overcome escaped, exploding outward in a huge sigh of relief.

"You're sure about the tattoo?" the sergeant asked. "She may have told you she had one. Have you actually seen it for yourself?"

I nodded. "Yes, and you wouldn't miss it."

As we were leaving, I turned to look at the sheet-draped young woman on the table. "What happened to her face? It appears to be more than water damage."

"She was caught in the rocks. The incoming and outgoing tides battered her without mercy. Did a lot of damage, it did, to her head and shoulders."

"I'm glad I couldn't identify you as my friend," I said to the dead woman, "but I hope someone who loves you will claim you and lay you to rest in a lovely garden."

"Sometimes no one claims them," Sergeant Jones said. "It's like they're little more than rubbish to be thrown away."

"If that's the case with her, please see she's buried somewhere nice and send the bill to me."

"You mean that?"

"Yes, I do." I laid my hand on the sergeant's forearm. "Will you do that for me?"

"Yes, I will. I thank you on her behalf for your kindness."

"I'm sure Dr. Curtis would want it, too." I took a deep breath. "And now, I must return to Dolgellau."

"I'll have the constable drive you."

"Thank you, Sergeant. You've been very kind."

"I'm relieved that she wasn't your colleague. I hope we find her in good health, and soon."

"Thank you."

I turned my back, and without another word to Terry, hurried the constable along.

PJ was still missing, so I had work to do.

Chapter 15

Kim and I were running along the beach below the cottage in Newport, dodging sea grass and ocean-polished stones. She wore a black, one-piece swimsuit that looked stunning on her. I couldn't wait to get it—and her—wet.

With each stride, we came closer to the incoming tide. The waves surged and foamed, sliding across the damp sand at our feet. As one large wave broke, I nudged Kim toward it. She slipped and recovered, but not before getting her shoes and ankles wet.

"Yeow! That's so cold." She hopped from one foot to the other. A devilish grin creased her face. "Come here, you."

I couldn't escape her firm grasp, and seconds later we both splashed into the water.

"Ahh! It is cold. But it feels great. Doesn't it feel great?"

She lifted one soggy shoe. "The water feels good, but I'm not sure this gritty sand is going to do anything special for these Nikes."

"Then take them off," I said, laughing. "I'll hold you up."

While I held onto her waist, she yanked one off, but another wave caught up to us. Thoroughly soaked now, I gasped and swallowed a mouthful of saltwater.

Kim screamed.

"Hey, it's okay. I'll get you." I reached out my hand, but she fell away with another scream, this one more desperate.

"Kim!" I sat up in total darkness with the thin blanket tangled around my legs. "Kim?" Sweat dampened my neck and chest, plastering the T-shirt to my body.

In a rush, it all came back to me. I was still a captive, and I'd had a nightmare. There was no ocean, no Kim. Just me, alone in this basement room.

I heard the scream again. A woman, in pain.

This time, I wasn't dreaming. Sweet Jesus. Was it Sarah?

I pitched sideways off the cot, stumbled to the door, and pounded against it. “Open up, damn it! What’s happening? Sarah! Are you okay?”

Nobody answered me. My hands stung from beating against the solid wood, but no one came to the door. I pressed my ear to its surface trying to hear something, anything, but I only heard the thumping of my heart.

A scream in the night wasn’t a good sign. But they wouldn’t hurt her, would they? They needed her to take care of me.

I fumbled for the light switch and blinked when the dull light illuminated my cellar room. Shivering with cold and fear, I returned to the cot and pulled on my jeans. With the blanket pulled up around my shoulders, I waited, but all was quiet. There were no more screams, no heavy footsteps, and no voices. Only silence.

* * *

I heard a rustling noise in one corner and opened my eyes. I hadn’t intended to fall asleep, but somewhere between the screams and the rustling, I must have dozed off. There was daylight in the room now in addition to the overhead light, which I had left on. How could I have gone back to sleep when Sarah might be hurt?

The rustle came again. Out of the corner of my eye, I saw a small brown mouse venture out of the shadows, scamper toward my dinner tray, and sniff at the remains of last night’s meal.

I watched in fascination as he sat up on his haunches and surveyed his surroundings. We looked right at each other, or so I thought.

“Sorry, fella. There’s just a crust or two of bread and maybe a crumb of cheese.”

He dipped his furry muzzle into what was left of my cheese sandwich and came up rubbing his whiskers.

“Good, huh?” I whispered. “I’ll try to get you more for breakfast.”

He snatched up the bread, raced into the shadows, and vanished as quickly as he had arrived. I smiled. I wasn’t alone in this prison. I had a roommate. Then, I shuddered. Wait a minute. What was I thinking? It was a mouse, second cousin to a rat, like those ugly things that were in the shed where Kim and I hid at the Morrison estate. But this was different. He was cute and hungry and a survivor. I could learn a lot from the little guy.

The door rattled and my guards entered. "What's going on?" I asked. "Why didn't you come when I called you earlier? Where's Sarah? Is she okay?"

"Shut up. You ask too many questions." Garlic Breath's dark eyes glared at me from the ski mask.

"What have you done to her?"

Woodsy gathered my shoes and wool shirt. "Come with us. The boss wants to see you."

"Wait. Wait a minute." This was something new, a change from the routine. Fear made a tight fist in my stomach. Don't panic. Think tough.

"Don't I get to use the bathroom or eat breakfast first?"

"Shit!" Garlic Breath gripped my shoulder in his meaty paw and gave my whole body a shake. "Always a pain in the ass, aren't you? You can use the john, but the only way you'll get breakfast is to fix it yourself."

His nicer companion handed me the shirt and shoes, then glanced at his partner. "Hey, maybe she could fix us all something to eat."

"Sure." I smiled at him, as I slipped into the shirt and pulled on the shoes. "I'd be—"

"I said shut up, damn it." Garlic Breath's thick fingers clamped around my cheeks and jaw, daring me to speak further. "The boss is waiting. We'll figure the other stuff out later."

He pulled me upright and yanked my hands behind my back. The straps dug into my wrists, irritating the old wounds.

"Is this really necessary? You two are twice my size." I tried a glare of my own, but it was lost on them. They were too intent on getting me upstairs to meet their boss.

"Sorry, miss. It's the boss's orders," Woodsy mumbled by way of apology.

We shuffled along in single file with me between them. "And we certainly wouldn't want to disobey the boss, would we?"

Garlic Breath turned around so suddenly that I slammed into him and bounced a few steps backwards. Talk about a brick wall.

He grabbed a fistful of my shirt and twisted it at the neck, forcing my head upward. His breath fouled the air between us. "You shut your yap, bitch. Not another sound."

Sensing that he was at the end of his minimal allotment of patience, I decided to keep my pithy retorts to myself and climbed the steps in silence. Pastel-striped wallpaper lined the sides of a narrow hallway in what I thought might be an effort to make the windowless passage lighter and brighter. It failed on both counts.

I was hustled into what was probably the dining room. A large wooden table commanded most of the space in the center, and four sturdy chairs with woven seats surrounded it. There were a couple of brown-toned pastoral prints hanging from the walls, and some thick, dust-covered drapes hung at the window, blocking out most of the daylight. Compared to my basement prison cell, the upstairs felt dry and warm. Though a large ceramic lamp was lit, the ambience was not at all friendly.

We entered in silence. Playing the part of a defiant captive, I held my head high and kept my posture erect. Both guards had prodded and poked me along our journey upstairs, and I bristled at the unsolicited contact.

Woodsy's touch was innocent enough. He seemed intent on keeping me from falling and out of reach of Garlic Breath's roaming hands. Resentment built inside me with each little pinch or squeeze from that oversized animal. The creep drew a chair away from the table, turned it sideways, and, using a combination shove and grope, forced me to sit. My butt slammed against the hard seat, and my bound wrists scraped along the wide slats of the chair's back.

I gasped in pain.

When he patted my cheek, I tried to bite one of his fingers. He snatched his hand away before I could connect, so I settled for a murderous glare.

He winked at me behind his mask.

A tall, well-built man entered the room. He wore a black ski mask and a tailored black suit. Armani? No, that new French designer, Rene Delacorte. This thug had good taste in clothing, not that it helped me any.

Designer Suit dismissed his men. He made a show of closing the door and leaning back against it, arms folded. I could see the shine of matching gold pinkie rings on his well-manicured fingers.

We stared at each other for several seconds.

I swallowed.

The room grew warmer. A trickle of sweat formed at my neck and slid down between my breasts. I could feel my underarms dampen. Geez, I needed a shower. My body odor alone could probably knock him out.

That thought brought a tiny grin, which I suppressed.

The more we stared at each other, the more familiar he seemed, but I couldn't quite place him. Had we met before? I didn't think it was prudent to ask that question.

I wondered if he carried a gun, or if he had ever used one. Visions of a Mafia enforcer drifted into my mind, but I squelched the thought. Surely, that couldn't happen here in Wales, this peaceful, idyllic place. Besides, I didn't know any Mafia enforcers. At least, I didn't think I did.

We continued our visual standoff. What was with the silent treatment? Was he trying to scare me? If so, it was working.

He unclasped his arms and walked to the edge of the table, stopping just a few feet from where I sat. I kept my eyes focused on his, summoning the courage to endure whatever would happen next.

"Priscilla—"

"That's Dr. Curtis to you."

Sometimes the best defense is a strong, in-your-face offense. Sometimes.

His head bobbed, conceding a point to me in this freaky tennis match of wills. "Very well, Dr. Curtis. I'm afraid you have not been our most cooperative guest."

"Guest?"

"Yes. My associates inform me that you complain about your accommodations."

"It's a cold, filthy cellar, with a lumpy cot and a blanket so thin—"

"You demand special privileges."

I gritted my teeth, seething. "Christ! I wanted to take a shower, wash my hair, and brush my teeth. That's only basic—"

"And you speak most discourteously to them."

"What? I can't believe this! Listen, they deserved whatever I said to them!"

I leaned forward in my seat, mustering all the bravado I possessed. "Let me tell you, Mr. whoever-the-hell-you-are, I am not a guest here. I'm a prisoner. I was abducted—painfully I might add—and brought to this shithole without makeup, a change of clothing or even a toothbrush. If it hadn't been for Sarah, I'd have perished from neglect. Where is Sarah, by the way?"

"Her whereabouts shouldn't concern you."

The way he said it made a chill skip along my spine.

"I see." It took all my strength to return his volley.

"And here's another thing. I'm only fed whenever the mood strikes one of you. Then, when you add being mauled by a lecherous—"

"That will do, Ms. Curtis." Heaving a weary sigh, he pulled out a chair and sat so close to me that our knees touched, making my stomach tighten.

"That's *Doctor* Curtis to—"

"I need to tell you something right now," he said, ignoring me. "It's for your own good."

He stretched out a hand and tucked a loose strand of my hair behind my ear. I kept my eyes focused on his eye slits.

"I'm listening."

"You will not make demands, nor will you hinder the progress of our plans. If one of my associates happens to think impure thoughts about you, the other will keep him in line. You will not be harmed as long as you obey us. Do you understand? We hold all the cards."

"Is that so?" I said in a low, even voice. I tried to make it a growl. Kim would have growled.

His hand dropped. I heard a metallic click, and a switchblade flashed before my eyes.

I flinched. *Jesus. Take it easy.*

The blade glistened when he waved it in front of my face. I swallowed again and watched as he slid it along the front of my wool shirt, slicing neatly through the stitching of three buttons, and moving it upward along my chest.

I sat paralyzed as the blade pierced my T-shirt near the collar, making a V-neck in one quick upward thrust. The blade tip paused in the hollow of my throat. It was so close to the surface of my skin that I dared not even swallow.

"You will make no further trouble. Is that clear, Ms. Curtis?" His voice had deepened.

When I hesitated, the blade bit into my flesh. I felt a stinging pain, and a trickle of blood seeped along the top of my T-shirt.

"I can't hear you."

"It's clear," I managed to whisper.

"That's much better."

Game, set, and match to Designer Suit.

He pulled the knife upward, wiping the blade on my cheek. I sank back in my seat, finally understanding the game. It was all about power. He had it. At the moment, I didn't.

"Now that I have your attention, here is what I need to discuss with you. We haven't had much success with our ransom notes and calls."

I didn't respond.

"It appears that your father has received numerous contacts from crackpots all over the world."

Dad was stalling so the police could try to locate me. Just what he said he'd do in this event. I permitted myself a tiny smile.

"Oh, don't get too cocky, Miss Curtis. We have another plan in mind."

"If it involves taking a picture and sending it to my father, you can forget it. He'll say that he has no way of knowing if I'm still alive."

Designer Suit shifted in his seat, continuing to hold the knife, but not as menacingly as before.

"You seem to know your father very well."

I shrugged. "We talked about security and what could go wrong and… stuff." I didn't enjoy talking about this eventuality when it was obvious that something *had* gone wrong.

"What would he think of a video tape of you giving him the details of our ransom request? Would he believe that?"

"I imagine he would, if he knew that I was still alive and in reasonably good health."

I couldn't tell through his mask, but I think that amused him. "You'd need a shower, to show you were in good health?"

I gave him a thin-lipped smile. "It would be a nice goodwill gesture."

"Yes, I can see that." His tone was patronizing, but if it meant getting clean, I didn't care. "We will prepare a message for your father, and you will deliver it right here in this room. The owner of this house is away for the next three weeks. We've already checked on that. He has some video equipment that I'm sure he won't mind us borrowing."

His chuckle was soft, but I could imagine the self-satisfied smirk on his face. I recalled my exploration of the medicine cabinet. Yes, the resident, and the town in which he resides. I had wondered if Peter Gibbs was connected with these men, but now I felt certain he had no idea what was happening here.

I thought about this videotaping idea and what it could mean in terms of my possible escape. Each night before drifting off to sleep, I had drawn up plans and then discounted them for one reason or another. There just might be a way to turn this situation to my advantage, if I could do this video on my terms. I would have to resist a bit first, and make it look like it was all their idea.

"My associates will prepare a message for your father," Designer Suit continued. "We will videotape you reading it. He will receive the tape, give us the money, and you will be released at a time and place of our choosing. Is that understood?"

"Perfectly."

"Excellent."

"Except for one thing."

"What's that?"

"My father doesn't make deals with kidnappers. He has to be handled with finesse. He won't pay a ransom easily."

"Not even to save his only daughter?"

"Especially not for that." I could only hope these people were familiar with our turbulent history from reading tabloids, and had not learned of our recent reconciliation. It was probably crazy to try to change their minds about a ransom, but I had so little leverage, anyway. I figured stalling on my end might help.

"You don't think you're worthy of being ransomed?"

"How much are you asking?"

"Ten million."

"*Dollars*?"

He nodded.

"No way." I shook my head in disbelief. "You've got to be kidding. My father is a tightwad. You'll never get that much from him. Sorry to disappoint you and the boys."

"Are you saying we shouldn't even try?"

I shrugged. "It won't be easy, that's for sure. I mean, you can't just have me read a demand for that much money and expect him to cave in. It would take some time to get that much money together." I tried to look sad. "I don't see how your video scheme will work, not for all that money. I guess you're screwed, and I am, too."

Designer Suit stood and looked away, obviously pondering. Finally, he turned back to me and pulled something from his pocket. "I'm going to show you some pictures, Ms. Curtis. I think they may convince you to cooperate with us. We could even give you a say in what you tell your father on the tape. We'd have to approve the script, of course, but I bet you'll be able to convince him to pay the money. See, it's not just your life in jeopardy. If we don't get the entire ten million, others will suffer."

What the hell was he getting at? I decided to press him on the issue. "I think you're bluffing."

The knife flashed again. For one heart-stopping moment, I was afraid that I'd pushed him too far, that it was all over. He reached around and cut the bindings at my wrists. I bit down on my lower lip as my numb arms and hands tingled back to life, and flexed my fingers until some feeling returned.

So far, we had played a game of verbal tennis, which I lost, and a game of force-the-captive-to-request-a-ransom-payment, which I planned to go along with, grudgingly. Now, he was confusing me with something else. Who was manipulating whom? This guy was plenty shrewd.

He held up a handful of photos and then dropped the first one into my lap. It was a shot of the inn where Kim and I were staying. I was surprised, but recovered quickly, keeping my gaze on him. "So?"

"The second one." He flipped over a photo of Kim and me outside the Bragdy Cambrian Brewery in Dolgellau.

"Someone has a lot of free time on his hands." My eyes returned to focus on him, though a slight tremor went through my hand when I examined the picture. Kim had been right. Someone was following us around. Small comfort that was, now.

"Still think we're bluffing?" He dropped the third onto the vacant chair beside me. I snatched it up, unable to breathe.

"Pup? No! Oh, God, no!" Our pet was lying on his side in the inn's front garden, a patch of dark soil underneath him. His eyes were half-open, and his tongue lolled to one side of his mouth.I surged toward Designer Suit, my hands balled into fists.

"You bastard!" The words caught in my throat. "You goddamned, filthy, rotten son of a bitch!" I couldn't seem to get enough air into my lungs. Tears welled up and spilled down my cheeks, but I kept going at him, trying to beat him to a bloody, unrecognizable pulp with my bare hands.

He took a step backwards and flicked open the switchblade.

I halted when the blade tip waved in the vicinity of my neck.

"Sit down," he said, in a quiet, controlled voice. "I'm not finished with you. What happened to the animal was to demonstrate that we mean business."

I sank into the chair and lowered my head, still crying.

He grabbed a handful of my hair and yanked upward, forcing me to look at him. With his other hand, he shoved the final picture into my face. Kim and I were in the inn's back garden, hand in hand.

"Now listen to me," he said.

I viewed him through a film of tears.

"You will make the tape, Priscilla. Or we'll kill her, too."

Chapter 16

I sat at the table under the bright floodlight while my kidnappers prepared to shoot the film we were going to make for Dad.

I didn't know why we needed the spotlight. The heat was making me sweat. Well, that and my nerves. At least I'd gotten a shower, shampoo, and new toothbrush out of the deal.

If only I'd listened to Kim. My eyes started to tear up, I missed her so much, but I couldn't think about her now. I had some serious work to do.

Designer Suit had gained my cooperation in making the video. All it took was a threat to my partner and the killing of our beloved pet. Now, I couldn't wait to send my loved ones a message, one I hoped would lead them straight to me. I had to be clever about it, though, or I would endanger everyone.

They were fiddling with the camera, looking so weird in their multicolored ski masks. But if I didn't see their faces, I couldn't identify them, and they'd have no reason to kill me once they got the ransom. They probably just wanted to get the money and get out of Wales.

I kept trying to convince myself that soon I'd be back in the arms of my loved ones. And I wanted to comfort Kim. She'd be distraught over losing Pup.

"Okay, Blondie, do your thing. And no funny business." Garlic Breath moved behind the camera, which was mounted on a tripod at the end of the table.

"Would it be okay if my hands were untied? You could chain my ankle to the table leg, like you've been doing. I talk with my hands, you know." It galled me to have to beg him for anything.

He looked over at his boss, who gave a slight nod. "I guess we can do that for you." He took his time ambling along the edge of the table to my side. With an exaggerated sigh, he cut the bindings around my wrists, taking the opportunity to put his hands on my butt when I leaned forward.

I ignored him and flexed my fingers. Then I slipped out of my wool shirt, grabbed the script, and cleared my throat. It looked like I was going to have only one chance, so I'd better get it right the first time.

I took a final glance at Designer Suit, who had moved out of the camera's range to a position along one wall. Woodsy was at my back and to the right, guarding the door, just in case I planned to pick up the end of the table and bolt for freedom. Designer Suit gave me a nod, Garlic Breath counted down from three, and the red light blinked on. I straightened my shoulders, wet my lips, and tried to smile.

"Hello, Father. It's me, PJ." I spread my hands and gestured. "As you can see, I'm alive. A little shaky, but alive."

I read from the text, embellishing in a few spots. "My amigos, here, are demanding a ransom of ten million American dollars, to be delivered in three days. They know you're on the way to Wales, so they're sending this tape to your London office. The drop-off location for the ransom will be disclosed later, before the deadline."

I placed the script on the table, folded my hands on top of it, and stared into the camera lens.

"Father, I know I've been a pain in the ass for quite some time, and that it is your policy to refuse to pay ransoms."

My hands parted, and I gestured again. It helped me to imagine that Dad and Kim were sitting just behind Garlic Breath and the camera, listening.

"Normally, I would agree with you, but I have been persuaded to ask you—no, to *beg* you—to reconsider." While I said this last sentence, I stroked the collar of my T-shirt, hoping it looked casual enough. I wanted Dad and Kim to see the dried blood there, and know that these guys were serious about their threats. "I'm not permitted to explain further, but Pup's death... was..."

I stopped and looked away, swiping at some unplanned tears. The loss of our pet left my emotions raw, and I took a deep breath before starting over. "Pup's death was a warning to all of us that these people mean business. If we ignore that warning, several of us will suffer. Please pay close attention to my words. I don't mean to *harp* on the subject, but lives are in danger here."

I paused and looked down at the script before continuing. "They've read the newspapers and monitored the radio and television reports. They're not happy that you've brought the police into this, Father, but they understand that you received many bogus messages. They're willing to overlook your foolishness if you obey their orders and work directly with them. They're reasonable, but their patience is limited."

I tried to smile. "Finally, please don't blame Sandy or Max because I'm missing. I take full responsibility for disobeying orders and leaving the hotel without an escort. Take good care of the staff." My lip quivered, and I could barely choke out my next words. "I love you all."

"Aww, so touching." Garlic Breath switched off the bright light. When he turned away from me to pack up the camera, I gave him the finger.

Now that the hard part was finished, my mouth was parched. I looked over at Woodsy, who was still guarding the door. "Could I please have some water?"

"I'll get it," the boss said. "In fact, I'll get something for all of us. Keep an eye on her." He left the room and returned with three bottles of Bass Pale Ale and a bottle of water.

Designer Suit and Garlic Breath began a discussion of various ways to send the tape to my dad, and Woodsy was ordered to return me to the basement after I finished my drink.

My head ached from the stress of taping the ransom message. I sat and wondered if I would be rescued, and if Dad, Kim, and the police would pick up on the clues that I'd included in the message. The chance was probably slim, but I refused to give up. My attention focused on what I could do to escape.

I was no longer heavily sedated like I had been when I first arrived, but on all trips out of the basement room, my ankles were shackled and one or both thugs escorted me. The door to that room was solid and the lock frustratingly unpickable. My best bet for escape would be during an excursion upstairs.

I wondered about Sarah, too. I hadn't seen her since the evening before the night of screams. She had been so kind to me. With a little more time, I'd bet I could have convinced her to help me escape. Now, that wasn't an option.

Since my capture, a subtle change had developed in my daily routine. Sometimes, I was allowed to come upstairs and fix a meal for all of us. I didn't know how to prepare a lot of things, but I guess it was a cut above what they could do for themselves. I thought about escaping during those times, but so far, one of them had always been with me, and the others were close by.

I drained my bottle of water, and after a brief trip to the bathroom, I was led back to the basement. I reflected that the one tiny window in the bathroom was nailed shut, just as Woodsy had told me.

Besides, I had tested it early in my confinement, while Sarah was accompanying me.

After unshackling my ankles, Woodsy lingered in the doorway of the room. I could tell he wanted to chat, but I wasn't feeling very sociable.

"I'll come and get you in time to start our supper tonight."

"Yeah, okay." Thinking about the bathroom window and Sarah had dampened my spirits. For the first time since my capture, I seriously questioned my chances of escape.

"It's going to be spaghetti and meatballs. You can fix that, can't you?"

"Yes, I'm fairly certain I can boil water without burning it and heat up canned sauce with meatballs already in it."

"Good."

I flopped facedown onto the cot and folded my arms under my chin. I had no appetite for such a meal.

"You know what I really miss?" I muttered.

"What?"

I was surprised that I had spoken out loud, and I was even more amazed that he had lingered long enough to hear and respond. I rolled over onto my back, hands tucked behind my head. "I miss the inn's nice hot cups of Earl Grey." I also missed a certain hot-blooded archaeologist, but I kept that thought to myself.

"I could probably fix some sort of tea for you."

"That would be very nice of you. I would be happy to make it myself, but I seem to be confined to my quarters right now."

He rubbed his chin through the ski mask. "Let me check on something, miss. I'll be right back."

He was gone so long that I had almost fallen asleep.

A soft tap on my shoulder jolted me awake. "We can have some tea. Get up and come with me." His voice was almost gentle.

He shackled my ankles together, and we climbed the steps to the kitchen, where I went through the motions of putting the kettle on. I pulled two mugs from the cupboard and shuffled about finding the other necessities. I listened for signs of Garlic Breath or Designer Suit. They didn't seem to be around, but I heard a radio playing in another room. The announcer was reporting the latest cricket scores, and I thought about Trevor and Geoff.

Once the water had boiled, Woodsy chained my ankle to the kitchen table, and we sat down to tea. I studied him as he drank his beverage.

“Forgive my asking, but how did a halfway decent guy like you get involved in a mess like this?” I gave him a smile and took a long sip. It wasn’t Earl Grey, but it warmed my insides.

“You don’t really know me, or you wouldn’t think I was decent at all. Besides, it’s a long, boring story.”

“I’ll soon have to start our supper, but in the meantime, I have nothing else to do and nowhere to go.” I rattled my chained foot and he grinned.

“Okay. I’ll give you the short version.” He leaned back in his chair. “When I was about fifteen or sixteen, I worked for my uncle in his store, sweeping up and stocking shelves.”

“Whoa,” I said and held up my hand. “That’s too short a version. Where did you live, and what kind of store did this relative have?”

He sat up straighter. “You really are interested?”

I nodded, smiling. “Sure.”

He finished the last few drops of his tea with a belch. “Beg your pardon, miss.”

“Hey, no problem.”

“It was a delicatessen in North Jersey. You’ve never heard of the place, so I’m not going to be any more specific.”

I drained my mug. “Fair enough.”

“Okay. So here I was at the store, working my ass off for minimum wage or less. Uncle Leo made a decent living with the hot pastrami, ham and provolone on rye, and all that, you know?”

I nodded, salivating.

“But one day a guy comes in and pulls Uncle Leo aside. ‘Want to make a quick fifty bucks?’ he asks my uncle. ‘Sure,’ my uncle says. ‘Who I gotta kill?’”

Woodsy and I grinned. Sounded like a Mafia tie-in to me.

“Turns out, this guy is starting up a numbers racket in the neighborhood, and he wants a place with a phone for a few hours, on account of the cops are hassling him at his other place of business.”

“Oh, dear,” I said.

His fingers drummed on the tabletop.

“Yeah. ‘Oh, dear’ is right. Before we know it, the cops are all over the place. This guy gives me his little black notebook and all sorts of cash and tells me to go to Camden or Cape May—anyplace in South Jersey—and lay low for a few days. So I did, but there’s six hundred and seventeen dollars in the bag he gave me.”

Woodsy spread his arms wide. “That’s a lot of dough for a sixteen-year-old kid from the streets, you know?”

“A lot of dough,” I agreed. “Were you tempted to keep it?”

"Hell yeah, I was tempted. I did keep it. Big mistake. Somebody squealed to the cops, and this guy found out where I was. Before I knew it, I had all sorts of people after me."

"What did you do then?"

"I did the only thing I could think of. I hopped on the ferry to Lewes, Delaware, took a bus south to Ocean City, Maryland, and got a job on a fishing boat until the heat died down."

"What did you do when you ran out of money?"

"You're a smart one, you know that?" Woodsy eyed me carefully. "I wouldn't have expected someone as rich as you to worry about the likes of me."

"It's not that I'm worried, but I've lived on my own and had to earn my own way. So, I do understand that the money runs out fast. My father and I didn't get along for many years. Still don't. He thinks I'm wild and irresponsible."

"Huh? I didn't know that."

"Yeah, that's why I'm not sure he'll think I'm worth ten mil."

"He'd better. I'd hate to see the boss hurt a nice girl like you, but he will. He's a bad one."

"Yeah, well…"

I glanced at my watch. "I'd better get started on our meal. Maybe you could finish your story a little later."

"Sure." He stood up and took our mugs to the sink. "Only there's not much more to tell. I liked working on different boats and around the docks, but I fell in with the wrong crowd and had some close brushes with the law." His hands balled into fists and then relaxed. "But, I've never been involved in murder before. You have to believe me."

An uneasy feeling came over me. I wanted to ask the obvious question, but I was too afraid of the answer.

"No sir. Never a murder." He bent to free my ankle from the table leg.

I went to the counter, took a pot from under the sink, and added water to boil for the spaghetti. Woodsy opened the jars of sauce and slid them toward me. Our hands made contact. "You don't have to go down with these guys," I told him. "You aren't like them. Not really. You still have a conscience."

He made some sort of noise and walked away from me. "I've gone too far to turn back now. Nobody'd believe me anyway."

When Garlic Breath and the boss walked in, Woodsy's demeanor changed and our conversation ended.

I prepared the meal and washed the dishes when we finished, feeling like a modern-day Goldilocks living with three seriously dysfunctional bears.

Chapter 17

"So far, she's still alive, Kim. And she seems to be in relatively good health."

Frederick's words came as such a relief that it sapped my remaining energy. I had been living on the raw edge of my nerves ever since PJ's kidnapping, and it didn't help that I was still weak from that dratted flu. I dropped onto the bed, unable to speak.

"Are you okay? Kim, answer me. Are you all right?"

He was still on the telephone, and I needed to respond. "I'm fine, really. It's a big help to know that she's okay, at least for the moment. But how do you know that she's—" A bout of coughing stopped me for a few moments. "Sorry, Frederick."

"Are you sure you're okay, health-wise?"

"Yes, I just have this lingering cough. It's getting better, though."

"No matter what else happens, you have to take care of yourself, you hear me?"

"I am, and I will."

"Good. Now, to my news. First of all, I'm here at my London office." He went on to explain that he had a videotaped ransom demand and had expressed the original to the Welsh police, along with instructions that Terry and I be allowed to view the tape at any time. He felt that PJ, by her body language and careful wording, was sending out clues, but he was unable to decipher them.

"I'm planning on staying here a day or two. I feel more productive here in London, at least for the moment."

"I feel better, Frederick, knowing you're closer."

"Should you need me, I can be there in less than an hour. And by now, you've met Dr. Terry Simms. She's done some amazing work for various law enforcement organizations."

"Yes, I've met Dr. Simms." I hoped he wouldn't notice the venom in my tone.

"You and she can examine the tape for clues."

"Her specialty is forensic anthropology, so I'm not sure how much help she'll be."

"With just a three-day deadline, we can use all the help we can get. Besides, someone in the Los Angeles office recommended her because she helped solve a difficult abduction case where everyone else had failed. Apparently, she possesses a sixth sense about such things."

From observing Terry's work in South America, I knew that she had uncanny insight. I couldn't deny the fact that she was a brilliant scientist and seemed to connect with ancient people on a purely cognitive level. Evidently, that skill worked equally well with the criminal element.

"Frederick, you said the kidnappers gave you three days to get a ransom together. We have to find PJ before the deadline."

"We will. And if we don't, I'll have the ten million ready to transfer."

I sighed as I recalled reading about cases in which, despite payment of a ransom, the outcome was tragic.

"Don't worry. I have the police back home tracking the whereabouts of all my known enemies."

It was the unknown ones that worried me the most. "When can I expect to see you here?"

"I don't really know, but before the deadline. Listen, keep good thoughts. I love you, and we both love Priscilla. That has to count for something."

When I hung up the phone, I lay back on the bed exhausted, but feeling more optimistic.

* * *

I was to meet Terry at the police station, where they had set us up with the necessary viewing equipment. The room was small, but airy, with two open windows. Outside, in an untidy little garden, roses bloomed, their fragrance wafting into the sparsely furnished room. A television and tape player had been set up on a long table that was scarred with numerous cigarette burns. Two swiveling, rolling, office chairs, a smaller table, and three metal file cabinets completed the furnishings.

In addition to the tape, we were provided with yellow notepads and pencils. I would have preferred to look at the tape in private, but PJ was Frederick's daughter and he was sending in all the troops he could muster. With her vast forensic experience, Terry was, in my opinion, overkill, and a slap in the face to the local authorities who had so far gone out of their way to assist us. But Frederick was leaving nothing to chance.

"Good morning, Dr. Blair." Terry entered the room with all the panache of a prima donna. She was impeccably dressed in brown linen slacks, a chocolate-colored turtleneck, and a suede jacket.

I acknowledged her arrival with a nod.

"I trust you slept well?" A taunting smile creased the edges of her mouth.

"Let's get on with it, shall we?"

"Kim, we may as well face the fact that we're working together. For the sake of your friend, why don't we forget the past and concentrate on getting her back?"

"I'm all for that." I forced a smile. "You'll have to forgive me for being gruff, but I've been under a lot of stress lately. On top of all that, you and I have our own baggage."

"Maybe it's time to rid ourselves of some of it."

"Yeah, well… "I took a seat in front of the television and picked up a pencil. "Are you ready to go with this?"

She pulled a chair up next to me. "Let's do it."

As we watched and listened in rapt silence, my heart went out to PJ. Seeing the fading bruises on her face, the dark splotches under her eyes, and knowing that behind her mask of defiance she was scared, it was all I could do to listen to her words. The sound of her voice, strong and resolute at first, then wavering at times, sent tears rolling unchecked down my cheeks. How I missed her! If only we could find out where she was.

Terry was all business and either did not, or pretended not to notice my distress. We focused our attention on the tape and watched it all the way through without comment.

"You know her, what do you think?" she asked, as I rewound it for another viewing.

I dug into my pocket for a tissue. "I believe, like Frederick, that she's clueing us in to something." I paused to blow my nose. "But what? And then there's the bit about Pup's death. What is that all about?"

"What, indeed?" Terry pushed her chair back from the table and crossed her leg, ankle over knee. "If we had the answers, we could ride in with swords drawn and rescue her."

"Don't make light of this situation. PJ is in serious danger."

"I'm not making light of anything. I'm just saying that if we could read her clues we could, with the help of the local police, go get her."

I bit my lower lip and sighed. "I'm sorry. I'm just worried to death about her, and your presence is adding salt to old wounds."

"Forget who I am, okay? I'm here to help in the search, not irritate your fragile ego."

I was halfway out of my chair before I could stop myself. "Wait just one bloody minute, Terry Simms."

"Uh oh, you're picking up on local cusswords." She smothered a grin. "They are so expressive, don't you think?"

"Not expressive enough." I sank back onto my chair and folded my arms.

"Come on. Let's just concentrate on finding PJ and getting her back safe and sound."

"I'll accept that."

"Then, when you have her back, if she's all that you say she is, I just might give you a run for your money."

I slammed the table with my fists. "You know, for one fleeting moment, I thought—"

She waved her hand, dismissing my resentment. "Hey, I know what you thought. Let's get back to this. What do you think? Did you see anything obvious in the tape?"

I counted silently to ten. When I was composed, I consulted my notepad. "Okay, I wrote down three things. The first is when she says: 'Father, I know I've been a pain in the ass for quite some time.'" I looked at her. "Frederick and PJ mended fences months ago. They get along wonderfully now, so why is she saying that unless it's to clue us in to something?"

Terry tapped her full lips with her pencil. "She's letting us know that there's more to her words than the obvious." She made some notes on her yellow pad. "Maybe she has a good reason for wanting her captors to think she doesn't get along with Daddy Dearest."

"Hmm. Going back to Pup's death, he got into some kind of poison the other day, but he's okay now. Very much alive and well."

"For some reason, they've convinced her that he isn't alive and well."

"He wasn't bad enough to take to the vet. I wish now that I had. If he was deliberately poisoned, we might have been able to trace the substance to an individual."

"Forget what happened to him for a minute and concentrate on why it happened. It's possible the poisoning was a coincidence, although I don't think so. What bothers me is why she thinks Pup is dead. Someone made her think that way. That could be a strategy to rattle her and force her cooperation."

"He looked dead when Trevor found him, but he recovered rapidly. If the poisoning was deliberate, whoever was responsible could have taken a picture."

"And showed the picture to PJ." Terry stared at me for a few seconds. "Does she care for the animal the way you do?"

"If she thought Pup had been killed, it would break her heart."

Terry stood and paced the width of the room. She was disturbing my orderly train of thought, and I wished she would sit down. She seemed to be focused on the project, though, so I swallowed my bitterness and turned back to my notes.

"What really puzzles me is this reference to Sandy and Max. It sounds as if she's referring to the bodyguards, but their names are Trevor and Geoff. No connection there that I can see. The only Sandy I know is a young man who worked with us in the Superstitions." I leaned back in my chair and crossed my legs.

Terry stopped pacing. "Could he be behind this?"

"Who? Sandy? Don't even go there. He's a colleague and a close friend."

"That doesn't mean he couldn't have spearheaded something like this."

"Damn it, forget Sandy, okay? Besides, he's someplace in Greece now."

Terry shrugged her shoulders, removed her jacket, and flopped onto a chair. "I just don't want to leave any stone unturned." She stretched her long legs and put her feet up on an empty box.

I couldn't help but admire her perfect figure. Her sleeveless turtleneck revealed tanned arms with well-defined muscles. That she worked out with weights was obvious. Then I noticed how the material stretched enticingly over a pair of large, firm breasts. My eyes lingered for a moment on the outline of her nipples. Delicious buds, straining against the fabric. I remembered a time when my mouth sought the sweet taste of those same buds. I tore my reluctant eyes away. Some snakes were beautiful, too, but their bite was deadly.

"Okay," Terry said, a smile playing around her sensuous mouth, "let's get back to the tape and go over it again, slowly and carefully."

Had she noticed me checking her out? I cursed myself for the moment of weakness. She didn't hold a candle to PJ.

Halfway through the second viewing of the tape, Constable Richard Williams brought us a pot of tea and a plate of cookies. "If you need anything else, just give us a nod," he said, placing the tray at the other end of the worktable. The police had been most accommodating. I wondered whether it was due to Frederick's influence, or simply because the local constabulary was more in tune with people's feelings than their American counterparts. Cups and saucers, yet. PJ would be so impressed.

I poured the tea. Thinking of my partner reawakened the sense of helplessness that threatened to destroy me. I had to change the subject, force some normalcy into my life for a few minutes, or I'd go crazy. "So, what have you been doing lately?"

Terry allowed her fingers to brush my hand as I handed her the teacup and saucer. She smiled when I drew back as if I'd touched a hot wire. Damn it, there had to be a way to convince Frederick that she wasn't needed here.

"For the past few weeks I've been in Toronto, helping to track down a serial child-killer."

"You're using your expertise in criminal cases rather than in antiquities?"

She shrugged her muscular shoulders and spread her arms. "I was tired of living in the past, though I'm still dabbling in antiquities. Pots and things. There's money to be had there."

I folded my arms across my chest. "The ancient world is where it's at for me, but not because of any money. On the contrary, there's satisfaction in being a starving archaeologist."

"You always were overly righteous, stuck in your own little time warp."

Her condescension made me bristle, but I held my anger in check. "Thanks," I said. "And since where I am now is no longer any business of yours, let's get back to work."

"My, are we touchy today, or what?"

I wanted to grab her by her long, aristocratic neck and choke the smirk right off her luscious lips. Instead, I took my tea and sat down in front of the console. Without waiting for her to reposition herself, I leaned forward and stabbed the play button.

Terry sat down with an exaggerated sigh. She rolled her chair closer to the table, and together we studied the flickering image.

"It's a lousy copy," she said, after a few seconds. "I don't know how they expect us to work within the detail of the image."

"It is a poor copy, probably second or third generation, and the original could have been less than perfect."

"Stop *there*." Terry leaned forward. "Back up a little."

I did as she requested.

"Why is she shaking her hands like that?" Terry asked, as we replayed the part in question. "Is that a mannerism of hers?"

I shook my head, backed up the segment, and played it through again. "Probably nothing. I can see she's nervous, though she's hiding it pretty well." I backed it up again, then let it play through the segment and beyond.

"Shit!" I said. "Look at that." PJ was pulling the neck of her T-shirt. "Is that blood?"

Terry scooted closer to the screen. "It sure looks like it. Go back again."

We studied the sequence repeatedly. "I noticed some old bruises on her face, but it looks like there's a scratch on her throat. Could that be the reason for the blood?"

"I guess they mean business."

I felt a wave of nausea pass through me and tried breathing through my mouth. "I never doubted they did."

We replayed the segment, but other than seeing spots of what appeared to be blood on her shirt and the scratch on her throat, we saw nothing that would help us.

Each time the tape ended, we rewound it, and started over, stopping where necessary and repeating, searching for something, anything, that would tell us where she might be held. We scanned the background, hoping to see something in the room, a picture perhaps, or a calendar on the wall behind her, that might be a clue to her whereabouts. But the shots were tightly framed; there was nothing obvious.

"What about this part?" Terry asked. "When she asks her father to pay close attention to her words, she says she 'doesn't mean to *harp* on the subject, but lives are in danger.'"

I gave her a questioning look.

"That word, harp. It's not that common. Why the almost exaggerated emphasis on the word?"

I chewed my lip and felt a tiny bubble of excitement swell inside me. "You know, you're right. I don't believe I've ever heard PJ use it in that context before." Something about the word had triggered a brief recognition in my brain, but I couldn't quite put my finger on it.

"There has to be something we're overlooking, some hidden clue she's giving us with that expression. And I wonder whose lives are in danger, other than her own, of course?"

"We're getting closer," I murmured, rubbing my chin, "but we still haven't connected." I slammed my fist against the table. "It's so damn frustrating."

Terry put her hand on my arm and gave it a squeeze. "Patience, Kim. Rome wasn't built in a day."

"But we only have three days to find her." I sat up and stabbed the play button again. "We need to really focus."

She picked up her pencil and turned to a fresh page on her pad. "I'm ready if you are." For a fleeting moment, I was thankful for her expertise.

We ran the tape back and forth until our eyes were bloodshot and I had the mother of all headaches. A search of my bag yielded a couple of outdated Tylenol tablets. I was sure they had lost some of their potency, but I swallowed them anyway.

"Look," Terry said after another couple of hours of intense viewing, "we're so tired now that we're liable to miss something even if it leaps onto the table and slaps us in the face. What say we call it a night and start fresh in the morning? We can stop somewhere for dinner."

"We only have three days, less than that now, before the ransom is due."

"I know that, but right now we're both too damn tired to be of use to ourselves or to PJ."

"I suppose you're right, but no dinner." I gathered up my supplies. "I'm going right back to the inn."

Her fingernails drummed on the tabletop. "You have to eat, and so do I. Since we're working together, what's wrong with keeping each other company over dinner?"

I wasn't happy about it, but I had no real reason to decline, except for the headache, which had eased. "Where do you have in mind?"

"Now you're talking. I found a great little pub where they serve a lamb stew that is out of this world."

* * *

We chose a well-worn oak table in the back room. On the other side, two men in overalls and tweed caps were conversing in Welsh. I found the singsong resonance of the language fascinating. In the far corner, an older couple spoke in hushed tones. Conversation and laughter drifted in waves from the bar. A well-endowed barmaid in a gauzy peasant blouse arrived to take our order for stew and ale. Except for the modern dress of the patrons, the ambience could easily have been Elizabethan.

"Tell me, what do you and your little concubine do when you're not digging through piles of dirt? Other than the obvious, of course." Terry gave me a saucy wink.

I started to rise from my seat. "I'll leave right now if you're going to talk about her like that. She doesn't deserve such treatment."

"All right, I'm sorry. It was a cheap shot." Terry put her hand on my arm and coaxed me back down. "Come on, you know me. You know how I like to kid around."

"Yes, I know you too well."

I picked up my glass and savored the robust taste of the British ale, enjoying its nutty flavor as it slid down my throat. "There's nothing in the world to compare with the European ales," I said, more to myself than to my dinner companion.

She raised her glass. "I'll drink to that. Cheers!"

I was hungry for the first time in days, probably because I was finally feeling better physically. More than that, though, I was at least doing something constructive. Knowing that Frederick was covering all the bases helped, too. We would find her. I dared not think otherwise.

Food would help. I hadn't had a decent meal since before I'd come down with the flu, and I certainly hadn't eaten much since PJ had been taken, either, so it had been several days. I smiled.

"What's so amusing?" Terry asked.

"My eating habits have been very erratic, what with the flu and the kidnapping. PJ would tan my hide if she knew."

Terry's smile was wicked. "Mmm, would that be with the aid of chains and handcuffs, or would she just strip you naked and use a bullwhip?"

I could feel anger rising inside me. "That remark doesn't deserve an answer."

"Why not?" She drank some of her ale, wiping the froth from her lips seductively with the tip of her tongue. "I've found that pain heightens and prolongs the sensation, if you know what I mean."

"I'm not one bit interested in your sensations."

"A little jealous perhaps?"

My look froze her into silence. She shrugged and turned her attention to her meal. I unclenched my hands and inhaled the delectable aroma rising from our plates.

Besides chunks of tender lamb, the hearty stew contained potatoes, peas, carrots, mushrooms, and even a few turnips. It was served with a platter of brown soda bread. We each ordered a second glass of ale, and I endeavored to keep our conversation centered on work. Terry, on the other hand, seemed bent on making it personal.

After swallowing her last bite of stew, she wiped her mouth and put down her napkin. "Can I ask you something?"

I buttered my last piece of bread. "You can ask. Whether I answer remains to be seen."

"You always were the cautious one."

"So ask."

"Do you really think it's all over for us?"

I stared at her. "What are you suggesting?"

Her long, tapered fingers traced the lip of the empty glass. "Sometimes, I'd like for us to be together again."

"I don't believe you." I tossed the bread down on my side plate, shaking my head. "Why, when I'm in a perfectly stable, loving relationship, would I want to repeat previous mistakes?"

She wrapped both hands around her glass. "We were happy for a while, very happy."

"For a while, until you revealed your true colors."

"We could make things work."

I drained the last of my ale and put my glass down. "Terry, understand this. I'm in love with PJ. We have something special going, and we intend to spend the rest of our lives together."

"You listen to me, Kim." She pointed her finger like a dagger at my chest. "I'm giving you good advice. There's an age difference between you two."

I knew she was baiting me, trying to force me to lose control, but I wasn't about to give her the pleasure. "We've discussed that, and it doesn't matter."

"By the time she's the age you are now, you'll be applying for Medicare. Do you really think she's going to stay with an old woman? Use your head. You'll be lucky if she sticks around for five years."

My fist pounded the table, causing heads to turn in our direction. My voice lowered, but I gave my anger free rein. "Enough! This is the last I'm going to say on this subject. We have pledged ourselves to each other. Do you understand? That's the way it is, so drop it."

Terry shrugged. "Don't say I didn't warn you."

* * *

It was a beautiful night for the stroll back to our digs, but the air smelled of rain, and the moon played hide-and-seek with the fast-moving clouds.

"Goodnight," I said when we arrived at my place. Terry was staying at a hotel farther down the street.

"Okay." She touched my sleeve. "You've convinced me that you and PJ are going to live happily ever after. But she's not here right now, and you're lonely. I can see it in your eyes." She lifted her hand to caress my cheek, and her voice dropped to a seductive whisper. "Let me comfort you tonight, for old times' sake. If PJ is half the woman you say she is, she'll understand. She'll know how alone you must feel, how afraid."

We stood opposite each other, bathed in the glow of the inn's entrance lights. Terry was stunning. Gazing at this tall, captivating woman, I could see why I had fallen in love with her all those years ago. And she was right; I was lonely. It would be comforting to snuggle up to a warm body tonight. In the glow radiating from the inn's leaded windowpanes, her trim form was delectably inviting. Her expensive, snug-fitting pants and jacket accentuated her sensuality.

I recalled how she looked without clothes and how good she was in bed. She played her lover like a fine musical instrument, lifting her until the final crescendo burst in a dizzying array of colored lights, sensations, and sounds. Yes indeed, Terry was good in bed, but PJ was better. Her spirited lovemaking was initiated by love, not lust. That made one hell of a difference.

"You just don't get it, do you? When you're in a relationship, you remain true to your partner, no matter what. Sure, I'm lonely and in need of loving. There's nothing I'd like better than to have someone in my bed tonight, but that someone has to be PJ. End of story."

Terry patted my cheek. "You're too good to be true." Her laugh was taunting. "See you in the morning, my dear," she called over her shoulder as she walked away, then she stopped and turned. "I thought you might be hard to get along with, but I brought my toys—just in case."

"Good night, Terry."

* * *

I undressed slowly, thinking about what she had said. I was aware of the age difference—just short of fifteen years—and while it did not affect our relationship now, what of the future? As we aged, the difference would become more evident. PJ wouldn't leave me, of that I was sure, but what if my health broke down? Would she feel trapped? Would she yearn for younger company? Was I being fair to her? Damn Terry for having put those thoughts in my mind.

I reached into the bedside stand and pulled out PJ's medallion. Remembering the circumstances surrounding our discovery of the two Amazon medallions and the snakes that slithered harmlessly by us that day, I was certain it had been a message from beyond the grave, from Marna, myself in another time. The medallion glowed faintly in my hand. I felt our connection more strongly than ever.

Tears welled in my eyes, and my body ached for PJ. The two medallions represented an invisible thread between us, a thread that would not, could not, be broken. I caressed it, touching it to my lips.

"Oh, PJ," I whispered to the darkened room, "what are you telling us?"

I buried my face in her pillow and sobbed until there was nothing left in me, and fell asleep with the medallion clasped in my hand, the chain woven securely through my fingers.

Chapter 18

I stretched out on my cot, fingers laced behind my head, trying to ease the unpleasant knot in my stomach.

Fear.

It never seemed to go away, especially at night. When things were quiet, there was nothing to distract me from my situation. I stared at the exposed floor joists overhead, and my thoughts turned to a more pleasant subject.

Kim.

I'd done what I could. If she and Dad were able to find the clues in the tape, they just might get here in time. If not, then I didn't want to think about that.

In the meantime, I was working on a way to escape. As much as I loved Kim, I couldn't put all my faith in her ability to save me from my own mistakes, and this one was a whopper.

There was a remote possibility that Dad would pay the ransom or make it look like he had, and my captors would set me free. I wasn't holding my breath on that, however. If I could be patient, my best hope would be to get away when the timing was right.

For a while, I considered making Woodsy an ally. When he mentioned murder, though, I was convinced it was too late. He had already crossed the line. I couldn't bring myself to ask if the murder he mentioned was Sarah's, but it probably was. One murder could easily beget two in a criminal's warped mind. I thought of Garlic Breath and shuddered. His mind was about as warped as it could get.

I had to stop thinking such sickening thoughts right before sleep. I needed to remember the other option—escape. It wouldn't be easy, but I didn't see any other way.

I gave my pocket a protective pat. Each time I visited the bathroom, I palmed several Ambien tablets, crushing them into a fine powder once I returned to the privacy of my basement cell. Peter Gibbs sometimes used envelopes as bookmarks in his reading material. One of those now held my cache of tablets. I discovered that

I could slide the envelope with its fresh supply of pills under one leg of my cot and then climb on the mattress. Voila! Instant pulverized medicine. If I was asked to fix a meal and was unobserved for any length of time, I could doctor their food and drink with the drug. It was a risky plan, but if the guys were drowsy enough, I thought I could get away. I had to be ready.

But once out of the house, where should I go? Were we in a village, or some distance from one? If this place was near a farm or house, I could knock on the door and get help. What if they thought I was a crazy person, or looking to rob them? Considering how I looked right now, I didn't think I'd trust me enough to invite me inside.

We had approached the critical point of negotiations on the ransom. We assumed the tape was in Dad's hands by now, and these guys were anxious to make a collection. The only bad part that I could see was that Designer Suit had provided Woodsy and Garlic Breath with handguns. The switchblade remained the boss's weapon of choice, and a vicious weapon it was.

I rolled to my side, tucking one hand under my pillow and curling the other against my chin. This was my usual sleeping position. The only thing missing was a warm, naked body spooned against my back and a protective arm hugging me and occasionally tickling my belly.

I thought about Kimmy a lot. Was she feeling better? Was her flu all gone? I hoped so. What was she doing right now? Was she thinking of me, too?

I shifted again and felt the piece of paper crackle inside my bra, where I had tucked it for safekeeping. Call me a sentimental fool, but when I finished working on the videotape script, I got the chance to write Kim a note. Woodsy was guarding me while Designer Suit and Garlic Breath argued over who would deliver the tape and who would pick the drop-off spot. The conditions weren't perfect. My leg was chained to the table, and Woodsy rarely took his eyes off me, but while pretending to work on the script, I managed to scribble a message to my love, just in case things didn't work out.

Alone in the dark, I recalled the words I had struggled to write.

Dear Kim,

If you are reading this letter, it probably means that I am dead. I wanted you to know that my final thoughts were of you and the love we shared. Although it's been less than a year, it was the best time of my life. I hope it was for you, too.

Once we got to know each other, we seemed like a pair of old friends who were meeting again after a long separation. It was weird and a little creepy at first, but comfortable and relaxed once we stopped fighting the attraction. We discovered that we had a lot of unfinished work to do, like finding your Amazon family and figuring out how our destiny meshed with theirs. I guess you'll have to do that work alone now, until we can meet again in some other, better place.

You made me so happy, Kim. I hope you were happy with me. I tried to tell you often enough how much I loved you. Please don't grieve for me. Move on. I'll have our love for comfort wherever I am. I'll find a sunny beach somewhere and wait for you at the water's edge, writing our names in the sand.

You're on my mind and in my heart. And I will love you...

Always and Forever.

PJ

My throat tightened and tears filled my eyes. It was always worse at night, when my defenses were weaker. Loneliness and fear grew like twin vines inside me, threatening to choke off my hope and render me helpless. I tried all sorts of things to fight it. I prayed, read, gave myself pep talks, and slept with the light on. But the fear always returned. The only way I could get relief, the only way I could sleep, was to punish myself with physical exercise. I performed sit-ups and crunches until sweat trickled into my eyes. I ran in place until my knees weakened, and I did push-ups on the cot until my arms trembled with fatigue.

Peter Gibbs had several books of Celtic myths in his bookcase, and I delved into them, reading until the words blurred and ran together on the pages. There were thick volumes on Welsh heritage, Druids, warriors, bards, and ancient symbols. I read until my eyes burned, and the mental or physical exhaustion engulfed me like a shroud, releasing my mind and body to the blessed oblivion of sleep.

I'd often dream of Arthur's return—to help Kim vanquish my evil kidnappers and restore me to my place at her side. In my dreams, Kim's battledress was decidedly Amazonian, and her trusty steed looked a lot like Pup, but night after night, they arrived in the nick of time to help me. Together, we fought our way to freedom.

Tonight was no different; however, I had the added distraction of physical need. It was my own fault. I knew that thinking about my partner, especially in Amazon leathers, would arouse me. It always had. I resisted as long as I could, but my body had gone too long without my lover's touch. I was only human, and I knew what I was missing.

"Damn it, I want to be with you tonight." I shifted onto my back and hugged myself. "I'm trying so hard to be brave, but God, I miss you and I need you."

I turned my face into my pillow and sobbed.

* * *

There was a scraping noise in the corner where the bookcase stood. I rolled over and sat up, careful to make no further sound. Either the light had burned out, or I had turned it off before falling asleep. Though disoriented, I was alert enough to realize that my mouse friend was on a nocturnal food raid.

"Hey there," I called softly as I reached out for the switch. The room was bathed in ghostly light.

The mouse retreated quickly to the sanctuary of the old bookcase, but soon he reappeared.

He needed a name. Maybe, since he was brown, I could call him Brownie. I didn't even know if he was a he or a she. Brownie should work either way.

"Hey, Brownie. You don't mind if I call you Brownie, do you?"

I pulled a roll out of my pocket and broke off a piece. "I saved this from supper. But you probably have some starving mouths to feed behind that wall someplace, so you need it more than I do."

He sat up on his haunches. I could see his whiskers twitching. "Come on. I know you want it. You don't have to be afraid of me. We're buddies, right?"

I tossed the bits of bread off the end of the cot and waited. He took a few tentative steps toward the food and halted. "Okay, so it isn't cheese this time. I'm sorry. I can't give you gourmet meals every night."

He stuffed a piece of bread in his mouth and scampered back to the bookcase. One second he was there, the next he'd vanished. In an instant, he was back for more.

"Ah, I knew it. You have a family under there, don't you, Brownie?"

He approached the edge of the cot, emboldened by the smell of food and soothed by my soft, familiar voice, or at least I hoped so. I felt a tiny weight as he sprang onto the mattress. "Come on, fella," I whispered, holding out the last morsel of bread. "Sorry there's no butter on it. But, at least there's none of that Marmite crap." He crawled up my blanket-covered leg, took the bread from my hand, and paused to stuff a wad into his cheek. His head dipped just as I mentioned the Marmite, and I laughed. "I know. That stuff looks like roofing tar and smells like dirty socks. The man who owns this place has jars of it stashed away." I shuddered, and Brownie retreated. "Sorry. It just gives me the creeps thinking about it."

He scurried back to his hidden sanctuary. "Bye, Brownie. I'll try to get some cheese for you in the morning."

I turned off the light and stretched out under the blanket. If Kim could see me now, she'd never believe it. Training a mouse to take food from my fingers.

The thought made me smile, if only for the moment.

* * *

The noise was soft, but I heard it. Too big to be Brownie this time. My heart thudded in anticipation and I sat up. In a voice that surprised me with its strength, I said, "Whoever you are, come out of the shadows and show yourself. I'll fight you if I have to."

A human shape materialized at the foot of my bed. It was a woman, wearing some sort of battledress made of skins, feathers, and metal. She glowed with a soft, internal light that formed an aura around her body. A mask covered the upper part of her face, but I glimpsed a flash of white from her eyes as she approached me.

I groaned. "You're not Kim. It's supposed to be Kim coming to my rescue. Damn it, I can't even get my dreams to work right."

"Hush and be still," said my nocturnal visitor. She placed a firm hand on my shoulder and pushed me flat on my back.

I tried to sit up. "Not another Amazon. I've been around Kim too long, I must be losing it." I peered at her familiar shape in the semi-darkness. "Wait a minute, I've seen you before. You're the one who popped up unannounced in Arizona last fall, aren't you?"

"Keep your voice down."

I took her hand, which was surprisingly strong, shoved it aside, and forced myself back to a sitting position. "Okay, I'm keeping my voice down. Answer me. Are you the same one?"

"I am." She sat beside me on the cot.

My patience had worn thin. "What do you want? Why are you here?" Geez, I was having a conversation with an apparition. Again.

She reached for my hand, but I snatched it away. "We were afraid you had lost hope, little one. All that weeping."

I stood up and pulled on my jeans. I had slept in one of Sarah's old shirts while my underwear, socks, and T-shirt dried on a nearby chair. The air in the basement was cold, sending goose bumps along my arms. "Jesus Christ! I've been a captive here for almost a week. If things don't go right, I'll be shot and dumped in a hole somewhere. I think, under the circumstances, that I have a perfect right to be upset."

"Of course you do, but you must not show the enemy your vulnerability."

"Don't patronize me. And stop treating me like one of your warriors. I'm not an Amazon like you and Kim. Sometimes, I feel weak and—"

"Oh, but you are," she said, interrupting me.

I stared at her, watching the feathers on her tight leather costume sway as she moved. The whites of her eyes were bright behind her mask. "What? What am I?"

She gave a light laugh that was part snort. "An Amazon, of course. Didn't you know that, little one?"

I sat back down on the cot because my legs had lost their strength. "That's ridiculous."

She shook her head and grinned.

I wondered what she looked like under all those feathers. She didn't have any weapons. I'd bet I could yank that mask off her face and see for myself. Oh, hell, she'd probably kill me with her bare hands.

"If only you had worn the medallion," she said in a soothing voice, "you would have seen the visions. I could have come to you sooner. Your questions would have—"

I held up my hand. "Whoa. Enough. You people may be able to invade Kim's dreams and convince her that she is one of you, or was one of you, but I'm not such a pushover."

This time she laughed out loud. "I told my superiors that this assignment would be difficult, but I had no idea."

"You can't tell me a piece of metal has such powers. And for your information, it has a faulty clasp, so I couldn't wear it." I stood and folded my arms across my chest for emphasis.

Her voice dropped. She spoke slowly, as if speaking to a child who could not comprehend. "Very well. Whatever you say. We will deal with that later. I am here now to give you hope and a message from your soul mate."

My heart tumbled in my chest. "A message from Kim? Is she okay? Does she—"

The Amazon put her hand on my arm. "This time *you* need to whoa."

I sat down again on the cot and finished pulling on my socks, taking a deep breath as I did so. "All right, then. Is she okay?"

"Yes, except for missing you and worrying about you, she's fine."

My eyes filled with tears, but I smiled through them. "Thank goodness. Do you know if she's been able to see the videotape yet?"

She pressed her lips together and shrugged. "Videotape? I know nothing of this. I'm sorry. My superiors told me that she was angry, worried, and determined. That's all."

I nodded. "That will be enough. When Kim is any one of those things, she's a force to be reckoned with."

The woman tucked a stray strand of my hair behind my ear. "Her concern—indeed, our concern—is with you, little one. Are you strong enough to survive this?"

"You tell me." I stood and began to pace the length of the room. "I have to be, don't I? I'm aware my options are limited, but I have an escape plan."

"Good."

I spent a few minutes explaining what it was, and she seemed to think it could work, though she preferred that I overpower the men and kill them with their own guns.

"Shooting is not an option for me," I told her. "I'm the running-away type."

She laughed. "You may be surprised."

"Well," I started to say, but she stood up and made a silencing gesture. "What is it?" I whispered, the hair rising on the back of my neck.

"I am called back now, but I'll be watching over you, little one. Is there anything you wish me to tell your soul mate? It might be possible to get a word or two back to her."

I told her about Peter Gibbs and the name of the town, but Welsh was not the Amazon's native tongue. She had enough trouble with English. "Just try to get her to read the travel brochures on the table by our bed."

She gave me a smile of relief. "All right, brochures, whatever they are. I'll see what I can manage. Be aware that it takes an enormous amount of energy for me to appear in your world, but I'll do what I can." She faded into a wisp of pale amber smoke, and then vanished completely.

As I stared at the empty space her body had occupied, I detected the faint smell of old leather and campfire ashes. I reviewed our conversation, and my stomach did a Texas Two-Step. "Holy shit! She said I was an Amazon, too." I thought back to Arizona and the Amazons sleeping on Superstition Mountain. They were real, archaeologically speaking, but I wasn't sure where I fit in.

More light filtered down from the window well. I sat back on my cot and waited for one of the thugs to come and escort me upstairs.

One thing was certain. If I was really an Amazon, it was time I started acting like one.

Chapter 19

The day was gray and rainy, typical in this part of the world, but that was the reason the grass grew so green and the flowers were so prolific. My mood matched the clouds more than the grass, the rain more than the flowers. As long as PJ was a captive, held under who knows what conditions, every day would seem dismal.

My image in the mirror looked gaunt. Black circles under my eyes attested to my sleeplessness, and red eyes evidenced the tears I had shed during the long, lonely hours.

I took a quick shower and dressed. Arwel handed me a message as I was walking through the lobby. It was from Terry, saying that she would meet me for breakfast at Sally's Café.

"Shit!"

"Is something wrong?" Arwel looked at me with concern.

"No, not really. May I use your telephone?"

She slid the instrument across the counter toward me. I know I should have used the pay phone, but this was quicker, and Arwel didn't seem to mind.

I'm in no mood for this, I thought, as I dialed her number to decline her invitation. Having breakfast with her was so low on my list of priorities it wasn't even there. Couldn't she see that I was more concerned about working on the tape than I was about eating?

Damn it, there was no answer, which left me no choice but to join her.

I stepped outside into a light drizzle. When strangers gave me cold stares, I realized that my own expression must have mimicked the swollen dark clouds that threatened to turn the drizzle into a downpour.

I pushed open the door to the restaurant and a small, tinkling bell announced my arrival. Terry was already seated at a table in the alcove of a bay window. White lace half curtains on the small-paned windows shielded the diners from people passing on the street. It was cozy and private, but did little to lift my foul mood.

I nodded a greeting and sat down, noting with irritation that Terry appeared fresh and rested. She wore a pressed pair of faded jeans and black knee-high boots. Her soft pink shirt was open sufficiently at the neck to allow full view of cleavage and the hint of a black lace bra.

She gave me a quick once-over. “You look like roadkill. I wouldn’t want to touch you with a long pole.”

“That’s fine with me. Let’s keep it that way, shall we?”

“Good God, woman, what is the matter with you? Is my baby lost without her little bed warmer?”

I leaned toward her and lowered my voice to a menacing growl. “That’s enough! You’re here only because Frederick requested it.”

She recoiled in a huff. “I know that.”

“And since you’re getting paid a bundle for your services, Frederick expects you to do your job to the best of your ability. I’m going to be watching to make sure you do just that.”

“I know what’s expected of me, and I’m doing it.” She gave me a seductive smile. “Aren’t I?”

Everything had a double meaning with her.

“Hear me loud and clear, Terry Simms. I’ve had just about enough of your antics.”

“What antics?”

“You’re here to do a job, nothing more.” I dropped my voice, speaking slowly for emphasis. “And while you’re here you will treat PJ with the utmost respect. That goes if you’re dealing with her in person or speaking about her. Furthermore, you will treat me with the respect due a colleague. I will treat you respectfully, too, as a colleague. And that’s all there is.”

I picked up the small, neatly handwritten menu.

She sighed and picked up hers. “Whatever you say, dear.”

The paper crackled in my hands. I wanted to wipe the smirk off her face with my fists, but the waitress arrived at our table before I could embarrass myself by making a scene.

Two middle aged women and one older woman, seated by the inner wall, stared at us as politely as they dared, dropping their eyes when I glanced their way.

I ordered tea, dark toast, and a soft-boiled egg. Terry ordered a pastry.

Though I was in no mood to appreciate my surroundings, I had to admit that the café was delightful. The walls were papered in tiny rosebuds against a white background, and a collection of antique teapots was displayed in two glass-fronted cabinets. White lace cloths covered the eight small, circular tables. In the center of each table, white vases of different sizes and designs contained small bunches of flowers.

I'd have to bring PJ here when this was all over. She'd love the atmosphere. It was so British.

The thought of my missing partner filled me with despair, but Terry didn't seem to notice. She chatted about her work, her travels, and a wealthy woman she had met in Rio, who was, according to her, head over heels in love with her. I listened just enough to add a nod here and there or to say "Is that so?" or "Indeed." The rest of the time I sat in morose silence. Her life was of no interest to me whatsoever.

The food arrived, and I focused my attention on the beautiful brown egg, served in a proper British eggcup. The cup itself was a dainty piece of bone china, trimmed in pink rosebuds. Accompanying it was a small silver utensil that neatly clipped off the top of the egg.

How civilized. When had we Americans decided that boiled eggs should be smashed and served like a semi-solid soup? We could take a lesson from our British friends.

This egg was cooked to perfection. I spread my toast liberally with chunky orange marmalade, thinking that, under other circumstances, I would have enjoyed the rather simple, but delightful meal.

* * *

By the time we stepped outside of the café, the rain had stopped. A gentle breeze felt warm and soft against my face. Since my heavy shirt and pants felt uncomfortable in this milder temperature, I suggested that Terry go on ahead to the police station while I returned to the inn to change.

I knew that I didn't have to worry about Pup, who was quite safe with Geoff, so I climbed the twisting narrow stairs to our room. Arwel and her staff had been in to make the bed and tidy up. I looked around and was struck by the emptiness. Once, this room had been a source of solitude for us and a respite from our wild escapades through the Welsh countryside. I remembered driving along the coast, hiking over flower-blanketed hillsides, and exploring countless shady glens with PJ at my side.

Her clothing hung where she had left it, in the wardrobe and draped across the wooden chair by the bed. I didn't have the heart to move any of it. Leaving everything as it was made me feel that she had just stepped out and would be right back.

A stack of travel brochures had been scattered over the nightstand, but someone had straightened them into a neat pile. As I pulled on my cargo pants and a lighter shirt, I found myself staring at those folders, feeling a prickling sensation at the back of my neck. I swore the stack seemed to glow. I rubbed my eyes and took a deep, steadying breath.

"Damn, what is happening to me? I must be losing my mind."

I looked around the room and then back at the pile, afraid to approach it. The glow intensified.

"This is insane. *I* must be insane. Can grief drive a person crazy?"

Faint laughter seemed to bounce from wall to wall. Then a softly vibrating haze materialized into a form over our bed. An Amazon. Not Marna. Not a warrior, but no less an Amazon.

"Who are you?"

"Shh," the voice cautioned. "Those parchments. You must read them." Her hand gestured toward the end table.

"The travel brochures?" My mind refused to function. "You want me to read those? Why?"

"You must," she said, her voice fading out. "For your soul mate."

A sob caught in my throat. "For PJ?"

The image vanished.

I turned in a circle, searching for her, but there was no one in the room but me. "Please. I have to know. What is in these that I should study them now?" There was no answer. "I don't have the time."

The stack no longer glowed. I picked up the pamphlets and flipped through them. Was PJ sending me a message? Was there a clue in here somewhere?

I stuffed the brochures into a tote and left the room, determined to read every word in them if it would bring us closer to finding my partner.

I saw Geoff in the lobby with Pup. "Trevor is on the telephone," he said, "following up on some leads. Nothing of importance. A lot of people claim to be eyewitnesses to this or that. Most turn out to be cranks, and when it comes right down to it, we end up in the same old dead end."

I wanted to lie down and cry. "You'd think that in a place this small, someone would have seen something, some little thing that would give us a clue."

"Don't give up, Dr. Blair. Something's going to open up soon."

"It has to be soon, or else… " I choked on the words.

Geoff squeezed my shoulder. “Here, now. Hang in there.”

I paused a moment to calm myself. “I’ll take Pup with me. You and Trevor have enough to do without tending to him.”

“He’s been no trouble at all.” Geoff patted Pup’s head and handed me his leash.

* * *

The tape played back and forth as we searched its contents for any clue that would lead us to PJ. Constable Williams kept us supplied with tea, and he gave Pup water and dog biscuits from a stash he kept in his desk drawer for the K9 corps. During each break, I studied PJ’s stack of travel brochures. Many were of locations we had already visited, but there were some of places we had hoped to see together before we left Wales.

A lump formed in my throat. There was still time for that. There had to be.

“She refers to her captors as amigos,” Terry said, bringing me back to the present. “Maybe she’s telling us that they’re Latinos.”

“Or Americans, since she stresses that the ransom be paid in American dollars.”

“Then there’s Sandy and Max.” I stood up and arched my aching back. “Who are they?”

Terry’s gaze tracked me as I paced beside the table. “You know Sandy, and so does PJ. It wouldn’t surprise me if he’s behind this whole thing.”

“You’re wrong,” I said. “Sandy, PJ, and I are close friends, and he’s a successful scientist.”

“Successful, maybe. Poor, probably.” She poured another cup of tea for herself. “The lure of money has led many a young man into a life of crime.”

“No way. Not Sandy.”

“Okay, okay.” Terry took a sip and stared silently into her cup.

“Are you going to sit all day reading tea leaves, or are you going to come up with some worthwhile suggestions?” I sat back down and opened my notebook.

“Patience, darling. Goodness, what am I saying? You never did have much of that, did you?”

“Damn it!” I hit the table with a clenched fist. “Time is wasting while you’re busy with your little games.”

“I’m not in any hurry. After all it’s not my little tart who’s—”

Terry grabbed my arm before my hand connected with her cheek. "I do love to see you burn, you know."

I pulled away from her, reaching for my cell phone.

"What are you doing?"

"Calling Frederick to tell him I want you off this case. He's not getting his money's worth."

"Oh, come on, where's your sense of humor?"

She tried to look contrite.

I glared at her.

"All right, I'll get down to business, but you can't blame me for taking advantage of a rare chance to niggle at you. Call it payback."

I ignored her last remark and responded instead to the first one. "You had damn well better get down to business."

I was so furious by this time that I wanted to cry, but I wasn't about to give Terry the satisfaction of seeing me fall apart. I faced her. "Just remember that you're being paid to help find PJ. My relationship with her has nothing to do with your assignment. Do you hear me? It has nothing to do with it. Now cut the crap and get to work."

Terry stared at me with intense dislike before rewinding the tape, so that we could start again.

It felt good to be off the uncomfortable chairs, so we remained standing while waiting for the tape to rewind.

"Let's think about those names again." Sandy and Max, Sandy and Max. I ran the names through my mind. "There has to be a connection, but what? Sandy and—wait a minute. Peter. Maybe that's it. Sandy is a nickname. His real name is Peter, Peter Arnold."

"So what's that supposed to mean?"

"I don't know."

"Are you hiding Sandy behind his alias? Sandy didn't do it, but Peter Arnold did. Is that it?" Her laugh was taunting, daring me to react.

I did, whirling around and this time connecting.

Terry turned in the nick of time, avoiding the full impact of my hand. As luck would have it, Constable Williams chose to appear at that very moment. I was mortified by my action and by the fact that the constable had witnessed everything.

"Here now, Dr. Blair, Dr. Simms, what is going on?"

If I hadn't been so embarrassed, I would have found his startled expression comical.

"Nothing," Terry said. "I provoked her by being my usual bitchy self."

The constable looked from one to the other of us. "You're sure that everything's all right?"

"Fine," Terry said, and then turned to me. "I'm sorry. I was just trying to get your goat."

"I apologize for slapping you. That was uncalled for." I felt like a jerk for acting just the way she wanted me to. In her mind, it was a small victory. "I haven't been myself lately," I added.

"I'll get a fresh pot of tea," Constable Williams said, backing through the door.

Terry and I looked at each other. Then we laughed at how we must have looked to him, and that he apparently believed pouring more tea into us would solve everything.

When he returned, we were studying the tape once more.

"Constable," I said, trying to resolve a question that had been nagging at me. "I remember hearing something about a place where harps are manufactured, or used to be. Do you know of anything like that around here?"

The young man thought for a few seconds and his expression brightened. "Yes, Llanrwst." He helped us locate it on the map. "It was once known for its harps."

"Thank you." My smile matched his.

"Want to fill me in on this?" Terry asked, after the constable had left.

"Remember, you pointed out the emphasis on 'harp' in PJ's words: 'I don't mean to *harp* on the subject.' It didn't occur to me then, but she and I were planning on doing some more sightseeing while we were here. She mentioned going to this place where they used to make harps or sold harps, or something. I thought there was a pamphlet about it, but so far… Geez, I wish I could remember what she said about it."

"Never mind, we have the name of a town which may or may not mean anything." She made a notation on her pad.

I went to the door and called to Constable Williams. "Is there something about a shaking bridge connected with Llanrwst?"

"Oh yes, Dr. Blair," he said, returning to our open doorway. "The Shaking Bridge dates back to 1636. Though it has been modified since then, it's still quite a landmark."

"Thank you, Constable. You know your local history well."

"It's a hobby, Dr. Blair. I hated history when I was in school, but I love it now."

"I think we have to have history of our own before we can appreciate history in general."

"Yes, quite so."

"I think we may have stumbled onto something," I told Terry, after the constable left.

She gave me a puzzled look. "What's with this Shaking Bridge?"

"PJ was shaking her hands. Maybe it was another way of identifying the town where she's being held."

Terry tapped her teeth with her pencil. "Hmm. Pretty clever. Okay, let's see what we have." She took one of the yellow pads and wrote Llanrwst, harps, and Shaking Bridge in capital letters. Underneath that, she wrote the names Sandy and Max, then on the next line, Peter Arnold. Next, she wrote Max with a big question mark. She slid the pad over to me. "This is like an algebra problem, and Max is the unknown quantity."

"Exactly. It's been obvious all along what PJ was telling us, but we didn't see it." I dropped my head into my hands and rubbed the bridge of my nose, feeling the onset of another headache. "Now if we can just find out how Max figures into the equation."

"Then we put the names together, come up with the right combination, and go to Llanrwst."

"But without knowing who Max is, we're up a creek."

I stared at the names on the yellow pad while Terry left to go to the bathroom. We were missing something obvious. I doodled around the neatly blocked name. "Wait a minute."

I was on the cell phone, holding for Frederick, when Terry returned.

Once I heard his voice, I couldn't contain my excitement. "We may have a line on something, but we don't have all the pieces yet."

"Quickly, what is it? I'm supposed to deliver the ransom in three hours."

"Believe me, I haven't forgotten." I felt that trickle of fear along my spine, and I glanced at the old clock ticking away on the wall. It wasn't reassuring. "I've just got one or two pieces left to fit into the puzzle."

"Kim, I need to know." His normally calm voice quivered, and I knew—we both knew—that we were reaching a point of no return.

"I'm not sure yet, but I'll explain as soon as we complete the puzzle."

"What can I do to help?"

"I think I've heard you speak of a Max something or other."

"Yes, Max Gibbs, my VP in charge of Grant Evaluations. Don't tell me he has something to do with Priscilla's kidnapping. I've known him forever."

"No, nothing like that. She mentioned Max as a clue, just like she mentioned Sandy."

I hung up after assuring Frederick I'd get back to him the moment we had something he could use.

I filled Terry in on the conversation. "I don't know why I didn't think of him before."

She added Max Gibbs to her list. "Okay," I said, pointing to her pad, "let's take those two names and mix them up a bit. Max Arnold is a possibility, or Peter Gibbs."

"Could be Arnold Gibbs," she added, "or Max Peter or Peters, Max Arnold, or Arnold Peters."

"Let's see if the constable can run down our combination of names and locate a match in Llanrwst."

Terry took a clean sheet of paper and wrote down the various combinations. While she took it out front to the constable, I poured us another cup of tea. I was getting as bad as the Brits with my tea fixes.

"He's calling Llanrwst as we speak," she said, when she returned. She proceeded to do some stretching exercises while I ran through the tape once more.

Less than fifteen minutes had passed before the constable came in. "There's a Peter Gibbs who owns a cottage on the outskirts of Llanrwst. He's not there now. It seems he spends most of his time in London. He has some very uninspiring government job."

Terry straightened up. "I wonder where he is right now. I'd sure like to talk to him."

"He's at work," the constable said. "I took the liberty of finding that out."

"Good man." She gave him an expansive smile.

"Please get him on the phone." I looked at Terry. "Do you want to talk to him, or shall I?"

"Be my guest."

Within moments, I was talking to Mr. Peter Gibbs of Llanrwst. "No," he told me in clipped English accents, "I haven't been back to the cottage for three months. I have a contract here, and it doesn't run out until the end of the month."

"We have reason to believe that criminals are keeping a woman hostage in your cottage."

"My God!"

"Who else has a key?"

"No one. I sometimes hire a cleaning service, but I was called back here so suddenly that I didn't have time. I have the only keys here with me."

"And your call back to London was legitimate?"

"Why yes. Although, come to think of it, my boss seemed surprised to see me so soon. I thought it a bit strange, because he was the one who must have issued the call back. I put it down to his being preoccupied with a heavy schedule."

I wondered if his call back to work had been part of an elaborate setup.

After gaining as much information as I could from Peter Gibbs, I told him that the police would be in touch after they had investigated the situation. Then, I hung up.

I looked from Terry to the constable. "We have permission to search his property, breaking in if necessary."

"I'll get right on it," the constable said. He hastened out of the room.

"Good." Terry gathered her gear.

"He told me his place was well-concealed behind a grove of large trees. He likes his privacy."

"So would the kidnappers, I'll wager."

Her words sent a shiver down my spine.

"I'm going to Llanrwst with the police," I said.

Terry faced me, clutching her jacket and supplies. "Okay, then. I'm with you. Let's do it."

I sat down for a minute, going over all of this in my mind.

"Now who's wasting time? What's the matter, Kim?"

I looked at my watch. "We have less than three hours to coordinate this rescue before the ransom deadline."

"Okay then. All the more reason to get going."

"You don't understand." I was sure she could hear the panic in my voice. "This is our one and only chance to save PJ. What if I've figured it wrong? What if we're on the wrong track?"

Chapter 20

I finished off fifty crunches and thirty push-ups while waiting for my captors to escort me upstairs. Sitting on the lumpy cot, my body coated with a light sweat, I longed for a fragrant bath and my favorite back-scrubber.

Would I ever see Kimmy again? I shivered and wiped my eyes with my shirtsleeve. Sweat? Tears? Probably a mixture of both. The exercise made my body feel stronger, but there was little I could do for my spirit.

This was the day of the ransom pickup. Time was running out. What if this escape plan of mine didn't work? I was way out of my depth here. Had I considered all possible angles, covered all the things that could go wrong?

I felt heat across my chest. My heartbeat quickened.

Stop it, I told myself. This was no way for an Amazon to think. An Amazon was fearless. And that was precisely why I was no Amazon. I was only a hair's breadth away from a panic attack right that moment.

I looked around the room for a trace of my late-night visitor, then stood up and practiced some kickboxing moves. Shit. I was so rusty.

The butterflies in my stomach were on an acid trip. It didn't help that I was jumping around the room so much.

My roundhouse kick flew too close to the bookshelf and made it wobble.

"Oops! Sorry about that, Brownie—and family." I groaned. Now I was talking to a mouse and his offspring. At this rate, I'd be ready for the loony bin before lunch.

I sat back down on the cot and looked at my watch. My bladder was sending me faint alarm warnings. "Damn it. On top of everything else, guys, you're late this morning."

The door rattled and I caught a glimpse of Brownie scooting out of his hole in the corner, coming to mooch some food from me at the worst possible time.

Garlic Breath saw me looking toward the bookcase. "Something interesting going on over there, Blondie?"

I stood up to face him and made a shooing motion to Brownie behind my back. "Nothing's going on, except you're late and I need to get to the bathroom."

"Ain't that a shame." His false sympathy and dogged interest in what was happening behind me heightened my anxiety. "I think I need to see what's so fascinating about that bookcase."

He tried to go around me, but I stepped into his path. Brownie must have sensed danger. I could hear his toenails scratching across the floor, making a noisy getaway. Garlic Breath grabbed my shoulders and pushed me aside. "There's something over there."

"It's nothing. Really." I shoved against his chest, trying to delay his advance.

"The hell it is."

We wrestled for a second or two more. "Blondie, this is a cute little dance you're doing with me."

"I'm not dancing with you, damn it, I need to go upstairs."

"Shit! It's a rat. Right down in the corner there."

"No, idiot, it's not a rat." I continued to push him, but he backed away and his hand moved quickly to his belt. The action was so fast that all I saw was the flash of a shiny blade flying through the air. I heard a thud, a sickening squeak, and a thrashing of toenails against the baseboard.

Garlic Breath was gleeful. "Gotcha, you little rat."

I tried to go to Brownie's aid, but Garlic Breath snagged my T-shirt collar and dragged me back. "Don't go near it, bitch. I'm saving you from that filthy animal."

"Let me go!" I pushed at him, but he locked his arms around me, and his chest heaved with mocking laughter.

I glanced at the far wall, hoping against hope that Brownie had somehow escaped this brutal assault, but the knife had found its target. The tiny body was pinned to the baseboard. Brownie's legs twitched weakly and then stilled.

Tears slid down my cheeks. It was all my fault. I tamed him, taught him that he was safe with me, and now he was dead.

A sob caught in my throat.

Garlic Breath released me in disgust. "I can't believe you're crying over a lousy rat."

"He was a mouse, an innocent little mouse." I swiped at my eyes. "The only rat in this room is you."

"Whatever. Come on, it's time for breakfast."

I straightened my shoulders and glared at him. "Why'd you have to go and do that? He wasn't hurting anything."

"Ah, shut up. Turn around and put your hands behind your back."

"You're a bastard and a bully," I said, turning around as instructed.

"Yeah, that's what makes me so irresistible." He slipped a pair of handcuffs on my wrists and squeezed them shut before giving my butt a squeeze. "Right, cutie?"

Woodsy appeared in the doorway. "What's taking so long?" He looked at his partner and then at me. "Any trouble? I thought I heard a noise."

Garlic Breath twirled me around and cupped my chin in his meaty hand. "We'll attach your ankle chains when we get upstairs." He turned to Woodsy and gave a hearty laugh. "I just did a little pest control. See over there?" He pointed to the far wall. "Our prisoner was threatened by a filthy rat."

Woodsy spotted Brownie's body and made a noise under his ski mask. I couldn't tell if it was sympathetic or congratulatory. It didn't matter, anyway. Brownie was dead and would never again scamper across the blanket to pick up crumbs of bread and cheese from my fingers or cheer me with his bewhiskered expressions.

"For some reason, she isn't very grateful about it, though."

Garlic Breath tried to hug me, but I stepped away and glared at both of them. "Can we get this show on the road? I assume you want something cooked for your breakfast."

"Let's go." Garlic Breath gave Woodsy a soft punch on the shoulder. "I guess the rat's too small to fry up."

Woodsy groaned. "Come on, you've done enough damage down here." He started to guide me up the stairs to the bathroom.

"Shit, I almost forgot to get my knife back." Garlic Breath tossed the handcuff keys to Woodsy and retreated to my room. "Go on ahead. I'll catch up with you in a second."

We climbed the stairs in silence.

I think it was then that I realized how tenuous my existence really was. I had lost my mother when I was young, and while I was devastated by the loss, I hadn't given a lot of thought to my own death. We can be here one day and then, the next day, the next hour, be gone forever. Brownie had taught me something about the fragile nature of life, both human and animal.

Woodsy opened the bathroom door, checked the interior, and unlocked my handcuffs. "Watch yourself around him," he said.

"Thanks for the warning."

He closed the door behind me. Garlic Breath must have climbed the stairs, because as I hastened to empty my bladder and wash up, I could hear their voices.

The discussion grew louder, more strident. This was new. What could they be arguing about? Curious, I edged to the door and put my ear against it.

"—not what I signed on for, Charlie. It's murder, plain and simple."

"Who asked for your opinion? Shut up, asshole."

"It's not necessary, that's all."

"They're paying us to carry out orders. It's as simple as that. You're too damn soft on her anyway."

Her? Were they talking about me?

"I'm only saying—"

"Say all you want, Bert, but when the boss wants her dead, we'll do it."

Christ. The butterflies were back on their acid trip.

"I'm just saying she doesn't have to die. We've kept the masks on. She can't identify us."

"It doesn't matter. She's a liability. If you haven't got the guts, I'll have to do it. But I'll have a little fun with her first."

"Shit, Charlie, your idea of fun is—"

There was a loud snort, and their voices dropped.

Jesus. I could imagine. My mouth went dry. My heartbeat drummed in my ears. This was the plan all along. Collect the ransom and eliminate the witness. My mind refused to consider the in-between part.

After a moment, their voices rose again.

"Shit, I can't help it if I get urges. You can see she's got a good body."

"You should know, you've felt it enough."

"You're welcome to party along with us, Bert."

"I'm just saying we could do it another way, is all. She doesn't have to die." Woodsy sounded almost as sick about the situation as I was.

"Come on, it'll be fun. You, me, and her. If the boss wants a piece of the action, the more the merrier. And then, who cares? She'll be out of our hair forever."

His wicked laugh caused a revolution in my stomach. I rushed to the toilet and vomited. With shaky hands, I splashed water into my mouth and over my face, telling myself to take deep breaths. At least the butterflies were gone. I had probably flushed them all away.

How would an Amazon get herself out of this situation? I looked around the bathroom. Rape and murder were on the agenda, and no armed, leather-clad Amazons were materializing to give me a hand.

Thanks a bunch, ladies.

Okay, there was still the escape plan. Put the Ambien in their food. I'd start with breakfast and keep it going with each meal.

* * *

It was hard to tell whether or not the plan was working. Aside from a few yawns over the scrambled eggs, there was little evidence that the men were weakening enough to permit my escape. I spent the rest of the morning pacing my room, reading and thinking, examining the rest of my powdered sedative, gathering up my meager belongings—just in case—and listening for Designer Suit's return.

* * *

Bert brought me upstairs for supper. I appreciated his verbal attempts to dissuade Charlie from raping and killing me once the ransom had been paid, but I knew I couldn't count on his physical support when the time came. Charlie was as big as he was and twice as mean. He wouldn't hesitate to use force if his plans were challenged, and he'd already demonstrated his prowess with a knife. Designer Suit controlled his men when he was around, but soon Charlie would have complete freedom to deal with me in his own delightful way.

I shuddered. I knew I couldn't count on anyone but myself when the time came.

I took mugs and supplies from the cupboard and put the kettle on to boil. After I set the table, I stared out the kitchen window into the evening shadows. The yard was small, with lots of tall trees and thick hedges. I could detect the remains of a once cheerful garden, its few remaining flowers now brutalized by a horde of bullying weeds.

Just like Brownie and me. We were the flowers in that pitiful garden, and these guys were the weeds. I sighed. We probably never had a chance.

A lump of self-pity formed in my throat.

Charlie entered the kitchen, glancing around to see if we were alone. He had strapped a gun to his belt along with his knife and a set of handcuffs. Though I could hear Bert stumbling around in the next room, I didn't want to be alone with Charlie. Nervous sweat dampened my neck and underarms.

"Come on, Blondie." He gave my butt a rub and slipped his arm around my shoulders. "Are you going to fix us something to eat or stand around admiring the scenery?"

Something snapped inside me, and along with fear, I felt a surge of anger. It was all I could do to keep from telling him what he could do with his filthy paws. He was hungry. I'd give him something with a strong dose of Ambien.

I forced myself to smile at him. "How about tomato soup and grilled cheese sandwiches?"

He grunted his approval and slid his arm down off my shoulder toward my breasts. I shuffled away from him, opened the cupboard, and searched for bowls, spoons, and plates. "If you don't have anything else to do, you can set the table."

Charlie laughed. "Oh, I can think of lots of things to do."

"I'll help you, miss." Bert crossed to my side and took the plates and bowls. At my suggestion, Charlie found utensils for us in the drawers. I started the soup and grilled the sandwiches, sprinkling Ambien in small pinches whenever the men weren't watching me. Most of it went into the soup.

"Blondie, hold it right there."

Charlie must have seen me sprinkling the last of the Ambien.

My heart stopped.

"What's that?"

I struggled to speak over the dryness in my throat. "What's what?"

He walked over to me and stared into the pot. Ambien residue still floated on the surface of the soup. "What's that stuff you put in there?"

I made a pretense of looking where he was pointing, my brain working frantically to come up with a plausible response. "Oh, that. It's just a little garlic powder to spice up the soup. It's so bland without something to enhance the flavor."

He seemed surprised. "How'd you know I like garlic?"

I smiled. "Oh, just a guess." That, and the fact that he reeked of it. He probably used garlic-flavored toothpaste. "Anyway, I think it's ready. Let's sit down and eat."

They helped me put things on the table, and then Bert unhooked one ankle chain and attached it to the table leg. The men made idle conversation as we ate. I poked at my sandwich, never chewing much of it, concentrating on my tea, the one thing I hadn't doctored.

Bert tried to hold up his end of the discussion, but started rubbing his eyes. He propped his head up with both hands.

Oh, shit! It was working, but on the one guy who might help me.

By the time we finished the meal, Bert's head was resting on his folded arms.

Charlie blinked and rubbed his face. "Geez, my eyes feel itchy." He stifled a yawn and rose on unsteady legs.

Noticing Bert's fatigue, he shook his head. "Looks like it's just you and me, Blondie. Let's go downstairs and get you settled." He took his gun and placed it in one of the kitchen drawers. "Wouldn't want this to go off accidentally."

He bent to free my ankle from the table leg. I started to stand, but he grabbed my right wrist and slapped one end of his handcuffs over it, locking the other end onto his own wrist.

A spasm of fear shot through me. "What are you doing?"

He touched the side of my face with his free hand. I could see his mouth widen behind the hole in his mask, exposing big, uneven teeth, his attempt at a seductive smile. "I've got a little party planned just for the two of us."

My heart thrummed in my ears. "Shouldn't I finish the dishes first and put away the leftovers?"

"That can wait. This can't," he said, patting his crotch. He tugged me along toward the stairwell.

I fought him every step of the way, squirming and dragging my feet, but he was too powerful. By the time we entered the basement room, we were both sweating.

He leaned me against the door and held both my hands in his handcuffed one long enough to turn the lock.

"Gotta have some privacy for this little party." His breath was hot against my cheek, and the scent of garlic tickled my nose. "Now, cutie, we can do it easy or we can do it hard. It's your choice."

"I'd sooner not do it at all."

He laughed and wrestled us both over to the cot. "Oh, that's not an option. You're going to do it, all right." He climbed on top of me and peeled off his ski mask.

"Now, isn't this more comfortable?"

"For you maybe. Your breath makes me want to puke." I turned my head to the side and gagged.

"You know, Blondie, you're a feisty little bitch. I think I'm going to enjoy this."

The mask was off. He didn't care if I could identify him because I wasn't getting out of here alive.

With that ghastly thought ringing in my ears, I memorized every feature of his face, from the blue eyes, brown hair, and thin nose down to the small mole right above his lip, just in case I survived.

I bucked and twisted, breathing hard in an effort to fight him off. He used his free hand to unbuckle his belt and unzip his pants.

"Come on, you'll enjoy it more if you relax and stop struggling."

I continued to thrash and wriggle beneath him, growing more desperate with each passing minute.

Damn it! Why wasn't the Ambien working?

Whenever he removed his free hand to tug at his pants, I tried to roll away from him. He'd stop and grab my free hand, and we'd stare at each other, sweating and writhing.

"Admit it, Blondie, I turn you on. Don't I?"

"You're a pig."

He growled. "Aw, now you hurt my feelings. I was only trying to give you a little present." His pants were low enough to reveal patterned boxer shorts. I felt a hard lump grind into my abdomen.

I smirked at him. "Little being the operative word."

Charlie raised his free hand and slapped me across the mouth. I blinked back tears and choked on bloody saliva.

"You're going to pay for that, bitch." He grabbed at the neckline of my T-shirt and ripped it down the middle.

While his hand was otherwise occupied, I pushed against him with all of my remaining strength and managed to slide to one side. Anger replaced my fear. "Get off me, you sick pig."

"Oh, you like to play rough, huh?" His movements were slowing, fumbling, but his attitude remained belligerent. He made a clumsy swipe at my breasts, trying to unhook my bra, but his finger caught in the gap between the cups and slipped out. "Little bitch. I'll give you more than you bargained for."

"The hell you will." I brought my knee up hard and connected with his thinly covered "little present."

"Aghhhh!"

"That's for Brownie, you bastard."

His free hand cradled his injured anatomy. I used the heel of my unrestrained hand to smash the underside of his chin and nose. This new wave of pain brought him right off the bed, yanking both of us to the floor. He crawled to his knees but got tangled in his pants and fell flat. I pounced on his back, struggling with him until he stopped whimpering and fell asleep.

My handcuffed wrist throbbed from the lurch off the bed, but I managed to ignore the pain long enough to locate the key in his pocket. I freed myself and slipped the empty cuff around Charlie's other wrist. Feeling a lot braver now that he was restrained, I couldn't resist patting him on the cheek. "I know you like your women feisty, but if that's your idea of foreplay, forget it."

I collected the wool shirt and buttoned it over my shredded T-shirt.

Bert was asleep at the table when I tiptoed by the kitchen. I hadn't been able to find my shoes, so I had to watch where I stepped. The back door opened silently. I held my breath and slipped outside. It was late, nearly dark. The yard was a complex maze of shadows. A path, overgrown with weeds and wild flowers, led to a stone wall near some shrubs and old fir trees.

I took several deep breaths of clear, clean air. Freedom!

Which way should I go? I flipped a mental coin and chose the right side path. I had taken three or four steps, when a strong arm wrapped around my waist and a hand clamped across my mouth. I bit down on a finger and encountered metal. The gold pinkie ring nearly cracked my tooth.

"Ouch! How did you get loose?" Designer Suit's breath tickled my ear.

I stomped down on his instep. He hopped a bit, but hung on to me. In frustration, I jabbed his ribs with my elbows and kicked back at his shins.

"Shit!" he said. "Damn it. I'm in no mood for this."

We wrestled together in sweaty frustration. "First the goddamned ransom never got transferred, and now this."

Panting, I strained to free myself from his determined embrace. I managed to knee him in the groin but not hard enough to incapacitate him.

His grip loosened, and he let go with a stream of curses that would make a sailor proud. I pulled away from him and ran, all the while fearing the bite of his gleaming switchblade in my back. There was a loud noise from somewhere in front of the cottage. It sounded like a bullhorn. I took a quick glance back and saw for just an instant that Designer Suit had pulled something from under his jacket and was pointing it in my direction.

The stone wall was right in front of me. I leaped to the top, heard a loud crack, and felt a sharp pain. I landed on the other side, took a few more staggering steps and noticed a pond below me. The ground was spongy. My legs wouldn't work properly. Was I faltering, or was it the sucking motion of the boggy terrain? The sky and ground began to spin. My escape plan had failed.

I tumbled face-first into a genuine Welsh bog.

Chapter 21

I called Frederick and told him about our interpretation of the tape and of our plan to go to Llanwrst. He put me on hold.

"I'm having the jet readied now," he said, when he came back on the line. "I'll fly into Caernarfon and hire a helicopter from there." I pictured him in his London headquarters, arranging everything with masterful efficiency.

"How long will that take? We're so close to the deadline."

"I know. I'm as concerned as you are, but arrangements are going on as we speak. I'll be in Llanwrst when you arrive, or soon after."

"What about Geoff and Trevor? Should I contact them?"

"I'll let them know what's going on," he said. "They reported to me that they've been cooperating with the authorities, but this is past the bodyguard stage. Let the police see to it."

Tears welled up in my eyes. "I need you, Frederick. I don't know how I'll handle it if things go wrong."

"I know, and just in case, the ransom is ready for transfer to a Swiss Bank account at a moment's notice."

I watched the constables collect their equipment while they talked in calm, confident tones. Terry glanced in my direction, but I turned away from her and partially covered the telephone receiver. My hands shook. "What if we're wrong? Everything is a matter of interpretation, and that's far from an exact science."

"Then we will have done all we can. But keep the faith, my dear. There's still time, I think, to pay the ransom."

I knew he was struggling, too; his faith was cracking and he wasn't that sure about the ransom. I could hear doubt in his voice. He was trying to put up a brave front for me.

"I feel so helpless," I said. "I've never been this afraid of anything before." I heard someone on the other end speak to him.

"I have to go now," he said. "I'll call the police and make sure they're well-prepared for any eventuality."

"I'm sure they are, Frederick. They seem very efficient."

I was a complete mess, but trying to be positive for him. It didn't matter though. He hadn't heard, having hung up without as much as a goodbye. That frightened me more than anything. Damn it, if Frederick lost hope, who would keep me from losing mine?

I couldn't think that way. I mustn't give up. Not now. I had to have faith in my powers of deduction and sense that I was on the right track. I was feeling PJ's influence. Call it ESP, but I knew that she was with me on this.

Moments later, I received a call from another police squad. This was a team from Aberystwyth, headed by Detective Chief Inspector Doreen Edwards. Her assistant, our old friend Sergeant Blodwyn Jones, would stop to pick Terry and me up on the way.

* * *

Two police cars pulled up. A boyish-looking constable was at the wheel of the leading car, with DCI Edwards in the passenger seat and Sergeant Jones in the back. In profile, Edwards resembled a spinster schoolteacher I once had. That thought didn't reassure me. Terry climbed into the second vehicle, which Edwards said held a constable and two Emergency Medical Technicians. I wasn't comforted by Terry's presence, but at least she wasn't riding in the same car with us.

I slid into the backseat next to Sergeant Jones. Pup lay at my feet, leaving me little wriggle room.

"Is this all?" I asked the stern-faced Chief Inspector.

"All from our jurisdiction," she said, giving me a look that would peel paint.

"We'll be met by a unit from the North Wales Police," Sergeant Jones said. "We're working together on this one."

It made me feel better to know that we would have reinforcements.

My mind filled with unsettling thoughts about PJ's situation. Sergeant Jones covered my hand with hers. "Don't worry, we'll find her."

"I want to believe that we're on the right track, but this is all guesswork. What if we're wrong?"

"You can't think that way. Your friend gave some good clues on the tape. She knew you could decipher them because you know her better than anyone else does."

I swallowed the lump in my throat and swiped at my eyes. "I just can't go on much longer knowing that PJ is in the hands of those creatures."

"For what it's worth," the sergeant said, her voice dropping to a whisper, "I understand the depth of your concern. I really do."

"Thank you," I said automatically, but when I looked into the sergeant's eyes, it was clear that she was sharing more than what her words alone conveyed.

I managed a smile. "It's good to know that someone here understands the bigger picture. I don't feel so alone with someone standing by, someone to lean on. Just in case."

She gripped my hand. "Stop torturing yourself like this. Think positively."

Sergeant Jones was the only person besides Frederick who understood my anguish and knew the depths of my fear for PJ's safety.

I stared out of the window into the dark night. It rained intermittently, and the road was a black ribbon in front of us. The undulations in the tarmac were clearly visible in our headlights.

Fieldstone walls on either side of the road threatened to close in on us. Despite the conditions, the police vehicles made good time.

I mentally urged PJ to hold on; the troops were coming. A whole damn convoy was converging from the south and from the north, just to get her out. In other circumstances, she'd find the image amusing. I was too worried to see anything humorous about it.

The red and blue flashing lights cast an unnatural glow on our immediate surroundings. I took a deep breath. Why did I feel like we were entering the gates of hell?

* * *

As we closed in on our destination, Edwards ordered the police to cut their lights and separate, so the vehicles wouldn't look so conspicuous. When we arrived at the cottage, I could see that Peter Gibbs really did value his privacy. The shrubbery, and a tall, thick hedgerow between the house and the road, provided ample concealment for a surprise invasion.

An unmarked van was waiting when we arrived. Two plainclothes officers and six armed, uniformed officers got out of it to meet with us.

One of the plainclothes officers, whom Sergeant Jones identified as another chief inspector, huddled with DCI Edwards. Their voices were quiet, but much arm and hand action animated their conversation as they planned their strategy.

Everything moved in slow motion—except the clock, which continued to tick in real time. I could hear it inside my skull. I closed my eyes and prayed that we were in the right place and not too late.

Sergeant Jones put her arm around my shoulder and whispered close to my ear. "I wish I could assure you that everything will be okay. You know I can't do that. I can tell you, however, that I have a good feeling about it."

"Thank you for your honesty and your encouragement."

She took out her sidearm and checked the load. "I always hope I won't have to use this, but one never knows."

"That's right. Your police don't normally carry guns."

"I'm afraid terrorists and drug trafficking have made our lives a lot more dangerous these days. We use firearms when the occasion calls for them."

I thought about PJ being caught in crossfire between the kidnappers and the police, and I shuddered. "Have you ever had to use it to kill?"

The sergeant looked at me for a moment before nodding.

The reality shocked me. "It's almost dark. What if you have to shoot? She's so short, you might not see her."

"Try not to worry. We only use that kind of force as a last resort."

DCI Edwards also had a sidearm, as did the driver. Every member of the contingent from the North Wales jurisdiction was armed, two with automatic weapons.

How many people were in the house? The bicycling witnesses saw only two men. There were probably more.

"We'll resort to heavier weapons only if something goes awfully wrong," Sergeant Jones said, sliding out of the car.

My head already ached with tension; I didn't want to think anymore about anything going wrong.

I got out with Pup and waited in silence while the detectives and constables looked the situation over and discussed strategy.

Again, everything moved with agonizing slowness except my watch. I wanted to spur them into action, urge them to hurry. Didn't they know that time was running out?

I held Pup on a short leash. "No," I said firmly, but quietly, when he started whining. I suspected that with his highly developed wolf intuition, he sensed that PJ was close by, and I was hard-pressed to hold him. I knelt beside him, and he looked at me with his big yellow, all-knowing eyes. *You can feel her presence, can't you?*

I looked around for Frederick, but didn't see him anywhere.

* * *

There was a flurry of activity, and someone announced over a bullhorn that the house was surrounded.

Nanoseconds later, the sound of a single shot pierced the night. "Oh, shit!" I screamed.

Then a searchlight revealed a man standing in front of the house, holding a handgun. He fired several shots, then only clicks could be heard. One officer was hit, but the other bullets went wild. The rescue team surrounded the shooter. They disarmed and cuffed him and sat him near a tree under guard.

There didn't appear to be any movement in the house. Three officers, including Sergeant Jones, drew their weapons and stormed in. Moments later, they came out dragging two handcuffed men, neither of whom showed any resistance. They were deposited next to the first shooter, where they slumped to the ground.

The sergeant reported to DCI Edwards then turned to me. "She's not inside. We're going to question these three while the others do a more thorough search of the house and grounds."

My heart sunk into my shoes. If she wasn't here, then where was she? Unless she was already… I didn't want to think about that possibility.

Questioning the men revealed nothing. The first one arrested snarled something about the bitch not living to tell about it.

Hot tears bubbled from my eyes.

I heard a helicopter flying in circles overhead. I knew it had to be Frederick, and was relieved to know that he was here. Whatever happened now, we would go through it together. The pilot aimed a bright shadowless spotlight into the yard, and then around the area, looking—I presumed—for a place to land. An open field across the road provided space away from the trees.

Pup was pulling at his leash and whimpering. "No," I said, giving it a tug. "You've got to sit still." With an unexpected lurch, that knocked me off my feet and freed him, he took off. I thought he was going to tear the prisoners apart, but he bypassed them without missing a stride and jumped the stone wall.

"He's onto something!" I yelled, following as fast as I could, vaguely aware of Terry and Sergeant Jones joining the chase. When I came to the wall, I bounded over it in a manner I wouldn't have thought possible, had I been in a rational frame of mind.

The moon, reaching peak fullness, was hidden behind the clouds. I couldn't see much in the dark without a flashlight. Somewhere ahead of me, Pup whimpered.

"I'm coming!" I cried. My side ached, and I was breathing in great gulps of air.

The ground was spongy; with each step, I sank up to my ankles. I pitched forward twice, my arms sinking almost to the elbows in mud. The sergeant caught up to me and shone her powerful flashlight into the darkness. "Over there," she said, taking off at a stumbling run. Terry and I followed as quickly as we could over the soft, uneven ground. We caught up with Sergeant Jones, who was in mud up to her knees, helping Pup drag what appeared to be a lifeless body from the murky water. We hurried to lend a hand.

It was PJ. My heart stopped. All but blinded by tears, I fell on my knees beside her. With shaking hands, I wiped the muck from her face, my mind blank, while the sergeant checked for a pulse.

"She's alive," she said, "but her pulse is thready and she isn't breathing."

For a moment I couldn't comprehend what she was saying, and then it came to me. PJ was alive! My mind started working again. "I know rescue breathing techniques."

"Good, then you can help."

With Terry's assistance, we started to roll my partner onto her back.

"Wait!" Sergeant Jones's command stopped us. "Bloody hell. She's been shot in the shoulder." She indicated a wound that was barely visible through all the mud.

I quickly ripped a strip off my shirt and handed it to the sergeant who pressed it against the wound. "Dr. Simms, hold this, will you. Keep the pressure on while we get her onto her back. We need to get her breathing."

Terry looked like she would just as soon be somewhere else.

Sergeant Jones fumed. "Where are those medical blokes?"

We eased PJ onto her back while Terry held the makeshift pressure pad in place.

My actions were robotic. I felt empty-headed, unable to understand the most basic instructions.

"Come on, Kim, don't lapse out on me now." The sergeant's command galvanized me into action. I whipped off my cardigan and covered PJ with it. To help guard against shock, I thought, though I wasn't sure it would help a whole lot.

I wiped PJ's lips and cleaned the inside of her mouth with my fingers.

Sergeant Jones nodded for me to begin.

I moved PJ's head back, tilted her chin upwards, pinched her nose shut, and breathed two quick breaths into her mouth. Her lips had never felt so cold.

Come on, sweetheart. We had to get oxygen into her lungs.

The sergeant put her ear against PJ's chest and felt her neck for a pulse while I breathed into her mouth, one breath every five seconds, just enough to raise her chest, but not to force air into her stomach. PJ made a choking noise. We turned her onto her side, and she spewed out a stream of mucky water.

Just then, the two medical technicians, weighted down with equipment, slogged through the ankle deep mud to join us.

I heard the sergeant mutter under her breath, "And about bloody time, too."

They paid no attention, just pushed us out of the way and started working on PJ.

Now that I was no longer tending to PJ, the horror of what had happened hit me. My knees buckled, but the sergeant's firm grip kept me from sliding to the ground.

I felt Frederick's strong arms engulf me. "She's in good hands now," he said, hugging me despite the slime that coated much of my body. "She'll make it. She's a fighter."

"I know, I know," I muttered to myself and anyone else listening. "She's as stubborn as they come." I giggled with relief. "I'm sorry to be getting all this mud on you."

"Think nothing of it."

In my peripheral vision, I thought I saw an Amazon, a fully armed warrior, saluting me with her sword. "Marna, is that you?"

"What's that?"

"Oh, nothing. I was just thanking the Goddess for her intervention."

"While you're at it, thank her for me, too," Frederick said.

I rested my head against his chest. "I will," I whispered. "I will."

The medical helicopter arrived in less than five minutes, but every second seemed like an hour. It landed next to Frederick's craft, and two more flight medics joined ours. They discussed PJ's situation, then all four prepared her for flight.

Frederick moved away to speak with the pilot. I stayed close to where they were attending to PJ and hugged the mud-covered Pup. If it hadn't been for him—well, I didn't want to think about how different the ending could have been. I kissed his muddied muzzle. "Another couple of minutes, Pup." He whined as though he understood. Perhaps he did, on some level.

A familiar voice broke into my thoughts. Terry had spotted Frederick walking back toward me and sidled over to intercept him. I focused my attention on what was happening to PJ, but I couldn't help overhearing their conversation.

"It looks like we arrived in the nick of time," he said. "Thank God for that. I don't know what I would have done if I had lost her now."

"I'm relieved," Terry said, "that things turned out so well." I turned slightly, just in time to catch her extending her hand. "It's been a pleasure working with you, Mr. Curtis. Don't hesitate to call on me again."

"I owe you a debt of gratitude. You and Kim cracked this case, not the police. They were just backup." He looked toward his daughter, now strapped onto a stretcher and ready for transport. "She and Kim are my family. They're all I have."

"You don't seem bothered by their relationship."

I turned to find her watching me, a smirk on her face. What a bitch. She was always looking for an opening, an opportunity to make trouble. She didn't realize that Frederick knew about PJ and me being partners, and she wanted to be the one to break the news. The joke was on her.

Frederick didn't notice us glaring at each other. "Why would it?"

"Oh, I don't know. Some people—please don't misunderstand." Terry was speaking in that sweet, cloying voice she used when she was up to something. "I'm not being derogatory. I'm just curious, wondering about a parent's take on the situation."

It was hard for me not to jump up and slap her silly.

"Kim has been good for Priscilla," he said. "She's part of the family." He looked again at his daughter, and his expression grew wistful. "She used to be a handful, especially when she was younger, but she's settled down since she's been with Kim. She's in good hands. I worry a lot less about her these days. Besides, this way I get two archaeologists for the price of one." His little joke was lost on Terry.

The medical team carried PJ across the road with Frederick, Pup, and me following close behind.

"One of the policemen was shot," I said. "Is he all right?"

"He's was just winged. He'll be fine."

"I'm glad to hear that, and I know PJ will be glad, too." They loaded her into the waiting helicopter.

Frederick called out to her, saying he loved her.

I doubt she heard him above all the talking and the idling of the rotor blades. I wasn't sure if she was conscious.

Frederick dipped his head and spoke into my ear. "I've made arrangements for you to fly with her."

"What about you?"

"Only one of us can go, and she'll need you to be there more than her crabby old man."

Again, I was close to tears. "Thank you."

He hugged me. "Besides, I have plenty to do here. You just tell that little girl of mine that I'll see her later, when I'm sure her kidnappers are locked up tight."

I left Pup with him and climbed into the helicopter.

When I reached for PJ's hand, it was warmer than it had been. She didn't open her eyes, but managed to squeeze my fingers. She knew I was there, and that was comforting for both of us. I sat quietly beside the medic as he dressed her wound, administered oxygen, checked the IV, and kept tabs on her vitals. The rotor revved, and the helicopter tugged against gravity. With a roar, it finally lifted into the air. Looking down at the cottage, I could see that a small crowd had gathered. This was likely the most excitement the villagers had experienced in many years.

We banked into a turn, and my eyes darted toward PJ. The mixture of wet soil and vegetation on her body and clothes produced a pungent, disgusting odor inside the aircraft. Every inch of her clothing was mud-caked, torn, and bloody. Beneath the oxygen mask, her face was pale, bruised, and etched in grime. Her beautiful blonde hair was now black and matted with goo, but to me, she was the most perfect creature on earth and more beautiful than ever.

Chapter 22

I was running along a path, pursued by hounds that raced ahead of a stranger who was dressed all in black and riding a pure white stallion. The hounds surrounded me, yelping and jumping up on my flowing gown. I was irritated because the fabric was thin and delicate, and the animals left muddy paw prints all over me.

The horseman caught up to us and dismounted with a flourish. His armor gleamed in the sunlight, and his long sword clanked against his powerful thigh as he approached me. When he flipped up his visor, I could see merriment in his eyes.

"Well now," he said. "What brings a beautiful maiden out here in the wilds, so far away from hearth and home?"

I tried to speak, but no words came out of my mouth. It was important that I let him know that I wasn't afraid of him or his rowdy hounds. The more I tried to talk, the more the animals barked and snarled. One darted behind my legs and tripped me. Astonished at the pain, I cried out and fell to the ground, rolling all the way into a sacred well. I was finally able to speak, and my futile, belated shouts echoed against the surrounding stone walls.

There was someone else in the well. A man, dressed in a tunic of animal skins and wearing a braided gold torque around his neck, splashed about, treading water. His hair was long and flowing, his beard and mustache thick and brown. A short-handled axe was still clutched in his hand, and the tip of a sword handle was visible at his hip. I wondered why he didn't drop the weapons; it would make him more buoyant in the water.

I started to explain that to him, but he brandished the axe and shouted something at me. The language was ancient, though I interpreted what he had said into modern Welsh. "Cymru am Byth!" Wales Forever! Before I could respond, he spoke again in that ancient tongue, and again I understood his warning. "Fair maiden, you must leave. Swim to your knight and escape. The druids need a pure soul to sacrifice, and if you tarry, I fear for your life."

I did my best to assure him that I wasn't anyone's fair maiden or any druid's sacrifice, and I definitely wasn't a pure soul. He muttered something else and dropped from sight.

I bobbed around in water up to my shoulders, searching the moss-covered walls for some sort of vine to climb up or some uneven stones that my fingers could grasp. There was nothing obvious.

With a mighty roar, the Celtic warrior surfaced again. Before my astonished eyes, he changed into a wolf. Shit. I'd never believed in this shape-shifting business, but I'd just seen it happen. One second he was a solid Celtic chieftain, the next he was a powerful, dark wolf.

I struggled to swim away from the wolf, but he opened his jaws and sank his yellowed teeth into my shoulder. My body stiffened in pain, and my arms stopped thrashing. The wolf and I slid under the water. I opened my mouth to scream, but only bubbles and gurgling sounds came out.

I made one last effort to rid myself of the wolf, the pain, and the cold, dark water. The well had turned into a bog, so I forced my head to the surface and gasped for air. Muffled voices reached me, but I couldn't understand the words. I sensed that the voices were directed at me, though. One voice sounded particularly familiar.

I knew that voice. A woman. One who meant a great deal to me. Kim! It was Kim, and she was upset.

I wanted to tell her not to worry. I was here. Well, I was somewhere. I had to open my eyes and talk to her.

I concentrated on that not so simple task, and found that I lay in a bright yellow room, covered by starched white sheets, naked except for one of those skimpy cotton gowns. IV tubes secured with adhesive tape poked out of various orifices, hooking me up to a monitor and some kind of fluid drip. I was tucked into a huge, adjustable bed, with my left arm in a sling and my left shoulder swathed in bandages. Kim sat in a chair to my right, but her upper body was propped against the edge of my bed and her chin rested on my leg. Her eyes were closed, but her lips were moving.

Jesus, she looked exhausted. Poor thing. I couldn't tell whether she was awake or talking in her sleep. She hadn't done that since the Amazons visited her in Arizona, or she them. I never knew for sure how that happened.

"Please," she murmured, giving the sheet over my thigh a squeeze.

"Ow!"

Her head flew up and her eyes widened. "PJ! Oh, God. PJ." Tears dribbled down her cheeks, startling me. Kim didn't cry—at least, not often.

"Hey," I said, keeping my voice low. "It's okay. Really, it's okay."

She wiped her eyes and gave me the most radiant smile. "You're awake. Finally."

"Come here." There was a tube attached to my right arm, but I managed to tug at her shirt, pulling her closer to my face.

She realized what I wanted, but hesitated. "Your lip's all puffy. I don't want to hurt you."

"Kiss me. Now."

She grinned and leaned over me. "Geez, you're so demanding."

We shared a long, pleasurable kiss that left us both breathless.

I patted her wet cheek. "I sure missed that. And you, of course." I smiled through my own tears. "For a while there, I thought I'd never see you again."

She took a long, shaky breath. "You and me both, kiddo."

"Snuggle up here beside me," I said, and she lost no time in complying.

"So where am I?" I asked, when we were ensconced in each other's arms as much as tubes and bandages allowed.

"In the hospital."

"I figured that much. Where exactly is this hospital?"

"Aberystwyth, I think. I'm a bit fuzzy on places right now because it was dark and I came in with you on the helicopter. I do know that it's been a long day and night."

"Yeah, you look wasted."

"Ha! That's a good one. You should see yourself."

"Do I look that bad?"

Her lower lip trembled, and she shook her head. "You look fantastic."

"Yeah, right. I bet you say that to all the kidnap victims."

A nurse came in carrying my chart and a white plastic bag on which my name had been printed with a large black marker.

Kim slid over to the edge of the bed. The nurse eyed my partner, but spoke to me. "How's our patient doing?"

"Our patient's doing well enough, I think," I said.

She placed the bag at the foot of my bed and checked the numbers on the monitor. She fiddled with some of the tubes and wires before making notations on the chart. After a few seconds, she smiled. "Yes, a nice steady pulse. That's what we like." She slid the metal end of her stethoscope under my gown and pressed it against my chest, listening.

"Good. Very good."

I glanced at Kim, who was nodding her head.

"Are you able to sit up, Dr. Curtis? I'd like to check your back."

Kim helped me sit forward so the nurse could do more listening. She had me take several deep breaths and cough a few times. My ribs felt sore, but other than that, I had no discomfort except for the ache in my shoulder.

When I was able to lie back down, the nurse made more notations on my chart. "It's amazing," she said, smiling. "Your lungs are first rate. No fluid at all. If I hadn't been told that you'd been plucked from a briny bog, I'd never have believed it."

"Oh, it happened all right," Kim assured her. "I helped fish her out, and she was one slimy creature."

I gave her a look. "Thanks for your insightful comment, Dr. Blair."

"No problem," Kim murmured.

The nurse folded my chart and slid it under her arm. "Which reminds me..." She picked up the bag. "You were wearing these when you were brought in here. We dried them out as best we could."

"Oh, burn them or toss them out," I said. "I never want to see any of that stuff again."

Kim stood up and took the bundle. "I'll take care of it, thanks."

"Your father and the police are waiting to talk with you, Dr. Curtis, but I'll give you both a bit more time alone before allowing them in."

"Thank you," I said. "You're very kind."

She moved to the door. "I'm Gwen. Just ring if you need anything, luv."

Kim sat down on the bed and was poking around in the bag. She pulled out my filthy shirt, pants, and underwear.

"You don't need to look at that stuff. It's gross."

"What's this?" Something crackled at the bottom of the bag. Kim pulled out a stained and wrinkled piece of paper—the note I had written her.

"Oh, that. It's nothing, really." I felt my cheeks flame with embarrassment. "Let them get rid of all that."

She smoothed the paper out on her lap and examined it as if it were an ancient parchment. "It's a note of some kind. In your handwriting, if I'm not mistaken."

"It's just something I wrote while I was there at the cottage. I didn't mean for—"

"Shh." She continued to read. I watched in fascination as her eyes slowly filled with tears, and they spilled down her cheeks. Her mouth quivered, her eyes scrunched up. When she had finished reading, she bent her head and covered her face with her hands.

"Honey?" I tried to sit up.

Sobbing, she turned to me and tucked her head into my good shoulder. "Oh, PJ. Oh, my—"

"Hey, I didn't think my writing was that bad."

"It's beautiful. I'm... It's just that... Oh, God. Where's a tissue?" She located one on the bedside table and blew her nose. "Sorry, it all came down on me at once there. Reading that note and realizing what could have happened to you. To us." She rested her head against my chest. I held her with my good arm.

"It's okay. Really." I stroked her hair and kissed the top of her head. "We're here, we're together, and we're fine."

My big, tough Amazon warrior. I fell in love with her all over again.

Dad tapped on the door and entered. Kim wiped her eyes and sat back beside me on the bed. He hugged me gently, placing a kiss on my forehead before doing the same to Kim. "Some night, huh?" He smiled, and all the worry lines on his face relaxed.

"Some week," Kim said, her voice husky.

I cleared my throat. "I just want to say how sorry I am for all the trouble I caused."

Trevor and Geoff tiptoed through the door.

"Hey there, PJ. Glad you're in one piece." Trevor looked around the room. "Coo, look at the size of the telly."

"Good to see you awake," Geoff said to me before admiring the television propped high above our heads in one corner. "Say, do you suppose the test match is on now?" he whispered to his fellow cricket fan.

Kim sighed. "If it isn't cricket, it's darts in the local pub. The remote's over there on the table."

"Hey, that's right." I looked at her and then at the guys. "We haven't collected on our bet yet. You two owe us each a pint of *really* expensive ale."

They laughed and took seats on either side of my bed, while Dad perched on the mattress by my feet. Kim remained sitting at my right side, holding my free hand.

"When the doctor says okay, we'll make good on our bet," Geoff assured me. They took turns filling me in on their part of the investigation and rescue, ending with the fact that the police would be in to get my statement, and that the kidnappers were now in custody. I was happy to hear about that.

I told them in general terms what I remembered about my captivity and ended by apologizing again for causing them so much grief.

"And my biggest regret," I continued, with a catch in my throat, "was being responsible for Pup's death."

"But you weren't." Kim squeezed my hand.

"No. If I hadn't gotten kidnapped, those bastards wouldn't have killed him."

Kim reached for her purse.

Dad smiled at me. "You didn't cause Pup's death, because he isn't dead."

"They gave me a photo. He was lying in the garden and—"

"Arwel? It's Kim." My partner had taken out her cell phone and apparently dialed the inn. "Can you do me a favor and bring Pup to the phone?"

Arwel must have laughed or questioned Kim's request.

"I know, but PJ doesn't believe he's alive."

A moment or two elapsed before Kim thanked her and put the phone in my hand. "Talk to him yourself, if you don't believe me."

There was a snuffling and whimpering on the line, and I started to grin. "Pup? Sweetie, is that you?"

He gave a loud yelp and started panting into his end of the phone line.

"Oh, Pup." I felt tears trickle from my eyes again, but they were joyful ones. "I'm so glad to hear you, buddy."

His response was a long whine ending in a tiny woof.

"Yes, Mommy wants to come home and tickle your belly, too." Everyone in the room laughed. "As soon as they let me out of here."

I heard a scraping of teeth against the telephone's casing. Arwel came on the line. "PJ, it's good to hear your voice, but I'm afraid Pup is going to chew up the receiver if I don't ring off now."

"No problem, Arwel. It's good to hear your voice, too, and thanks for taking good care of my pal." I looked over at Kim. "Of both my pals."

Arwel assured me that it was no bother at all, and then hung up.

"Feel better now?" Kim asked me.

I beamed. "Much."

Her expression grew serious. "You know we never would have found you in time, if it weren't for Pup. Another few minutes could have been too late." Kim's eyes glistened with fresh tears, and I shuddered.

Trevor and Geoff left then, promising to keep an eye on things, both in the hospital and back at the inn.

Another person joined our merry group. She was tall, red-haired, and brown-eyed, and set off warning bells in the recesses of my mind. Friend or foe? I couldn't remember, but she looked familiar and very attractive. She nodded, smiling at Dad and Kim.

"Oh, I guess you two haven't been formally introduced." Kim stood, and the woman came over and took my hand. "PJ, this is Terry Simms."

Now I remembered. She had dropped by Kim's motor home that night in Arizona, outing Kim in front of Sandy and me. What the hell was she doing here?

The woman gave my hand a gentle squeeze and in a voice oozing with sensuality said, "I'm delighted to finally meet you, PJ. You've kept us pretty busy this past week." She glanced fondly at my partner.

Uh oh. What was that all about?

"I guess I have at that," I said, keeping my tone neutral. "Nice to meet you, too." Maybe.

A doctor marched in with Gwen at his heels, and they shooed everyone out.

Dad tousled my hair and said he'd be close by if I needed him.

Kim squeezed my hand. "I'll be back when the place empties out," she whispered. "Save my spot."

"Always," I assured her.

Gwen pulled the curtain up around the bed, while Dr. Coyle undid my hospital gown to examine my shoulder.

"Now then, young lady. Let's have a look at this nasty hole, shall we?" He probed and poked at the front and back and had me move my arm around.

"Does that hurt?" he asked after each maneuver. He had a thick, dark mustache that made me think of Tom Selleck.

"When I move it around. Mostly, it's just sore and stiff," I told him.

He wrapped a fresh bandage diagonally across my shoulder and around my chest. "The good news is that you are a very lucky young lady. It could have been much worse, but it's doing very nicely and doesn't seem to be bleeding as much. Furthermore, the antibiotics seem to be holding the inflammation at bay. That's good news, too." He looked at me and waggled his eyebrows. "You know, jumping into a bog is not the recommended procedure for treating gunshot wounds." He clicked his tongue against his teeth. "Most unsavory places, they are. Too many bacteria floating about in them."

"Believe me, Doctor, I didn't plan on doing that. I just couldn't make my legs move fast enough to avoid it."

He finished the dressing and had Gwen retie my gown. "I think we'll continue on with the painkillers," he told her. "Give her a good night's sleep. She's healthy and fit otherwise, and rest will do her a world of good." He made a notation on my chart and handed it back to Gwen.

"I'll see to it, Doctor."

He smiled at me. "Right you are then, young lady. We'll have you up and about in a day or two. In the meantime, try to limit your visitors. We haven't had this much excitement around here since the Queen's last trip."

He and Gwen walked out of the room discussing my convalescence and possible physical therapy.

I gave my shoulder a gentle twist and winced. I wouldn't be throwing darts at the pub anytime soon, that was for sure.

There was another rap on my door, and two uniformed policewomen entered. I recognized Sergeant Jones from the Aberystwyth area station. She gave me a cheery smile and a thumbs-up. Her companion was also a woman, but rather austere in appearance. A young man rushed in carrying a tape recorder. He set up the machine on the side table and pinned a microphone to the neckline of my gown with trembling fingers. A faint scent of peppermint hung in the air between us. My mind flashed back to odors of garlic and the fragrance of pine. Peppermint was a decided improvement.

"Begging your pardon, miss. I trust I didn't pinch you," he said, his cheeks pink-flamed.

"You're doing just fine, thanks."

He took out a steno pad and prepared to take notes.

"Good morning, Dr. Curtis. It's good to see you looking so much better." Sergeant Jones began the interview by introducing me to her superior, Deputy Chief Inspector Edwards.

The DCI nodded in my direction, then cast a harsh glance at the young man. "Phillips, are you ready?"

"Yes, ma'am."

"Very well, then. Let's proceed, shall we?" She and Sergeant Jones took seats and identified each other, and me, for the record. "Tell us what happened to you from the time you left your room at the inn to go into Dolgellau for medicine for Dr. Blair. Don't rush. We want to know everything you can remember."

"I'll do my best," I told them and began my story.

An hour later, I sank back into my pillow, drained. My throat was dry, and my head pounded with the strain of reliving the events of those days. I even told them of my strange dream and the Celtic warrior who appeared in it. Once the police had finished with me, I closed my eyes and let my mind wander, pondering each question, each response, and then releasing it. I remembered how this day had started for me, how happy I had been to regain consciousness and see Kim waiting for me.

There was a rustling beside the bed, and I opened my eyes to find my partner slipping out of her jacket and removing her shoes.

"And where the hell have you been?" I asked, my voice showing more irritation that I meant to reveal.

"Hey. Do you have any idea how popular you are around here? The doctors, the police, your father, the bodyguards—I had to line up and get a ticket to see you."

She let out a hefty sigh and stretched out on the bed beside me, then gave me a long, lingering kiss.

"Mmm. That's the only ticket you'll ever need." I opened my mouth and welcomed her tongue. My body relaxed, and my concerns about Terry Simms disappeared. All my tension vanished, replaced by the warmth and comfort only my soul mate could provide. "I hope it was worth the wait," I whispered into her neck before kissing it thoroughly. "I didn't mean to sound so cranky."

"You're cute when you're cranky, and it was absolutely worth the wait." Her hands caressed my face and brushed my bangs from my forehead. "Tell me if I'm hurting you."

"You're not," I murmured.

"Did you answer all the questions the police had for you?"

"I did." My throat was parched from all the earlier talking. "Can you slide that water glass over, please? I need a sip or two."

Kim held the straw for me so I could drink. "Huh. That's funny. Your throat may be dry, but your tongue is nice and wet."

I chuckled. "Trust you to notice that."

"Of course. Wet tongues are important."

"Mmm. They are indeed."

"So, what did they ask you and what did you tell them?" She leaned her cheek against my chest.

"They wanted to know all about my trip into town for cough medicine and how I spent the week away from you. I told them that I ran off into the woods with a couple of bards, and we made up poetry and drank hot cider from bubbling cauldrons all week long."

Kim giggled. "Okay. I guess I should know better than to ask for details so soon after your formal interrogation. You will tell me everything eventually, won't you?"

I stroked her cheek with my free hand, curling a strand of her hair between my fingers. "I'll tell you everything, I promise." I hoped she was willing to do the same.

We dozed then, together, my mind forming a couple of unsettling questions before surrendering to sleep.

I trusted Kimmy, and I knew she trusted me. But I really wanted to know how her former lover got involved with this case, and just how busy the two of them were together during my absence.

Chapter 23

While PJ recovered enough from her surgery to be discharged from the hospital, Frederick and I spent our days scurrying from one police briefing to another. News came at us from all directions. I remembered feeling frustrated because I knew so little of what was happening while PJ was missing, but now I was bombarded with information from all sides.

We spent all of one morning in DCI Edwards's office with Sergeant Jones and various constables, listening to the most current findings. Frederick pulled his chair close to mine so that he could reach out and give my knee a reassuring squeeze from time to time.

Sergeant Jones sat off to one side, taking notes in her usual quiet and efficient manner. Edwards, her superior, was a cold fish and a chain smoker. She appeared competent, though, and wasted no time in getting down to business. Since we weren't there to pass the time of day, that was fine with me.

"The one that Dr. Curtis nicknamed Designer Suit is really Martin Patterson." DCI Edwards exhaled a stream of cigarette smoke. "By his own admission, we now know that he was the individual who impersonated Lord Morrison. That's probably why Dr. Curtis thought she knew him from somewhere."

Frederick and I murmured our surprise.

"He kept his face covered and made no attempt to use an English accent while speaking, to prevent her from recognizing him."

Edwards crushed her cigarette butt into the already overflowing ashtray. After pulling a pack of Players Cigarettes from her pocket and laying it open on the desk in front of her, she continued. "Interpol is quite familiar with him. He has a long record of extortion and armed robberies."

I watched her fiddle with the wrapper on her cigarette pack until I wanted to jump up, snatch the vile-smelling things out of her hands, and hurl them across the room.

High stress level? Not me.

"Despite having two jail terms under his belt," she said, "he latched onto an opportunity to move into the big time with murder as the bottom line. In addition to all of that, he's suspected of being involved in antiquities black marketeering. So far, he's outsmarted us on that score. We haven't been able to prove anything, nor have we been able to identify any other gang members." Edwards placed a fresh cigarette between her lips and lit it, giving the match a brisk wave to extinguish it.

"During our interrogation, he admitted forcing Morrison, at gunpoint, to write to you," Edwards said, looking at Frederick, "to request your daughter's help with a personal problem."

Frederick grimaced. "No wonder the letter looked authentic to us. Poor John."

The DCI consulted her notes. "The original idea was to grab Dr. Curtis when she arrived at the estate and hold her for ransom, but he was forced to rethink his plan when she arrived with Dr. Blair."

"Then why didn't he just kill me, too?" I asked. "He'd already killed or been responsible for the deaths of four people that we know about, so what's one more?"

"I can't answer that," Edwards said, tapping the ash from her cigarette.

She protected us from the criminal element, I thought, but who protected our lungs from her habit?

"We've found that the criminal mind can be both brilliant and stupid at the same time, Dr. Blair. The ironic thing is that if he had killed you, we very likely would never have found Dr. Curtis."

I gave an involuntary shudder and thanked the Goddess for stupid criminals.

"We were concerned all along that he planned to kill Dr. Curtis and disappear with the ransom. Her report verified this."

Finding the DCI's comment too painful to accept, I stopped listening for a moment and watched her instead. She took a final drag on the cigarette, expelled the smoke from her nostrils, and snuffed the butt alongside the others in the ashtray.

Dragon Lady belching fire, I thought. PJ's sometimes-misplaced sense of humor was rubbing off on me.

"There is no honor among men like that," Edwards was saying. I wondered if I had missed something during my lapse of concentration.

"And the other two?" Frederick asked. "Who are they?"

"Small-time hoodlums who have been in and out of county jails. They were lured by Patterson and the promise of big money. Now they're implicated in these murders, so they're going to spend a long time in more secure surroundings."

"I've been wondering," Frederick said, "if there was some connection to any of my business ventures. I've made some enemies along the way."

"I don't think so," Edwards said. "Rich and successful men are always targets, but it's my belief that Patterson is an opportunist who found other willing parasites to go along with his scheme."

Frederick stood as our briefing came to a close. "I'm very grateful to you and all who were involved in Priscilla's recovery. My daughter is very precious to me."

"We didn't do it alone," Sergeant Jones said. "You and Dr. Simms found the clues on the tape and presented us with a viable lead."

"Everyone working together resulted in a successful investigation," DCI Edwards said. "The police cannot always do it alone."

"It appears," I said, my mind racing ahead of my words, "that these people went to great lengths to get PJ out of the country... to get her here. Why? Why didn't they just grab her in the States? Why involve the Morrisons?"

"No doubt," the DCI reached for another cigarette, "they did their homework and were aware of the Curtis Corporation's security, which is known to rival even your own government's security measures. They didn't plan on being caught, hence the elaborate scheme." She paused to light up. "Their mistake was in underestimating your ability to discover their hideout and our ability to launch a successful rescue."

I found it difficult to believe that these people were capable of such elaborate planning all by themselves. It had crossed my mind that perhaps Terry was involved, but I had no real evidence and dismissed the idea as too outlandish.

"I... *we* will be forever indebted to you for providing a successful conclusion to a traumatic event in our lives. Thank you for your help." I looked toward Sergeant Jones, who was closing her notebook and sliding the pen into its sleeve. "And thank you for your support."

We started to stand, but Edwards waved us back to our seats. "Before you leave, there's one more thing, and this will be of special interest to you, Dr. Blair. You were right when you said there were ancient remains in that glass coffin."

"Oh?" I leaned toward her.

"They were removed. Part of Patterson's plan, I suppose. We found them, mostly disintegrated, in a cardboard box."

"Exposure to the air and mishandling would have done that," I said. "What a shame."

"Despite their condition, they've been sent to London for forensic studies. Perhaps you would like a copy of the report when we receive it."

"Thank you, yes. I would."

She looked toward Blodwyn. "Make a note of that, Jones."

"Yes, Chief," the sergeant said, opening her notebook again.

"We've processed a lot of evidence at the Morrison estate," Edwards said, as we were leaving, "and located the stolen car in which Dr. Curtis was transported. That, plus her testimony, would have certainly convicted them, but it looks as though this trio will save us the cost of a trial. They've been singing like canaries ever since we incarcerated them."

Frederick frowned. "I've been focused on Priscilla and her injuries so much I hadn't thought about anything else. What will Patterson get at court?"

"Probably several mandatory life sentences. We don't have the death penalty here."

I glanced from one to the other. "It doesn't seem right. Among them, they've taken four, maybe five lives. We know for sure that he murdered the Morrisons and the two servants whose bodies were discovered in the garden pond."

"Yes, he's already confessed to the killings. I agree with you both, but all those crimes were committed on British soil."

"But there may be another one, here. PJ told us about a younger woman who took care of her for the first couple of days. She was a captive, too, and disappeared under mysterious circumstances. Her name was Sarah something."

"Yes, I know. It's in her report." Edwards sighed as if she had enough to deal with without another body to account for. "You have to remember that Dr. Curtis is not yet herself; she could have imagined the threat to the young woman."

"Priscilla may not be herself at the moment," Frederick said, "but I know her. If she thinks this woman was a victim, I wouldn't dismiss the possibility."

"I didn't intend to dismiss anything," Edwards said, softening her voice. "I only meant to caution you about the accuracy of facts obtained from someone who has suffered severe mental and physical trauma. We will, of course, investigate all possibilities."

"And what about the servants who greeted us at the estate that day?" I asked. "There was a gatekeeper, a housekeeper, and a maid that we know about, and there was someone in the groundskeeper's cottage. They must be part of this whole thing, and adding them into the equation makes for quite a gang."

"Minor players," she said, "but we haven't overlooked them. We'll find all who were involved. It might take a little time, but we *will* catch up with them."

For the first time in many days, I broke into a broad grin. "I believe you will, Inspector. I do believe you will."

* * *

Sergeant Jones walked out of the building with us. Frederick thanked her again for her assistance and left to attend to some business matters. I knew PJ would be resting, so I invited the sergeant to join me for lunch at Sally's Café. She accepted without hesitation.

While we waited for our order to arrive, I noticed that the sergeant acted a little shy now that she was outside her law enforcement environment. She stirred her tea, added a little more sugar, and stirred again, staring in silence into her cup. When she removed her hat and put it on the empty chair, I saw how brilliantly her red hair caught the light. She was a homespun beauty; slightly reserved, but salt of the earth.

We maintained a companionable silence while she continued stirring her tea, staring into her cup.

"Sergeant—"

She looked up. "Blodwyn, please."

"All right, Blodwyn, I want to thank you for being there for me. I was having a tough time handling everything."

"I know you were," she said, smiling.

At that moment, the waitress arrived with lunch, and we realized how hungry we were. Blodwyn had ordered steak and kidney pie, which looked and smelled delicious. I, being less adventuresome, had the sausage roll. Spiced to perfection, the sausage was wrapped in a cocoon of flaky pastry. Both entrees were served with thin-sliced cucumbers and tomatoes on a bed of crisp lettuce leaf.

Blodwyn asked for my fork. "You mentioned that you'd never eaten steak and kidney pie, so I want you to taste this. It's very good, and I guarantee you'll like it." She dug the fork through the crust into the rich brown gravy, and speared a piece of steak and a piece of kidney. I hadn't been too sure about the kidney until I tasted it. That one bite was sufficient to convince me that I had to have one of those delicious entrees before I left Wales.

"Mmm-mm. That *is* good."

"Told you so," she said, her eyes sparkling.

We ate in silence for a few minutes, each of us savoring our entrees.

"So, tell me about yourself," I said.

"Not much to tell, really. I was born in Haverfordwest—that's down south. My parents were killed in a motorcar accident when I was quite young. I always wanted to be in law enforcement, so here I am, working my way up the ladder."

"How do you get along with Edwards?"

"All right. She doesn't share much of herself, and she's a stickler for job performance," Blodwyn said and grinned, "but that's all right, too. I've learned a lot from her."

"I wish for her sake she'd stop smoking like she does."

"I do, too. We all do. We've tried to convince her of the benefits of stopping. But she says, 'It's my life, and my lungs.'"

I set my fork down and wiped my mouth on the cloth napkin. "Then it's not for us to worry about her."

Blodwyn sighed. "I suppose not."

"But you, now. I have no doubt you'll reach the top of that ladder."

A rosy flush enhanced the sprinkling of freckles across her cheeks. "Thank you."

We had both decided on the Chocolate Log Roll for dessert. When it arrived, we took one look at the rich cream oozing from between the circles of moist chocolate cake and grinned at each other.

"This is no way to act in a lovely tea room," I said, smacking my lips, "but I'm going to do it anyway." I scooped up some cream with my finger, and popped it into my mouth.

Blodwyn's eyes sparkled as she broke into a very un-sergeant-like giggle.

"Lunch is my treat, I insist," I said when the bill was delivered, along with three candied blossoms for each of us.

"Thank you, but that's not necessary."

"Perhaps not, but it pleases me. Let's just say it's a token of appreciation from PJ and me."

"Very well, then. Under those conditions, I accept."

"One more thing," I said, afterwards, when we were standing on the pavement outside the café. "What you said that night about 'understanding' meant more to me than you can ever know."

Blodwyn leaned close to me and spoke in a low voice. "I hope that someone would do the same for me if the love of my life were in trouble."

I raised an eyebrow. She replied to my unspoken question with a nod. After a quick hug, we parted company. I watched her walk away, back toward the police station. Yes indeed, Sergeant Blodwyn Jones was an asset to her chosen profession. And I could stand around and wonder who the love of her life was that needed her protection, but right now, it was time for me to check in with the love of *my* life.

Chapter 24

Keeping my eyes closed, I stretched and wiggled my toes under the soft, sweet-smelling sheets. It felt wonderful to be out of the hospital and sleeping in our own bed. I turned my head to the left and opened my eyes, and saw that I seemed to be the only one in it at the moment.

There was a scribbled note on the pillow where Kim's head normally rested. It told me that she and Dad were at the police station, attending another briefing. I closed my eyes again, letting my mind drift along, taking a mental inventory of my aches and pains. I was lucky, very lucky. My overall health and fitness would help to speed my recovery. The shoulder was sore, but not as stiff as it had been yesterday. Either I was healing well, or the painkiller was keeping me oblivious.

Pup meandered to the side of the bed and rested his head a couple of inches from mine. He was alive. I still had trouble believing that. I scratched his ears and rubbed under his chin. His mouth flopped open and a wet tongue slathered my cheek.

"Ah! Bad breath! Thanks so much. And good morning to you, too, sweetie." I rubbed my cheek dry.

With a tiny whine, sounding more like a Pekingese than a wolf-Shepherd mix, he poked his nose under my hand.

"Please tell me you don't have to go outside. I don't think I'm up to walking you around the garden just yet." He tilted his head at an angle and made a snuffling sound.

"Good, then. I'll take that as a no, and I can snooze a bit longer."

He huffed out a sigh and dropped to the floor beside the bed with a groan.

"Just give me five more minutes, okay? I'll call over to see if one of the guys can take you for a walk."

His yawn ended in a hi-pitched gurgle.

"I'm going to take that as a yes."

In exaggerated slow motion, I turned onto my back and stared at the ceiling, thinking about our time here in Wales before the kidnapping, and what had happened since my rescue. There were so many holes in my recollection of the shooting and near drowning. One second I was on the wall, looking over my shoulder at Designer Suit as he raised the gun toward me, and the next I was waking up in the hospital after a puzzling dream.

I remembered Kim hovering over me, looking like she had lost her best friend. I guess she had, or thought she had. I know I'd feel that way, if the situation were reversed.

A tiny piece of the dream came back to me, nagging me about another presence in that bog. When I first mentioned it, Dad thought it was the medication giving me hallucinations. I wasn't so sure, and Kim didn't comment. Wales had cast a spell over me and my memories. I'd experienced some of the best and worst moments of my life in this country, all within a few short weeks. I even halfway believed that I had conversed with an Amazon in the cottage.

"I don't think I'll mention the strange Amazon vision to Kim," I muttered. "She's so into it that she doesn't need to be encouraged."

"Who are you calling strange?"

The voice came floating down to me from a spot above the dresser. Pup stood up and growled, but lapsed into silence with just a shake of his spine, as if obeying a silent command. Then he sat motionless beside the bed, while I focused on a small, amber cloud that grew larger and more human in shape.

Oh, geez. Not again. It was the painkillers this time. It had to be.

She sat on top of the dresser, her long, leather-clad legs draped over the edge. "It's not a potion. Your wits are about you, little one, at least as much as they ever can be."

I made an effort to sit up. "What's that supposed to mean?"

She laughed and took several deep breaths that emphasized each ripple and curve on her muscular body. "Now, that's more like it." She glanced to her left and to her right. "The medallion is here. I can feel its power. Why won't you see that it helps?"

"Jesus Christ. Why is it always the medallion? I told you back in the cottage that I'd wear it again when we get the clasp repaired. In case you haven't noticed, we've had a few more important things to do recently."

"Oh, I've noticed." She folded her arms across her nearly naked chest. The leather bra encasing her well-rounded breasts had to be at least two sizes too small, but I wasn't going to object. In fact, I found the vision quite alluring.

"Put it on as soon as possible, little one," she said, quickly returning me to the reality of the moment. "It cannot protect you if you don't wear it."

I sighed and sank back onto my pillow, resigned to the fact that I was having yet another conversation with a long-dead Amazon, albeit a good-looking one. "I know. You've warned me often enough. To hear you talk about it, those medallions could cure cancer, AIDS, and a host of the world's maladies."

"I only know what I have heard from the storytellers."

My wounded shoulder burned. I gave it a gentle rub, trying to ease the throbbing. "Could we move on to something else? Like why you're here again, picking on me?"

With catlike grace, she dropped from the dresser top to the foot of our bed, her eyes a bright bluish gray behind her mask. I really wanted to get a peek under there sometime.

She smiled. "You don't have enough faith yet to see under the mask. You will when it's time for you to do so."

"Jesus. You can read my mind."

Her hand came up, halting me. "No, not exactly, but the more I know you, the more I can imagine what you are thinking at certain times."

"Isn't that peachy." Was she reading it a minute ago, when I was admiring her breasts? Oh, shit.

She sat at the foot of the bed on Kim's side, ran her hand across the blanket, and gave my foot a tap. "You have questions, don't you?"

"Wouldn't you?"

Her lips twitched. "Yes, I believe I would. What can I tell you to ease your mind?"

Pup stood up and gave a tiny woof as a knock sounded on the door. I looked at my Amazon visitor. "That's probably Arwel or one of the bodyguards. Do you need to dematerialize or something?"

"No need. She won't be able to see me."

"She?"

"It's a woman holding a tray of food."

"That would be Arwel with my breakfast. Why can't she see you?"

The woman leaned back on one elbow, sending her abdomen into rippled relief. "We choose to allow only selected people to see us, especially when we're on a mission."

I nodded as if I understood, but I didn't. Not really.

The knock sounded again, harder this time.

"Come in," I called.

Arwel's tray contained a pot of tea, a soft-boiled egg in an eggcup, and several buttered scones. "Bore da, Dr. Curtis. How are you this morning?"

"Feeling stronger every day, thanks to you and Cook." I sat up and she tucked an extra pillow at my back so I could eat.

Arwel looked around. "I thought I heard voices."

"You did. I was talking to Pup."

"Oh." She didn't sound convinced, but she unfolded the napkin and placed it across my stomach, as was her habit when she brought me a meal. She then poured my tea and added just the right amount of cream and sugar. "Anything else I can do for you?"

I took a sip of tea and a bite of scone, pausing to lick the melted butter from my fingers. "Yum." After chewing and swallowing, I remembered Pup and his morning walk. Arwel assured me she would take care of that.

"Find your leash, Pup." He padded to the chair and snatched it up between his teeth. "Good boy. Arwel is going to walk you this morning."

He waited patiently while she fastened his leash, and pranced beside her in barely contained ecstasy as they both tried to fit through the door at the same time. Arwel and I laughed. "I'll have him back in just a tick," she assured me as they left.

My Amazon companion stared at the closed door. "A truly magnificent specimen, and so devoted."

I laughed. "You're talking about Pup, right?"

Her head tilted and a sly grin appeared. "Of course."

"Why don't I believe you?"

"You had questions? I can't stay much longer."

"Okay, then. Question number one. When you visited me in the cottage, you said you'd protect me."

"Yes."

"I was almost raped and took a bullet through my shoulder during my escape. You call that protecting?"

She slid further toward me. "We did the best we could, little one." Her hand rested lightly on top of my injured shoulder. "You will remember that I was concerned because you weren't wearing the medallion."

"Yeah, I remember. The medallion and all its powers, yadda, yadda, yadda."

"And I suggested that you use a weapon on those men if you got the chance. You failed to act like a warrior."

“Because I’m not a warrior, and I told you that the gun wasn’t an option. Killing them was out of the question for me.”

“They would have killed you in an instant. Your back was facing that man when he fired. To shoot at your enemy’s back is the sign of a coward. Would you like to know where the wound would have been if we hadn’t intervened?”

“Really, it’s not necessary.”

She tapped her index finger between my breasts.

“Jesus.” My mouth went dry. “You’re sure?”

She nodded, withdrawing her finger. “And I was the one who instructed your soul mate to read the parchments beside your bed. You called them brochures. One of them helped lead her to where you were imprisoned.”

“I guess I owe you and your people my gratitude. Thank you for saving my life.”

“Our pleasure, little one. You can thank your four-legged friend for finding your body in that pool.”

“It’s a Welsh bog.”

“And your soul mate for breathing life back into your lungs.”

“I have thanked her. Many times.”

Her smile lingered as she stood up. “One last thing and then I must leave.”

Her hand slipped under my nightshirt and moved across my bandages. The sore shoulder stopped throbbing; the pain vanished.

“Wow! How did you do that?”

With a dismissive wave of her hand, she stood and returned to the dresser where she stared into the mirror, her back toward me. Her body shimmered into the familiar amber cloud that had heralded her arrival. Her voice was the last to go. “The medallion, little one. It will protect you far better than I. It will help make a believer out of you.”

“I’ll wear the damn thing,” I said to the empty air. “As soon as the clasp is fixed.”

I finished my breakfast, musing over the strange connection between our Amazon visions and the Celtic mystique that had surrounded us during our visit to Wales. No doubt about it, this place was filled with memories and energies of long-dead people. But was I ready to believe I was actually hearing and seeing these things? Or was I under the influence of powerful painkillers? If I told Kim about what happened, she’d try to convince me of things that I wasn’t yet ready to accept.

I climbed out of bed and eased the tray onto the dresser. Sunlight filtered through the green-glass window of our cozy room, and the wood flooring felt warm and comforting under my bare feet.

My shoulder didn't hurt. Was it really the dream warrior's touch, or just my own desire for the pain to cease? The medication sure didn't work that fast.

I shook my head, bewildered. It was probably better for me to stop thinking about the past and enjoy the present.

I'd try a short walk around the garden after my bath. If I was lucky, a sexy archaeologist would return in time to accompany me.

I pulled on my robe and struggled with the old wooden dresser drawer that contained our underwear. That drawer had stuck from the first day we arrived. Kim and I thought about putting our panties in another one, but solved the problem by leaving it partially open. She must have forgotten and pushed it in too far.

I entered the bathroom and turned on the hot water faucet. Kim had located a carved wooden stool for me to use when I had to bathe or use the toilet. I still felt like the place had been designed for Paul Bunyan and his blue ox, but after a week in that basement wearing the same clothing and with just a hint of wash water, I relished each and every amenity at my disposal.

As the hot water flowed into the old tub, I returned to the bedroom for pants and a top. I chose a large flannel shirt of Kim's, so I could pull it on over my bandages.

As I started back into the bathroom, a knock sounded softly on our door.

"The tray's on the dresser, Arwel," I said, but Terry Simms greeted me when I opened the door. She was most apologetic for disturbing me while I was dressing.

"No problem. I've been meaning to talk to you anyway." I turned off the bath water, and she sat in our overstuffed chair while I perched on the edge of the bed.

She cast a glance toward the rumpled sheets and then back to me. "What did you want to talk about?"

"We were interrupted in the hospital before I could thank you for your part in my rescue. You and Kim did a wonderful job of deciphering all the clues I threw at you."

"It was nothing, really. You were very clever and brave to have risked doing it. I'm glad I could help." She moistened her lips. "I must admit you're looking really good considering all you've been through."

"Thanks." I couldn't stop a flush from warming my cheeks. "I've had lots of rest and an abundance of TLC."

Terry smiled in a rather seductive way, I thought, or perhaps I was just imagining it. She did have a very sensual aura about her. Her green silk blouse was unbuttoned to reveal plenty of cleavage, and her black knit slacks fit her shapely hips and thighs like a second skin. Knowing the history she and Kim shared did nothing to boost my confidence. It took little effort to imagine them together, bodies entangled in various sexual scenarios, pleasuring each other in ways I had yet to learn.

"If there's anything you need or want," she murmured in a husky voice, "I'm here for you." She fiddled with the thick manila envelope she held in both hands.

"Um. Thanks, Terry, but Kim is taking good care of me."

She looked a bit uncomfortable. "I see. That's fine, then." She stood and walked a few paces away from me, keeping her back turned. "I can't believe that you are so understanding and forgiving about the whole thing."

"Sorry, I don't follow you. What 'whole thing'?"

When she turned toward me, she looked surprised and then embarrassed. "Oh, dear. I thought you knew. Kim didn't tell you about us?"

My stomach clenched. I didn't like where this conversation was headed. "What about you?"

She put a hand over her heart, as if holding back a tumultuous secret. "It really just sort of happened, you know."

"Terry. What happened?"

"Uh, while you were in that dreadful cottage, we had to work together, for long hours, going over the tape, looking for clues."

"Damn it, Terry, spit it out!"

"We had dinner together."

I exhaled in giddy relief. "Oh, is that all? For goodness sakes, I'd have expected you to eat a meal together."

"That's not all."

"Oh." There was a faint buzzing in my head that left me disoriented for a few seconds. The room grew warmer. My heart thudded in my chest, and I told myself not to listen further, not to believe her. "Go on," I said in a strangely detached voice.

"When we walked back here from the pub, we started talking. She told me how lonely she was, how she needed comfort, a woman to warm her bed."

I pressed one hand against my stomach, feeling as though I'd just been kicked. This couldn't be true. Not my Kim.

I stared at her and shook my head. "You're lying."

"I wish I was." The look she gave me might have been compassion or pity. It was hard to tell. "I told her it wasn't right, but she insisted. I've never been able to resist her."

"No," I whispered, still shaking my head. "Damn it, no."

I could see moisture in Terry's eyes. Either she was one hell of an actress, or… Oh, God.

I needed to be alone, to think about this. "You'd better leave." I moved toward the door and grabbed the knob.

"I'm so sorry. You'll never know how much I regret what happened that night."

"I don't want to hear any more."

"I'm only telling you for your own good. Kim was a horny animal. She started tearing off my clothes as soon as we got here."

"Terry, that's enough." I yanked the door open. "Get out of here. Now!"

She moved toward the dresser. "I'll go, but I have to leave these papers for Kim. They're police business."

She turned her back to me. I wasn't the least bit interested in whatever she had to do. Her words had turned my world upside down, and I wanted her gone.

"I'm sorry I've upset you," she said, folding the now empty envelope and heading toward the door. "I just didn't want any secrets."

I couldn't look at her anymore. I stared at the floor, trying to compose myself. My hand shook as I held the knob. "Get out of my sight before I sic Pup on you." That was an empty threat. Pup was still out with Arwel.

Terry sighed. "I'm sorry that's the way you feel." With her head held high, she walked through the doorway.

"How the hell do you think I feel?" My eyes filled with hot tears. I slammed the door shut and leaned my forehead against the cool wood, my chest heaving.

Terry was a bold-faced liar. Kim loved me. She'd never betray me. She'd never sleep with her, even under these circumstances.

I wanted to believe that so badly, and yet...

* * *

I moved to the bathroom as if in a trance. The bath water had cooled. I pulled the plug and watched it swirl down the drain.

I folded my arms and dropped my head, letting my forehead press against the cold porcelain rim of the tub. Life had seemed so blissful an hour ago. Now, I had so many questions, doubts, and fears. Terry was a beautiful, experienced woman. She and Kim had been intimate for several years before I entered the picture. A lump formed in my throat. Oh, geez, did Kimmy do what Terry said she did?

I knew how I felt in that cottage without Kim. I was so desperate one night that I took matters into my own hands, so how could I blame her for seeking physical comfort, especially from a former lover? She had no guarantee I was ever coming back alive.

Tears dribbled down my cheeks. I sniffed and tried to swipe them away. I turned the water on full force to drown out the sound of my sobbing.

A hot bath wouldn't solve this problem, but I had to start somewhere. A long soak would give my mind and body time to absorb the blow, as unfair as it was, and try to decide what to do about it.

I put a waterproof covering over my bandage, shed my robe, and lowered myself into the steaming water, tilting my head back against the tub's cool surface.

It took so much courage to love someone, to give your body and soul to someone, to be so vulnerable. Kim knew this. She remembered how she felt after Terry left her for someone else, and how it hurt so much to be betrayed. She'd been through it. How could she do it to me, knowing the anguish it would cause?

I squeezed my eyes shut and tried to rid myself of the vision of Kim and Terry together.

The more I tried, the harder it became.

Chapter 25

Enjoying a delicious meal with Sergeant Jones had put me in good spirits. We had shared candid thoughts on the investigation and what PJ and I needed to do to get our lives back on track. From Blodwyn's suggestions, I gathered that life had not always been rosy for her and that some of the comments she made were from personal experience, though she didn't go into detail.

I took the long way back from the café, strolling along the cobblestone paths and enjoying the warm summer sunshine, making mental lists of future work projects and social activities.

Now that our business here was nearly complete, I guessed we wouldn't be seeing much more of Blodwyn. That was too bad. I'd like to count her in our circle of friends, and I'm sure that PJ would, too. Circle of friends! That was a joke. With our moving around so much, our circle was small indeed, but there was no reason it had to stay that way.

Oh, we had our colleagues from the Superstitions, but that wasn't the same. They were just starting out and were scattered across the globe. Our most frequent contacts with them came in the form of e-mails, postcards, and hurried phone calls. I hoped that some day we could settle at the ranch and discover the sociability there that we lacked in our present situation.

Listen to me, talking about social interaction. Me, the consummate hermit, the loner, the lover of solitude.

The social thing was really more important for PJ than it was for me. And Santa Fe was a lively town. PJ should thrive there. She was the extrovert in this relationship, though she had obviously brought me out of my shell—the shell that Terry clamped shut when she left so suddenly, shattering my faith in people and my ability to love. PJ, bless her heart, helped me live and love again.

I followed the winding path along the ridge until it met the inn's long circular drive. In a few more seconds, I was up the steps and through the heavy wooden door. The aroma of fresh baked bread welcomed me, and Arwel smiled a greeting from across the vestibule. She was busy registering a couple of guests, so I waved, crossed through the sitting room, and climbed the stairs.

If I hadn't been so stuffed from lunch, I might have been tempted to make a detour to the kitchen for some tea and toast. Right now, though, my interests lay with a certain blonde beauty.

I let myself into the room quietly, thinking that PJ might be napping. I wanted so much to tell her about the meeting with the police and about my luncheon with Blodwyn, as well as a dozen other things of lesser importance. We hadn't had much time to really catch up, and I yearned for quiet time to reconnect with my partner.

The doctors had cautioned Frederick and me about future reactions that PJ might suffer due to the kidnapping. They suggested we find her a good therapist and attend sessions ourselves. Her father knew a specialist in trauma and Post-Traumatic Stress Disorder. He had already made some initial calls to set up appointments for when we returned to the Boston area. In the meantime, he and I decided to be discreet when discussing the ordeal with PJ.

God, how I'd missed her. I needed to recharge my core and spend some overdue quality time with her. She was my tonic.

She wasn't in bed, so I checked the bathroom. I found her in the tub—head tilted back, eyes closed. I thought she might be asleep, so I paused for several seconds, admiring her body. She had lost some weight, and there were still ugly bruise marks along her ribs. A piece of plastic protected the bandage on her left shoulder, keeping it dry, but her breasts, only partially submerged, drew most of my attention. How I longed to put my hands on those beauties again.

"Hi, sweet treat," I whispered, leaning close to her head. The kiss, intended for her lips, landed off to the side when she jerked awake.

"Jesus, you startled me," she said when I swept some strands of damp hair from her forehead.

"Sorry. I didn't mean to scare you." Her right arm moved to the wound, effectively covering her breasts. I couldn't tell if her gesture was a response to pain or sudden shyness. "You okay? Your shoulder aching?"

"I'm just tired, that's all." She sat up straighter. "I'd better get out. The water has cooled."

She averted her eyes in what appeared to me to be a deliberate attempt to avoid mine. Something was wrong, and she wasn't telling me what.

I picked up her towel. "Would you like help getting dried off?"

"I can do it myself." She pulled the old-fashioned plug from the drain before climbing out of the tub and snatching the towel from my hands.

"What—" I swallowed my words, heeding the little voice that warned me that it was not a good time to confront her. "You know, I'm pretty tired myself. While you're finishing up, I think I'll go lie down and relax a bit."

"Yeah, you do that. Relax a bit," she said, awkwardly drying herself off with one hand.

I wanted to help, but I could tell that she would rather I didn't. Her attitude was puzzling. It hurt me to see her acting this way, as if I were the enemy.

I took a deep breath. Patience, I told myself. She'd been through a week of hell. It was no wonder she wasn't herself.

I paused in the doorway on my way to the bedroom. "You know something?"

Her head came up and we made eye contact. "What?"

"I love you."

There was a second or two of uncertainty in her eyes. "Yeah, that too."

Now, I was really concerned. Her usual response would have been that she loved me, too, or something cute and suggestive. What was going on with her?

I was confused by her attitude and unsettled by her avoidance of the L word. PJ had never hesitated about saying she loved me, or in demonstrating how much.

I sat on the side of the bed and removed my shoes and shirt before stretching out with my hands folded behind my head. It was just my overactive imagination. She'd be out here in a minute, ready as always for a kiss and a bit of snuggling.

I must have fallen asleep, because when I awoke, the sunny room had turned gray. Large raindrops splattered against the glass, creating a wavy, streaming effect. PJ was sitting in the chair, in her terrycloth robe, her bare feet drawn up beneath her. She had an open book in her lap, but she didn't appear to be reading.

I yawned and stretched, turning onto my side with a smile. "Sweetie, come lie down beside me."

At first, PJ acted as though she hadn't heard me. Then, as if in a trance, she did as I asked, stretching out on her back and staring at the ceiling.

I put my hand on her arm, but she made no move to acknowledge me. To hell with the sensitivity stuff, I needed to get to the bottom of this.

"I know something's bothering you. Why don't you want to talk about it?"

When she turned to look at me, her eyes were red. She'd been crying.

"Won't you tell me, sweetheart? Is it something I've done?"

"Humph!"

"PJ, I'm worried about you."

"You are?"

"Of course I am."

Two delicate tears trickled from the corners of her eyes. "Am I too young for you?"

"What?"

She sniffed. "Not experienced enough?"

"Where the hell did that come from?" I sat up and pulled her to me. "Whatever put such a crazy idea into your head?"

Her body stiffened, but she didn't draw away. "You were lonely when I was gone, weren't you?"

"You know I was."

She took a long, shaky breath. "You wanted a woman to share your bed."

"Yes, I did."

"At least you're honest enough to admit it." PJ moved away from me, rolled off the bed, and went to the window. Even in the glass's wavy reflection, I could see that she was trying hard not to cry.

"Yes, I wanted a woman to share my bed." I followed her to the window, gripped her gently by the shoulders, and turned her around. "You."

"Me?"

"Of course you. Who else?"

She paused and seemed reluctant to answer. "What about Terry?"

"What about her? She and I were over long before I met you. You know that."

"That's what you told me." She glanced downward and took a deep breath.

"What's this about?" My grip on her right shoulder tightened.

"Terry was here during this whole ordeal. I wasn't."

"Yes, she was. And for the record, I didn't call her in on the case. Your father did. She and I went to dinner together one evening after working all day to decipher your tape. I did not see her socially at any other time."

PJ's sullen expression didn't change. We stared into each other's eyes for several long seconds.

"You know better," I said. "I'm surprised you'd even consider there was more to it than that." I was angry that she would think that I had been with Terry, and especially while she was a captive and in so much danger.

"Then why—" She stopped and bit her lower lip.

"Why what?"

She tried to twist away from me. "Nothing."

"How can I come clean with you, if you won't do the same?"

"Then you admit that there is something to come clean about?" Her green eyes bored into me.

"No, I don't." Where was she getting all these cockamamie ideas?

"Come here." I pulled her back, taking her in my arms, smelling the clean scent of her skin and kissing her tear-filled eyes. I murmured soothing words and rubbed the tip of her nose with my own until she smiled. Her body relaxed against me and her head found its familiar spot under my chin.

I felt we were back on track, now. Whatever crisis was bothering her had passed.

"Why don't you get dressed?" I said softly. "And if you're up to it, we can take a little drive. They tell me there's a place about ten miles up the road where they have the best stewed eels."

"Yuck!"

I was delighted to see a smile, however brief. "Then how about some fresh-baked trout?"

The smile widened. "That's more like it."

I gave her a final squeeze and kissed the top of her head. "Okay, you get dressed while I hop into the tub."

I took a quick bath, still missing the showers I was used to, and preferred. I had just wrapped myself in a towel and was coming back to the bedroom, when PJ confronted me. Her stance was belligerent, and her eyes sent spears of anger through me.

"Only *me* in your bed, isn't that what you said?"

"Yes."

"Then, what the hell are these?" She threw a pair of bronze-colored briefs onto the bed.

"They're not mine. I don't have any undies that color." Come to think of it, PJ didn't either, so who the hell did they belong to? A knot formed in my gut.

"Pick them up. Look at them. Look at the initials."

What was going on here? Neither one of us had any initialed briefs.

"What's the matter?" PJ asked, her eyes blazing fury. "You've handled them before. Why would you hesitate now?"

I reached for the briefs. On the right side of the front, in delicate gold stitching, were the initials TS. "Terry Simms."

"Bingo! You got it in one!"

I turned to stare at her. "Where did you get these?"

She tugged at the dresser drawer with her right hand. "Right here in this stupid, damn drawer." After it failed to move more than a few inches, she slapped at it and turned back to me. "You need to smarten up and destroy the evidence before wifey finds it, don't you think, sweetie?"

"You think I put them there? *You* tell me where they came from."

PJ's whole body bristled. "Don't insult my intelligence by denying that you slept with her."

"But I didn't!"

She advanced toward me, the index finger of her right hand stabbing the air in front of my face. "You were probably so horny you had them off her before you even got to the bed. Maybe you and she were rolling around on the floor, or you were on your knees in front of her and she was up against the dresser."

"Shut up!" I grabbed her finger and held it still. The tone of my voice halted her tirade in mid sentence. "Terry was never in this room with me. Do you hear me? Never." I released her finger and stood back, taking several deep breaths, my mind whirling. "Which brings me to only one conclusion." I picked up the panties and flung them into a corner. "And that is, that you and she were here, together. That it was you and she making love. Then, too late, you found the briefs and realized they'd be a dead giveaway, so you concocted this wild story about Terry and me to cover your own guilty ass."

Her mouth dropped open. "What?"

"You've had plenty of time alone since you were released from the hospital."

She was stabbing her finger at me again. "Don't you dare turn this around on me."

I shook my head slowly, the knot in my gut growing tighter by the second. "It explains why you've been reluctant to let me touch you or make love to you. It had nothing to do with rough handling by your captors, did it? That was just an excuse. I see it all now. You were getting what you wanted from Terry."

"That's the most ridiculous—"

"Stop it!" My head was pounding. "If you wanted out of this relationship, why didn't you just say so, instead of planning this elaborate, overly dramatic scheme?"

"You're crazy!" Her voice choked. She put her hand on her stomach and closed her eyes, fighting back more tears.

I snatched a pair of cargo pants off the hanger and a Welsh, fisherman-style sweater from the drawer and dressed in a daze.

"I'll send for my stuff later." I grabbed a waterproof anorak off the hook inside the door.

"Kim, wait. I want to know why. Where are you going?"

I slammed the door behind me, her words still echoing in my head.

In truth, I had no idea where I was going.

* * *

I stood in the courtyard, stunned at the sudden and unexpected turn of events.

PJ and Terry! Just the thought of them together turned my stomach. I couldn't believe it, didn't want to believe it, but the evidence was there—in the underwear and in her false accusations.

It was undoubtedly Terry's doing, but why would PJ fall for her line? I had credited her with more sense. "I guess you never know." My words were lost in the driving rain.

The normally picturesque village was shrouded in a gloomy pall. I walked through the pouring rain, losing track of time, oblivious to the dampness that soaked into my bones and chilled my soul. The very real possibility of hypothermia didn't enter my mind until later. My heart was breaking; any other ailment paled in comparison.

The huge raindrops were like tears from the sky, joining those that trailed down my cheeks.

How could I have been so stupid… not to know, not to have guessed?

Terry must have been with her just this morning. I was in that drawer early, when I first got up and dressed. Those briefs weren't there then.

I walked along the wet, deserted street, overhead lights reflecting in the slate gray pavement. With no destination in mind, I splashed through puddles I didn't even see, my saturated clothing weighing me down.

So, that was why she was taking such a late bath, to wash away the evidence.

I choked on the thought. PJ and Terry.

"No!"

I felt sick and betrayed. The once arousing vision of PJ lying naked in the tub now disgusted me. All I could see was both of them together, all over each other, making love. The image of Terry exploring PJ's secret places, the ones I thought she shared with me alone, left me swallowing hard, unsuccessfully fighting nausea.

I stood at the river's edge watching the wild water gurgling, burbling, and leaping over and around the boulders in its path. Despite the obstacles, the river kept moving.

That's what I had to do: keep moving. But how could I do that when I felt so devastated, so betrayed?

I was older than PJ and had sometimes wondered whether she was uncomfortable with the difference in our ages. But damn it all, Terry was only five years younger than I was. Age couldn't have been that much of a problem. Five years is five years, though. And Terry was here, providing an easy way for PJ to end our relationship.

Damn it, why couldn't she have just talked to me about it? There had been no warning of her discontent, no previous distancing between us.

Terry was worldly, smooth, and good-looking. She had a line that would snag even the most reluctant of women, or men, for that matter. She used them, too, whenever it was to her advantage.

She had even tried it on me again. But she found that I was on to her little games. Maybe I shouldn't be so surprised that she got her hooks into PJ. Terry would play with her awhile until she'd had enough, and then she'd discard her, as she had me. By the time PJ realized what was happening, Terry would have destroyed her, too.

* * *

Finally, I returned to the inn. I didn't want to face Arwel or any of the staff, so I let myself in through a back door. My pants were waterlogged and my hair plastered against my skull. Shivering, I summoned up the courage to knock on Frederick's door. I didn't know what else to do, where else to go.

Luckily, he was in and alone. He took one look at me, and his mouth fell open. "What the hell happened to you?"

My teeth were chattering and my voice was husky, but I managed to blurt out, "PJ and I—it's over."

"Come in, woman. You'll catch your death." He refused to listen to anything I had to say until I went into his bathroom, removed my wet clothes, toweled myself off, and wrapped myself in a thick warm blanket that he had pulled off the bed.

"Here, drink this," he said, when I came out, handing me a tumbler of scotch. It burned going down, making my eyes water on top of the tears.

Frederick listened patiently to my halting story, including the part of my having lived with Terry at one time.

He looked uncomfortable. "I hate to say this, but you're right about one thing. They were together this morning. I know that because Terry left a note for me at the desk, saying that she had just left Priscilla. That was around eleven-thirty. I didn't understand then, and I still don't, why she felt the need to tell me that she had been to the room, unless—"

"Unless she wanted to be sure I knew about their liaison."

"Damn it! I thought that daughter of mine had finally settled down. Sometimes, she doesn't use good sense."

"Frederick, your daughter is considerably younger than I am. Perhaps she feels I'll hold her back as I get older."

"Nonsense."

"Something pushed her into Terry's arms."

"Look here, I want you to move into the adjoining room. You can use it for as long as you're here. It's right through that door. But first, I'm going to insist you have something to eat. Then, I'll fetch some of your clothes."

"I'm not hungry, Frederick."

"I'm sure you're not, but I insist. A bowl of Cook's hot soup and some fresh baked bread isn't a cure-all, but it will do wonders for the chill."

I wasn't just chilled to the bone; I was chilled to the depths of my soul. I doubted that soup could fix that.

Frederick opened a cupboard and pulled out a soft bath towel. "While I'm having the kitchen rustle up something for you to eat, I want you to soak in a warm tub." He handed me the towel and his tartan wool robe.

"Thank you," I murmured, tears stinging my eyes.

He gave me a hug. "Things will look brighter after a hot meal, Kim, and after you've rested."

"If you say so." I turned on the bath water, and he left on his errands.

Frederick's soft, well-used robe smelled faintly of his distinctive aftershave. When I put it on after my shower, I found it strangely comforting.

Chapter 26

When a knock sounded on the door, I hoped it was Kim returning to apologize for her part in our fight and separation. Even though I was still very angry and confused about what had happened, I was prepared to forgive her.

It was Dad, however, who filled the doorway.

"I just came to collect Pup and pick up some of Kim's clothing," he said, as he entered the room. If he noticed my puffy eyes and tear-stained cheeks, he refrained from commenting.

How the hell did he get mixed up in all of this? I was too exhausted to ask.

Without a word, I yanked the wardrobe door open, found Kim's suitcase, and slammed it onto the bed. Dad stooped to give Pup lots of tickles and scratches, and I felt a pang of guilt. I'd neglected our pet during the aftermath of the fight. The poor baby had kept a low profile, avoiding my unpredictable outbursts of anger and anguish, preferring to curl up in the corner with his muzzle on his paws.

I'd like to keep Pup with me, but he was Kim's friend first, and she had every right to claim him. My God, had it come to that? Were we about to divide our jointly owned possessions, the things we had accumulated so lovingly together? Not that Pup was a possession. No animal was. But was he the first step in the rending of our relationship?

My stomach tightened, and I was momentarily breathless from the lump forming in my throat. I shook my head and choked back angry tears.

All because Terry mattered more to her than I had ever thought possible. Damn that woman to hell and back.

I spread Kim's suitcase open, picked up her neatly folded articles of clothing, and pitched them into one side or the other. I kept my back to my father. If I faced him, I'd lose my composure, but his uncharacteristic silence was an irritation.

"I suppose you're going to tell me I'm being pig-headed and that Kim is the best thing that ever happened to me."

"That's what I'd like to say, but I think you already know that, so I'll settle for telling you that she's staying in one of the empty rooms in my suite."

Oh, so that was how he got involved. She needed a place to stay when she left me. A few stray tears escaped, and I swiped at them. "Good. I'd hate to think of her roaming the streets in weather like this."

Dad cleared his throat. "I'm afraid she already did. When she arrived at my door, she looked like somebody's drowned puppy dog."

I made an involuntary sound that he might have construed as concern. Of course, it wasn't. She had betrayed me, damn it—going back to her old flame. I was the injured party here; at least, I thought I was.

Truthfully, I wasn't sure what had happened to us. I know we fought and parted, and now I felt like shit.

"I know you're concerned about her, Princess."

"I am not. She's a big girl. She can take care of herself." I folded my arms across my chest and stared at the window where rain ran in rivulets down the green-tinted glass.

He sighed, and I imagined him folding his own arms. "Princess, I know you're upset, and I have no right to interfere."

"Right. So don't." I finished packing Kim's suitcase, smashed its sides together, and fastened the latches. "This isn't Carlos or any of the fiascoes of my youth, Dad. You can't solve this problem for me."

"I realize that, but I'm willing to listen to your side of the story if you want to tell me." The floor squeaked as he took a step toward me.

When I didn't say anything, he moved closer, pulling me around and into his arms. "Come on, I know you're hurting."

I hugged him back and rested my head against his chest.

Damn it, he didn't play fair. How could I wallow in my misery if he wouldn't keep his distance?

For several seconds we stood together. I sniffled and struggled with my emotions. He plucked a few tissues from a box on the dresser, so I could blow my nose.

"Dad, it was so awful." I told him what happened, ending with the most critical piece of information. "Kim and Terry had a history before I came along."

He rubbed my back and kissed the top of my head. "I know. Kim told me all about it. I wish I'd never contacted that Simms woman. I should have known her availability was just too convenient, but she was so well-recommended."

I looked up at him. "Don't blame yourself. It was bound to happen sooner or later. Terry knows Kim better than I do. She knows all the things that Kim likes, how to satisfy her every—"

"Whoa." He pulled back, one hand gripping my good shoulder. "That's a bit more information than I want right now."

I gave him a tired grin. "Sorry."

With a light touch on my cheek, he brushed a few new tears away. "Just let me say that Kim loves you, Princess. Only you. And this is tearing her apart inside. Just as it's doing to you."

"Then why doesn't she come and talk to me?"

"She's stubborn." He lifted my chin. "Almost as stubborn as you are."

"Do you believe her?"

"I do. More important, though, do you believe her?"

My father was a good judge of character. If he thought Kim was telling the truth, then…

"I want to, more than anything. I love her so much." Tears leaked out again, trailing down to my chin.

He dabbed my cheeks with a tissue and kissed my forehead. "Give her a little time. This is all a misunderstanding. She'll be ready to talk when she's calmed down."

"Okay, I'll try."

I found Pup's leash, clipped it onto his collar, and crouched down to bury my face in his furry neck. "I'll see you soon, I hope. Maybe we could share custody of you."

"He and I don't want to get in the middle of this." Dad picked up the suitcase and took the leash from me. "Come on, Pup. Let's go cheer up your other mother."

Pup gave me a tiny swish of his bushy tail.

"Thanks, buddy," I said. "I appreciate your support."

* * *

Arwel brought me a tray of meat, cheese, and granary bread.

"If there's anything else you need, Dr. Curtis, just ask."

"Thanks." I couldn't quite meet her gaze. There was an awkward pause. "Nothing right now, thank you."

I played with the food, rearranging it on the platter, but my appetite was nonexistent. With a sigh, I gave up all pretense of eating, put the tray on the dresser, and prepared for bed.

Since my wound had been aching ever since my antics with Kim's suitcase, I swallowed enough pain medication to help me sleep through the night.

No Kim and no Pup. I was on my own. Who was going to help me get ready for bed?

Luckily, one of Kim's old button-down shirts was hanging in the bathroom. I slid my good arm through the right sleeve and gathered the other around my sore shoulder, leaving several of the uppermost buttons unfastened to accommodate my bent left arm. Kim's distinctive spicy scent lingered on the fabric, filling my heart with longing. I turned down the bedcovers and switched off all the lights, except the one next to Kim's side of the bed.

Not quite ready to sleep, I sat on the bed and stroked Kim's pillow, clutching it awkwardly to my chest to inhale more of her scent. Was this the first of many nights that I would have to sleep in a big, empty bed?

When a light tap sounded on the door, I figured it was Arwel returning for the tray and I went to answer it.

"Terry?" My chest tightened. Thrumming sounds filled my ears. "What the hell are you doing here?"

"Hi, PJ," she said, keeping her voice low. "I'm sorry to barge in on you like this, but I felt so bad about what happened. I just wanted to see if you were going to be okay." She was dressed in slim-fitting slacks and a silk blouse, accessorized with a pendant and a flashy ring with a blue stone. The exotic fragrance that clung to her body was probably meant to allure and attract, but it turned my stomach and left me feeling anxious.

As she stepped through the doorway, I blocked her path. "Look, Terry, I don't mean to be rude, but I don't want to see you right now. In fact, I was just about to go to bed."

"I see. I won't stay long, then." She glanced at the bed. "Unless you want me to join you."

"What?"

"Oh, I'm kidding, of course." She favored me with the same sensual smile I had witnessed in the hospital, took off her jacket, and tossed it onto the chair. The tiny hairs on the back of my neck tingled. "You know, PJ, I give a pretty mean backrub. Perhaps it would help you sleep better tonight."

I shook my head, temporarily speechless.

Her laughter startled me. "You needn't be afraid of me." She reached for my right hand. "I never bite on a first date."

My stomach tightened, and I yanked my hand free. "I'm not in the mood for this."

"What are you in the mood for?"

Her gaze traveled down my body, lingering on the area that displayed an immodest amount of my chest.

Damn it. Why hadn't I grabbed my robe before I went to the door?

She looked at my face again. "Poor thing, you've been crying, haven't you?" She flashed a sympathetic smile, and her hand slid along my arm before I could snatch it away.

"What? Oh, um—"

"Let me guess." She took a step toward me, and I retreated. "I'm good at this." She licked her bottom lip. "You and Kim fought, she stormed out, and now you're devastated." She touched my cheek; her fingertips were warm against my skin. "Am I right?"

"No." I took another step backwards, but my legs bumped up against the side of the bed. "Listen, Terry, you'd really better go now."

"Come on, PJ. We're having a friendly conversation, that's all, getting to know each other better." She sat at the bottom of the bed, while I remained standing. I realized that the painkillers were starting to dull my reflexes and affect my thinking.

"I'm here to make amends, if I can," she said. "PJ, please, sit down, or lie down. You look like you're about to collapse."

"No, I'm fine." I did sit on the edge of the bed, though, just to ease my tired legs. "It's the pain medicine. I took some before you arrived, and it's making me drowsy."

She smiled and scooted close enough to rub my back and shoulder. "You really need to lie down, sugar. Does your wound still ache?" Before I could react, her fingers tugged at Kim's shirt, pulling it off my shoulder and exposing my breast.

"Hey!" I pushed her hand away and covered myself.

"Sorry, sugar. I'm only trying to help. Don't be embarrassed. You have a beautiful body, at least what I can see of it." Her hand moved slowly along my arm. "I bet I can make that shoulder feel better. I can make all of you feel fantastic. How about I show you something Kim used to love?"

"No." Her coming on to me was creeping me out. I stood, and used a more authoritative voice. "You've done quite enough damage already. Now, leave me alone."

"You're such a sweet thing, but you're not playing the game right at all. I came here to say I was sorry. I thought maybe we could get to know each other a bit better, you know, and it would make you feel better."

"Not tonight. Not any night, for that matter."

She pushed herself off the bed and approached me. "Kim isn't here, you're going to sleep alone in that big bed, and I'm finding you extremely attractive, even injured and dressed in that hideous shirt."

I stepped toward the door, and she followed me.

"You want to stop the fun before it even gets started."

"That's right. I do."

"That hurts my feelings, sugar, and I'm not used to being rejected."

I took a long, slow breath, trying to stay patient. "I'm sorry about that, but I don't like this game you're playing."

"You don't?"

"Not at all."

She put her hands on her hips. "Listen to me. I'm offering you something very special."

"And I'm refusing you." I turned the knob and opened the door. "So, get the hell out of my room."

"I'm so much better in bed than that old fossil. I can't believe you'd turn me down."

"Believe it."

"Very well, if you insist." She started out, and then quickly turned around. Before I could move, she had her arms around me and my good arm pinned to my side. Pain knifed through my wounded shoulder.

"Ahh! Jesus! Stop it!"

Terry kicked the door shut with her foot, forced me back up against it, and pressed her body into me. I could feel her warm breath against my neck.

We struggled briefly. She kissed me on the mouth, and I twisted my head to one side. "Stop it!" I squirmed and twisted, trying to free myself from her grasp.

"Come on, sugar. Get naked and show me that tattoo on your ass. You know you want to."

I ignored the pain in my shoulder and pushed that arm against her, creating a few inches of space between us. "I want no such thing."

Her lips parted. She lunged at me, kissing my mouth, cheek, and neck.

I gagged.

"Baby, relax. Enjoy yourself."

She was too damn strong for me to fight one-handed. And on top of everything else, I thought my wound had reopened and started to bleed. My call for help ended in a strangled yelp when Terry's hand clamped down on my mouth.

"No, no, sugar. No noise. This is our little party. We don't want any company."

I wrestled with her in a vain attempt to get free.

"God, you fight like a little wildcat." She let go of my mouth and put her cheek against mine. "I bet you're a spitfire in bed."

"You'll never know. Now, *back off*!" I was sure Terry could feel my strength draining away. Holding me with one arm, she used the other to pull my shirt open and paw at my chest, making soft mewing sounds. When she tried to put her mouth over my breast, I broke away long enough to deliver a solid punch to her eye. We both cried out in pain.

"You little bitch!" She backhanded me hard across the mouth, splitting my lip and bringing tears to my eyes. I bent over and clutched my jaw with my aching right hand.

"God damn it, that hurts." Terry picked me up and tossed me on the bed, where I lay on my back, gasping.

"Help! Somebody help me!" My shouts were feeble now, and I was shivering from pain.

Terry climbed on the bed and straddled my hips.

"Why are you doing this to me?"

"Shut up. You hear me? Just shut up." Her chest was heaving, her breath coming in great gasps. "I didn't want to hurt you, I really didn't. I just wanted things to be the way they were with Kim and me, but you were in the way. So, I'm going to change the rules and split you up for good by having a little fun with you."

I swallowed some bloody saliva. "Kim and I had a fight, but we'll work it out. It's not over between us."

"She's too old for you anyway. You're better off without her." She lowered her head and clamped her mouth over my exposed breast, applying her tongue and teeth to my nipple.

I felt nauseous, and the room was spinning. Pain and panic had me gasping for air. "Stop! You're crazy. You've got to stop—"

Wham! The door crashed open with a tremendous noise and Kim burst into the room like a human dynamo. She seized Terry by the shoulders and tossed her to the floor. Harsh barking and fierce growls bounced off the walls.

"I'll handle this, Pup! Go to PJ."

Shivering and whimpering, I curled into a fetal position. The bleeding wound was making me light-headed. If I moved too much, I was afraid I'd pass out.

Pup came to me, and I held on to him as tightly as I could with my good arm. Deep-throated growls rumbled in his chest. If ordered, he would have torn Terry to pieces. I was afraid Kim was going to do just that all by herself; she was pummeling Terry's face with her bare hands.

"Kim, no!" I cried.

Terry cowered and covered her face with both hands, trying to talk between the blows. "Ow! Stop. PJ came on to me. I didn't want to—out of respect for—"

"You lying bitch!" Kim smashed Terry's nose, and blood splattered over both of them. "Don't talk to me about respect. You don't even know the meaning of the word."

"Please stop. You're going to kill me."

Kim readied another punch. "I *should* kill you."

"Please, Kimmy," I said, "you've got to stop."

"Stay out of this, PJ. It's between Terry and me."

My father and Geoff dashed into the room.

"My God!" Dad snatched up a blanket and covered me. "Easy. Don't try to move."

"What the bloody hell?" Geoff stared at my face.

"Go call an ambulance," Dad said to him. "I'll handle Kim."

Kim resisted Dad's efforts to restrain her, but after some persuasion, she lowered her swollen fists and stepped back, leaving a battered and blood-smeared Terry lying on the floor.

Kim turned her attention toward me, and her rage seemed to drain away as quickly as it had taken hold.

"My God, PJ. Are you okay?" Her eyes glistened with tears. She cradled me in her arms before lowering me down on the bed and propping a pillow under my head. Using an extra pillowcase, she stanched the flow of blood from my shoulder. Even with the blanket covering me, I couldn't stop shivering.

"I'm so cold, Kimmy."

"It's going to be okay." Kim brushed my bangs back and placed a tender kiss on my forehead. "Help will be here in no time."

"I know, but first, I want to tell you—."

"Don't try to talk now."

I clutched at her, feeling her strong arms around me, moving gingerly across my back and shoulders.

"Where does it hurt, sweetheart?"

"My shoulder, my head…" I flexed my fingers. "My right hand." My breast. Oh, Kimmy. Terry's tongue… her teeth…

I started to cry.

"Oh, baby, I'm so sorry." Tears spilled down Kim's cheeks and dripped from her chin. "If I hadn't been so pig-headed—"

"No." I stopped her apology. "I doubted you. It's my fault. I'm so incredibly sorry. Can you ever forgive me?"

She pulled me to her breast, ruffled my hair, and kissed the top of my head. I could hear the rapid beating of her heart. "Of course, little one, though I don't blame you one bit. We'll talk more, after we get you fixed up. Damn that woman! What the hell is the matter with her? She's always been flirtatious and full of herself, but this is far out even for her."

I heard Dad's voice and Arwel's, too, saying something about shock, but my head was spinning and darkness closed in on me. From a long distance, I heard Kim shouting, "Where the hell is that bloody ambulance?"

I had a vague awareness of several strong hands probing me from different angles. I remembered ripping and tearing sounds, cold metal against my chest, a tightening on one arm, and then relief. I felt sharp pricks of pain and heard confident voices murmuring soothing words above me. I was lifted onto a stretcher and sank comfortably into a cozy, warm corner of my mind, free of pain for the first time in what seemed like an eternity.

* * *

Light flickered behind my eyelids, and hushed voices penetrated my subconscious. Though I couldn't quite understand the words, the voices were familiar. Other senses came to my assistance.

Antiseptic smells. Stiff sheets pulled snug against my body. A tube taped to the back of my hand. Shit. I was in the hospital. Again.

Details came flooding back to me. Terry. The attack. Kim and Pup charging to my rescue.

I needed to open my eyes. I had to tell Kim that I was sorry we fought. I was an idiot not to realize that Terry was behind it all. Kim had to forgive me. Damn it, why wouldn't my eyes open?

"Hey there, beautiful." Kim's voice penetrated the haze.

I felt her touch my arm, and I opened my eyes as she leaned over the bed railing to kiss my cheek.

"Welcome back, little one," she whispered.

I blinked back an onslaught of tears. "I'm so sorry."

“Shh.” Two fingers brushed across my lips. “You have nothing to be sorry for.”

“I was so stupid. And I was too weak to stop her.”

“It’s over now, and you’re safe.” She blotted my cheeks with a tissue and kissed me again, on the mouth this time.

Her lips grazed my cheek and touched the tip of my nose, making me smile.

“That’s more like it.” She grinned and gripped my free hand. “You’re going to be fine, you’ll see. Once you get your strength back, we’re going to be better than ever.”

My smile faltered. Somehow, I didn’t think it would be that easy.

Chapter 27

PJ was still sedated when I entered her hospital room. I tiptoed to the side of her bed and stood by the railing, watching her chest rise and fall with each gentle breath, assuring myself that she wasn't in any discomfort.

Her face was pale beneath long straggly bangs. She'd want a haircut as soon as we got back to Boston.

The bruise along her jaw was changing from red to purple. Damn Terry! I wanted to do a number on her jaw. My wish for revenge turned into a smile of satisfaction. Hell, I had already done a number on her face she wouldn't soon forget. I giggled, and wondered if she'd need a nose job.

PJ looked so fragile, lying there with tubes and attachments hooked up to her body. The doctor had assured Frederick and me that the intravenous fluids were precautionary, keeping her electrolytes balanced, and that the catheter would be removed as soon as she was ambulatory. The medical mumbo-jumbo gave me a headache, and it scared me to see her so still, so vulnerable.

I was supposed to be her Amazon warrior, her protector. If only I'd been quicker getting back to the room, I could have stopped Terry from hurting her. My throat tightened. If only…

I rested my hands on the bed rail and found it cold to the touch. It felt like a barrier between us. What other barriers had come between us because of Terry and her vicious tricks?

I felt another flush of anger and struggled to compose myself.

I had to focus on PJ. She was going to need plenty of support when she woke up.

As if hearing my thoughts, she moved her hand in my direction and sighed. I slid my arm between the bars of the rail and tickled her fingertips.

"Hey there, beautiful." Gently, I stroked her forearm. "Welcome back, little one."

She stirred. I watched her soft, green eyes open and immediately flood with tears. Her stammered apology sent daggers of guilt straight to my heart.

I reached for a tissue to dry her tears.

"It's over now, and you're safe." I kissed her, then kissed her again.

"You're going to be fine, you'll see. Once you get your strength back, we're going to be better than ever."

She accepted my words but didn't seem convinced that all was well. The PJ I knew and loved was never this passive.

I relaxed a little after the doctors came in and told us that physically she was going to be okay. She'd spend one more night in the hospital and then be released to my care.

* * *

After a few days of recuperation, PJ was getting stronger, but I could see that the traumas of the kidnapping and Terry's vicious attack were affecting her mental state. I hoped that time and good therapy would fix that. Meanwhile, I intended to distract her with some short trips away from our room, to reconnect socially.

PJ had always loved eating out, talking to people, visiting friends, shopping, and seeing shows, but for the past few days, she'd confined herself to our room with only me for company. To nudge her out of seclusion and back to the real world, I'd made dinner reservations for the evening.

I held her jacket as she slid her arms into the sleeves. Judging from the amount of grimacing going on, she was still in pain from her wound. It would take some time before her shoulder returned to normal, and the slow healing had to be frustrating her.

There were smudges of fatigue under her eyes, and her face was pale from too much indoor confinement. She needed to get out and start living again.

We needed to be working, but projects weren't a dime a dozen and there wasn't anything in our sights for the immediate future. Oh, how I missed the years of searching for the lost tribe. I sighed. Something would materialize. It always did.

Inviting PJ out to dinner might be premature, but it also might boost her spirits. Damn those men, and damn Terry, for what they did to her, taking the sparkle from her eyes. Damn them to hell.

"I'd like us to go to Sally's Café for dinner," I said, a reassuring smile plastered on my face. "But if you don't feel up to it yet, just say so."

She poked me in the chest, forcing me backwards. Apparently, she wasn't as weak as she looked. "Stop fussing over me. Honestly, Kim, sometimes you're like a mother hen. My shoulder's not that bad today. I even have a bit of an appetite."

"Okay, if you're sure." I held out my right hand, and after giving me a puzzled look, she shook it. "We'll go tonight then, and I promise not to act like a mother hen."

"It's a deal." She flashed me her familiar lopsided grin.

"But it's cool and damp outside, so maybe your heavier jacket would be better."

"Cluck, cluck."

I raised both hands in surrender. "Okay, point taken. I won't say another word."

She scooped up her shoulder bag, and we left our room. "Promises, promises," I heard her mutter, as we descended the narrow stairs.

I couldn't help it. I loved her so much.

* * *

Although the café wasn't crowded, we asked for a table in the rear where we could talk without being overheard and PJ could ease herself back into civilization. As we were led to it, heads turned and watched us, but most diners returned to their conversations after a few polite glances. Since the story of PJ's kidnapping had been publicized, they more than likely knew who we were, and their curiosity was understandable.

Muted talk mingled with sounds of tinkling glasses and clinking silverware to provide background noise as we soaked up the Welsh atmosphere.

PJ spied the collection of teapots. "Oh, aren't they gorgeous? I wonder if they're for sale."

I shrugged. "We could ask, though I imagine they're part of the owner's private collection."

She admired them a second or two longer, and then focused on me. "No matter. The whole place is so enchanting, so very Welsh."

"Wait until you taste the food." I gave her a wink. "The aromas alone will put pounds on you."

PJ frowned. "Ah, yes, my weight. We're back to that topic."

"I'm sorry. I didn't mean anything."

"Now then," a smiling young waitress said, handing us each a menu, "how are you ladies today?"

We murmured a few noncommittal words and smiled back at her. She had striking blue eyes and reddish blonde hair, pulled back into a ponytail.

I took a quick look at the menu, but neither of us needed any time to decide on our orders.

"Steak and kidney pie for me, please," I said.

"And I'd like the trout cooked in white wine and lemon juice." PJ looked at me. "Should we order tea, or do you want something stronger?"

I smiled at her and turned my head toward the waitress. "A pot of tea will be fine, thank you."

She finished writing our orders and reclaimed the menus. "I'll be back in a tick with your tea, ladies."

When the entrees arrived, I insisted that PJ try a bite of mine. She sampled a small portion, but wasn't impressed.

"I'm sorry you had to wait so long for your trout," I told her, dabbing a drop of gravy from my lip. "We had to weather a storm before we could land those babies."

She rolled her eyes. "Yeah, like we went out and caught them."

"True, but with all we went through before getting to this point, we might as well have gone fishing for them."

I hadn't fly-fished in years. It was something I had enjoyed until work assignments, Amazons, and other complications got in the way. I imagined a perfect fly-fishing holiday with PJ.

Fly-fishing was poetry in motion. I could visualize the line sailing through the air, over the fresh, clear water, the sun glinting on its arc. It took a lot of skill to get the lure to land at exactly the right spot—fooling the fish into thinking the colorful critter was the real thing.

It was a battle of wits between fisher and fished.

Archaeology was a little like that: a battle of wits between the ancient world and the modern one. Reading the past was much like reading the habits of a fresh-water trout; it didn't want to be caught any more than the past wanted to be revealed.

I heard the soft clink of a spoon against my water glass. "Kimmy, oh, Kimmy… Is there anyone home?"

"Sorry, I was far away."

"Yeah, tell me about it."

"Actually, I was thinking about fly-fishing."

“Fly-fishing?” Her eyes widened, and I noted the lopsided grin before it disappeared.

“Yeah. Do you like to fish?”

“I don’t know. I can’t remember ever doing much of it.” She rubbed her chin, thinking. “There was one time, now that I think of it, when I was little.”

I smothered a laugh.

She frowned at me. “You know what I mean. Okay, when I was younger. Dad took me on a boat, and we went deep-sea fishing. That wasn’t much fun, really. I had to get strapped into a special chair and hold this enormous rod. My arms ached and my hands were bent into claws.” She gestured with curled fingers. “It took forever to reel the stupid fish close enough to the boat, and then the men threw it back anyway.” She wrinkled up her face.

“This would be a lot different. Would you like to try?”

She reached across the table and gave my hand a squeeze. “Kimmy, with you, I’ll try anything.”

I placed my other hand on top of hers. “Then we’ll do it.”

“As long as you take care of the fish and the worms.”

“We don’t use worms in fly-fishing. We use lures.”

PJ reclaimed her hand and took a sip of tea. “Okay, whatever.” She put the cup in its saucer and rubbed her palms together. “Now that’s settled, what’s for dessert?”

“Dessert?”

“Yeah, you know, those gooey goodies you drool over before devouring, then regret having eaten when your pants get too tight.”

“You have such a romantic way of putting things.”

“Dessert, my dear. What about dessert?”

How could I resist her? I was putty in her hands, and overjoyed to see her so animated. Besides, she needed the extra calories. I picked up the dessert menu and made a show of perusing the list.

“I’m having apple-cinnamon cake,” she said, as if to spur me into action.

“Okay, I think I’ll have blackberry and apple pie with custard sauce.”

“Ooh, that sounds good, too. Maybe we can split and have a little of both.”

I raised an eyebrow. “You mean if I let you taste mine, you’ll let me taste yours?”

The sexual innuendo struck us both at the same time, and we grinned lecherously. I was encouraged to see a hint of the devilish PJ returning. She leaned across the table to add something naughty, but was interrupted by the waitress asking if we had decided on dessert, or sweet, as she called it.

"We're going to share," PJ said with a straight face. "We're going to taste each other's. Can we do that?"

"Oh yes. We have many customers who like to taste each other's sweet."

I spluttered as her perfectly innocent remark caught me in the act of swallowing water.

* * *

After dinner, stuffed and contented, we strolled along the quiet streets and stopped beside the river. We stood silently, arms around each other, and watched the moonlit water gurgle and bubble its way downstream. I thought about that other night when—wet, angry, and brokenhearted—I had looked at the river and wished I could lose myself in its depths. I glanced at PJ standing beside me, her arm still snug around my waist, and knew that drowning in the river's murky depths was no longer an option.

"Look at that clean water," she murmured. "I wish I could pour all the sordid memories of the past few weeks into that river and let it cleanse my soul completely."

I hugged her against me, defying any other sordid thoughts to defile her. "You're safe now, little one. Nobody's going to hurt you while I'm around."

She tilted her head upward to smile at my bold declaration. "I appreciate the sentiment, but as we've both learned the hard way, there are no guarantees of safety in this world."

"Yeah, I know. There will always be criminals. But even beyond them, there are always people like Terry lurking about, ready to make trouble. She wasn't always that way. A few years into our relationship, she wanted to experiment more, if you know what I mean, but we were able to compromise. Something in her has changed in the past five years, and not for the better."

"Kimmy, that's probably more than I need to know about you and Terry."

"Sorry."

"But I've been meaning to ask you something."

"What, sweetheart?"

"Why on earth did you tell her about my tattoo?"

"I didn't. Why would I have a need to? Oh, wait a second. She was at the morgue the day I had to look at that young woman's body. I told Sergeant Jones you had a tattoo, and no doubt Terry heard me."

"Jesus. The police know about it, too?"

I chuckled. "Yeah, but they're sworn to keep things like that confidential."

"Okay. I guess that makes sense, then. But you'd think Terry would have given you some privacy, just in case it was me."

"True."

"Anyway, given the circumstances, I forgive you."

"That was so hard, PJ, going in there, terrified I'd see you on that cold slab." A chill slid down my spine. "I don't know what I would have done if—but enough of that."

I traced gentle circles against her back with my fingertips. "How are you doing? Are you still feeling anxious?"

"Every once in a while it comes over me, that's all. I used to be fearless, you know, but now…" Her voice trailed off. "My confidence is shaken. I feel so weak and helpless at times, and these scary thoughts worm their way into my brain."

"Oh, honey." I brushed her bangs aside and kissed the top of her forehead. "The doctor your dad found will help you with all of that."

"I hope so. She's supposed to be an expert in mental trauma." PJ's eyes glistened as she looked at me and then away. "Is that what I have now? Mental trauma?"

I wanted to assure her she was as strong and confident as she'd ever been, but I knew she had changed. "Some, I guess," I told her. "But, it's understandable, considering what you've been through."

"I don't like it. Not one bit. The time in the hospital was bad enough, but it turned out that getting shot was only the beginning of the problem."

We turned and headed toward the inn and our warm, safe room. As we walked, I analyzed my own feelings of inadequacy. While PJ and I had been separated, first by the kidnapping, then by her hospitalization, I had floundered in a haze of anxiety, fear, and rage. The final couple of days that she spent recovering from Terry's assault were among the worst in my life.

PJ wasn't the only one who had come away changed. I was different, too. I blamed Terry for disrupting part of our lives, and I wanted her punished.

My former lover had been arrested, courtesy of Her Majesty, but had posted bail and disappeared. I was furious at the leniency of the Welsh judicial system, and wondered whether she would show up for the hearing or flee to the States or some other part of the world. Terry had almost succeeded in destroying PJ and me, but despite her efforts, we *were* together and we *would* heal. I had faith that in time, we would recover all we had lost.

We had both learned a serious lesson in trust. It wouldn't be that easy again for anyone to drive a wedge between us. I squeezed her hand as we strolled along. After a few minutes, I stopped and nudged her up against a stone wall, where I lowered my head and planted tiny kisses along her jaw.

She giggled, tilted her head, and moaned in pleasure when my lips found the hollow of her collarbone and lingered there.

"Are you sure there's nobody watching us?" she asked, her voice a husky whisper.

I looked in all directions. "Not a soul in sight."

"Good." With a sigh, she pulled my head down and delivered a moist, open-mouthed kiss to my waiting lips. Our tongues tangled in a delicious duel over familiar territory, as the river raced along nearby, all but ignored.

We spoke little as we wandered slowly toward the inn. Just being together was what we needed after all we had been through. Words were unnecessary when our innermost thoughts were in tune. Besides, it would only burden PJ to know about my inner turmoil. Her recovery was of primary importance.

* * *

"Who was on the phone?" PJ perched on the edge of our bed and towel-dried her hair, perfuming the air between us with the scent of raspberries.

Her terrycloth robe, cinched at the waist, covered an extra large T-shirt. I felt a pang of disappointment when I realized she intended to sleep in the shirt again tonight. Months ago, when we first became lovers, we had decided to sleep nude whenever possible. It had been an enjoyable, comfortable, and quite practical arrangement for those times when the urge to make love overcame us.

Since the kidnapping, however, PJ clothed herself in some sort of shirt or gown at bedtime. We were just about to hurdle this awkward barrier and return to our preferred sleeping attire when Terry attacked her, and we lost all the progress we'd made.

I knew I had to be patient, that PJ would work her way through this new difficulty. In deference to her feelings, I began wearing my comfortable, well-worn scrubs again. It would only be a matter of time, but meanwhile, I ached for the feel of her warm body draped across mine as we slept. So much time had passed since we had been intimate, and I knew just how much I was missing. She had awakened a whole new vista of sensual delight in me during the past year. Damn it, I wanted it back. I wanted her—plain and simple.

"Kimmy?"

"Hmm?"

"Earth to Kim. Are you in there?" PJ finished drying her hair and settled the towel across her shoulders.

"Sure. You asked me about the phone call."

"That's right." She patted a spot on the bed beside her. "Come here and tell me what has you so jumpy. Did something happen?"

I sat down and took her hand. We smiled at each other. "Nothing happened as far as I know. Blodwyn called and wants to talk with us. I invited her for tea tomorrow afternoon."

PJ squeezed my hand. "That'll be nice. I like Blodwyn a lot, and I know she was a big help to you and Dad when I was gone."

"Yes, she was." I noticed that one of the ties of her robe lay across her bare thigh, just a few tempting inches from my hand. What if I gave it a tug, just enough to loosen her robe, and then, what if I slid my hand under her shirt? Would she let me?

Soft green eyes glanced downward, and her cheeks flushed.

Was she reading my mind? We were often able to do that, but maybe this time I wished she couldn't.

"Kim?"

My head lifted.

"You want to untie it?"

My breath escaped in a rush. "Oh, I want to do much more than that."

Her hand closed over mine, her thumb sliding across my knuckles. "I know this has been hard on you. You've been so patient with me, but I just can't seem to sort out my emotions."

I reached my free hand up to touch her cheek, and my thumb rubbed her lower lip. "I understand. And I'll wait as long as you need me to."

She kissed my thumb and took it into her mouth, biting down gently before releasing it.

Oh, baby. Liquid fire scalded my insides.

"Go ahead. I'd like to try 'a bit of a cuddle' as they say around these parts. If you're ready for bed, untie my robe, and we'll see how things go, okay?"

Her smile was so sweet it brought tears to my eyes. "You mean it? You're not just feeling sorry for me?"

"Actually, I'm feeling sorry for me. I miss being with you, too. This thing with Terry robbed me of my pleasure, too."

I kissed her and felt my heart thudding against my chest. "I'll make a final bathroom stop and check on Pup to see if he needs to go out." I left the bedside lamp lit. PJ's blonde hair shimmered in its soft glow, lifting my libido to a higher level. "Wait right here, okay?"

She giggled. "Okay. I won't go anywhere."

After taking care of Pup, I changed into a nightshirt, finding it less restrictive than the scrubs, and pulled back the covers. PJ slipped out of her robe and wrapped her arms around me. "I think," she murmured against my neck, "that we might be too warm in these outfits tonight."

"Whatever you say." I grinned and held my breath as she unfastened the first few buttons of my shirt. It was slow torture of the most exquisite kind, and it lasted just two more buttons before I yanked the shirt over my head and tossed it on the floor.

Her hands moved over my skin, stroking and caressing, her words a steady jumble of husky endearments. I leaned back on the pillow, pulling her down on top of me with a contented sigh. "At last."

PJ braced herself with her right arm, lowering herself to kiss me on the lips, chin, neck, and all the way down to my breasts. Either she was ignoring the pain in her shoulder, or her left arm was stronger now. I reached up and traced the edges of the dressing through her shirt, remembering how close the bullet had come to taking her life.

She moaned and pressed her warm mouth against my breast, jolting me back to the present. Without further conscious thought, my hands were in her hair, raking through thick, golden strands. I wished the sensation would go on and on. It felt wonderful, but we weren't quite back to normal. She was still wearing that infernal T-shirt.

"There's still something in the way here."

She pushed herself up and back, straddling my waist. "I think it's time. Help me get this off, will you?"

"With pleasure."

I slid my hand under her shirt and lifted. She pulled her left arm out of the sleeve and tugged the garment over her head. With a soft moan, she stretched out on top of me.

"Oh yeah," we murmured together, and laughed, as our breasts mashed and mingled in comfortable reunion.

Eventually, we resumed kissing and touching, stroking and fondling. Our bodies heated with the friction of such passionate attention, and glistened with a thin film of sweat. At first, it was scary and awkward. I let PJ lead the way and take me as far as she thought possible. I had removed my briefs and was sliding her bikinis down over her hips when she trembled.

"What is it? Should I stop?"

She broke contact, lifting herself up on one elbow. "I'm sorry, I can't. I just can't yet." Her chest heaved, and I felt her tears dropping onto my breasts.

"Shh. It's okay. It's going to be okay." I stroked her back, making tiny circles against her smooth skin. "You're doing fine."

She raised her head, and I saw the tears on her cheeks, the agony in her eyes. "I love you. That's what hurts so much. I've never stopped loving you."

I tried to pull her body back down on top of me. "I know, and I love you, too. Make no mistake about that. We're going to get beyond this. A little more time is all we need."

"Shit! I hate what I've become." Her face twisted into a grimace. "What's wrong with me?"

"Absolutely nothing."

"Then why can't I make my body and my brain work together? Damn it, you're my lover. I want to show you how much I love you, but I can't."

"It will come. You just have to allow more time."

She slid off me and rolled onto her side, crying harder, pounding the pillow in anguish.

"Hey, there." I put my arm around her waist. My body thrummed with intense need. I took several deep breaths and willed certain areas to stop tingling. Oh, geez. This was torture.

Sensing my thoughts, PJ turned and embraced me. "Please, let me help you. I know you're hurting, and I can take care of your needs. I know I can do that much. I wish I could do everything."

"I love you and I want you. Right here, right now. But our lovemaking is a shared experience. I want you to enjoy it, too."

"Shit. I'm so pathetic."

"You stop that. Don't you think that, or say it ever again. You're the love of my life, the best thing that ever happened to me. I love every inch of you. Do you hear me?"

Except for sniffling, she was silent.

"PJ? Look at me."

I stared into her watery eyes until she gave me one of her lopsided grins. “That’s more like it. Now, why don’t we curl up together and get some sleep? Are you okay like this, or do you need to put your shirt back on?”

“I think I’m good this way, unless you want me to put it on.”

“I want what you want, and I think we’ve made great strides tonight. We really have.”

She plucked several tissues from the box on the bedside table and blew her nose. I switched off the light, and we pulled the covers up around us.

PJ’s lips were warm against my neck. “I love you, Warrior Amazon. No one else in this world would have such patience with me.”

I ruffled her hair and kissed her forehead. “I love you, too, shortstuff. And you’re well worth the wait.”

Chapter 28

Blodwyn poured two steaming cups of tea and handed them to PJ and me. We were gathered around a small table in one corner of the spacious dining room. A dozen or so of the inn's guests sat at tables around us, enjoying afternoon tea.

Dressed in civilian clothing, a heather green sweater and black slacks, Sergeant Jones made a congenial, less intimidating addition to our group.

"Here, try some of the fresh ginger biscuits." She reached for a couple of still warm cookies. "They're incredible."

I took a sip of tea and leaned back in my chair. PJ, sitting beside me, had been unusually quiet since Blodwyn's arrival. I wondered why. Maybe she would participate more once the refreshments were served.

She took a ginger cookie and passed the plate to me.

"Thank you, sweetie." I selected one of them and one of the shortbreads. "I'm going to miss Cook's baking when we leave."

"Mmm," Blodwyn said, biting into a flaky tart. "I probably gain half a stone every time I come over here."

PJ drank some of her tea, but I noticed that her body had tensed. Was she expecting to hear more bad news? As if there could be anything more, after what we'd already been through.

Not one to let the grass grow under her feet, my partner came right out with the question that was obviously on her mind. "So, what brings you here, Blodwyn? Is this official business?"

The policewoman opened her shoulder bag, pulled out a large manila envelope and placed it on the table in front of us. "I'm afraid it is a bit of business, but I do have some other, more personal things to discuss."

PJ put her cup in its saucer and folded her hands in her lap. "Then we'd best get to it."

"Right." Blodwyn picked up the envelope. "I'd like you to take a look at a photograph, PJ, and tell me if you recognize the person."

She slid the envelope away and the image of a smiling, blonde-haired woman appeared. She was standing in a garden and wearing a pastel sleeveless dress.

PJ gasped and reached for the picture. "It's Sarah," she whispered and then bit down on her lower lip to stop sudden tears. "Why do you have her picture? Is she dead? Is that what this means?"

Blodwyn glanced at me and then back to my partner. "I'm afraid so. Some campers discovered her body several days ago. We've been working with her mother and relatives to piece together what might have happened to her."

PJ wiped her eyes. "You know her full name, then?"

"Yes. It's Sarah Evelyn Worthington. She was thirty-two and worked in the area as a housekeeper for various families, including the Morrisons."

I reached for my partner's hand. "Are you okay? Can I pour you some more tea?"

"I'm fine, Kim." She looked at the picture again. "Sarah Worthington—a couple of years younger than I am."

Blodwyn tried to take back the picture, but PJ was reluctant to release it. "I had a hunch it was your Sarah," the sergeant said gently. "The timing was right, and your description fit. I'm truly sorry."

"Do you know what caused her death?" PJ's voice was soft, but persistent.

Sergeant Jones glanced in my direction. I sensed that she'd rather not divulge such news at the table in the middle of tea.

I shrugged. When PJ was on a mission, there was no stopping her.

"She was shot," Blodwyn said finally, managing to reclaim the picture and return it to the envelope.

PJ chewed her lower lip. The room was silent except for the sounds of bone china clinking against saucers and soft voices presumably chatting about civilized activities, murder not being one of them.

"I'd like to speak with Sarah's mother," PJ said in a matter-of-fact way. "Would you give me her telephone number?"

"Normally that wouldn't be done."

PJ gripped her hand. "Please, Blodwyn. Sarah was kind to me. It's important that I speak to her mom."

The policewoman and I shared a look.

"If you can manage it, I think you should," I said.

"Very well." She consulted her notebook, wrote a number on a slip of paper, and slid it along the table.

PJ took it and stood up. “If you’ll excuse me, I’ll make the call right now.”

Before we could say another word, she was across the room and out of our sight.

Blodwyn gave me a quick grin. “Doesn’t waste any time, your woman.”

I smiled. “Not when she’s got her mind made up, no.”

We poured ourselves another cup of tea and sipped slowly.

“Blodwyn, I don’t believe you told us the whole story just now.”

“Why would you think that?” Her eyes wouldn’t quite meet my own. “I’ve told you the main thing, that she was shot. Allegedly, but most probably, by one of the men who kidnapped your partner.”

“We could assume that, because PJ identified her picture, but there’s something else you’re not telling us about Sarah.”

Blodwyn fidgeted and glanced at the doorway to the drawing room. “I didn’t want to say it in front of her, you understand.”

I leaned forward. “What?”

“Before Sarah was shot, she was raped, rather brutally.”

My stomach tightened. The recently swallowed tea and cookies now threatened to reappear. “Oh, shit.” I shuddered and closed my eyes, trying my best to shut out the image that appeared in my mind. I couldn’t, no matter how hard I tried.

After several seconds, I forced myself to look at the sergeant. “Thank you for sparing PJ that information.”

“It may come out sooner or later at a trial. But for now, it would only disturb her more.”

“Yes.”

“She really needs to see a therapist, Kim.”

“I know. And she will, once we return to Boston. Her father has made arrangements.”

“You’ll make sure she goes?”

“I will.” Though it might take an act of Congress.

“Good. Now, one more thing.”

“Good grief, what else could there be?”

“You should go, too.”

I stared at her. “Me? I don’t need a shrink.”

“Take it from me, you do.”

Furious denials formed on my lips, and my belly heated in anger.

Blodwyn raised her hand. “Before you get all huffy with me, listen. I know what I’m talking about. You both need counseling, or your relationship will suffer.”

“Our relationship is none of your damn business, Sergeant Jones.”

She smiled, despite my outburst. “Probably not. But I’m making it my business long enough to tell you something. I know from experience what trauma like this can do to a couple.”

“PJ is going to be just fine.” I took the napkin from my lap and wadded it between my fingers.

“I pray that she will be,” Blodwyn said. “And what about you? What about all that anger you’re carrying around inside?”

“We just need a little time to sort things out, to get away together.” I spoke with my teeth clenched, trying to keep my voice under control.

“Kim. Listen to me, okay? Get your knickers untwisted long enough to hear me out.”

I tossed the napkin on the table and laced my fingers together in my lap. “Fine. You seem bound and determined, so go ahead.”

“Four years ago, I was in just about the same situation that you’re in. My partner was attacked and raped one night on her way home from work.” Blodwyn’s face flushed as she spoke. “Jemma fought her assailant, but in the end, it didn’t matter. The only thing she could do to stay alive was to let him do whatever he wanted to her. And he did.”

“I’m so sorry. Though PJ managed to avoid being raped, I know how you must have felt. It must have been hell.”

She bit her lip and gazed past me, blinking back tears. “It was all of that and more. I was crazy with anger. I could have ripped the bastard’s heart out of his chest and stuffed it down his bloody throat. My rage was so strong that I couldn’t function. Not as a copper, or a lover, or even as a human being. Jemma and I barely spoke to each other, we hurt so much. She was keeping all her pain bottled up inside, only I was blind to it, you see. I mistakenly thought time was the healer of all things.”

I was embarrassed to hear such intimate revelations from her, and afraid to admit that she had struck a nerve. Could my rage be that unyielding?

“The department insisted on counseling. I resisted for many days, telling them I was all right, that it was Jemma who needed help. We would be just fine as long as she received treatment. Isn’t that what you’re telling yourself right now?”

I stared at my folded hands. “No, it’s not like that at all with us.”

"Very well, lie to me. But don't lie to yourself or to PJ. See that she gets help, and then get some for yourself. Both of you need to work on this together, or things may never be the same between you."

Her expression scared me. There was a crack in her professional veneer that threatened to reveal old, painful wounds.

"You seem to be functioning okay now, Blodwyn." I gave her a tiny smile. "Did you have a hand in catching the rapist?"

"He was caught, but it wasn't from anything I did. Jemma went to several psychiatrists before she could even bring herself to return to her job. I went to the department counseling service after our relationship fell apart." Her voice caught, and raw emotion spilled out. "I was with you through all of this, Kim. I know how you feel about PJ and how she feels about you. Don't let what happened to Jemma and me happen to the two of you."

My brain finally registered the anguish in her words. I was expecting a happy ending to the story. I was all set to nod my head and assure her we would not let anything happen to us, once she assured me all had been fixed in her life. But then I sensed that her story was not going to end happily, and my mind reeled at the thought of losing what PJ and I had together. Surely that wasn't possible, was it?

"Please, Kim," Blodwyn was saying, "you need to listen to me."

"I hear you, really I do. But tell me how it all turned out for you and Jemma. Didn't the counseling do you both some good? You were able to patch things up, weren't you?"

"Why do you think I've been badgering you so? This is serious. Trauma like what happened to Jemma and PJ doesn't get fixed without professional help. I was lucky enough to get aid from a very wise and caring doctor. I was able to work through my anger issues."

"Good. What about your partner?"

She looked down at her hands. "I'm afraid Jemma wasn't as lucky. Her pain was too deep. She never got over the incident, and our relationship fell apart."

My mouth dropped open. "Oh, no. I'm so sorry."

Blodwyn raised her head, eyes glistening. "That's not the worst of it. I could have accepted the fact that Jemma couldn't love me the way she used to, if only…" She took a shaky breath and started again. "If only she'd gone on living."

"What? I don't understand."

"She couldn't live with the pain of it all, Kim. She took an overdose of barbiturates and died before I could get her to hospital."

I felt like a cannonball had slammed into my gut.

Blodwyn bent her head and pressed her hand to her eyes. "I thought our love would last forever," she murmured.

And always, I thought. Forever and always. Just like PJ and me. Oh, God.

I reached across the table and gripped her free hand until she regained her composure.

PJ returned and gave us both concerned looks. "Everything okay back here?"

"Yeah," I assured her in a husky voice. "How about you?"

She sat down and folded her hands. "I talked to Mrs. Worthington. She's a lovely woman. She sounds so much like Sarah." Her voice cracked. "Anyway, she said it would be okay if I went to visit her." She looked at me. "Do we have time before we leave?"

"I think we could make the time."

PJ focused on the sergeant. "Will you take me to see her? I'd like to have you there when I tell her what I have planned."

"I imagine I can. Just tell me when it suits you."

PJ gave her a huge smile. "I will. Thank you."

I tapped her hands. "Are you going to let us in on your plans?"

"Sarah told me about wanting to finish nursing school. It was her dream to become a nurse and help others. Her mother was divorced and couldn't afford to pay the tuition, so that was why Sarah dropped out and went to work, taking cleaning jobs around the area."

"Poor thing," Blodwyn said.

"Yes," PJ agreed. "I'm going to keep in touch with Mrs. Worthington, and make sure her bills get paid, but my real goal is to start a nursing scholarship in Sarah's name at the college she was attending."

"Great idea," I said.

The sergeant nodded. "I'm sure it will give Sarah's mother some comfort to know that her daughter's name and ideals will live on through such a program."

PJ beamed. "That's settled, then. Are we all finished now, or do you have something else to discuss?"

Gripping her briefcase, Blodwyn looked at her intently. "I think I'm finished. I'll let Kim fill you in."

"Okay," PJ said, but she was clearly puzzled.

Blodwyn's gaze shifted to me. "Tell her everything we talked about."

"I will. She'll know if I try to keep anything from her, anyway."

PJ touched my arm. "Now you have me really curious."

Blodwyn brushed some crumbs from her lap. "What we spoke of had to do with my personal experiences in a similar situation. I've also observed, and Kim agreed, that you haven't been quite up to par lately."

PJ let some irritation show. "I see. And how, exactly would you—"

"Wait, please" Blodwyn held up her hand. "I'm not trying to criticize. I'd just like you both to move beyond this terrible time in your lives and remember Wales with fondness."

"We had great memories before all the nasty stuff happened," I told her, coming to my partner's rescue.

"And we found this place enchanting," PJ assured her.

Blodwyn nodded. "It is enchanting, magical even. But you've been cheated out of so many wonderful experiences."

"It's okay, really."

The sergeant turned to me. "No, it isn't. What happened to both of you never should have happened."

PJ took her hand. "Blodwyn, we appreciate what you're trying to say, and we want you to know that we don't hold Wales responsible. We've visited a lot of great places here and enjoyed everything."

"I'm glad, but I can't help thinking that you deserve more. Please promise me you'll come back again soon and let me show you all the places that I know and love."

PJ and I shared a look.

"Thank you," I said. "I'm sure we would love to take you up on your generous offer."

"Good." Blodwyn nodded. "That's settled then."

I looked around the sitting room, surprised to discover that we were the only guests left at tea. "In the meantime, we'd better get going. I think Arwel and Mavis want to clean up in here."

"Right you are." Blodwyn shouldered her purse. "Thanks to you both for a lovely visit. PJ, ring me when you want to see Mrs. Worthington."

"I will. Thank you for your friendship, Blodwyn. It means a great deal to both of us."

"Yeah," I said. "I appreciate everything you've told me."

She our hands and smiled. "It's been a pleasure getting to know you both. I just wish circumstances had been different."

"Getting to know you has been one of the good things about our trip to Wales," PJ said, as we walked Blodwyn to the door.

We said goodbye to her and climbed single-file up the narrow, spiral stairs to our room. Pup needed a walk, and I had a strong suspicion that PJ would accompany us, firing questions at me left and right.

Tact wasn't my strong point. I knew Frederick was in favor of this therapy plan. PJ went through it before, years ago, but I wished I could say that I was comfortable with the idea of letting a shrink pick at my brain. Just the thought made me shudder.

PJ put her arms around me. "Cold?"

"No, I was just thinking about something."

When we opened the door to our room, Pup greeted us like long-lost family. We ruffled his fur and tickled behind his ears. "Ready for a walk, boy?" I asked, taking his leash from the dresser top.

Pup yelped an answer.

"If you can wait long enough for me to pee, I'd like to join you," PJ said.

"Sure." I gave her a weak smile. Oh, boy. I was in for it now.

When she had closed the bathroom door, I knelt and attached Pup's leash. "You're going to be the only one who enjoys this walk, my friend," I whispered into his ear.

He gave my chin what I took as a sympathetic lick.

Chapter 29

Two days later, Kim and I were up early, driving the Rover along the winding country roads surrounding Dolgellau. We had scheduled several important activities for the day, beginning with a visit to the grave of Kim's "mermaid," the Jane Doe from the morgue. Kim had offered to provide her with a proper resting place, despite some local resistance to burying an unidentified person in the churchyard. The granite headstone, a rush order, was simple, but beautifully carved.

Fair Mermaid, it read, *may you rest in peace forever.*

My partner knelt to brush some debris away from the gravesite. "No one claimed her, so I named her Fair Mermaid because she was found in the water."

"Why 'fair?' Was she fair?"

"She looked a little like you, which is why I was called in to identify her." Kim stood and put her arm around me. "They thought she *was* you."

I gave her waist a squeeze. "Oh, right. You told me a bit about that time. My memory has so many holes in it these days."

She touched my cheek. "Have patience with yourself. We'll get through this together."

"I know we will. But I'm sorry you had to go through that alone."

"They say that suffering builds character, don't they? And to be honest, Blodwyn was there supporting me when I viewed her body, so I wasn't quite alone." She took the bouquet of white roses I was holding for her and laid them at the base of the headstone.

"She met a violent death, you know," Kim said. "A young life with so much potential, wasted."

"You did a nice thing," I told her, trying to avoid tears. "Providing her with a decent burial is probably the nicest thing anyone ever did for her."

"As you did for Sarah. In a way, they were part of our lives, Sarah and the Mermaid. Now they'll be remembered in a positive manner."

We stood wrapped in each other's arms for several minutes, listening to the birds and the breeze as it whispered through the leaves of a nearby oak. Kim was probably reliving the time she had been called to see this woman in the morgue. Now, at least, the woman was covered in green grass and shaded by the branches of a friendly old oak. It was a pleasant place to spend eternity. And Arwel, bless her heart, had promised to bring flowers on special days and lay them on the Mermaid's grave.

"We've both had the unpleasant task of identifying or viewing women who were killed by sudden, violent means." I reached up and touched Kim's tear-stained face. "Am I heartless to be glad it wasn't me who died?"

She took my hand and kissed it. "No. I couldn't have survived such a tragedy."

"I'm sorry she still has no name. At least I got to see Sarah's mother and tell her how brave and kind her daughter was during her last hours on earth."

Kim steered us back to the Rover. "I'm sure that was a comfort to her. And the nursing scholarship you're planning to set up in Sarah's name will be a lasting tribute to a life that ended much too soon."

I took a deep breath and filled my lungs with the scent of flowers and freshly cut grass. "It was the right thing to do. I promised Sarah I'd help her once we escaped, but—" My voice cracked and tears slid down my cheeks. "It's a damn shame."

Kim rubbed my back as we stood beside the vehicle, looking back on the hillside with its row upon row of weathered, moss-covered headstones. "It is, indeed," she said.

* * *

We found a level patch of grass overlooking the graveyard and we spread our picnic blanket there. Sunshine warmed our bodies, and birds continued to serenade us with their melodious songs. As my partner opened our basket and prepared plates of food, I closed my eyes and tried to absorb the tranquility.

"A penny for your thoughts." Kim sat down beside me and put two plates of fruit, cheese, sandwiches, and Scotch eggs in my lap.

I held our plates while she pulled two bottles of lemon squash from the basket that Arwel had packed for us.

"You've gone silent on me for the past half hour. Do you want to talk about it?"

She traded a bottle for her plate, arranged herself on the blanket, and kept her eyes focused on me as she chewed on a watercress sandwich.

I shrugged. "You know that I'm going to be like this for a while."

"Like what? Distant?" Kim took a swallow of the lemon drink. "This quiet version of you is unnatural."

I finished off an egg and licked my fingers. "Damn, I'll miss these when we go back home."

"PJ, if you don't want to talk about what's bothering you, okay, but please don't change the subject on me."

"You're right. I have been thinking a lot about things. It comes over me, and I can't always block it. Sometimes my body and my spirit feel numb. My brain just zones out."

Kim put her plate down on the blanket and scooted closer, taking my hand in hers. "I'm sorry. I'm trying to accept this situation, really I am. But if you keep silent… I mean, maybe I can help, if you'll share some of your thoughts."

I gave her hand a squeeze. "You're the best, Kimmy. You know that, don't you?"

"Well, if you say so."

"I mean it." My throat tightened, but I was determined to get the words out. "I love you so much. Especially now. And I thank you so much for putting up with me."

Her hand caressed my face and slid to the back of my neck, giving it a gentle scratch. "You know I'm here for you, little one. I'll always be here for you, no matter where *here* is."

I leaned back against her hand, and she reached across my shoulders, pulling my head down to her chest.

"Maybe I can say it if I don't look at you," I mumbled into the fabric of her crisp cotton shirt. "If I just start out and don't worry about getting it right, maybe I can manage."

Both her arms tightened around me. I could feel the warmth of her body and the strength of her love seeping into my pores, giving me courage. "Just start any place. I'll keep you safe, and I won't say a word unless you want me to."

"Okay." I took a steadying breath. "As you know, I've always been a confident person, never worrying much about my safety. Maybe I was just supremely naïve."

She gave me a sympathetic grunt, but otherwise remained quiet.

"Now I've got this weepy, snot-nosed condition going on." I broke our embrace long enough to fish a tissue from my pocket, and blew my nose before laying my cheek against her breast. "That sucks, big time."

I felt her chest rise as she smothered a chuckle.

"I'm afraid. And I can't sleep without experiencing at least one scary dream a night, sometimes more." I rubbed my hands against her back. "I know you're aware of that because I wake you up whenever I have one."

Kim's heartbeat thrummed beneath my ear, and I took a moment to close my eyes and inhale the familiar scent of her skin. "But then, you hold me and kiss me whenever I have them, so the nightmares might not be such a hardship." I tried to laugh, but only a strangled snort came out.

"Hmm." My partner was doing her best to remain silent and let me express myself.

"Kimmy, I'm really hesitant to tell you this because I know how you'll react. I know how you feel about them already, and you know I'm skeptical." Her body stiffened. "I'll tell you what happened. I'm going to blurt it all out, and then we can talk about it, okay?"

"Go ahead." Her response was soft, restrained.

"It started when I was in that cottage, and it happened a couple of times."

She made a growling noise in her throat. "Is this going to make me angry?"

"No. Probably not. I… uh, saw an Amazon."

"What?" Kim's outburst startled me.

"Wait. Just hear me out, okay? You promised to keep quiet until I finish what I need to talk about."

"I know, but that was before I knew what you were going to say." She stroked my cheek and smoothed a bit of hair behind my ear. "You go ahead, little one. I wasn't expecting you to mention an Amazon. Can I ask if it was Marna?"

"No, I don't think it was. She wore a mask over the upper part of her face. It had feathers and beads and stuff. The rest of her body was— whoa—right out there, though."

"Hmm."

“Leather bra, short pants with a flap, lots of bare midriff. Sometimes she wore sandals, sometimes boots. Jesus, she must have been a forty double D. Her breasts were spectacular, and her legs went on forever.”

“Humph! This is fascinating.”

“I’m just telling you what she wore.”

“Which wasn’t very much, I take it.”

I broke free of her embrace and stood up, intending to walk back to the Rover. “This was a bad idea. You’re focusing on all the wrong stuff.”

She sprang up and reached for my arm. “Me? You can’t fault me for—”

“For what? I’m trying to tell you about this Amazon who came to talk to me.” I could barely suppress my anger.

“Is that all she did?” Kim’s eyes darkened. “Talk?”

“Yes, damn it.” I pulled away from her. “I thought you’d be pleased.”

“I am. But I’m also a bit surprised.”

“This isn’t working. We should probably go back to the inn.”

Kim looked down at our plates. “But you haven’t eaten your food.”

“I’m not hungry anymore.” I folded my arms and stared across the silent gravestones. “We should just go on back.”

Kim knelt to gather the remains of our meal, packing everything neatly into the basket, then folding the blanket and tossing it over her shoulder. “I’d better let Pup visit the bushes for a bit before we leave. You want to take the basket back to the Rover?”

I sat in the passenger seat with my head in my hands, while Kim finished with Pup. What was wrong with me? Why did the Amazon’s wardrobe become the issue? Why couldn’t I tell her what happened without it turning into a fight?

“In you go, fella,” Kim said. “In the back and settle down.” Pup bounded between us and flopped into the rear.

I glanced at Kim as she pulled on her seatbelt. She turned to meet my gaze. “Buckle up.”

“Wait. I want to apologize for what happened.”

She bit her lower lip and shoved the key into the ignition. “I’m sorry, too. I guess I wasn’t ready to hear about some scantily clad woman making nocturnal visits to your room.”

“It wasn’t like that.”

She paused with her hand on the key. “Then how was it, exactly?”

I closed my eyes for a couple seconds and took a deep breath, composing myself. As I spoke, I watched Kim carefully. “She told me I was an Amazon, too, just like you and Marna. I thought it would please you. Only, I told her that wasn’t possible because I wasn’t a warrior, not a real one. She wanted me to kill those men with their own guns, and I refused.”

Kim looked shocked. “Wait. She told you to kill them? I can’t figure out what’s going on.”

“I don’t have the killer instinct.”

“That’s the first thing you’ve said that makes sense to me.”

I caught myself smiling. “I agree, but it happened. She kept telling me that I would be safe, that the Amazons were watching out for me, for both of us. When I asked for more information, she said it would all be made clearer to me later on.”

“Really?”

I nodded, and Kim’s expression softened.

“One time, I wondered what she looked like under the mask, and she read my mind, or seemed to. She said I would find out about that later on, too. It was so spooky.”

“I can imagine.” Kim stared at a spot beyond my side window, remaining quiet for several seconds. “I think I’d better tell you about a strange visit I had during our search for you. I think your mysterious visitor came to me in our room one day and made me take another look at the travel brochures.”

“That’s right. She told me she gave you that message.” I shuddered.

“Yeah, there was a yellow glow right above them and a presence of some kind.”

“Spooky, right?”

“Incredibly.”

“Anyway, I’m glad I told you about it. I’m still not convinced she was there, nor am I truly convinced about any of this Amazon stuff. But everything she said was…”

Kim waited, but I couldn’t bring myself to say the rest—how my nocturnal visitor swore that the Amazons had altered the trajectory of the bullet away from my heart at that critical moment.

“Are you okay now?” She gave my knee a squeeze.

“Yeah, I guess.” I gripped her hand and our fingers interlaced. “I’m sorry, Kimmy, but I’m afraid to let myself believe in them. Because, if I do, it means that they have some sort of control over us, and over our lives, like we’re being manipulated.”

“Like puppets?”

I let out a shaky breath. "Something like that. It's as if they're hiding in the shadows as we live our lives, deciding what happens to us."

"Maybe it's a good thing to have Amazons in our corner. I won't say you and I didn't experience some scary times this past year, but we've also had some great things happen to us, too, starting with the fact that we met and fell in love."

"You think we were destined to do that? Did some shadowy Amazons bring us together?"

"Perhaps."

"I guess that could have been a good thing."

She patted my stomach. "More than a good thing. A great thing."

"Hey." I caught her fingers just as they approached my ribs. "You tickle me, and I'll sic my Amazon on you."

She laughed and started the Rover. "I bet my Amazon can beat up your Amazon."

I shook my head. "You're crazy, Kimberly Blair."

"Yeah?"

"Uh huh, but I wouldn't have it any other way."

* * *

"Before we turn out the lights," Kim said, as she tucked me into bed in our cozy room at the inn, "I have something for you. Maybe it will ward off the nightmares tonight."

I yawned. "You know I have no control over them."

She pulled a couple of small boxes out of the dresser drawer. "I know, but humor me. Open this one."

"What on earth did you get me?"

"PJ, please, just open it."

I sat up and brushed back my bangs. "Okay, gimme."

Kim laughed. "That's the woman I know and love."

I glared at her, but I couldn't help a delighted yelp when I spied my medallion on a brand new silver chain, nestled on a bed of soft cotton. "Oh, good idea." I held it up to the light. The medallion twirled and glittered. "And it's engraved."

"Yes, I had the jeweler put something on each of them."

I examined the back. I saw the word "*Forever*." "Oh, Kimmy." Tears blurred my vision.

"Uh huh. And mine says, '*Always.*'"

I wiped my eyes and struggled to sit up straighter. "Can you help me with it? I still can't raise my left arm that high."

"Sure thing." She gripped the medallion in her hand and grimaced. "Damn thing still heats up like it did when we found them up in the Superstitions. Remember that day… with the snakes?"

I laughed. "I had to pee right in the middle of it." She laughed, too. "Yes, I remember. All of it was so weird."

I felt the metal cool to my body temperature and settle under my nightshirt, midway between my collarbone and the tops of my breasts.

Kim leaned over and peered down. "Mmm. Wish I could rest right there, too."

I pulled back, depriving her of the view. "I just bet you do. Come on, bend your head down and I'll help you get yours on." I picked up her medallion and gasped. "Jesus, it's almost hot. How does it do that?"

"Beats me."

I fastened the chain and kissed the back of her neck. "Now, warrior, we can get some sleep."

Kim turned off the light and slipped into bed beside me. Wordlessly, we snuggled together, my back against her chest, her arm draped protectively across my belly. I could feel her heartbeat synchronize itself with mine as we drifted toward sleep.

Her lips brushed along the back of my neck. "Mmm. You smell so good."

I turned in her embrace and breathed in her scent. "I could say the same for you."

"Comfortable?" Kim's warm hand rubbed across my ribcage.

"Yes. Thank you for getting the medallions fixed and for adding those words."

She kissed the top of my head. "You're welcome."

I rotated my body enough to kiss her, leaving my lips parted, granting her tongue access.

We both sighed after a thoroughly enjoyable kiss.

"You took your pain pills?" she asked.

"Yeah."

"Damn. Enough of this, then. We'll wait until you feel more alert."

I gave her a final peck on the cheek and returned to my original position. "Sorry, love. I'll soon be sleeping like a drunken slug."

Her hand slid up and tousled my hair. "As if we knew how a drunken slug sleeps." She brought her arm down to my belly again, but not before finding my left breast and giving it a gentle squeeze.

"Ah." I sighed. "No fair." A bit of drool leaked onto my curled up fist. Geez. If I wasn't blubbering, I was slobbering all over the place.

Kim's steady breathing lulled me, and her warm body soothed me far better than any painkiller. I let my mind float along on a feathery current, searching the immediate area surrounding our bed for unwelcome spirit activity.

If there were Amazons out there controlling our destiny, they were giving us a respite tonight. With unspoken thanks, I focused on my body's internal rhythm, tuning it to match Kim's gentle breathing, and reached out for sleep.

Chapter 30

On the morning that PJ and I planned to leave Dolgellau and our comfortable room at the inn, we rose early to finish some last minute chores. I wanted to check e-mail on my laptop, and PJ needed to complete her packing.

I watched as she gathered souvenirs, clothing, and toilet articles, stuffing them into several travel bags. She rummaged through a pair of dirty cargo pants, pulled out what looked like a smooth stone, and slipped it into the right front pocket of the pants she was wearing.

"What are you doing?" I asked.

"Oh, I just discovered the stone you found for me at the sacred well. You know, the one that was guarded by the hawthorn tree and the fire-breathing dragon?"

Geez, that seemed so long ago. "You said it might bring us luck. Too bad it didn't."

PJ zipped her bags and lined them up on the bed. "I didn't have it with me during the kidnapping. Maybe things would have been worse if you hadn't found it at all."

"Perhaps, but it's hard to imagine that our luck could have been any worse."

Despite all that had happened, we had seen much of beauty in this small country, and the people had been extraordinarily hospitable. Maybe PJ's stone helped with that. We would never forget many of the men and women we had met during our stay. If only we had gotten to know them under different circumstances.

I turned my attention to the laptop. We had an e-mail from Frederick, who urged us to return immediately to Boston to spend a few days with him. He needed some quality time with his daughter and she with him.

That would work out well. While they were enjoying each other's company, I'd have time to catch up on my writing projects.

DCI Edwards sent an e-mail with an attachment of the forensic report on the remains that Morrison had kept preserved for so long.

For all intents and purposes, they were gone forever, but testing what little was left dated them to approximately the second or third century B.C.E.

Damn. What a loss that was to the scientific community. But with careful preservation of the compromised remains, who knew what additional information they might offer to archaeologists of the future?

PJ came up behind me, wrapped her arms around my shoulders, and kissed me lightly on the cheek. Her hair was still damp from the shower, and she smelled like a dew-sprinkled garden of spring blossoms. I drew her to me and had her sit on my lap while we read the rest of the report together.

"What a waste," I said, thinking about the destruction of such valuable remains.

"Unfortunately, that kind of thing happens more often than we know."

"Yeah. And then there's the issue of your mysterious man in the bog. I really believe you saw something."

"I wish I knew. Maybe it was my overactive imagination, or maybe it was some kind of a vision prior to my imminent death."

I shifted to support her weight more comfortably. She was lighter after her ordeal, but I was happy to see that she was gaining some of it back. Much as I admired her rippled abdomen, I didn't want to feel her ribs every time I squeezed her. "If there were remains preserved in the bog, they would have been soft tissue, nothing skeletal. The acidic conditions break down the bones while leaving the soft tissue intact."

"Are you thinking of a further search?"

I couldn't tell if PJ's question was encouraging or discouraging. Probably a little of both. As an archaeologist, she'd be curious, but after all she'd suffered, her heart might not be into it.

"Not me," I said, giving her thigh a rub. "I've had my fill of this place for a while, and I don't really have a lot to go on. But it's a perfect summer vacation project for some first-year archaeological students I know, and their professor."

"So you're going to slough it off on some unsuspecting first-year students?"

"That's the general idea."

PJ giggled.

"What?"

"Whoever he is, if he's buried in that bog and they find him, they can just roll him up, stick him in a backpack, and transport him to the lab that way."

"There are times when your sense of humor flirts with the weird."

She played with the top button on my shirt. "I know. I'm a mass of contradictions these days. But if you can't laugh at ill wind, then you're going to get lost in the storm."

"True." I tightened my hold on her. "I don't care how much wind we get, kiddo, I'm not losing you, not ever."

We sat silently, holding each other for a few more seconds, then finished reading the report from DCI Edwards.

I tapped a spot in the text with my finger. "Look at this. There were weapons, too. A sword and an axe. I wonder why those guys didn't take them when they removed the body. They could have sold them for good money on the black market."

PJ leaned her head back against my shoulder. "Except for their leader, they weren't very bright, you know, the bad guys. Scary, yes. Bright, no."

The report went on to say that the design of the weapons and the markings on them were Celtic in origin. I brought up the pictures that accompanied the report.

"Oh, geez." PJ's breath caught. I could see the color drain from her face.

"What is it? Are you okay?"

"The Celt in the bog had those weapons with him."

"That same design would have been used by many Celts."

"Not the design, Kim." She pointed to the axe. "Magnify this area."

I brought it up.

"There. That irregularity on the handle." PJ ran her finger over the image. "It looks like it's been chipped." She kept her finger poised over a spot in the photo. "I saw this axe before, with the Celtic warrior, chieftain, figment of my imagination, or whatever he was, in the bog."

"Sweetie, you were hallucinating."

She covered her eyes, fingers probing and squeezing her temples as if fighting a sudden headache. I could feel the agitation in her body. "I'd like to believe I was, but—"

"But what?"

"The chip in the handle. I can't deny that."

"Easy, there. I'm not saying you should."

"Jesus." PJ's voice quavered. "What's going on here? It's like this guy is—was—talking to me, sending me a message."

She looked at me, on the verge of panic, her expression pleading for an explanation, preferably a reasonable and logical one. What could I tell her?

"Maybe he was using you to send a message. Stranger things have happened."

"To you, maybe, like the Marna thing and the dreams. It all happened to you. I was there, and I know it was real for you because you lived with the lost tribe of women in your dreams for so long. But I don't have that extrasensory perception or whatever you call it. I'm here, solidly planted in this place and this time. I have no past lives trying to catch up to me."

There were tears in her eyes as she waited for me to convince her that this wasn't happening, but I couldn't. I could only console her the best way I knew how, by taking her into my arms, kissing the top of her head, and brushing away the tears as they spilled onto her cheeks.

I didn't cope too well with tears, especially PJ's. I launched into lecture mode, offering her the most expedient thoughts my poor, panicked brain could conjure up. Perhaps putting an academic slant on the situation would make it less personal.

"Okay, think about it. You recognized the marks on the axe handle without a moment's hesitation, so it's obvious that you've seen them before. Somewhere, in some time frame."

She sniffled against my neck. "But I'm a pragmatic, garden-variety archaeologist. I don't deal in the paranormal. At least I didn't, until our Superstition project. Frankly, it scares the bejeezus out of me."

I could see that PJ was seriously frightened. She got up and began pacing.

I turned my chair and sat with my back to the laptop. "All right, let's say for a moment that it was an extraordinarily vivid vision, and that he was communicating with you at some level. What was his message?"

She raked her fingers through her hair, giving the ends a tug.

"What if he was identifying himself as the mysterious Celt in Morrison's glass coffin? With his remains destroyed, he had no way of communicating with the modern world, no archaeological path for us to follow back into his time." PJ bowed her head, probably remembering her encounter. There was fear in her eyes when she looked up. "So he came to me. I don't believe for one moment that is what happened, but how else can I explain the weapon?"

"First of all, there's nothing to be afraid of. Okay?"

"Easy for you to say."

"Let's consider for a moment, that the story about his being discovered in a bog is true. If it happened to be your bog—"

"It's not my bog."

I held up my hand. "Okay, it's not your bog, but let's say for the sake of argument that it's the same one. It's quite likely he would have left something there, a spiritual energy force. Psychics tell us it happens often enough, especially when someone dies a violent death. They tune into something like that when they help the police solve crimes." I shook my head, denying my own explanation of things. "Though we don't know that he died violently."

"Oh, he definitely did."

I stared at PJ. Her face was pale, her eyes haunted. "How can you be so sure?"

"Because when he appeared to me, his weapons were drawn and his sword was dripping blood."

I pulled her onto my lap again and drew her head to my shoulder. It was obvious that she was still fragile from her ordeal and needed careful handling. I gently rocked her, hoping it would calm and reassure her. "There's nothing to be afraid of, you know. We're all capable of receiving messages from out there, but most of us never do. Our minds are too cluttered."

"Are you saying that my falling into the bog provided him with a way of telling his story? That I was a conduit for him?"

"I can't know that for a fact, but who am I to deny it? Stranger things have happened to us, or at least to me. Perhaps our working together has increased our power and allowed us to see beyond the here and now. We're either blessed or cursed with something that's beyond explanation."

PJ groaned.

I stroked her head. "The Superstitions, the Amazons, Marna and me, and now this. Think about it. There are no logical, earth-based answers."

PJ stood up. This time, thank goodness, she didn't appear as agitated, and she didn't start pacing.

"We know one thing for sure, though," she said in a calm voice. "Morrison's missing corpse was not Owain Glyndwr."

"I've decided," I said, turning back to the computer and powering down, "that looking for the bog man is no project for first-year students."

"You're right about that." PJ dropped to the floor and folded herself into a yoga position.

I wished I could do that. "Have you finished your packing?"

She closed her eyes and took a deep breath. "Yes, I'm ready whenever you are."

I slid the laptop into its travel case and put it on the bed. "Let me take Pup for one last visit to the garden and kennel. Then we'll be on our way home."

Still in the lotus position, she propped her chin up on her hands. "So much work to be done when we get there. You have your book chapter to finish, and I have therapy."

Pup danced around my legs in anticipation of a trip outdoors. "Why don't you join us? You could use a bit of sunlight, and we can say goodbye to the roses and butterflies."

She smiled at me and got to her feet. "Just as long as we don't see any dead Amazons or Celtic warriors along the way."

I took her hand. "Pup will protect us if we do, won't you, buddy?"

A low growl and a lolling tongue were his only responses.

* * *

Arwel had taken such good care of us in our time of need that parting with her left us saddened. We exchanged goodbye hugs in the foyer, breathing in the delicious scent of baking bread. It had been the first aroma we associated with the inn, and it would be our last memory as we departed.

"I hope we will see you again," Arwel said with sincerity.

"I'm sure we'll return sometime," I assured her, "but it won't be for a while. The horrors are too fresh in our minds to contemplate another visit anytime soon."

"I understand," Arwel said, in her musical Welsh accent. "I'm sorry that bad things happened to you here in my country, and in my village."

It was a shame that so much evil had marred our visit to Wales. The faces of almost everyone we had met were so open and outgoing, and we could honestly say they were there for us when we needed them most.

"Just remember that the ones doing the bad things were Americans," PJ said.

"That's right," I added. "The Welsh are in no way to blame for what happened to us here. Besides, without your help and that of Sergeant Jones, things would have been even harder to bear."

"I did what I could, and I'm sure the sergeant did, too."

"If we do come back," I said, "I'll insist that we be given the same room. It was delightful."

"You shall have it without fail." Arwel made us wait while she gathered a bag of snacks for our drive back to London. "Some biscuits for you, Kim, and a few of those Scotch eggs you enjoy so much, PJ. There are some goodies for Pup, too."

I smiled at her. "You're a treasure, Arwel. Give our best to Mavis and Cook."

She blushed and assured us she would.

PJ gave her a parting hug and murmured her thanks.

* * *

We stowed our bags and drove along the winding road to the ridge overlooking Dolgellau. At the top of the hill, we pulled over to take a final look at the picturesque village nestled in the valley below. We gazed in silence, remembering all that we had experienced.

PJ's hand rested on my thigh. I covered it with mine. She closed her eyes, and I could see tears escaping down her cheeks. She made no effort to stop them.

She was no longer the young, playful woman that I knew so well. She had aged as the often-harsh realities of life caught up with her. We were both forever changed. But we had survived the pain, and we were better prepared for the journey ahead, wherever it took us.

As if reading my mind, she gave my hand a squeeze. "So, are we moving anytime soon?"

Smiling, I started the Rover up. "You seemed a bit upset."

"Just one of those mood swings." She reached into her pocket and retrieved the small, smooth stone I had given her. She held it tightly in her fist. "This has a calming effect."

"Good. If it can't be lucky, it can be calming." I patted her thigh. "Is it okay for us to leave now?"

The lopsided grin appeared. "Actually, I thought maybe you wanted me to drive this time."

With a laugh, I shifted into gear and we roared over the hill. “Not on your life, little one. And not on mine, either. With you at the wheel, all the calming stones in the world won’t protect me.”

K.C. West

Victoria Welsh

About the Authors

K.C. West and **Victoria Welsh** met online several years ago. Despite living on practically opposite coasts of the United States, they found plenty of common ground in their interest in writing.

K.C. lives in the East with her husband and two daughters.
Victoria is a poet and writer. She and her life partner reside in the Southwestern United States.

The authors are hard at work on the next book in the *Shadows* series. You may write to them at:

kcwest2004@hotmail.com
victoriawelsh22@aol.com

Blue Feather Books is proud to offer this excerpt from the exciting sequel to *Celtic Shadows*:

GREEK SHADOWS

Coming soon, only from

Bluefeatherbooks LIMITED

www.bluefeatherbooks.com

"Stay, Pup."

The light from the lamp on my hard hat reflected in his yellow canine eyes. He crouched obediently several feet from me, but he didn't relax. I had a gut feeling that the room was off-limits and that we shouldn't go in there, but with her usual enthusiasm, PJ was not to be deterred. She had already ventured inside. And really, what could be the harm? I swept my fear aside, took a deep breath of stale air, and squeezed through the crack in the rock.

When I reached PJ's side, she was exploring a faded fresco of a panther on the far wall of what looked like a rounded, naturally-formed room. She had pulled a soft-bristled brush from her daypack and was gently removing the dust of time from the animal's eyes. They glowed like burnished gold. It was an unnerving sight—raising the hairs on the back of my neck and setting Pup on edge. Even though he couldn't see me behind the rock wall that separated us, he must have sensed some supernatural vibrations, because he was showing his displeasure with alternating whines and growls.

"It's all right," I called back to him. "You stay out there. We won't be long." My voice was not as firm and confident as I would have liked, but he settled into infrequent whimpers.

My nerves were on alert. I turned to PJ. "Did you hear that?"

"It's just Pup." She finished cleaning the fresco's surface, replaced her tool, and wiped her hands on her cargo pants. "What's gotten into him, anyway?"

"No, something else, muffled and far away. Do you hear anything?"

She shook her head. "Like what?"

"Thunder."

"There wasn't a cloud in the sky when we left the surface, and even if it were thundering, we wouldn't hear it in here."

A strange sensation struck me, and I didn't feel right—not sick exactly, but not well. It began with my head and moved downward through my body, leaving me paralyzed.

"Are you all right?" PJ's voice sounded close, yet far away. As if I were having an out-of-body experience, I saw her guide me to the stone wall for support, but couldn't feel anything solid at my back. "Are you feeling okay? You're scaring me."

I was scaring myself. What was happening? I was so hot and dizzy. "I don't know, honey. I just don't know." My mind refused to focus on anything.

"Kim, please, what's the matter? Are you sick?"

Unable to answer, I reached out for her, but something pulled me away, catching me up in a whirlwind. I could only watch as PJ grew more and more distant, finally becoming just a blurred speck. Though I couldn't hear her voice, I could feel her panic.

I held my hand out to her, but she was out of reach, and then, out of sight.

There was a whirling kaleidoscope of color: rainbow waves and shooting stars as everything swirled around me, and my mind shut down.

When I came to, I was sitting on the ground in the middle of a strange and beautifully pristine meadow. It was peppered with hundreds of yellow, red, and white wildflowers. Fighting a bout of vertigo and ignoring the churning of my stomach from what I could only describe as a weightless journey, I attempted to stand, and promptly sat down again.

There was a roaring sound like heavy surf crashing onto a beach, but as far as I could see there was no beach, no surf. The roar grew louder until—as mysteriously as I had lost her—PJ appeared on her knees beside me.

"What the hell happened?" she asked. I noticed her eyes were wide with fear. "God, I feel so sick. Where are we, anyway?"

"I don't know where we are or how we got here, but here we are." I looked at the abundant flowers surrounding us. "You have to admit, it's beautiful."

"That's what worries me. Are we dead?"

I stifled an urge to laugh. "Hardly." I felt at peace, and yet I was troubled, as if by guilt for putting us both in this predicament.

"Then how did we get here?" PJ brushed some dirt from her arms and clothing. She sat back on her heels, frowning at me. "Where is this place? And how do we get back to where we were?"

"Why would you think I'd know that?"

"Kim, you know I have absolutely no sense of direction, so give me a hint."

"I've no idea, and thinking about it makes my head hurt." Still feeling slightly dizzy, I staggered to my feet and offered PJ my hand. "Up you go."

She clasped my hand and grinned at me. “I wonder what Susanna, the wonder therapist, will have to say about this dream.”

“You’re sure it’s a dream?”

“Of course. What else could it be?” As she turned to face me, her gaze drifted to something over my left shoulder. Her face paled. “Don’t look now, but we have company.”

I turned and studied them. From this distance, they appeared to be warriors—ancient warriors—about a dozen or so in number.

So, this was a dream after all. Or was it?

“Who are they?” PJ tightened her grip on my arm.

“I don’t know. They’re too far away to tell, exactly.”

“Do you think they’re friendly?”

I swallowed hard. “Possibly, but I have my doubts.”

She took a deep, tremulous breath. “Kimmy, I’m afraid.”

“So am I, darling. So am I.”

Blue Feather Books, Ltd.
P.O. Box 5867
Atlanta, GA 31107-5967
(678) 318-1426

CPSIA information can be obtained at www.ICGtesting.com
Printed in the USA
265920BV00001B/27/A

9 780977 031863